THE JOKER

THE JOKER

by

Elena Bruck

York House Press

978-0-9791956-8-6

York House Press
Soundview Plaza
1266 East Main Street, 700 R
Stamford, CT 06902

For my family

Acknowledgement

To my editor and friend Lisa Halliday without whom this book would not be possible.

"The second angel poured his bowl into the sea,
and it became like the blood of a dead man."
Apocalypse

"An awful demon
Saw I in a dream: all black, white-eyed...
He called me to his cart"
The Feast in the Time of Plague, A. Pushkin

1

She hadn't even been attracted to him at first. He had a languid way about him, out of sync with the party, which was merry with music, candles and freshly baked cookies served on large aluminum trays. She didn't like his friend either, a blue-eyed morose type slackened by heroin and punk rock, with needle marks that she recognized on his hands with her professionally trained eyes. Other than her friend Robin from the hospital she knew no one and was waiting for the alcohol to kick in. She'd had one Margarita already and was on her way to get a second glass. The languid guy emerged in front of her unexpectedly, wearing a sly and welcoming smile.

"I'm Greg," he said. "Bored?"

She shrugged neither yes nor no. Music made it hard to talk and hear. They danced, she drank, they smoked cigarettes. She began to feel dizzy and light and almost cheerful. It was New Year's Eve, a night to be happy and crazy. Greg was easy to be with – or maybe the Margaritas made it easy. She wore a skirt. She didn't object when he put his hand on her back and then on her buttocks, slightly lifting the fabric up. It was pleasant. They left early, as soon as the ball fell on Times Square and glasses were clinked in hopeful celebration of the future. How could it be, she said, that the step from one year to the next was only a second long? He shrugged his shoulders. How could it be that you live one moment and die the next?

While fireworks exploded in the sky they took a cab to her place in Stuyvesant Town. Streets were full, bars boomed with music, couples hugged and cabs swished by. Greg kissed her, fondling her breasts with cold palms and squeezing her nipples. She succumbed shyly, pressed into the cab's leather by his knee. He whispered something. She emerged from the erotic sea dazed.

"What?"

"What's your name?"

"Eva."

"Eva," he chuckled. "Eve. I'm Adam."

A stupid joke but she played along, "I want my apple first."

He laughed, heartily and excitedly, and ordered the driver to stop at the corner. Watching his long-limbed body stride into the deli, she considered escaping, but hesitated out of a strange sense of obligation. Greg returned holding an apple.

"So," he said as she bit into the juicy flesh. It sprayed her face with tiny droplets. "It's the beginning of time."

Upstairs, they took a shower together. He had a beautiful, boyish body, almost hairless, lean and straight, with a thin waist and firm round buttocks. In bed, his long hair tickled her face, and his hands were surprisingly soft. Their lovemaking was unhurried and sensual. "Eva!" he cried out when he came; she liked it and suppressed the temptation to call him Adam.

The next morning he didn't ask for her phone number. She took it stoically, telling herself that it didn't matter. Over the next few days, the memory of their sex lingered and she kept thinking about Greg despite herself. In the evenings she stayed in, hoping he would come or maybe leave a note. On the third night something rustled under the front door. Excited, she ran out of her room.

"What is it?" asked her roommate grumpily.

"Just a restaurant ad," Eva replied with false indifference. "Orchid Garden. Let's order?"

They did. The food was all right, of the popular Asian fusion kind.

Picking at soft, wasabi-spiced noodles with her chopsticks, Eva tried to remember Greg's face but couldn't, only the sensation of his hair brushing against her body. After a week she was cured of love but not of shame: There must have been something wrong with her if he didn't even ask for her number. Maybe her butt was too fat.

It was a cold January night, with snowfalls and frosty wind sweeping the city. Sitting in her office in the ER, dreamily gazing out the window at the dark wind-ravaged square, Eva wished she could leave, cross the street, and, escaping the noise of the city, enter the familiar surroundings of Stuyvesant Town, with its vast tranquility, elderly oddballs feeding the squirrels, and her own quiet apartment into which she had moved after her mother, Eleanor, had left for Paris in search of glamour and money five years ago. Eva closed her eyes and sighed, imagining how she'd run a bath and change into her pajamas, and then, warm and fragrant, recline on her sofa to watch the new episode of "24." It wasn't going to happen. She knew the night shift was going to be busy; the residents' wisdom and her own experience said that such evenings brought in a lot of the homeless. She clicked on the Internet Explorer icon to check her e-mail just as her beeper went off.

"Dr. Leigh!" she answered, intoning the firm, muscle-flexing competency she used in her hospital life.

The call came from the pediatric ER, and she rushed out to evaluate a ten-year old boy, overweight and clumsy, who cheerfully told her he had eaten a whole toothpaste out of curiosity. He appeared to Eva just like a normal kid, no trace of depression, a little bored with waiting in the ER and long over the shock that still lingered in his plump mom's eyes. His stomach had been pumped and he asked Eva hopefully, "Will I lose weight?"

"Sure, just don't drink too much soda. And no more toothpaste, okay?"

In the office again, Eva checked her e-mail. There were no personal messages, just medical news, a Delta SkyMiles statement, Citibank ads and spam.

Around eight she interviewed four homeless alcoholics seeking admission to get food and shelter for the night, all with the same story: "I hear voices that tell me to kill myself." "Are they male or female?" Eva would ask, and they would return her a blank stare. A "Mr. Jones" pulled off his boots and unbound the bandages around his feet. His toes looked like rotting tomatoes, red with black and white patches, the spaces between the toes full with maggots. Eva held her breath, overwhelmed by the stench and struggling to remain professional.

Late at night, red-eyed and heavy, she was called to see a recovering heroin addict on Methadone. His girlfriend had just passed away after taking one of his pills, too large a dose for her drug-naïve body. "I want to die!" he screamed when the paramedics arrived at his house and performed a useless resuscitation on the girl, trying to ease his despair. He was still screaming when Eva saw him, words impossible, pain tearing his vocal cords with shrill empty howls. She spoke cautiously and respectfully, letting her compassion glide over him until they found a sad melody through which to talk to one other and he settled down with the look of a forlorn child on his tired face. He told her his story, up to the details of the dress his girlfriend was wearing that night, the dress he'd bought for her at an Escada sale a month ago. Eva nodded and breathed deeply, trying not to cry with him. After he left, lucid and tamed by her tenderness, she stayed at her desk for a while, full of compassion and awe at the face of destiny – full also of pride at having been helpful, as if she, too, were one of fate's hands, a goddess of hope and forgiveness allowed to exist only in this screening room, devoid of her own personal history.

Between patients Eva ran out to get bitter, over-brewed coffee, which she cured with cream and sugar, and to smoke cigarettes, thumping her feet on the thawing snow and warming her freezing fingers on the hot cup. At four in the morning she finally retired to the on-call room where someone was already blissfully snoring on one of the cots. She made the bed and crawled under a thin blanket that smelled of starch and anti-roach detergent. Expecting to be paged at any time, she tossed and turned in a state of drowsy agitation until, just as she was dropping off, the beeper rang, bursting the silence with mechanical shrieks, and she jolted up, her heart thumping wildly.

"Dr. Leigh! I was paged!"

"This is surgery. We need a psych consult for a fifty-two year old female who refuses a procedure ..."

Eva was light and happy as she finally made her way home at noon, mission accomplished, excitement and tiredness mixing in one. Snow was everywhere, fresh and sparkling on the roofs of the cars and by the curbs. It was a clear, luminous day, and Eva laughed and sang along with Bryan Ferry on her iPod.

And there was Greg, waiting for her outside her apartment, drawing circles with his foot in the snow. His thin grey coat was open and hands were in his pockets. A red scarf was wrapped carelessly around his neck.

"I came by last night. Your roommate told me you'd be coming home around noon," he said timidly. "I didn't know you were a doctor. Do I disturb?"

"Come in!" she said, smiling and unlocking the door.

After avid lovemaking he made his introduction, which was not glamorous. Stuttering through his story he told her that he temporarily lived with his parents, worked as a waiter in Luca's Lounge, wrote songs and was a modern troubadour.

"A troubadour?" she repeated. "How romantic."

To refresh her memory she looked it up on Wikipedia, stumbling over the description of the infamous duke: *The Count of Poitiers was one of the most courtly men in the world and one of the greatest deceivers of women. He was a fine knight at arms, liberal in his womanizing, and a fine composer and singer of songs. He traveled much through the world, seducing women.*

"Seducing women!" she read aloud mockingly.

"I know. That reminds me, I wrote a song for you. A song for Eva."

And he sang his simple and sentimental song to her, and she was seduced.

Evas don't exist, just in fairy-tales.
Yes, my dear, that's fine, you may call me another name.
Is it the name of love? Is it the name of death?
Darling, just stop the cab,
and bring me a juicy apple
and a different, better name,
to deceive the serpent.

After Greg moved in with her, Eva was happy. The sense of vulnerability didn't leave her completely but was numbed by his attentive presence. They made love and talked for hours, and for those intense nights, full of life and dreams, she was grateful and forgiving. Something about her changed, she was more flirtatious and full of secret joy. And yet she lived on the verge. The feeling didn't leave her that this fullness of being could not last.

Eva's mother called from Paris, where she lived a slovenly, isolated life, getting fatter and more hypochondriac by the day, and complaining of imagined diseases, of the French, and of boredom. She had moved to Paris with her third

6

husband five years ago, then still a freshly plump woman, and stayed behind after he divorced her, fighting battles in court to get part of his family estate. The lawsuit dragged on in an unhurried European fashion, and over time Eleanor lost the will to return and settled into a small and greedy routine: spending Claude's money, bingeing on food, and worrying about getting sick. Conversations between her and Eva were always the same.

"Oh, thank God I finally get to talk to you," her mother would say, sighing loudly into the receiver. She was a master at sighing, at all its different kinds of heaves, inducing alternately guilt, compassion, and a shared sense of irremediable boredom and tragedy of existence. "My back pain isn't getting better," she'd said just the other day, and then paused, implying that Eva's advices of the previous week had failed her and therefore it was Eva's fault she wasn't improving.

"Mom, I told you to go to the doctor if you continue to have pain," Eva said with tired defensiveness.

"You're not listening! Doctors here are bad. And they don't understand me! They don't even try! It's not America. They're arrogant decadents, all of them."

"Then come back," Eva said, wishing guiltily that her mother would stay in Paris forever.

"Well, you live in my apartment now. Do you know how much money you're saving? Oh," she sighed again. "This city is so expensive. I wish *I* had a rent-stabilized place."

"Isn't Claude paying, anyway?" Eva asked irritable.

"Well, all his money goes toward the rent! I don't have friends because I don't have money to go out. And, of course, they don't like Americans here anyway. I told the grocer the other day, I am not Bush! Don't blame me! I can't even afford theatre tickets!"

You don't even speak French, why would you go to a theatre? Eva thought, but didn't say anything. "And the pains are killing

7

me. I think I have breast cancer. I sweat at night. I watched Dr. Gupta on CNN the other day. Did you know that night sweats are a sign of cancer?"

"Mom, night sweats are a general symptom, they're not specific for any illness."

"Don't you talk down to me!" her mother shrieked and then let out her longest and most miserable sigh, followed by a tense silence.

"Okay. I've got to go now. Hope you feel better," Eva said flatly.

"How's this boyfriend of yours? What's his name again?" her mother went on as if Eva hadn't said anything at all.

"Greg."

"Yes, the Russian. Is he working yet?"

"He works in a bar."

"In a bar! Be careful! Russians are crude, uncultured and alcoholics. Surely you know this. A Russian in a bar!"

Eva had hung up. Her resentment, sense of duty and pity for her mother bubbled in one pot, finding no outlet. She couldn't resolve it with Eleanor. Sometimes, she tried to love her mother and forgive her, remembering little good things of her childhood, the simple comforting intimacy of mother and daughter baking cupcakes together and then watching "adult" movies on TV, where men fought wars and women were kissed and then got pregnant, giving rise to little Eva's theory of procreation: The kissing couple's saliva would mix and go down to the stomach, where it would form a tiny baby that would grow over many months – much like "Grow the Monster" worked over a couple of days. At these memories Eva attempted to smile now, but they became juiceless and worn from frequent use over time.

Then the pain of an unloved and abandoned child would return. Having lost her father early, she was shipped from relative to relative, once staying under the care of a schizophrenic uncle of her mother's second husband for a month. The man, whose name escaped her now, was hunched, old and kindly in the clumsy way of someone who had never had a child. He taught her to play the piano, and while she pressed the keys, he sometimes mumbled to himself behind her back, filling her with affection and fear of his strange, rare illness. Mother had a terrifying presence: yelling, slapping, ignoring, and yet herself needy and craving of absolute love. "Do you love me more than anyone in the world?" she demanded daily of Eva, and, with downcast eyes, Eva would nod and say yes. Eva craved her mother's love. It took years for her to realize that Eleanor was too enveloped in herself. The world was there to serve her; other people were not real, and her little daughter was just a shadow of Eleanor's own self, existing to obey, admire, and serve.

It was still hard for Eva to talk about this to anyone. She would become breathless with anxiety, as if the omnipotent mother of her childhood could suddenly emerge in front of her and slap her back into nothingness with her perfumed, cruel hands. Eva would feel guilty. She had grown up feeling guilty and deserving of punishment, but also angry at her mother and entitled to love, and, in her other dimension, feeling an urgent, unbearable at times, sense of purpose. During those moments of inspiration teenage Eva would stand in front of the mirror and dance to the rhythms of the Pet Shop Boys, Michael Jackson, and REM. She could be strong and light only when she was alone. Among people she faltered, feeling awkward and ugly, just like Eleanor told her she was, daily and well into her adolescence.

Awkwardness still befell Eva frequently, although maturation helped her to feel more "normal." That was the word she used with herself: *normal.*

"Normal?" Greg laughed. "I haven't known anyone more normal than you. You transcend normalcy. You're beautiful."

"In med school, I interviewed a patient once and asked one of those naïve questions that med students ask: 'Why do you use drugs when it's so bad for you?' He was still a young man, but very thin, almost toothless, and sick. He closed his eyes and said with this explosive yearning, 'That first time I shot heroin I knew what people meant when they said they were normal.'"

"Wow! So, did you ever try drugs?"

"Not heroin. Although tempting, it was a cautionary tale. Also, I was afraid of the whole package that comes with it: needles, AIDS, abscesses, toothlessness. But I did try cocaine once, and LSD. And pot, of course. The last time I smoked I spent half the night in someone's bathroom staring at a doorknob unable to move, and that was it. Booze is good enough."

In college, Eva discovered another self. She learned to be gregarious in her dorm life, and sexy and attractive with her boyfriends. That second self co-existed with the first, always fighting for the upper hand in the battle for her self-representation. But only with Greg was it allowed to shine, casting her dark and guilty side into exile. She had never known such a pure joy of togetherness.

Sometimes, in those early winter evenings, snug under the old moth-eaten plaid on the sofa in the living room, lights dimmed and candles burning on the table next to their empty dinner plates, they would sip tea and play strange games that Greg called "psychological."

"If you had to live on an uninhabited island until the end of your days, and could choose just two companions, who would they be?"

"You, and ..."

They would giggle then, nervous and grateful, and content with the metaphor of marriage not chosen but thrust upon them by shipwreck or punishment.

She loved being adored, seeing herself through his eyes. Even when talking about her unhappiness, she was perfect, and confessions of imperfection were abstract, understood, and worked through like the accounts of Freud's cures resting on her bookshelves.

"You're my holding environment," she told Greg. They had just made love, and still breathing hard, Greg asked,

"What's a holding environment?"

"It's a concept adopted by one of the early psychoanalysts, Heinz Kohut. He believed that psychotherapy should offer a protective and loving environment to compensate for unhappy childhoods. His patients stayed in therapy for ten or more years, five times a week."

"Just five times a week? That makes me a super-holding environment," Greg whispered stroking her cheek.

Later, in the privacy of a shower, hot water gushing over her face, Eva felt skeptical of Kohut's theories. She wondered whether Kohut's method made an infant of a patient, creating dependency that could be very hard to break later on. Neuroses often went away without any intervention, and after ten years it would be impossible to say if it was therapy that helped or just life and chance finally kicking in. Wrapped in a towel, she stepped into the coziness of her living room. Greg lay on the sofa watching TV, his slippers overturned on the carpet. Eva stretched out next to him and wrapped her arms around his neck. Suddenly it seemed too cumbersome to explain the intricacies of her thoughts. Psychiatry had to remain whole, untainted by doubt and magical, transferring those qualities onto her. It was a conscious process. She was the shaper of her happiness.

One day Greg returned with a cat.

"Her name is Ska!" he said lovingly, scratching behind her peaked ears. The cat was white with brown spots on her sides and a black tail. She purred, rolling on her side, then walked to Eva's leg, brushing against it.

"Our building doesn't allow animals," Eva answered

cautiously.

"I know, but no one's going to find out. She's not going out, she's a cat!"

Ska stayed, and with her arrival Greg acquired a slightly different status in Eva's house, as if it weren't a cat but an engagement ring, holding promise and binding them together.

A couple of months passed. Greg became more relaxed and confident. He did not feel obliged to shave daily or comb his hair in the mornings, and he was less talkative. He often stayed behind when Eva left for work in the mornings, yawning while kissing her goodbye, his blue eyes dreamy and soft. He stopped announcing glamorous plans for each day, such as his attendance at recordings and rehearsals, and twice he failed to pay his half of the rent. Eva sometimes worried about these changes, but she was grateful for having him. In the evenings, they read and watched TV, her head on his chest, his hair tickling her face. They made love, and Ska would jump up on their laps, purr and brush them with her fur. Greg cooked and cleaned; from time to time he gave Eva a little smile or a quick warm embrace and it sufficed just to be together and comfortable without talking. It was the way of happily married couples, Eva thought. Greg was her friend, her cook, and her lover, great in all his roles.

Eva dreamed of going through a dark wet tunnel with a flashlight, running away from an invisible danger. Greg was with her, helplessly lagging behind, and repeatedly she had to urge him to hurry up. When the shrieking began, she yelled for help, sitting upright and with blood-chilling horror realizing that the screams were coming from Greg. It took a couple of seconds for her own dream to retreat and her scientific mind to kick in. Shaking his shoulders, she shouted,

"Greg, it's okay! It's just a bad dream! Wake up!"

But he wouldn't wake up. He continued to scream, piercing the air with the unnatural guttural sound of a hurt and frightened beast. Eva turned on the lights. Greg's eyes were half-open, his irises drowning behind his eyelids. He wailed and violently flailed his arms. With her orange eyes Ska watched from the corner, her back curved, and Eva shooed her away into the living room. It's a sleep terror, it will end, she kept telling herself. She held him, stroked his long blond hair and whispered tender words into his ear, although she knew he wouldn't remember them: neither his dreams and fright nor her tenderness. It felt liberating to do something good without the expectation of a payback. How had other women reacted? Eva wondered. How many of them had left him on account of this?

Greg shrieked for fifteen minutes, and then it ended as abruptly as it had begun and he drifted into a deep, quiet sleep. Eva tossed and turned for a while, leaving the lights on.

The next morning, Greg woke up in a foul mood and stumbled around the kitchen as if still possessed by his dream.

"You screamed last night," she said gently. "For a long-long time."

He stole a glance at her and nodded.

"Does it often happen?"

He put a slice of toast on the plate in front of her and poured a glass of orange juice.

"It happens once in a while," he said. "I was a 'lunatic' as a child."

"A lunatic?" she repeated and burst out laughing.

"That's what my parents call nightwalkers," he explained, blushing with a soft smile.

"They do? That's funny." Tenderly, apologetically, she stroked his arm, not letting him go.

"That's what Russians call nightwalkers," he continued in

13

a brighter voice. "Called by the moon."

"It was pretty awful. You should've told me."

"I thought that maybe once I met you it would go away."

"You flatterer! Do you know you're a flatterer, lunatic?" She laughed again.

"God, am I lucky to have a doctor for a girlfriend! Do you really have to go to work today, after working the night shift? We could cuddle a little and then go back to sleep."

It was tempting, and Eva took two sips of coffee before answering.

"No," she said. "I can't. I have patients scheduled."

"I love you. I mean it."

"You must have frightened off all the other girls," she said, her heart bursting with joy. She didn't feel the need to reciprocate, and was grateful for that. It was too early to talk about love. Love meant marriage and kids and living happily ever after.

Greg always got up with Eva, made her toast with butter and strawberry marmalade and a hot latte on the Nespresso machine he had purchased with her credit card shortly after moving in. In his striped boxer shorts and the torn pink t-shirt he slept in, he would move around the kitchen with a tired expression. Was it a ritual that saved him from guilt?

"You don't have to get up!" she suggested a couple of times. "Go back to sleep."

She remembered: That was how their living together had started.

"Go on, go to work, I'll clean up. Really, I mean it!" he said – and stayed on, first one day, then another, until his beaten suitcase arrived with its roaches and holey socks and he moved in for good. At the time, his idleness seemed a small price to pay. How big was the price, really, she sometimes wondered nowadays, trying to reason her way out of the flashes of irritation.

"All services provided!" Greg announced after each time he made love to her, cooked her dinner, washed the dishes or fed the cat. These announcements amused Eva even though she could sense he wasn't entirely joking. He said it flatly and mechanically, the way people mutter "fine" to the question "How are you?" She didn't grasp right away that he was defining himself in this unassuming way.

It irked her to return from work to see Greg still there, dazed and lazy from lying around all day, often with moisture in the corners of his eyes and his hair tangled as though he had just woken up. She wanted to shake him alive and make him do things: go to college, work, be ambitious.

"How can I look for a job if I'm a housewife?" he would retort.

"I didn't hire you, for God's sake! Just get off your butt and do something! Anything!"

Eva was efficient and mature in the common sense of these words, but she could also be prickly, with an edge in her voice that was loud and sharp, like a knife sticking out. She hated this voice for its shallow and squashed ugliness. It was partly the reason why it was so hard for her to discuss her differences with Greg. His deep and smooth baritone absorbed her little pricks like a river, leaving her helpless and frustrated in her inability to express herself. Her best arguments happened when she was drunk, and in time Greg came to learn that her pouring herself a third glass of wine over dinner often meant an imminent fight. His tactic was simply to agree with her, repeating and accepting the words she used to describe him – a psychological technique called mirroring. It had not come as easily to Eva in her professional training; Greg used it instinctively.

"I know I'm wasting my life. I wish I could figure out how to change myself. Maybe you can help me," he would say, and her anger would pass. Eagerly, he dreamed with her together about all the things that could be his someday, and this brought Eva an intense satisfaction, undiminished by her knowledge, deep-down, that he was a pleaser. Even when she yelled at him she wanted to weep and hold him and say she was sorry. He was soft, gentle. He loved her in a way of fairy-tales, like no one else ever had.

Trying to picture her life before Greg, Eva recalled an incessant hunger for life, an unquiet existence, empty and bare like a long white wall. She was happy now, and if she felt mad at times, it was surely her fault: her own ambitions she imposed on Greg, her overblown ideas of autonomy. She had to learn the art of kindness from him. Of course, sooner or later, he had to start a more normal life. But she had to be patient. She had in her the power of empathy and persuasion that made her a good psychiatrist. She would help him grow up. His idleness was a small price to pay.

2

Greg was from a Russian family. In this other life of his, his parents called him Grisha or, when the talk was serious, Grigory. He was five when they emigrated from Moscow, a child of repression and totalitarianism. This background added a new spiral of romanticism to Eva's feelings about him.

Next to his parents Greg became different in ways Eva couldn't fully understand. He was full of glossy aplomb and reassuring smiles and he lost his self-deprecating humor. Turning to Eva to explain or interpret, he smiled differently – sheepishly and sadly, an awkward apology in his eyes for himself and for his parents. He was embarrassed by how they dressed and by their home, by their accents and by little hints and meanings in their cautious questions that ran like avenues of irritation straight from his childhood, of which Eva knew so little.

Eva found Greg's parents endearing. Everything about their life seemed old-fashioned and cozy to her, even Greg's gentlemanly father Vladimir, a fussy, diminutive man who often looked frightened and perplexed at the same time and held strong opinions about life and politics. His favorite word with Eva was "wonderful." She looked wonderful no matter how tired; everything she said was wonderful; his wife Olga was consistently wonderful and the world was a wonderful place in which to live. Sometimes it seemed to Eva that Vladimir tried to cancel her out by acting agreeable, but she kindly ignored this. Vladimir was insecure. He had a thick Russian accent that she had to wade through to arrive at the meaning of his words. He was a self-made man. He endeavored to be pleasant. And, he was Greg's father.

Greg often told Eva different stories: of Vladimir's volatile temper, his drinking, his shouting sprees with Olga, his stinginess, his insomnia, his hatred for America. Father and son quarreled a lot on the phone. Although it was in Russian, of which Eva knew only a couple of words, she sensed that it was over the same topic that fueled her own arguments with Greg: work, future, responsibility. She remained quiet, studying Greg for signs of awakening. Maybe his father could bring the message home. Or maybe having several messengers would make a difference.

Greg's mother Olga was kind-hearted, musical and superstitious, often knocking on the wood and spitting three times over her shoulder whenever she wanted a wish to come true. Was she worried about Greg too? Eva often wondered, looking into Olga's calm eyes, which smiled at Eva through heavy-framed glasses.

There was no special occasion for this particular Sunday visit, and yet Greg was unusually excited on the way to his parents' house, talking non-stop and fondling Eva's hand affectionately on the train.

"What is it?" she asked, yielding to his caresses. It had been over a year that they lived together, but their lovemaking was as intense as in the first week, and she was silently proud of it. Erotic longing made her move closer to Greg. He laughed happily, touching her forehead with his.

"You're going to meet Anna today," he said.

Anna was a healer whom Greg's family had known forever. Years ago she and her husband had treated – and apparently cured – Vladimir's stomach cancer after his doctors had given him a death sentence. Greg had been fifteen at the time and could not remember all the details.

"Why didn't you tell me?" Eva asked. "I almost thought

you were planning to announce our engagement."

He turned red. "Sorry, I didn't think about that. But you wouldn't …"

"No, I wouldn't. It was a joke."

They fell silent, their hands falling apart.

Greg's parents lived in Bay Ridge, in a small townhouse they had bought years ago before the real estate boom. Vladimir owned a grocery store, which he had named Papa's Deli, featuring mostly Russian but also Spanish food to suit the neighborhood market. He ran it well, in his thrifty way, and Greg believed his father had amassed a small fortune. "My pension!" Greg called it. But if the Spasskys did have money, nothing of it showed on the surface. They continued to rent out their second floor and seemed never to buy any new clothes, frozen in the fashion of their youth.

In their modest two-bedroom Olga decorated the walls with striped wallpaper and put in dark wooden cabinets, massive bookcases, and two-ply curtains: breezy white to shield themselves from their neighbors' eyes, and heavy dark, pulled shut to block out the sun. On the floors were two large, worn-out carpets brought from Moscow; a smaller Eastern rug hung on the wall in the living room. Pots with plants and flowers crowded the window-sills and in the kitchen Olga nurtured a wide arrangement of different herbs: fresh dill, cilantro, rosemary, spring onions and basil sprouting out of long wooden crates built and painted green by Vladimir. Dried pumpkins of different shapes and colors sat on top of the kitchen cabinets year-round. When visiting children took them down to play, the gourds rattled and stained little fingers with a film of dust that covered them like hats of snow.

Olga met her son and his girlfriend heartily, planting three fragile kisses on Eva's cheeks as if Eva were a flower. As was customary in their house, Eva took off her shoes, even though it was a dry summer day. Olga offered fluffy pink slippers that Eva refused with an amiable chuckle.

Greg spoke softly with his mother.

"Anna's here," he said turning to Eva. They heard voices from the kitchen.

Holding hands, Greg and Eva entered, Olga following behind. The early afternoon light was streaming in from the window, and Eva could not see Anna's face clearly at first, just the full shape of her seated body. Anna and Vladimir rose. Greg and Eva were cordially greeted and seated at the table, already set for the meal.

"Anna is like our sister," said Vladimir seriously.

"Greg has told me about you," Eva said, nodding pleasantly in Anna's direction. Anna answered with a soft smile. Her plain face was framed by salt-and-pepper shoulder-length hair that made her look older than she was. She wore no makeup. Her gray eyes were clear and deep with a calm and friendly intelligence. And yet, there was something subdued in her shape.

"Would you like some cabbage soup, Eva?" Olga asked, and Eva nodded. Anna was watching her. When Eva shifted uncomfortably, Anna stretched her palm toward Eva without touching her.

"Anna and Ben saved my life," said Vladimir.

"Ben is my husband," Anna explained in flawless, almost accent-free English.

Eva was thankful when the soup was served. She did not believe in wonders, and, although she was curious, she did not feel like asking questions just now. Instead she said,

"Your English is so good."

"I have to thank Ben for it," Anna replied eagerly. "And for everything I am."

They ate *golubtsi*, chewy beefsteaks wrapped in cabbage leaves. Complimenting Olga on her cooking, Eva noted,

"Cabbage must be very popular in Russia."

They talked about food. Then, inevitably, politics.

"What do you think of Putin?" Eva asked innocently. Greg giggled.

"I wish you wouldn't start them on that!"

"My wife doesn't share my opinion," Vladimir explained. "But here is what I think: Putin is a criminal, and that's all there is to say."

Olga carried away the dirty dishes, dried her hands on her apron, and nervously settled down.

"*I* think Putin is a good president. Economy is growing, people's life improved, mafia is being ruled in," she said. "There is a lot of propaganda against Russia in America today. When Anna Politkovskaia was gunned down in her elevator, the press here did not even mention that in two days she was scheduled to appear in a criminal court hearing as a main witness. They wrote, she was a human rights activist opposing the war in Chechnya, and her biggest foe was Putin. Readers make conclusions. Politkovskaia had criticized Putin for a long time. Why should he be involved? It makes no sense to me. Or, take Berezovsky, the Russian billionaire who lives in London now. He is hailed here, but his hands are bloody. In the early days of perestroika, there were no honest businessmen in Russia, they were all mafia. They all killed," Olga talked quickly with a pleasant, defensive smile. She avoided looking at Vladimir who grew red and agitated and attempted to interrupt her several times.

"Finished?" he asked acidly. "I'll tell you once again: Putin is a criminal. Why he does all these things? Simple! To frighten. Like Hitler."

"You can't ..." Olga said helplessly opening her hands.

"Yes I can!" Vladimir shouted banging his fist on the table. "That's why there's no freedom of speech left, and all TV is state-controlled in Russia! What freedom always goes first? You tell me!" he challenged her, his fists clenched. Olga gave him a startled look.

"Yes, papa, we know, the freedom of speech." Greg turned

to Eva. "I told you, it's always like this with them. Who cares anyway? We're here now, a democracy that bombs others for freedom. Sorry, papa. Hakuna matata!"

Anna stayed quiet, not taking sides. Her face remained calm and friendly, which impressed Eva, who was drawn into the emotions of aggression and defensiveness against her will.

With the second bottle of wine, the tensions subsided, and Olga and Vladimir recounted their first meeting on a train to a ski resort in Uzbekistan.

"Olga was so beautiful that I proposed the same evening," he said, putting his thin, freckled arm around her shoulders. Blushing, Olga giggled.

Conversation was easy, and Eva, a little tipsy now, relaxed and lost the feeling that she was being put to some kind of test. They settled for tea in the living room, Anna next to Eva and Greg on the sofa full of laced cushions, Olga and Vladimir opposite to them in the armchairs.

"Card time," announced Vladimir, rubbing his palms. "Ready, Annushka? Eva goes first."

Anna took a deck out of her handbag, shuffled it, and asked Eva to draw a card for her blindly. Eva shrugged and pulled. King of Hearts.

"Were you a healer in Russia, as well?" Eva asked.

Spreading the cards in front of her, Anna smiled and began her story. As she talked, her voice acquired a detached and dreamy quality, as if she had forgotten about her audience, even though her hands continued to mix and spread the cards in perfect rows on the table.

In Russia she was a high school teacher, she said, a bluestocking teaching physics and algebra to pimple-faced youth. Now that life seemed to her a blur with islands of still pictures: her mother, her two aunts, the communal apartment with a yellow rusted bathtub and underwear drying over it, the family's daily squabble and bickering until

Anna's scandalous, unpatriotic emigration. The things she remembered were mostly small and insignificant: the smell of rotting onions and potatoes stored under the window sill, the crew-cut and khaki uniform of her boyfriend Igor, later killed in Afghanistan. Anna kept a couple of photos from the past, but that was all. It was too long ago. Her mother had been dead for years. Anna never went back to Russia. "Don't think I have bad memories," she added, her eyes downcast. "I think I was happy. People like the familiar. I was young, too. People are happy when they are young."

Harder times came when Anna arrived in New York, riding the last big wave of Jewish emigration. Her father David – yellow, grumpy, and disabled by renal insufficiency – met her at the airport. Other than him, she had no one here. "I was very lonely," Anna said, crossing her legs into a lotus position and shuffling the cards again. "But it was worth the loneliness." Everyone listened attentively, and she continued, lower and dreamier than before.

She descended into a hell of her father's petty tyranny and cultural isolation, her days spent caring for his endless needs, listening to reproaches and demands of gratitude to him for supporting her new life. She cried and learned English at night. Eventually she worked cleaning strangers' apartments and as an aide in a nearby Brooklyn hospital. She was just thirty-five but already saw herself as an old woman. "He wasn't a bad man, just confused and unhappy, and sick," Anna explained. "I felt young again when his coffin was put into grave and I threw a handful of earth on it. It was like a miracle. I wish I could say I had loved him." The funeral repast at the shabby one-bedroom apartment that still smelled of misery, urine, and medication was for Anna the best party she had ever hosted. She didn't allow herself to suffer guilt for her joy; it was the first time in years that she felt alive. It was at the funeral, through friends of her father's, that she met Olga, Vladimir, and little Greg.

Soon afterward, at her local yoga class, she met Ben. He was kind and generous, with a lingering smile, and she didn't care that he was odd: a vegan and a poet. She was not frightened when he confessed to conversing with ghosts, nor even when he claimed, in a poem, to be a "psychic prodigy working with energy." And then Ben discovered Anna's gift, and wrote her fate into another poem on a flowery *Thank You* postcard that Anna preserved carefully among her valuables in a jewelry box. She was to become a healer. She was to become his wife. She said yes to both. That was all; happiness just came to her, as if someone had stored it for her through all those parched years of misery. She couldn't wish for a different life.

Anna lifted her glazed, dreamy eyes to Eva. "That's it," she said. "My life. How about you? Are you happy, Eva?"

"I guess I am. Happiness is a big word," Eva replied uneasily, instinctively searching for Greg's hand. Anna's tale made an impression on her: her hardship, her honesty, her happiness – of which Eva felt jealous. *Am I happy?* Eva asked herself, leaning back, Greg's fingers stroking her palm. No, she decided; she was not. Suddenly the magic of Anna's story lifted and gave way to a nagging discomfort of being exposed to those around her as the unhappy one.

"Where is Ben now?" Eva asked, pouring more tea into her cup.

"He never comes here," Anna said quietly. "He's very sensitive to the environment. There's a hungry ghost in this house, he says. I don't feel it. But I'm not as powerful as he is."

"I don't believe in ghosts," Eva said bluntly.

"She's a doctor," Greg interjected by way of apology.

This irked Eva, and, turning to him, she asked, "Well, do *you* believe in ghosts?"

"I don't know," he said. "I've never seen one, but it doesn't mean other people haven't."

Anna had finished sorting the cards and was turning

them up one by one, humming to herself. Olga and Vladimir leaned closer. Anna uncrossed her legs and, with a gesture, invited Eva to edge closer to her. "Your destiny," she said.

Eva smiled, awkwardly accepting the invitation. "I don't believe in cards either."

"That's you, the Queen of Diamonds," Anna explained patiently. "Behind is pain, disillusionment, success, a journey overseas. Lonely girl, very lonely. A gathering coming, and an Ace of Hearts again next to Eight of Courts: a big prophesy you might not like. The King of Hearts and the King of Courts: difficult decisions. And the Joker coming in. Again. Not the first time I see it." Silently she turned the Joker over in her hands. "A man or child take your heart. A lot of pain is coming your way. A lot of Spades, a whole palette, and the Joker on top. But in the end you'll be fine with the King of Courts."

"I'm not following," said Eva. Olga and Vladimir's faces were worried and tense, as if she had been just given a bad diagnosis.

Anna looked at her soothingly. "Do you want to know?"

"I don't believe in cards," Eva repeated. "Excuse me, I need to use the bathroom."

Anna gathered the cards. "You will need my help one day," she said.

Eva shrugged her shoulders. She was annoyed. *You* will need *my* help one day, she wanted to say, but she kept silent out of respect to Greg's parents, who sat still and close to one other in the dimming light of early evening.

3

hortly before graduating from her residency, Eva went out to celebrate at Luca's Lounge, in the East Village, where Greg continued to serve tables twice a week. It was the middle of June, a soft summer evening full of tipsy songs, street bands and high hopes. On the way, Eva and Greg held hands, and, full of excitement, Eva walked close to him. "I love you," she wanted to say, but when she turned to him and their eyes met, she asked instead, "Isn't it great?"

"You graduating?"

"Everything. Life!"

Her colleague Robin was already at the lounge, fake gold chains dangling around her neck, her dress flying, her answers cryptic and funny. Eva's other residency classmates arrived soon after. Bill showed up wearing a hat and settled at the table's corner like a character out of Fassbinder, sipping his drinks, his face hidden in the hat's shade.

"Dr. Jacobs!" she called teasingly. "Come closer! Have you met Greg?"

As she introduced them to one another, she felt tense, as though Bill could by a remark, or a gesture render her love for Greg ridiculous. But just then Greg's friend Nestor, the one with the needle-marks, walked in, with his scrawny chicken neck, his pockmarked skin, and his nasal voice, and Greg turned to greet him. Nestor was wearing holey jeans that slipped from his hips and a Kinks t-shirt that hung sharply on his stooped shoulders. He was in an exuberant mood.

"I'm a *tigarassa*!" he announced, roaring. "Big tiger! In Spanish!" A waitress serving their drinks raised her eyebrows, and Eva gave a short derisive chuckle, displeased to see him.

"C'mon," Greg whispered guiltily. "He's a good guy; give him a chance."

Grazing the back of his hand with her fingers, Eva noticed how handsome Greg looked that evening. "Don't worry," she said. "I have manners." She put up a smile and kissed Nestor's cheeks, feeling the unevenness of his skin on her lips and breathing in the pungent reek of the cologne he had splashed generously on his face.

Nestor and Bill hit it off right away, cracking dumb jokes and discussing girls. Eva's classmate Kathy arrived, muscular, broad-shouldered, stressed, stains of baby food on her dress and above it all a nervous face. Before long she had taken out her cell phone and was shouting feeding instructions to her hapless husband, who had stayed home to watch their new daughter. Less than half an hour into the party she left with an embarrassed and angry smile.

"Children! How boring!" Robin said loudly and yawned. Everyone laughed.

Robin and Nestor sang karaoke songs, their voices amateurish, twisting like snakes around one another and upsetting the rhythm. Greg hopped onstage when *Lambada* came on, wrenching the microphone away from Nestor in a comic struggle. There was so much laughter that the rest of the girls also joined in on the dancing and singing, carried away by the group's enthusiasm. Shoes came off and the party reached its peak. Eva came face to face with Nestor. Vodka and excitement softened her toward him and she laughed, flailing her arms in the air. Nestor took her hands, pulling her hard toward his bony chest and then letting her fall back over his arm in a dramatic dip. Eva always found it hard to follow rather than lead, and she giggled, stumbling and panting.

"I need a cigarette!" she said at last.

"I'll come too," he offered, and they stepped out.

"Are you two still together?" Nestor asked then, bending to accept the flame that Eva held steady with her cupped palm.

"What do you mean?"

"You and Greg," he said nasally, exhaling smoke.

"Why shouldn't we be together?"

"It's just that he's, like, going out with someone else. Sorry to tell you."

Eva fell silent for several seconds. The sounds of music oozing from the lounge mixed unpleasantly with Latino pop blasting from a passing limo.

"Well that's news to me," Eva said finally, her mouth dry.

Nestor held a long pause, studying Eva with his brazen blue eyes.

"You should drop him. Go out with me."

"Sorry to tell you," she imitated Nestor passive-aggressively. "But it's, like, I don't like you."

"That's okay, no need to get angry. I ask, you say no. No bad feelings, okay?"

"And why should I believe you?" Eva asked, gesturing for him to stay.

"Everyone knows. Robin knows; ask Robin. Her name is Clair. A ballerina."

Nestor did not rejoin the party. The others were still dancing, Bill whirling with a microphone and trying to sing *Rigoletto,* to everyone's delight. Eva ordered a Cuba Libre and sat down heavily at the bar. Her legs were weak. She had been so happy just moments ago. "King of Hearts!" she said into nowhere, suddenly remembering Anna's prophesies. Greg, who had an almost supernatural gift for detecting distress in others, possibly spurred by a dirty conscience, pulled Robin offstage before approaching.

"Where's Nestor gone?" he asked innocently, Robin at his side.

"I don't know."

Bill came down too, unwittingly saving the evening. "I'm starving!" he said throwing his hat in the air and catching it with his head.

They ate at a table in the garden. Eva ignored Greg and made polite conversation with her classmates.

"I've just finished a biography of Kohut," she announced loudly. "It's a sad account of his life, really."

"Why?" Bill asked.

"Because of the ingrained deceptiveness of the human psyche. There's profound weakness in man that's not remediable, not even in one of the biggest and brightest and most influential representatives of the psychoanalytic movement, like Kohut. He was a Jew whose family perished in concentration camps, did you know that?"

"No! Kohut wasn't Jewish," Robin said with conviction.

"He was. And until his death he denied it and pretended to be Catholic. He got baptized and went to Mass, and lied about his origins when people asked him about them directly." Eva was aware of Greg's eyes upon her face.

"I thought you liked it! What about the holding environment?" Greg said. "You didn't tell me any of this other stuff!"

"Sometimes people don't tell each other everything."

They arrived home late and Eva cried in bed for a long time with her back to Greg. She resisted and yet craved his attention until Greg removed her clothes and turned her tears into moans.

"Nestor wanted to go out with me," she confessed then.

"Has he gone mad?"

"He said everyone knows except me that you're dating another girl, a dancer named Clair. So he assumed I was free."

"That's crazy! Clair is just a friend I met at a rehearsal."

That night Greg had sleep-terrors again. Eva didn't comfort him.

She slept in the next day and awoke with a hangover around noon. Greg was still in bed, curled up, his lips parted, his eyelashes trembling. Her hurt returned, made uglier by her headache.

After a quick shower she ran out with her cell phone.

"Robin! Hi!"

"Hi! What's up? Nice party yesterday."

"Nestor told me about Greg and Clair and said I should ask you, because you know."

"He said to ask me? Why me? I don't know anything!" Robin cried this out with a cheerful ease that was like armor around her.

"I want to know," Eva persisted, fighting the humiliation of having to beg for what she had the right to from her best friend – and for Robin's compassion. "He said everyone knows that Greg has been dating another girl."

"How can you listen to Nestor, darling? He's funny in the head. You're the psychiatrist, you must know!"

"I thought you were my friend," Eva said.

"Of course I am. And I'm telling you to forget it. Are you happy with Greg?"

"I don't know. I'm jealous."

"Don't be. Maybe Greg just kissed some unimportant girl once and that's all there was to it. Go out and kiss someone if it will help. Then forget about it."

"He kissed her?" Eva cried, and hung up.

With puffy eyes Eva got up for work.

In her office, bewildered and angry, she wrote an incoherent letter to Greg, explaining that she felt betrayed and asking him to move out of her place immediately. The part about her hurt feelings appeared pathetic to her on the second read, and she tore up the letter and cried again in helpless desperation. She didn't want him to leave her. All she wanted was to reverse the time and erase his betrayal from her memory so she could trust and love him innocently again. It must be love, she thought. Why else would she be so distressed? She tried to type up a case report for the SSI application, but her eyes kept gliding over the computer screen. She got up and paced around her tiny windowless office waiting for Mr. Harrison, her next appointment, to show up. Minutes elapsed slowly. She switched on the radio. The reception was bad, and she adjusted the antenna, twisting it in different directions without much success. Ad, another ad, war in Iraq, rap, Hurricane Katrina relief funds. She switched the radio off again and took a deep breath. The computer screen flickered indifferently, the clock continued to tick, and her patient was still not there. An emergency preparedness meeting was scheduled next. Seized by an irate inspiration, Eva dialed Bill's number.

"Hi!" she said, her voice hoarse from crying. "Do you have time for a coffee?"

Her heart jumped a little when she saw him come in, a rush of affection coursing through her blood. He looked tall, proud, and magnificent.

"What happened?" he asked, closing the door behind him. "Have you been crying?"

"It's okay," she said. "Let's just get a coffee."

Bill giggled the way he always did when something made him uncomfortable.

The emergency meeting was boring, and Eva kept shifting in her chair, chewing on her misery until a balding infectious disease expert took the stage to talk about Avian Flu.

"Influenza A, also called H5N1 virus, is an influenza A virus subtype that occurs mainly in birds, is highly contagious among birds and may be deadly to them. It does not usually infect humans except in cases of close contact with poultry or H5N1-contaminated surfaces. So why should we talk about it today? We're not in the poultry business, right?"

Even Eva managed a short laugh.

"In about 300 recorded cases of human H5N1 infections

there has been a staggering mortality rate: over fifty percent of infected people are dead within a couple of days. If H5N1 were to mutate it could gain the ability to spread easily among humans. Should infection with the human influenza A virus and the H5N1 occur in one individual, parts of the two viruses could combine their genetic material to create a virus monster. Or, during the adaptive mutation, the bird virus could slowly learn to attack the human cells. Then we could have a pandemic of horrendous proportions, possibly worse than the 1918 Flu – which was also a Bird Flu virus, by the way. So. Today we are going to talk about National Pandemic Influenza preparedness..."

"Fifty percent mortality," Eva whispered to Bill. "I didn't realize it was that bad."

"Don't worry, Dr. Leigh. There are so many other things to be scared about: global warming, terrorists, smoking. At least this one has a cure."

"What?"

"Tamiflu. Available at any pharmacy."

After the meeting, standing outside in a brightly lit square and sharing his cigarette, Eva asked Bill if he wanted to go out that evening.

"What about Greg?"

"We're breaking up."

"Oh. Sorry to hear that," he said, and she saw with satisfaction that he was not sorry at all. "I'd love to have a drink with you, Dr. Leigh."

He waved his hand at her and left, his hips swaying and his head held high. She watched him walk away until her beeper rang. Mr. Harrison had arrived for his appointment after all.

"Let's go somewhere quiet," Eva said when they met again in front of the building. Bill was, as always, late. "I just want to talk."

She didn't know what she really wanted, or why she had chosen Bill as her confidante, but she craved being with him now. The fact that they had long been attracted to one other bestowed on the moment a vague sense of freedom and possibility. She didn't think beyond that. It was just emotional upheaval, a melancholic force that drove her to Bill, like an affecting song sucking her in. Something in him invited her to sing that song out, freely, at the top of her lungs, and Eva yearned to talk endlessly, with insatiable inspiration.

Bill was dark and charismatic, with a sharp profile and laughing eyes. He was gifted with a photographic memory that allowed him to quote freely from every book and every song he had ever read or heard. That his opinions were often borrowed did not diminish his brilliance in Eva's eyes. She had almost fallen in love with him in the past, during their long talks well into midnight, but they had never even kissed. She thought she knew why. Bill was attractive and repellent at once. His fingernails were dirty and long and he often smelled like someone who took a shower just once or twice a week, despite being quite vain about his appearance.

Now, walking along with him in silence in the direction of First Avenue, it occurred to her that there might be something else to their not being together: His charisma and self-assuredness faded when closeness became palpable, not ruled in by the safety of social norms.

Bill walked, as if rushing somewhere, and swung his arms widely. He talked about music, his speech loud and uninhibited. Sometimes he sang a line or two in the flow of free associations that were hard for her to follow. There was a crazy disquiet in him, this moment exciting and tiring the next. Eva almost regretted asking him out.

They ate couscous at Mogador, then stopped at Pick Me Up on Avenue A, a cozy little café they had frequented during their residency years. Here, Eva could sip her coffee and watch people for hours, all the time dreaming of some other, vague and wonderful life where disappointments did not happen.

In the red streetlight two half-naked muscular boys swished by on their skateboards, followed by an elderly man on a strangely shaped bicycle from which hundreds of Puerto-Rican flags fluttered in the wind. The night was crisp and full of potential, and Eva's buried hurt sharpened her senses. As she and Bill approached the café, a heavily made-up woman emerged wearing a white lace dress and a straw hat, her bearing queenly and deliberate. Bill held the door for her.

There weren't many customers. A Moby record played quietly in the background. Eva ordered a glass of Pinot Grigio and a latte and sank into an armchair by a low, round table.

"Greg is dating someone else," she said in response to Bill's enquiring gaze. Saying it caused her a tearing pain, as though someone had ripped through her pride. Admission was humiliation, but she did it for the sake of friendship, for permission to spend the evening in Bill's company.

"I wish I could say why that happened or why we were together in the first place. Maybe I trusted him too much. Or maybe, and this is what's always in the back of my mind, I'm just not good enough. I mean my self-doubt. It poisons. The stupid thing is, I really tried to make this relationship work. Only yesterday I was debating with myself whether to tell him I love him. I was always afraid of confessions. Thank God I didn't. It just shows how little we know of other people's inner lives. They're all dark, murky waters, and in the end we're totally alone."

"You're a beautiful person," Bill said kindly, and through the gush of gratefulness, she answered,

"Thank you, but I don't believe it. I get bitter and snappy with age, and somehow numbed. I do feel more secure in many ways, but it's an ugly security, like building a house that you hate. It's becoming hard for me to trust people. You know this fear all girls have of not finding 'a man.' It's a cliché, really, a front to put on things which are so much more subtle and complicated."

"You could date anyone and you know it. I have no idea why you chose a schmuck."

"He is not a schmuck!" Eva retorted, stubbornly pressing her lips together.

"Sorry, I didn't mean to say it. He seemed like a nice guy. But you could do better."

"What's better?"

"Someone who cares about you more. Someone with ambitions. You've said yourself that you can't understand a person without aspirations. Right?"

"Right," agreed Eva. "But don't all roads lead to myself, after all? Why did I choose someone inferior to me in terms of achievement and yet someone so kind and loving?"

"Your father?" Bill suggested with a smile. "Sounds like an Oedipus complex to me. You told me once he died when you were young."

"He died when I was six. He fell out a window."

"How did that happen?"

"He was a counter-phobic and a fatalist. He believed that death would only come on its own time no matter how you much you tempt it. He walked on the balcony rail more than once. And that day he slipped. His best friend rushed over to see my father's fingers clutching the rail just before he fell."

"I'm sorry. It wasn't suicide?"

"I've asked myself that too. I don't think so. Who commits suicide when your friends are watching? Isn't suicide a private affair? No. I think it was fatalism that killed him."

"It must have been hard on you. Do you remember him?"

"Yes. He had sad, kind eyes. And he liked to carry me on his shoulders."

Bill was stroking Eva's hand, gently and yet with some

edgy detachment. She watched the coiling motions of his thin white fingers on her wrist, then withdrew her hand.

"It's okay. It was a long time ago."

"Are you a fatalist too?" Bill laughed at something unclear to her.

"No. I can't be a fatalist, can I? With my father dead of it?"

"Cause of death: fatalism!" Bill laughed again. "Sorry, Dr. Leigh, I hope I'm not being insensitive."

Eva sipped her wine, which had turned warm and a little too sour, and reflected on how typical this little psychological vignette was for Bill. He strokes her hand; she withdraws it; he feels hurt and ridicules her feelings.

"You are. But I'm not offended," she lied.

"So if you don't mind my analyzing you, does Greg remind you of your father?"

"No. He's more like my child."

"A child?" Bill snorted.

"Does it sound stupid?" Eva asked disarmingly. "I guess so. He's endearing like a twelve-year-old, and totally incapable of organizing himself toward anything. It's childish, isn't it?"

"Doesn't it irritate you?"

"Sometimes, I guess. I couldn't have a family with him, but there was always hope of him changing, or me changing him."

"That's rather childish too. People don't change, not easily anyway."

"No one said easily. People change in therapy, and in life."

"But why would you love someone who's infantile?"

"I think it's my low self-esteem. He's caring and kind. There's no power struggle with him. It's comforting. He's soft. Even his body is soft and hairless, like a boy's."

Bill unbuttoned his shirt to reveal the dense, curly chair on his chest. He pulled on it with a comically blank face.

"Hairy men are beastly!" he announced loudly and

turned around, looking for an audience. A red-haired girl at the neighboring table giggled silently, parting her fresh teenager's lips.

"I was not passing judgment on your hairiness," Eva said.

"Do you want kids?" Bill helped himself to a sip of her wine.

"I guess so. In the future. You?"

"Sure. I love kids. Isn't it marvelous that we both love kids?" he winked conspiratorially.

"Oh, cut it out, Jacobs! I'm baring my soul, and you're just being so impossible!"

He showed her the tip of his tongue and laughed again. Watching Bill's quick ape-like face Eva felt puzzled by his bullying playfulness, which she both disliked and enjoyed. He had been a bully as a child; she knew this. Someone who pulled girls' ponytails – Eva could picture it vividly.

"You're like a kid who's eaten too much sugar," she said. "God, I feel so depressed!"

"Don't be depressed, Dr. Leigh! Think about it like a psychiatrist, use a cognitive-behavioral approach. You're a beautiful and accomplished young woman."

"Sometimes I wonder whether I chose psychiatry to remedy my own insecurities. There is a study that showed that possessing a depressive predisposition makes therapists more compassionate. I guess it's true. Helping others has a healing effect on me, as if by giving kindness I'm liberating myself from fear and loneliness."

"There's a reason for all of us to have chosen psychiatry, Dr. Leigh." Bill ran his hand through his hair.

"Why did *you* choose psychiatry?" she asked.

"For me it was that or surgery. Both are like knives slicing in, taking out the tumor. Only psychiatry is subtler, more intellectually appealing. And of course you don't have to be on call every other night, which leaves time to live."

"What's your tumor, Bill?"

"Dr. Leigh! That was brilliant!" Bill shook her hand in a mock show of professional respect. His fingers were thin, tapering off at the ends, and bore black hairs sprouting from their backs. They were weak and neurotic hands, discordant with the Hellenic beauty of his body.

"Talking about psychiatry," said Eva, switching topics, "I had lunch with Robin recently and we played a game, picking psychiatric disorders to fit the personalities of our classmates …"

"What was my diagnosis?" Bill interrupted.

Eva laughed. "Narcissistic personality disorder."

"Oh, you have that too," he said dismissively. "Every achiever is narcissistic. Robin?"

"Manic."

"And you?" Bill asked.

"I thought you'd never ask! Depression. Nothing too interesting. It's a professional hazard to label yourself. It's like med students who become hypochondriacs as they study diseases."

"I've been through that. I thought I had testicular cancer, and Hodgkin's and what not. What about you?"

"No," Eva shook her head. "I've always thought my problems were mental. Although now that you mention it I do remember examining my moles in search for melanoma."

They laughed and regarded one another with affection.

A lanky blond man walked past their table, causing Eva's heart to jump. Feeling her glance upon him, he turned around, revealing his heavy features: a thick nose, a jutted jaw, a scar on his left cheek. Embarrassed, she looked away.

"See that man?" she said to Bill.

"What about him?"

"I thought it was Greg. I often mistake people for others. It's odd, isn't it?"

"Yeah," Bill said. "I do it too. It usually happens when I have a crush on someone. You must be feeling guilty about being with me."

He smiled. Eva rose to order them another round of wine. The stranger was standing in line in front of her. When he ordered, his voice was husky and tired, and for some reason Eva felt disappointed and tired herself. Greg was working at Luca's Lounge tonight and wouldn't be home until late. Eva wasn't sure which was stronger, her guilt or her desire to punish him. Her watch showed eleven o'clock. She yawned, covering her mouth and looking around. Bill was watching her. Back at the table, holding a glass of wine in each hand, she asked,

"Have you ever mistaken someone for me?"

"Many times," said Bill, pressing his lips together.

"Really?" she asked, grinning. Bill's lips curled into an ironic smirk but he remained silent.

"I'm flattered, Dr. Jacobs!"

"That was a long time ago," he said gravely, raising his left eyebrow.

Eva laughed, throwing back her chin.

"I wonder why I'm telling you about Greg anyway. It feels sick and exciting at once, like an itch."

"Sharing is always healthy," Bill stated philosophically. "Even when it feels sick. Imagine you live in a small primitive tribe and your hut catches fire, or there's an outbreak of Avian Flu. Why would someone come to your aid? It's the dopamine of compassion, the survival of the individual by group participation, programmed into our genes. One for all, all for one. That's why you're talking, and I'm listening, and we're both enjoying it. It's also why we practice psychiatry."

"You've convinced me, Dr. Jacobs."

Bill laughed a healthy, self-possessed laugh that made Eva envious of his gregariousness and the range of emotions that ran through him so fluidly, so easily finding their expression in his body. He was a perfect instrument of himself. Eva imagined a trumpet or a saxophone, a little too loud and brazen, just as proud and shining as his persona. She strived to be like him, and when they were together it seemed almost attainable. He pulled her up and gave her wings.

The café slowly emptied. They rose when the waiter started to overturn the chairs and rolled out a mop.

"Let's have a drink at my place," Bill offered.

It was fresh and windy outside. They walked in silence through the empty streets toward Bill's new apartment on Avenue B. Eva had never been there before.

"It's kind of messy," he warned. "I haven't unpacked yet."

Bill had lived in hospital housing on Third Avenue, a bright and welcoming place despite its clutter of books, records, socks and unwashed dishes. He'd had to vacate it at the end of his residency, a cause for much grumbling and aggravation with New York real estate agents.

"I always wondered why all our attendings live in Westchester," he muttered, finding his keys in his pocket. "Well, here's the answer. This is what we can afford with our fabulous doctor salaries!"

The new apartment was in a dilapidated brownstone, built at the beginning of the century for factory workers. There were garbage and rats on the streets, a shabby, covered with graffiti front door, and a staircase lit by a single bulb dangling from the ceiling. Amid a stale smell of cigarettes, Bill and Eva climbed three flights of stairs.

"Welcome to my palace!" Bill said pushing the door open.

It was dark and smelled pleasantly of book dust, like the second-hand bookshops Eva liked to visit.

"Let me turn on the light," he said. "Come in. Watch out for the boxes! Take my hand."

Bill's hand was sweaty. He drew her closer to him, and she put her head in the soft spot just below his Adam's apple, which hung heavily on his neck like a stone. He stroked her back and her hair. She was anxious and excited.

They kissed. Bill's tongue was quirky and sharp exploring her mouth. It was strange to be kissing him, both pleasant and revolting; it reminded her of her first kiss so many years ago. She kept her eyes closed. He switched on the light and led her to the bedroom.

"I love you, Dr. Leigh," he said in a stilted stranger's voice. Eva didn't answer. He unbuttoned her blouse and pressed his hands over her bra. She could hear him panting. They undressed. Her passion was gone, but she felt she had to stay. Maybe it would return, in time, as sometimes happened with Greg nowadays. She let Bill embrace her with a full body touch. He trembled like a string, infecting her with anxiety. He had the virile smell of an animal. His sharp beak-like nose kept awkwardly poking her cheeks.

"C'mon, let's lie down," he whispered, sensing her rigidity. She followed him silently, her wordlessness enhancing the sense of growing panic.

Bill lay on top of her, bringing her knees up, and there was something nice and tender about the way he did it, encouraging her to think that maybe this wasn't a mistake after all.

"Why are you so passive?" Bill asked, again in a stranger's voice, this time also bearing whiny and demanding notes. His erection was gone. Softly, Eva freed herself from his arms and sat up, draping a bed sheet around her waist.

"I think I should go," she said.

Bill was silent, and Eva rose, conscious of her body although it was dark. Bill stayed on the bed. Eva couldn't tell whether he was looking at her. While she laced her shoes, she heard him breathing hard, and paused to listen. A second later she heard him blowing his nose.

"Are you crying?"

"No," he replied nasally.

She switched on the light.

"Yes I'm crying," he said.

"I just want us to be friends. I'm afraid it will ruin our friendship."

"Bullshit! Bullshit!" he cried bitterly. Eva leaned toward him, gliding her hand over his wet face in a gush of compassion.

"Please, don't cry, I'm sorry."

Bill sobbed freely, abandoning his shame.

"Don't cry, it's going to be okay." She repeated this automatically, feeling cozy in her clothes, warm and safe from predators.

"Is it because of my erection?" he asked. "I told you I had problems."

Eva moved closer and took his head into her hands, stroking his oily bristles and the stubble on his cheeks.

"No, not at all, stupid!" she said kindly. "Of course not! It's just somehow not right. I can't explain it any better."

"I'm angry, I'm furious!" he cried, backing away from her. His eyes were moist and intense in the low yellow light.

"At me?"

"No man with a good hard-on gets into this friendship talk."

"But it's not because of your erection!"

"Then why are you going? Am I too good for you?"

Eva rose, dizzy and tired, feeling suddenly too distant to discuss feelings. She saw their two shadows on the wall, the dark round shapes almost immobile against each other. They could have been the silhouettes of love. But they weren't. They were just shadows. She had sung out her song. She had probably said too much. She knew she'd hurt him.

The city noise was dying outside; the wails of a faraway siren dotted the darkness. It was two in the morning. Eva thought of Greg, but that was an empty memory too.

The bed creaked, and Eva saw Bill rising. His erection had returned. She observed it with an almost scientific curiosity. Wrapped in the sheet, toga-like around his body, he looked like an ancient Greek.

"You have a Greek nose," she said. "I never noticed before."

"That's very Freudian. I thought you were looking at my penis."

"I was, too. You have an erection."

"Funny, isn't it? He forgave you. But I haven't yet."

Bill walked with her to the living room and, with a moan, fell into a large orange sofa.

"Sit down," he motioned, putting his feet up on the sofa's back. "Just for a minute."

Eva obeyed, sitting down on a box that cracked underneath her.

They sat looking at one another for a long time.

"Do you remember any poems?" he said finally. "I love poetry."

"T.S. Eliot?" she offered.

Bill nodded, and Eva began, first hesitantly, then drawn into the music of the words. As lines streamed out of her and drew her into a particular melancholic and elevated state of mind, she felt her anxiety leaving, her whole being tailored into the harmony of the poem:

April is the cruelest month, breeding
Lilacs out of the dead land, mixing
Memory and desire, stirring
Dull roots with spring rain.

"Beautiful, isn't it?" Bill whispered. He gestured for her to sit beside him now, on the sofa. Eva continued.

Winter kept us warm, covering
Earth in forgetful snow, feeding
A little life with dried tubers.

Now Bill moved his hand to the back of her neck, cupping it with his palm, then glided his fingers down to her breasts.

Eva paused.

"Go on," he said and she continued, haltingly, struggling to remember the words.

He ran his fingers over her t-shirt and sank them in her navel. She fell silent but did not stop him when he continued downward.

"Go on please," he said, and she obeyed.

Summer surprised us, coming over the Starnbergersee
with a shower of rain; we stopped in the colonnade,
and drank coffee, and talked for an hour.

He opened the button of her pants. She raised her hips to help him pull them down. He was slow, stroking her crotch, then sliding his fingers inside, separating her pubic hair.

"Don't stop," he said. She went on. When she couldn't remember the words anymore, she started over. A dizzying sweetness rose in her. She let her head fall back. She wanted it to go on. He felt her wetness. She spread her legs for him. A little voice in her woke up periodically, seeking explanation. She was grateful and guilty, were these emotions not enough? She was too lost to know what she wanted. What she wanted now was this. She continued to recite the poem.

Bill moved closer and guided her hand to his penis, knobby and hard under her fingers. She squeezed it with rising pleasure. She looked down at its blind pulsating hotness, which she held like a microphone, and realized she wasn't talking anymore, just moaning the music of the poem. Bill nudged her forward and down and she took his penis into her mouth.

"Good girl," he said through clenched teeth, breathing loud.

I'm a whore, thought Eva, and drowning in desire ceased to be herself. She imagined a blank room somewhere in Amsterdam, a bald fat customer she had to serve. She pictured the money he would pay her after it was over, a stack of foreign bills left on her nightstand. Then the whore's image became separate from Eva's: a peroxide blonde from Eastern Europe with heavy tits and a horny tongue. She was a queen, an anonymous young pussy, and she moaned together with the client, whom she called Hans. Eva inhabited the prostitute's juicy body, presenting her breasts, opening herself wider for Bill. He withdrew his fingers and then his penis from her and moved her aside to come by himself while Eva clutched his arm, whose joints and muscles she could feel moving back and forth while he ejaculated. Bill cried out. He didn't look at her. Her excitement waned but didn't leave her.

"Did you imagine I was someone else?" Eva asked.

Bill was startled.

"How did you know?"

"Tell me."

"No. Did you too?"

She laughed slyly.

"No, you tell me," he begged.

"You were a fifty-year-old fat and balding client in Amsterdam. I was a young blonde from the Ukraine with big tits. You had a stack of bills for me on the night table. You worshiped my body." The wave of excitement revived in her. She held his arm and spoke quickly to capture the moment.

"Oh," Bill replied, and Eva realized it was too late. Her heart sank with hurt as she watched him free his arm, then wipe up his sperm with the corner of a bed sheet. His face was smooth. "He sounds like a sexy man. And the money. That's a real turn on. Sorry. Don't have any for you."

Eva cringed and instinctively covered herself, suddenly sober and offended, as if she'd been slapped in the face.

"That's rude," she said stiltedly.

"Just joking, Dr. Leigh." Bill got up and walking naked across the room. "Gotta pee."

Eva gathered her things and quickly put on her pants. Her

45

foot stuck in the trouser leg and she pulled on it furiously. She had just buckled her bra when Bill came back, still naked, his slack penis swaying between his legs. He yawned loudly and widely like a hippo, not bothering to cover his mouth.

"Now your turn," she said.

She felt the need to keep talking, to put off the acknowledgement of her humiliation.

"What do you mean?"

"Your fantasy."

"Oh, that. It's boring stuff. Like you described, young, blond, large tits. No one old. No kids."

Eva buttoned her blouse, irritated and mute.

"So tired!" he said, picking up his boxer shorts.

"Well, it wasn't too healthy either. It wasn't me," she said.

"It wasn't you where?" he asked with impatience. He was standing, waiting for her to leave.

"In your fantasy," she said in a high-pitched defensive voice, raising her eyebrows. "You pretended I was a whore. You didn't make love to me."

"I don't have much luck with love."

Eva looked up at him.

"You don't get it? When I fall in love, I lose my erection. Girls find me boring, understandably so. When I treat them as whores, I'm as strong as a horse. Girls love me. What does it tell you?"

"I don't know. Never lose your erection?"

"That's good!" he grinned. "It was my line. You should have said, 'you must be afraid to love' or something touchy-feely that good insightful girls always say. It's what I expected from you."

"Right," Eva said. "I have to go now."

Eva walked home quickly, running away from her hurt. She felt violated like a rape victim. She hated Bill. The brisk walk brought her some relief. When she entered Stuyvesant Town, with its rows of identical houses and calm orderly lawns smelling of freshly cut grass, it was three in the morning.

Eva cautiously unlocked the door with a hand unsteadied by alcohol and emotion. It was dark and still inside. She turned on the light. Greg's shoes stood by the entrance, neatly lined up together. Ska didn't come to greet her, and Eva broke down in tears at this last symbolic betrayal. Quietly sobbing she dragged herself to the bathroom and locked the door behind her, turned on the water, and finally let down her guard. She took a long shower, rubbing herself with soap until it hurt, then frantically brushing her teeth, cleansing herself of the dirt and pain. Her vagina was still excited, and she masturbated a little, not thinking about anything in particular. The desire sparkled and went away and she let it go with an angry satisfaction. She hated sex. She hated alcohol. She hated T. S. Eliot. After the shower, she wiped down the misted mirror and applied her night cream. Giving herself a wooden smile she examined the wrinkles under her eyes, as she did daily now in a sad ritual of aging. *Thirty years old and so stupid*, she mumbled to herself. *Look at that son of a bitch.* Anna's prophesy flashed in her mind like a dark unclear sign. She pulled on her pajamas, tiptoed to the kitchen to pour herself some ice water, and settled in front of the TV to flip idly through the channels. That's how Greg found her, miserable, hunched over a TV set.

"Are you okay?" he asked. He stood timidly in the shade by the door, prepared to leave if she didn't want him.

"I'm okay I guess," she said. "Go to bed. I'm coming too."

In bed, lying at a safe distance from Greg, Eva listened for his breathing; it was relaxed and almost inaudible, spaced out in long intervals, and she decided that he was asleep. It filled her with emptiness and a silent rage. She didn't want him – and yet she still craved his love. Decidedly turning away, she resolved to cry, but tears wouldn't come. Furious thoughts boiled in her head. *Get out of here!* she wanted to scream. *Get out you piece of shit!* Punishing them both.

"Hey, Evy," Greg called softly, using his lovely name for her. "You want me to scratch your back?"

She didn't answer, but lay down with her back toward him. He moved closer and scratched her back in long tender strides, waiting for her to relax. On the verge of falling asleep she felt him kissing her hair.

"Sleep now. It will be okay. I love you," he whispered.

And she slept.

4

The days leading up to Eva's new job were full of good-byes. Her patients came with thank-you cards, tears and hugs, and story after story of the pain and little therapeutic successes they had lived through together. Eva was slightly uncomfortable with physical contact, but it also made her feel real in ways that words couldn't. Brushing aside a little voice critiquing her professionalism, she hugged her patients back.

A lot of paperwork had to be completed; charts had to be reviewed, corrected and returned, and this somewhat numbed the reality of separations. Eva worked, occasionally pausing to dream of the future and, refueled with the joy of anticipation, resumed her typing, organizing and filing. Always, like a buzz in the background, there was the knowledge of freedom and moving on – an aerial, sweet dream, carrying her away. Like a snake in the spring, she would leave her old self behind: her insecurity, her guilt, and Bill.

In these last days, Eva avoided Bill. The very idea of him became coated with the smells of his body, and she developed a physical aversion to him, senseless as an allergy. Rationally, in the days following their sex, Eva decided that what had happened was not that important. She had hurt him. He had erectile problems and these made him sensitive. He hurt her back. Eye for an eye. It was simple, really, and banal, no reason to be offended. And, serving its purpose, their crime had reunited her with Greg, for now she too was guilty, and they could continue loving each other on equal terms. Tooth for a tooth. Since the night with Bill Eva had been sweet with Greg in a vigilant and eager way. All could be healed and forgotten; they just had to try. She never mentioned Greg's affair with Clair again.

Beneath the simplicity, there were layers of darkness. Just the night before she dreamed of having sex with Bill and then awoke feeling Greg's hands stroking her body. Closing her eyes, she imagined herself a prostitute giving in to a different, cruel eroticism; when Greg whispered "I love you" she felt strangely irritated at him for disrupting the fantasy. Her subconscious was a moor into which she was afraid to walk. She dreaded what it might reveal: her basic guilt, worthlessness, badness? The labels didn't stick. She needed a leech-word to sap the pus, to become bloated with poison and fall away, leaving her light and healthy. But the word hid from her, while Eva hoped for the return of her innocence.

Bill's quick embrace on their last day felt dry and formal. They were standing outside the hospital building listening to the birds chirping in the park and to homeless women quarreling on a bench about money.

"Well, that's it," Bill said, shaking his head and smiling.

Eva nodded.

"Give me a call."

"You too. Let's stay in touch."

He waved at her, striding away. She lit a cigarette and watched his swaggering gait. *Are you the Joker, Bill?* she muttered to herself.

As the time of her new job approached, Eva grew nervous. The fact of becoming an assistant professor of psychiatry was disquieting, as if at any moment she might be accused of being an impostor and ridiculed. She knew she was good; her insecurity had nothing to do with her skills. But somewhere within her lived that picture of a bearded and mighty old psychiatrist who could read the mind's secrets. He was powerful and scary. He was God, father, authority.

Most importantly, he was flawless. He didn't cry at night. It was inexplicably disappointing to Eva that after all her years of residency the major metamorphosis she had waited for never happened.

"I understand it," Robin said. "It's an identity crisis. Many people feel like you, me included. Maybe it's because we didn't have a female role model during our training. It's so sad, really, that we live in a world of white men."

"Ah, Robin, don't start on the white men, please!"

"But it's true! You're just afraid to sound like a feminist."

"That too. It's ridiculous to be a feminist in an age of political correctness. It's passe."

Eva's new job started July 15th. Like most of her classmates, she became an inpatient attending, tending to the sickest at a city hospital. It was exciting at first, challenging and exhausting. Eva felt that the amount of paperwork was overwhelming sometimes, and she didn't have enough time for patients. She worked long hours. Yet, months later, when the first snow fell and the days began dying by the time she left work, her job became just what it was: A job. Eva became more efficient and skillful and usually left on time, but the way things were run bothered her. The social worker on the unit was lazy and spiteful. Administrative priorities such as the length of stay often trumped the ideal disposition for the patients, and Eva's own role in the process of healing was automated and faceless.

Was that what her life was going to look like in the years to come? Was that it? The upward trajectory of her long training came to an end and she was on her own – plateaued. Increasingly Eva began the days in a bad mood and had to pace herself to get to work in time. She returned home in the evenings exhausted – and worrying that she herself was becoming depressed. Looking for the meaning in her life, she tried to feel proud of being a doctor, of having a secure and reasonably interesting job and an unclouded tomorrow. She wanted to be positive. This was how people lived: dutifully and numbly. Growing up meant exchanging dreams for security.

Sometimes, on weekends, when Eva took long lonely walks through the neighborhood, she felt a quickening in her heart at the flash of an unclear inspiration; but soon, unsure what to do with her longing, she grew limp. Just a weird firing of brain synapses, she would tell herself. Fantasies were for kids. She had to accept her responsibilities and the "common unhappiness" which, she, like Freud, had become convinced, was the main and final part of human destiny. Only Greg was different and continued to play and have a jolly time. It was a mixed blessing.

She and Greg barely talked any more. From time to time, he made attempts to cheer her up with wine, dinner, and songs. Other times he sulked in the corner with the guitar on his lap, assuming she was angry with *him*. Eva let him think she was. It even seemed right to her that he too should suffer – for his silly happiness, and living off her money. She was tired and irritable. The banal formula of cultural pessimism echoed in her head: Life sucks and then you die.

Eva came home tired. Exactly one year passed since she became an attending. The mirror in the entryway revealed her face lit by the sidelong light of a corner lamp. Her face looked sharp and deflated, full of dark triangles. She smiled automatically, brushed the hair from her forehead, and walked into the kitchen. The fridge was almost empty.

"Greg!"

Greg came out to meet her, dressed in jeans and a blue shirt ornamented with red stitches running through it in chic disorder.

"Are you going out?"

"No. You gave me this shirt last Christmas, remember?"

Eva nodded.

"It's beautiful," she said, her face softening.

"I know. I kept it for a special occasion."

"I'm hungry," she said, sitting down. "Are you?" *He's found a job*, she thought hopefully, and straightened, trying to summon her joy.

"Let's order. I had a great audition today. It's a movie, I read the script. I think they're going to take me. Just a feeling!"

They ordered from the Republic and opened a bottle of Pinot Grigio.

"To your success!" she said, raising her glass.

Greg nodded and took a long, superstitious sip.

Eva studied his fresh boyish face. *Why does he stay with me?* she asked herself with a pang of pain. Something about him had changed, but she couldn't put her finger on it. His eyes were brighter and clearer than she remembered. He looked young.

"You look different," she remarked.

"You like it? I plucked my eyebrows."

Eva laughed. How easy. How funny.

"Do you think it was vain of me?"

"Hey, if it helps you get a job!" Eva opened her palms in a who-cares gesture. "Tell me about the part!"

Greg leaned back with an air of comic self-importance.

"It's about a homosexual guy who is trying to adopt a child," he said. "The story is a little cheesy, to tell you the truth, but I like it. That's what people want, right? Cheesy emotional stuff about little heroes. Ricard, the director, really wants me for the role."

"That's great," she replied. "Is Ricard gay?"

"I don't know. Probably. Real males don't go into the movie business, do they?"

"They do. But they don't necessarily make movies about homosexual men adopting children. Did he ask you about your sexual orientation?"

"Kind of. I quoted Freud. Said that eighty percent of the population is bisexual."

"Uh-huh."

"Well, what did you want me to do? Say I hate queers and don't want the part?"

"No, that's fine, really. It's great if it works out."

They fell silent, sipping their wine and watching one another.

"So how was your day?" Greg asked brightly.

"Same thing," Eva said. "There's a JACO commission coming to the hospital. The social worker smirks at me whenever I ask her to send applications for patients. She doesn't even see her patients because she's too busy gossiping and kissing her superior's ass."

"How can you let her behave like this?" Greg remarked. "Why don't you write a complaint?"

"It's not going to change anything! It's the way things are run."

"You don't know. You can't know if you don't try. You told me that yourself."

"Greg, you just don't understand. Please. Let's change the topic."

The wine made her tired, but she poured herself more.

"You're the doctor," Greg continued as if he hadn't heard her. "Kick her ass! I don't understand you!"

"No. You don't!" Eva stamped her foot. China trembled on the table. She covered her face with her hands. She wanted to buy into his dream again, into the life and promise blossoming on his face. But he was different. He was a deedless phoenix re-born daily with no purpose except to imagine the songs he would sing someday. Who was he to give her advice?

"You've never even held a job!"

Greg pressed his lips together.

"I'm sorry," she said. "I'm just stressed."

"You're not sorry," he said shortly. "You always do it."

"Do what?"

"You're a joy-killer. Whenever something good happens, you kill it. Like now."

Greg was right, and Eva turned away, crying.

Then, almost unwittingly, as if by chance, they stumbled into each other's arms. He kissed Eva's eyes and her cheeks where the tears had left their wet traces. She ran her fingers down his soft hairless flank, over his hard buttocks and then down toward his spread legs, and, feeling his hands over her breasts and hearing his first low moan, dissolved into a sweet and sweaty nothingness. Fights were like rains for their sex life, bringing freshness, grief and acute intimacy. Each time, Eva imagined, was a rehearsal for their last lovemaking, with the nostalgic intensity of savoring their bodies' here-and-now.

Sometimes there is nothing more erotic than saying goodbye.

5

Thanksgiving was celebrated at Olga and Vladimir's.

"Should I wear a dress?" Eva asked. "Everyone's going to look like in the old movies."

"Except for their waist sizes," Greg smiled. "But, of course, if you want to charm my father."

Eva pulled out an orange-colored woolen dress that she had bought when she was still in training, aspiring to look more serious and professional to her patients. For the past three years it had hung in the closet abandoned as she gained her professional confidence by other means. She vaguely recollected that she attempted to grow her hair long at about the same time as she purchased the dress. It didn't last, and she cut it short and went back to wearing pants, where she carried her keys in her pockets and the beeper on her belt.

The dress fit beautifully. Eva was a tall, slender woman with broad shoulders and a narrow waist; dresses in general flattered her body, which was a bit too wide at the hips. She admired herself for a second or two before becoming self-conscious and feeling desperately over-dressed.

"You look great!" Greg said, walking in, and the matter was settled. He wore a black t-shirt, a grey jacket, jeans, and red socks to match his father's (Vladimir loved bright socks), though on Greg they looked chic.

His parents' house was warm from the oven, and loud. Most of the guests, friends and relatives, all Russian, had already arrived. Olga cooked, dressed in a dark skirt that fell to just below her knees, a pink-and-white blouse, a string of pearls on her neck with matching earrings, heels, and an apron. Her loud and jolly sister Irina, the first of the family to come to America, was helping out in the kitchen, back to back with Anna, who gave Eva a warm hug as though they knew one another well. Anna's presence in the house filled Eva with hopeful tension, as if the stripe of her misfortunes could end with their second meeting. And yet here, in the hot and crowded kitchen, Anna looked ordinary and harmless, in her striped blouse and salt-and-pepper hair, blending in seamlessly with the rest of the company. A couple of other, middle-aged and elderly women were there too, to chat and cut onions and shell eggs. Men dressed in suits stood around the living room with their collars open, smoking cigarettes and talking politics, often inserting into their Russian heavily accented English words which, although understandable, sounded to Eva lost. The children, dressed for the holiday in suit pants and starched shirts, wreaked havoc in a bedroom, where they spoke loud and perfect English, ignoring the adults' Russian admonishments to behave.

"Are you okay?" Greg asked, handing Eva a glass of wine.

"I'm fine," she said, and he drifted off into a conversation with Irina, who loudly giggled, exposing a golden upper tooth.

Eva drank some more, talked to Vladimir, and attempted a conversation with Olga's mother using the few Russian words she knew. Before long Eva found Anna by her side.

"Your Russian is improving," Anna smiled. "How've you been?"

"The cards were right," Eva said half-jokingly. "I'm not happy. Work's not going well. Nothing is. Will you read cards for me today? Tell me all about good things."

"It's not the right day for cards," Anna shook her head. "Cards should be read at full moon. But changes are coming. I can feel it without the cards."

Eva was strangely disappointed, almost angry at herself for having asked for something she didn't believe in anyway.

"It's all so general," she said. "Changes are always

57

coming."

"Fortune-telling is like faith, you have to believe in it."

"I don't, and yet here I am asking you to read cards for me. Ridiculous, isn't it? Unhappy people tend to look for miracles, I guess. In the past months I've sometimes found myself blaming you for things that have gone wrong, like you caused them."

"Like Cassandra."

"Like Cassandra," Eva agreed. "People go to fortune-tellers to hear happy things so they can go on hoping. But you don't want to read cards for me today."

"It's not the right day for cards," Anna repeated softly.

"But changes are coming?" Eva asked ironically. "Well, you can't go wrong with this one!"

Anna smiled.

The table in the living room was expanded and covered with a starched white tablecloth adorned with red carnations and crystal glasses, small ones for vodka and big ones for wine. Water appeared in little dark-green bottles labeled Borjomi. It was fizzy and salty and made Eva's tongue burn. She was used to still water, but still water was never served at Greg's parents' home; Russians don't drink it, to Eva's surprise. Salads were served in crystal bowls, garnished with crushed egg-yolk, curly strips of carrot, and cilantro. The apartment smelled of heavy delicious food: onions, eggs, meat, mayonnaise. For their central Thanksgiving dish Olga cooked *pelmeni*, juicy dumplings filled with ground meat, "because my turkey is always so dry!" she lamented with a laugh.

After the table was set, guests settled into their chairs and the toasts began, first in English, for Eva's benefit, then in Russian, which Greg translated, whispering into Eva's ears. The toasts generally adhered to the idea of all things being "wonderful," as initiated by Vladimir, speaking first as head of the house. "I want to raise this glass to my wonderful wife of thirty-two, yes thirty-two years, who made this gathering possible and cooked all these delicacies, a real woman in form and content: beautiful, kind, strong and smart. To you, Olga!"

Greg rolled his eyes, and Eva giggled, covering her full mouth with her hand.

Toward the evening, Vladimir got up to talk again, a little unsteadily this time. A bottle of vodka on his side of the table was replaced by another, still frosted over and bearing the imprints of Olga's fingers. He sang a few lines from a song everyone seemed to know, then spoke in a loud, festive voice. Watching his flushed face, Eva thought it was the happiest she had ever seen him.

"Now, a philosophical toast!" Greg remarked a little too loudly, smiling at Eva with just the corners of his lips. "Freedom is hard work and respect. To America! Yeah right! Let's bomb the whole world into democracy!"

Vladimir's gaze shifted to Greg, and Greg turned red. Vladimir fell silent. All glances, one by one, turned to father and son staring at each other.

"Papa," Greg said continuing in Russian that no one translated for Eva this time.

"Why not speak English?" Vladimir replied. "Let's be respectful." He flashed Eva a remote smile. "This was coming for a long time, and it's fine, let's just say it so you know what I think. It's hard to talk to a grown-up son, he won't listen. So allow me, Grigory, to drink to your woman Eva, and allow me to ask for her forgiveness and express my deep appreciation that she cares for you and houses you. Thank you Eva! And, I am sorry, Eva, I want to add. I hope that my son is sorry too." He slightly bowed to her. "I know he is a good boy, good at apologizing, anyway."

The room was palpably still. Vladimir took another sip, his gaze fixed on Eva. He was poised. In heavily accented and meticulous English, with every word falling like a boulder, he continued:

"I was a somebody before. Here, I'm a nobody, just like the next neighbor. A simple grocer, that is. What I can't bear is that Grigory is a nobody too, a total loser. Because you know what it makes me? A double loser, a double nobody, because I failed myself and then I failed to bring up a son who would redeem us. Children are our future, we used to say. Do you know what I mean?"

Olga whispered urgently into his ear. He tiredly waved at her and took a loud breath to continue, but then, as if suddenly exhausted, dropped it and turned away from the table. Anna quietly took the glass out of his hand.

"Let's hear some music!" Olga announced with feigned cheerfulness. The CD player began to bark a rough song sung by a Russian bard, Vyssotsky.

They left in silence. Eva was shaken and confused by her pity for Greg, which was at odds with her simultaneous pleasure at his humiliation. *Maybe now he'll start working*, she thought, holding his hand and whispering kind, loving words.

Greg's mother called the next day to apologize. "What a sober man keeps in his mind, a drunkard has on his tongue!" she said. "An old Russian proverb."

They loved Greg and wouldn't leave him no matter what. He was theirs, painfully and wholly. Theirs was the guilt, the despair, the anger, the love, the hope.

Eva, on the other hand, could walk away.

6

Greg got the role that he auditioned for, and even though the job was unpaid, it raised their hopes. Eva liked the fact that Greg was occupied. It satisfied her desire to structure his life. For too long she had been living with a nagging splinter that he was alien to her in some basic way, causing her disquiet that lay apart from financial worries and her irritation at having to support him. Her long-winded psychological excursions into his character were futile, and she had learned to avoid the topics of his future. The job revived her expectations, and Eva left to work with a heart light as a feather. She felt inspired. Indeed, as weeks passed, she began thinking about getting another job. Life was not so bad, after all.

The script for Greg's play was too obvious and read a bit like a manifesto, but there was no better material for bonding. Greg played a middle-class nerd whose wallet gets stolen on the subway and who meets a married gay policeman and falls in love with him. Overcoming their identity crises, family problems and societal non-acceptance, they adopt a foster child. Reading lines aloud for Greg, Eva made faces, and sometimes altered the text for comic effect. Although the script was badly written, she loved it. It liberated her.

"Gay men love children too!" Greg read in a heart-felt voice. Huskily aping Sting, Eva sang:

"Russians love their children too!" And they cracked up, slapping their knees, Greg wiping tears with the back of his hand.

For Greg's birthday, Eva organized a small "rehearsal" party. Robin arrived first, a false moustache under her nose.

She greeted Greg with his own script's opening line – when Julio Rodriguez, the policeman, comes home after a night spent with his lover:

"I'm coming out!"

Greg froze, frowning in surprise, and held the door wide to let Robin and her new boyfriend in.

"Come in, come in."

"That's funny but it's not the line," Robin's boyfriend commented, baring strong white teeth and extending his hand to Greg,

"I'm Dan."

Dan was big and blond, with the massive dependable jaw of a Superman. Greg gave him a polite smile. By the way Greg held Dan's hand, Eva guessed that Greg's was sweaty and he was embarrassed about it. Hiding his hands in the pockets of his jeans, Greg turned to Eva.

"You're guilty of copyright violation, you know."

In a flash, Eva saw the evening falling apart. All her cooking and efforts to make it funny, to find lines for each guest to recite as he or she came in, was a disaster. She'd made a mistake. Greg felt that he was being ridiculed in front of a broad-shouldered, broad-smiled alpha male. Eva had forgotten how uneasy he became with men like Dan – how jittery and fidgety, almost in his father's way. Panicking, Eva caught Robin's glance and pressed her index finger to her mouth, making big eyes. Robin blinked, holding her golden eyelashes closed long enough for Eva to understand that not one more word from the script would spoil the party.

The guests proceeded into the living room and stood there awkwardly until Eva asked them to sit and brought out the wine. Robin had put on weight. Her red, knee-length dress, adorned with lace around the sleeves and printed with little elephants, did not flatter her round forms.

"Are you getting fat?" Eva asked affably.

Robin rattled with artisan Village jewelry and giggled

loudly, in an affected and disdainful way that Eva found attractive. Dan sat next to her, possessively holding her hand. When addressed, he answered with eager cheerfulness, like a good boy lost in a big man's body. He was a lawyer, he explained, dealing with corporate real estate. He went to Yale. He owned a house in the Hamptons but wasn't sure whether he liked New York well enough to buy a place here. He liked modern art and played the piano (an unusual touch, Eva thought, exchanging glances with Greg).

"You see," Robin commented with comic graveness. "Finally! Finally I found a real man."

Dan smiled indulgently and moved closer to her, their hips touching.

They ate little tramezzinis that Eva made, and avocado salad, and drank more wine. The conversation became livelier. When Eva carried out the dishes, Greg joined her in the kitchen.

"He's boring," he whispered, bursting with eagerness to share his opinion. His cheeks were pink and his hair tousled in an endearingly self-deprecating way.

"Like hell!" Eva agreed, laughing. They kissed.

"About the lines," Greg said. "It was really funny. I mean it."

Back in the room, Greg took a seat next to Robin.

"What's the next line?"

"Oh, that!" she smiled, glancing at Eva, who shrugged her shoulders. "Okay! Just to warn you: Eva gave me three lines to remember. So, don't expect me to recite the whole script."

Robin got up, straightening her dress.

"Stop staring, Greg! You're making me nervous! Haven't you heard of stage fright?"

"In fact I just finished reading an article about it in *The New Yorker*..."

"One more thing," continued Robin, evidently not suffering from stage fright at all. "Dan was supposed to participate, but

I made an executive decision to exclude him because he has no acting talent. I do all sides of the dialogue."

"Okay, okay!"

"*I'm coming out!*" *(in a deep voice)*

"*Coming out of what? Where have you been?*" *(furious housewife about to break the dishes, fists clenched)*

"*Coming out, Maria. It means …it means …*"

"*What're you talking about?*"

"*I'm gay.*"

"*You can't be gay, daddy. You're married!*" *(high-pitched daughter's voice)*

(Wife howling): "*You can't do this to me! I'm pregnant! We're going to have a baby!*"

Finished, Robin beamed proudly. Everyone clapped and cheered.

"You do have talent, you know! That last line … Wow! I almost believed you," Greg teased.

Now Robin bowed, the corners of her mouth curling in ironic appreciation.

"That's because it's true," she declared plainly, in her loud and fresh voice. "We're having a baby. Three months pregnant today."

Dan nodded affectionately and put his large, thick-fingered hand on Robin's belly.

That night Eva had difficulty falling asleep. She tossed and turned, the memory of Dan's hand – so still and secure – haunting her. Robin was pregnant. Eva had shrugged it off talking to Greg earlier, after the guests had departed and they went to bed.

"Don't you remember her proclaiming that kids are boring?"

"Oh yes. She also said she'll never get married. And now you're practically a bridesmaid."

"He'll make a good husband."

"Boring like hell, you said it yourself."

"Husbands are boring by default," Eva muttered, wrapping the blanket more tightly around her. "That's life. Life always wins."

"Or death always wins."

"I guess I meant that convention always wins," Eva corrected herself after a moment. "Even for Robin, with her bright dresses and tattoos and glass-bead jewelry."

Greg didn't answer, and, straining her neck in his direction, Eva heard a light musical snore.

"Don't sleep yet!" she cried, shaking his shoulder. He mumbled something, opened his eyes for a second, and turned around, smacking his lips. Reluctantly, Eva let him be.

A real man, Robin had said. Eva did not have a real man. She turned over on her belly and tucked her hands under her pillow. She was not happy for Robin. She felt betrayed and envious. She had no protective hand. No baby. But did she want to get pregnant? No, *no*! she thought with alarm. Kids are the end – the end of life. After much tossing and turning, she got out of bed and sat at the computer, angrily determined to find another job. There were many attractive offers, and, drinking the rest of the wine, Eva lost herself in vague dreams of the future.

Vladimir's seventieth birthday fell on a dark and windy Sunday. When Eva glanced out of the window, the snow drifts looked flat, heavy and gray, exposing miserable brown grass and patches of black pavement. It was quiet, in a desolate wintry way, and Eva went back to bed after a hot cup of coffee, enjoying the warmth of her blanket. Ska purred next to her and pressed her warm side to Eva's thigh. Absentmindedly, Eva stroked her fur and leafed through an old magazine.

Greg was gift-wrapping *The History of Jazz* in bright, glistening paper covered with motley balloons. On the television CNN reported on the war in Iraq.

"Should I wrap the bottle as well?" he asked. In a lazy voice, Eva replied,

"No. Who wraps bottles?"

They left the house in the late afternoon. The air was humid and fresh, the snow almost gone. They walked around puddles holding hands, each thinking about the night before. For the first time in a while, they had had sex.

Eva had stopped taking her pill a month ago. But she had not told Greg yet, and carrying the secret filled her with apprehension. In the circular thinking she developed around the subject, she tried to remember how it happened. First there was an article in *The New England Journal of Medicine* highlighting the risks of cardiovascular events for smokers over thirty taking the pill. Following this Eva had coincidentally forgotten to take her pill the next day, and the day after that – despite writing PILL on a bright orange Post-It affixed to the refrigerator door. On the third day she decided it would be a good thing for her body to find its natural cycle again and take a little break from medication. She honestly planned to tell Greg about it that night, but they had had an argument that she had provoked, as she remembered now – and when, after the fight, they made love, she didn't have the heart to ask him to use a condom. Later still, it became harder to talk about it, easier to pretend innocence … just in case. What the hell! She forgot to take her pill. These things happened all the time.

Robin walked around with a huge belly now. She was due in a week. The baby shower had taken place the previous weekend. Eva and her friends had bought a Bugaboo stroller in blue, for Robin was expecting a boy. Dan's huge hand kept stroking Robin's stomach. Eva averted her eyes and put on an overly cheerful manner, cracking jokes that won a few laughs and eased her own nerves. When she kissed Robin goodbye, however, there was a sense of disconnectedness between them. It was as if, subtly but deliberately, Eva had set out to hurt her friend and succeeded.

Now, holding hands with Greg on the way to his parents' house, Eva wondered if this was a good moment to tell him about the pill.

"This weather makes me nervous," Greg said as they approached Fourteenth Street.

"Why?"

"I don't know really. I reminds me of our last day in Moscow. I carried a heavy bag made of brown leather. My dad still has it somewhere. It's all ripped, the leather cracked. He never throws anything away. My parents were fighting about friends who owed them money. My shoulder hurt from the strap of the bag. I think I was crying, but they didn't notice."

"Poor little boy," Eva said tenderly, stepping closer to him. They halted at the crossing and kissed. A taxi drove by, slowly, looking for passengers.

"Let's take a cab?" he asked.

Eva stiffened. Did he think money grew on trees? Where did these rich man's habits come from? Certainly not Moscow.

"No," she answered coldly. "It's too expensive. We're not in a hurry."

"Why is it so terrible to take a cab once in a while?" Greg asked, letting go of her hand.

"Because we can't afford luxury," Eva said. "Please, don't talk like you don't know what I mean."

Greg sulked, and, looking at his sad profile, Eva decided not to tell him about the pill at all. She would punish him with secrecy, silence. The resolve brought her lightness, and immediately she felt cheerful again.

"Tell me more about Moscow," she said, taking Greg's hand in hers. He did not resist, but his hand was limp.

"It was a long time ago," he muttered.

They took a train to Brooklyn. On the ride Greg seemed distracted, and his hands, usually quiet, were restless. They didn't talk. Eva shrugged her shoulders, convinced he was still sulking about the cab, and continued reading an article about global warming that she had started at home.

"You have to read this!" she exclaimed from time to time. Greg didn't react, and she sighed – loudly, so that he might hear her through the rattle of the train and feel guilty.

When they were nearing Court Street station, the train jerked and stopped on the tracks.

"Jesus!" Greg said in a constrained voice. "Why aren't we moving? Are we still in the tunnel?"

Eva turned to him. Greg was pale; pearls of sweat clung to his forehead.

"Are you alright?"

"I feel sick. I can't breathe."

"It's a panic attack," Eva said. "Here. Breathe into the bag." Quickly she removed from his backpack the brown bag he had wrapped around the bottle of Champagne.

"Let's get out now?" he begged when the train finally moved and they approached the station.

"Avoidance is the worst thing. Once you start avoiding…"

But Greg was already on his feet and running for the door.

"Okay, okay, wait for me!" she yelled and raced after him to the exit.

They took a car service from Court Street.

"It's fine," Eva said once they buckled up. "Lots of people have panic attacks. Why didn't you tell me before?"

Greg shrugged. "You don't think I'm crazy, do you?"

"Of course not. Just unemployed. Again."

He nodded. The panic attack, now gone, seemed to have sucked all the energy from him. His hands were still moist. To cheer him, Eva kept talking.

"So Ricard said the movie might be shown in the Tribeca Film Festival?"

"That's what he said, yeah. I called him twice over the past week. He didn't call back."

"Maybe he's away?"

"No. Nestor saw him at Barfly. The movie sucks, anyway. No one's going to like it."

Eva continued holding Greg's hand, thinking of her own new job at the Bellevue outpatient clinic with fond gratitude. With patients, while supervising residents, at grand rounds and journal clubs she liked her professional self. She felt efficient, knowledgeable, and graceful. In fact, it seemed to her in this moment that life was just beginning.

Spring came suddenly. In a course of two days the whole city was blossoming, and Stuyvesant Town became a garden abundant with pink and white flowers, fresh tender leaves, and babies in strollers flexing their little feet, naked under the sun.

From the moment Eva woke up that Tuesday morning she felt nauseated. She had hid the fact of having quit her contraception for so long that the possibility of getting pregnant became in itself remote and dream-like in her mind. Her hands were uncoordinated when she locked herself in the bathroom. There was no blood, no tugging ache in the bottom of her belly, no period. Eva was nervous and excited – and thankful for being able to escape to work. En route she stopped at CVS and bought a pregnancy test.

The new five-story glass building where she worked was a strange place for psychiatric offices. Everyone passing below on busy First Avenue could see inside – a feature which hardly encouraged intimate exploration of the mind. One could draw the blinds, of course, but an effectively windowless space was no better. At the weekly staff conference Eva's colleague Sarah wondered aloud whether modern architecture shouldn't be free of such disadvantages.

"Maybe they couldn't afford the right kind of glass," Eva said, drawing laughs.

"I can't even wear skirts to work anymore," Sarah complained. "Every time I cross my legs I feel like some creep on the street is looking up."

Sarah was wearing a navy above-the-knee skirt and high boots. Her legs were crossed, exposing delicate round knees. She blushed, realizing the attention she had drawn to her legs, and pulled her chair closer to the table to hide them.

"Next topic," Roh Singh, the director of the outpatient clinic, urged, irritably jerking his head.

Roh Singh was a nice guy, generally, but his short temper and tics – he had Tourette's syndrome – were the inspiration for much ridicule among the staff. "Totally immature!" Sarah would say, sniffing at these jokes. She was right, of course. But Eva loved to parody Roh. It made her feel like a mischievous schoolgirl again.

"Let's get to our agenda before we run out of time. The diabetes clinic agreed to cooperate on the project of studying atypical antipsychotics and metabolic syndrome. Eva, you're on this. Inpatient psychiatry is complaining of the difficulty of making referrals. We need to work out our criteria for admissions. And Ely Lilly has invited the MDs to an educational lunch with Dr. Relkin, who'll be speaking about AD. We have to set a date if we're interested ..."

Feeling the urge to urinate and acutely aware of the return of her nausea, Eva rose and left. In the bathroom she removed the pregnancy test from its package. She read the instructions three times (one stripe nothing, two stripes pregnant), and sat down, placing the test strip under the stream of her urine. *One minute,* Eva thought as she drew in her breath to wait. It was agonizing not to look. The bathroom was silent and bare, its yellow tiles and fresh paint reflecting light off the walls. In what seemed like an hour's time, the minute passed. Heart thumping wildly, Eva looked at the strip. Two bright red vertical stripes looked back at her.

"Wow!" she cried at her reflection. "You *are* pregnant,

girl!"

She felt staggering, scary elation. The magnitude of what was happening had not registered with her yet; knowing it would, she didn't rush it. Tapping her shoes on the gleaming linoleum floor, she hurried to her office and dialed Robin's number.

"Hello?" Robin answered, and immediately afterward, Eva heard a high-pitched baby's cry. Spencer, a red-faced wrinkled creature, seemed to be gaining lung power.

"It's Eva," Eva said, her excitement diminishing. "Should I call another time?"

"It's like this around the clock. What's up?"

"I'm pregnant."

Oh my God, she thought through Robin's congratulations. The baby continued crying. *Oh my God. I* am *pregnant.*

"What did Greg say?"

"He doesn't know yet," Eva said. Robin cooed to the baby. The crying continued.

"Listen, call me when you can talk," Eva said, somewhat harshly, irritated by the senseless crying, and hung up. Her phone rang a second later.

"Dr. Leigh!"

"Tell him!" Robin yelled through her baby's howling. "Just tell him! Now!"

Eva returned to the conference room. Roh Singh stared at her admonishingly.

"Eva, could you please make an effort to be present here at the conference hour so I don't have to repeat myself?" His mouth jerked to the side, distorting his face, and he shook his head, as he always did when it happened in public.

Eva nodded feebly. Roh spoke again, something about policies, procedures, and budget cuts. Eva closed her eyes for a second. Greg. How could she tell him? Just go home and do it? Or call? He must be awake by now, aimlessly walking around the apartment, talking to Ska, half-listening to the TV.

Maybe it would be easiest to break the news over the phone and then say that she couldn't talk because a patient was waiting. It would give him some time to get used to the idea before they had to discuss it face-to-face.

"Eva!" Roh shouted. "What's going on with you today?"

Eva straightened her shoulders and snapped to attention.

"I was talking to you!" Roh said, waves of tics running over his face.

"I'm sorry!" Eva said. And then, before she could stop herself: "*I'm pregnant!*"

Eva and Greg arrived at the Flea Market simultaneously and immediately Eva wished she had chosen somewhere with a livelier, noisier crowd. They sat by a window. Nervously, Eva looked around at the restaurant's odd décor: there was a bicycle hanging over their heads and tattered teddy bears sitting on a shelf next to a scratched, rusty plate with a French street name on it.

"How was your day?" Greg asked gaily. Eva could tell he was making an effort to be upbeat after his own day of idleness. He yawned, he stretched. She guessed he'd showered just an hour ago. His hair was still damp.

Eva ordered a cranberry juice.

"You're not drinking?"

"I have something to tell you."

Eva took a deep breath. Her chair felt uncomfortable. What was the worst that could happen? He could leave. It would be bad, but she would survive. Could she raise a child alone? She didn't know. For her, as yet, the concept of motherhood was abstract. It was abandonment that she feared.

A sullen large waitress with a wide gap between her front teeth served them their drinks.

"So what did you want to tell me?" Greg prompted her.

The waitress took out a notepad and looked at them expectantly.

"Let's order first," Eva said. "I'll have the Gorgonzola salad," she said to the waitress.

"I'll have the salmon," said Greg.

When the waitress walked away, Eva smiled. Wanly, Greg smiled back.

"What is it?" he blurted out. "Why can't you just say it?"

"I just realized that you might be afraid too."

"Of what?"

"That I'm trying to leave you. Which is only funny because *I'm* afraid that *you're* going to leave me. A symmetrical fear, like a Rorschach blot."

"Why would I leave you?" Greg asked, playing with one of his shirt buttons.

"Because of what I have to tell you."

"Just say it!" he raised his voice.

"I'm pregnant." Saying it filled Eva with sadness. She felt she had broken the news the wrong way. She should have soothed his ego first. She should have said she loved him. Instead, she barely recognized her own voice; it wasn't her, it was like a robot speaking.

"I thought you took the pill," Greg said, confused and not yet comprehending.

"I was. But then I forgot."

"So," he started indecisively. "What are you going to do?"

"Make you a father?"

"Me?"

Eva waited, studying his face with hopeful patience. Greg shifted in the chair and blinked hard several times.

"It's a huge responsibility. I don't have a job."

"That's okay."

"But it's a huge responsibility!" he cried like a frustrated toddler.

Eva suppressed a surge of self-pity, determined to be

patient and motherly, as her role demanded.

"How could this have happened? You told me you took the pill!" he continued stubbornly, louder now, his thoughts clearer. She could hear a shade of indignation in his voice.

"I don't know, Greg. It just happened. It happens sometimes," she spoke quietly, hypnotizing him with her stare. "People have kids. It's not the end of the world. Robin had a child."

"But I'm not Robin," he said. "I'm me. I can't be a father."

The urge was unbearable. Eva held her tongue while whole sentences swished through her mind. (*You don't love me. It's all been just words. You want me to kill the baby? I don't need you. Go to hell. You'll never see your child.*) She kept silent, holding her ground.

"You want to keep it?" Greg asked sheepishly and blinked again, as if driving through a fog. "You never told me you wanted to have kids."

"I never said I didn't want to."

"It's something womanly, you know. You and Robin and all the others. You all say kids are boring, and the next second you're pregnant."

"It happened," Eva repeated. "It just happened."

"But why didn't you tell me?" Greg was getting agitated, his long fingers dancing in the air, his voice filling with a shrillness that sounded like her own.

"I'm telling you now."

"It's all because of Robin. It's a chain reaction!"

Again, Eva distinctly heard her own intonations, the piercing righteousness breaking through his friendly baritone. This is exactly how she sounds when she chastises him about not having a job. Now, like a boomerang, it was coming back at her: copy-cat revenge.

"This intonation," she said. "It's mine. You got it from me."

"What are you talking about!" Greg yelled, jumping up and banging the table with his palm. "Everything is yours: your house, your money, your baby, now even your intonation!"

"I'm sorry, I shouldn't have said it. I just found it interesting."

"Interesting! Interesting? I'll tell you what's interesting! You making me a father without even asking me! *That* is interesting! What am I? A pet?"

The heavy-set waitress moved determinedly in their direction. In her peripheral vision Eva could see other customers turning to look. They all knew that she was expecting a baby. She was proud and careless. They were their voiceless jury, to award Eva sympathy and Greg shame.

"Sshh!" Eva whispered, pressing a finger to her lips. "Calm down, please! How could I have told you? I forgot to take the pill, that's all. It was a surprise for me too. I just took a pregnancy test today." She spoke sincerely, her green eyes steady and luminous in the spring light.

"Guys," the waitress said. "This is a restaurant. Try to keep your voices down."

When the waitress's sturdy back turned to them, Greg whispered, leaning close.

"I don't believe you. You know why?"

Eva's heart skipped a beat. "Why?"

"Because if you found out today, you wouldn't be so sure you wanted kids."

"Analyze this!" she said with a smirk, derision coursing through her voice like poison. "Do you know how old I am? Tell me."

He shrugged his shoulders. "Thirty-one?"

"Right. Thirty-one. Do you think a thirty-one year-old childless professional should have an abortion when she gets pregnant? Don't answer without thinking. Consider it in the abstract."

"No. Absolutely not. You're right. Now let me ask you a question," his voice was firm. "Is it okay for an abstract female psychiatrist to inform her boyfriend that she's making him a father against his will and without his knowledge?"

Eva sighed. The waitress looked at her, but withdrew her glance when their eyes met for a second. Eva spoke, choosing her words carefully.

"It just happened."

Greg shook his head impatiently, indicating she didn't get the point. "It's all right, Greg," she said. "I wish we'd planned and discussed it beforehand. I want to keep the baby. I promise not to ask for child support." Dan's hand came to her mind, a steady faithful hand promising love and devotion forever. Eva allowed her face to predict tears.

"I need time to think it over," Greg said, rejecting the bait. "See you later."

He rose abruptly and then was gone in his swift, sweeping way, his food left untouched on his plate. Eva poked into it with her fork and chewed some salad, then a piece of salmon. Both were dry. For a second or two she stared into the nothing in front of her. Then she cried, unashamed in front of her sympathetic audience.

7

Eva was increasingly tired and heavy. Her pregnancy didn't seem real. Greg was back, and yet a part of him was lost to her. He was withdrawn. They did not return to the discussion of the baby, and Eva wondered whether it was this that felt so oppressive or if it was just a symptom of her changing hormones. She cried a lot, spending lonely evenings in front of the TV, Ska purring unfazed on her lap. From Robin, who was still fat and exhausted, she borrowed *What to Expect When You're Expecting* and read it avidly, straining for answers – but the book seemed written for Robins and Dans, its prose laden with boring cheer and chattiness. Eva felt lost. How had this happened to her? Why was she so miserable? *Should* she have an abortion?

She looked up a clinic in Midtown and after work one evening took a cab, getting off at the corner of Forty-First Street. Immediately she was met with slogans and prayers. Most of the protesters were men, many of them young, dispersed on the sidewalk, scrutinizing the women who passed with a hawkish intent to convert. *Abortion is homicide. Defend our Catholic church. Justice for all: born and preborn. Save Roe,* Eva read, looking disgustedly at pictures of tiny dismembered fetuses. *Stop killing my generation,* urged another poster, held high by a boy who could not have been older than ten. A man next to him, his face dark and creased (the boy's father? or his grandfather?), raised his poster, too: *God says Thou Shalt Not Kill.*

There was no need to check the address.

Eva did not intend to go in. She was just curious to have a look at the entrance, get her intuition going. The door was simple, glass and steel, a doorman in a blue uniform behind the desk. It looked plain and commonplace, a staid institution with dead fetuses hidden on the third floor. Pro-Lifers sized Eva up with their roentgen eyes, trying to determine how far along she was. She was about to flee when a couple approached the entrance. Eva watched them go in, a man and a woman, not young, not old. Their eyes were glassy; they didn't look around. The Pro-Lifers converged on them, chanting, *Abortion is murder!* The woman began to tremble. "*Go away!*" she cried back at them. Her companion pulled her in with a nervous jerk. The Pro-Lifers dispersed, boiling with near-triumphant excitement.

"I see you are a very nice person," a man's voice said close to Eva's ear. He spoke with a singing lilt she couldn't place. She turned to see the older man and his boy. Their shirts were open at the collars, revealing identical large crosses on golden chains.

"You don't have to do this," the man spoke mildly.

"I'm not pregnant!"

Gulping down tears, Eva walked away fast, not turning around.

Suddenly, as she was explaining CBT techniques to a new resident, she knew what to do: Greg needed proof, and rather than playing up her hurt feelings she had to take him to her appointment. He had to see the baby's heart beating. When she called him, Greg didn't pick up, and for some reason she became convinced that he was ignoring her on purpose. His youthful voice, light as a butterfly, greeted her on tape.

"Hi, Greg," she said, and at once felt overcome by a sense of futility. "Please come to the obstetrician appointment at five. It's at 32 East Forty-First Street, Dr. Bisquit, second floor. I'll be waiting for you."

Eva knew she failed. Then she snatched her cell phone up and searched for Olga's number.

"Alio!" Eva heard, the low friendly sound of a foreign accent.

"Hi! Olga? It's Eva."

"Eva darling, what happened?" Eva heard worry in that big calm voice.

"Has Greg told you anything?" Eva probed.

"No."

"I'm pregnant."

"What a wonderful thing!" Olga cried. "I'll be a grandmother!"

"I have an appointment with an obstetrician scheduled for today," Eva continued. "Can you find Greg and tell him that please?"

"Find him? Where is he?" Olga said, rolling her *r*s like Russians do in Cold War movies.

"I don't know. He slept at Nestor's," Eva mumbled, unwillingly assuming a victim's role – a role that would be all-too-well known by Greg's mother, a Russian woman married to a drinker, a teacher working as a receptionist.

"Tell me the address please," Olga said, her voice quivering with zeal and concern. She was mobilized.

It's going to happen. I am going to have a child. I'm not alone.
Eva dictated the address, slowly and distinctly, so there would be no mistake. Pacified by her unthought-of ally, lost in the fairytale of kind grandmothers, Eva felt lightened. Strangely, it didn't matter so much any more whether Greg came to the appointment. The might of Russia stood behind Eva, the sprawling devotion of Eurasia, all those low and capable voices, rolling their *r*s.

When Eva arrived at the obstetrician's office five minutes early, breathless and full with the jittery happiness of this first date, she caught a glimpse of a woman rounding the corner at the end of the block. Eva thought she looked like Olga, but of course Olga was on her mind. A moment later, Greg took her by the elbow, calling out in a loud voice,

"Eva! I'm here."

"I'm so glad you came," she said simply. They walked into the heavily decorated lobby with its dusty flowers, worn carpets and gaudy faux Renaissance prints on the walls. They stepped into the elevator, where they kept an amiable silence squeezed next to a yellowish woman wearing a head scarf (*chemotherapy*, Eva guessed) and the basketball-sized belly of a shy-looking young girl (*Am I going to look like that too?*). In the waiting area, while Eva filled out her health history and insurance information, Greg watched the other pregnant women and their contented-looking husbands. When Eva sat down, he took her hand; his face was open again. Eva reacted to this small kindness with an inner surge of gratitude. She was forgiven.

"How was your jam session?" she asked.

"Okay," he laughed, and then, pointing with his eyes to the girl they saw in the elevator, "I can't picture you like that."

"I can't either," she agreed and laughed too, riding her wave of happiness.

Dr. Bisquit was a plump, red-haired woman in her fifties who had intense eyes and a booming Italian accent. Her grip was dry and precise when she took Eva's and Greg's hands in hers.

"Eva!" she said. "What a nice name!"

"Thank you."

"A biblical name!" she continued, palpating Eva's belly.

Eva smiled politely. She shivered, now wearing only a patient's gown that flapped open in the back. The ultrasound machine was standing quietly by the bedside, awaiting its turn.

"So you're a doctor too. That's good, that's good. Psychiatry, huh? Interesting, yes, but crazy!" Dr. Bisquit smiled; Eva smiled back. "Now, let's look at the baby."

Eva lay down. She didn't turn to Greg, silently enjoying the mere fact of his presence. Dr. Bisquit applied the gel to her naked girlish belly, soft and vulnerable under the harsh lights.

"Ultrasound," she explained to Greg. Then: "Don't be shy, daddy. Come closer, look!"

Eva turned to look at the monitor, straining her neck.

"See? See that little heart beating? Perfect! It's perfect, Eva!" Dr. Bisquit declared this triumphantly, as if it were her doing. "You have a little healthy baby. I'll print a picture for you."

Eva felt love, love and wonder. She kept looking at the monitor. A little heart inside her? Two hearts, hers and the baby's. It was happening. She glanced at Greg, who raised his eyebrows in a gesture of surprise, as if to say "Wow! Imagine that!" They got two pictures, one for each of them.

Outside, when they had gotten into a cab, Greg whispered, "We didn't ask."

"Didn't ask what?"

"Whether we can have sex."

Eva laughed and laughed and couldn't stop laughing.

"You remind me," she said when she could speak, "of a patient who asked me once whether cancer is contagious."

"What was the answer?"

"You're kidding, right?"

They laughed more. *Do you still love me?* Eva wanted to ask, but kept the question to herself.

They had sex that night. Greg was careful and slow and had trouble coming. Her eyes closed, Eva summoned her prostitute fantasy; she couldn't come without it anymore. They did not speak about the pregnancy. Eva did not push him. It would come in due time, when her belly got big like the one on the girl in the elevator. Maybe then Greg would put his hand on her belly like Dan had with Robin, steadfastly and securely, and a different life between them would start. Greg would find a job. When Eva fell asleep, she dreamed about babies, and women disappearing behind street corners, and some vague, unidentifiable danger.

8

Having survived the news of Eva's pregnancy, Greg resolved to try and be positive. In return, he half-consciously expected a reward for his sacrifice. He wanted the nagging about the money and responsibility to stop. If he were a good boy, he would be loved. And it lasted for a while. Eva was friendly. She looked at him again in that old, shy and flirtatious way, her eyes clear and honest, her hips slow in the melancholy way he found sensual. They had sex, although it lacked the intensity and carelessness they used to enjoy, almost as if they were being watched by this invisible child who had destroyed their innocence. Or maybe it was just Greg. He was afraid to hurt the fetus, and resented it for his fears. Eva did not seem to care. But then, Eva was not the one penetrating. She was not the one who caused this trouble in the first place.

Or was she?

As Eva's term approached, Greg often replayed in his mind her story about the pill. But what could he do? He couldn't mention abortion; she'd never forgive him. It was one of those things he imagined stayed with people forever. So he hadn't said anything and now wondered if he should have. If not for him, she wouldn't be pregnant. He was the father. He was important.

Greg got lazy, lazier than before. Everything seemed put on hold, waiting for the change he didn't want to think about. He sacrificed his freedom for her. Surely she was thankful?

They came to talk about their baby as a she. He chose a name, Chantal, for it being strange, French and alien. Eva was surprised and repeated it again and again over her Yoga tea with its pungent irritating smell, one of her new healthy habits, and then said, "Okay. If you want." Chantal. Greg was not sure where he got the name, maybe from a movie or a book. It was a perfect name, not marked by ownership, beautiful and abstract, making the mere fact of her arrival remote, if not impossible. Taking walks around Stuyvesant Town, he studied little baby girls whose gender he recognized by the colors of their overalls. Girls have a special relationship with their fathers, or so he heard. They're sweet and quiet. He could imagine bouncing a little girl on his knee like all fathers did. He liked girls.

Once, crossing the road to the Oval, he saw a toddler girl falling on the ground. Aware of practicing his skills, he sped forward and picked her up. She was soft and light. Then she cried, her mouth wide open, showing him two little bottom teeth. He stroked her back with his huge-appearing hand, feeling terribly inept. The girl's mother arrived, thanked him, and lifted the girl with practiced ease. While she kissed her baby's cheeks, Greg watched. This mother was young and attractive, with a perfectly trim girlish body. Her breasts were small and firm under a light t-shirt. She didn't wear a bra.

"My girlfriend is expecting," Greg confessed.

"Congratulations! Boy or girl?"

"Girl," he said, and then added, confused, "Actually, we don't know yet."

"Good luck! Come on Stacy! Look at this full diaper! This needs to be changed, don't you think, sweetie?"

"I've never changed a diaper," Greg said, stealing glances at the mother's butt, outlined by tight shorts.

"Oh, it's easy, you'll learn!"

I won't! Greg decided. Diapers?! *No way!*

With growing panic Greg watched Eva gain weight, expand and mature into someone else who, like an impostor or alien, waited to devour him alive. Eva lost her beauty. She was fat, her pregnancy not obvious yet under clothes, her waist gone, her belly protruding, her face determined, devoid of that charming tentativeness he so used to like.

As the date of the fifth-month screening approached Greg grew more disconcerted. During the day, after Eva left for work, he spent hours watching Internet porn and masturbating, or loafing around the neighborhood, dazed and preoccupied, looking at women's butts and cleavage, lugging his guilty arousal wherever he went. Although his life was largely the same, something palpable had changed, as though Eva's pregnancy were a prohibition to dream. The future seemed to him ominous: a black hole.

He avoided his parents.

"You're becoming a man," his father had said sternly three months earlier, his mother nodding beside him with an encouraging smile. "Before you have a family, you remain a boy. After that, life changes, Grisha. Family means responsibility."

"I know, I know," Greg agreed and gave his mother the charming smile that always got him out of trouble.

"Well, that's good then. It's time for you to settle down. I found a job for you, Grigory."

"But I don't need a job, papa," Greg said, wincing. "I have a job. I have everything I need."

"Don't you want a real job?"

"I have a job, papa."

"What, serving drunks? Is that the kind of example you will give your boy when he grows up?"

"Please, don't start. I have to go. And I'm not having a boy, anyway. I'm having a girl."

"Silly boy," his mother laughed, sucking up to him with sweet giggles so he might do what they said.

"I found a job for you and you don't even have the respect to inquire what it is?" Vladimir asked harshly, his voice cutting through the stillness of the living room.

"Listen to your papa, Grisha," his mother said, despite how

pleadingly he looked at her. "He's right. Don't you even want to know what it is? You would like it. You'd be working with kids, gain some experience. You like kids, don't you?"

"Listen, folks," Greg announced with a swagger. "I appreciate your efforts, I do. But I don't want you to find me jobs. And to answer your question, mama, no, I don't like kids, I never liked kids, and I didn't plan to be a father either, in case you didn't know. It just happened. And now, I really have to go."

Greg rose from his chair, but even as he did, he knew that he was going to sit down again, pulled back like a wave in the ocean, a wave big and menacing and yet too weak to fight its own origins. He never learned to cross that line and be truly independent. Here was the chicken and the egg, all in one: he couldn't get up and leave because deep inside he was a coward – a coward his parents had made. For that he hated them.

"Grisha, just five more minutes, please," his mother started, interrupted by his father's quiet and methodical fury, an intonation carried forth from Greg's childhood: "Sit down!"

"Please," Olga pleaded, her voice anxious and cracked like old wood, her eyes big, the edges of her mouth looking down. She looked worn out, her wrinkles reflecting her dependency, her acceptance of defeat, but also her sad kindness and her need to be loved by Greg. *Moi samyi liubimyi*, she used to call him. My most beloved.

Greg sank down. He couldn't talk to his mother even if he wanted to be honest. He could only be loved by her and accept her love with all its different shades of worry. With his father, he could only listen, and if he listened well, he would get a little of Vladimir's dry affection in return.

The job they had found was at a nursery school, working with three-year olds, "having fun" as his mother described it, ten hours a day for thirty thousand dollars a year plus benefits.

"It's not for me," he cried. "Don't you see it yourself?"

"No, no, just listen," Vladimir insisted. Tiredly and obediently, Greg sat back. Vladimir continued in hushed and patient tones, subdued by his own effect. "You have to work there for a year, go to college, and get a degree in education. I figured it out. A school teacher makes a good living and has four months of holidays. Did you know that? Then you can play your music and do whatever you like."

Greg looked at his parents' faces, their eyes alight with hope, and wanted to weep.

"Right, dad," he said in English, which for him meant being different, rebelling, being himself. As he continued in English, he knew he had hurt them. "I'll think about it. Give me the address, I'll check it out."

"Why don't you speak Russian, Grisha?" his mother asked reproachfully.

"He thinks he's too smart for us," Vladimir interjected.

Greg never understood their reaction. Not that he didn't know that they would respond this way – when he was a child he had been slapped for speaking English in his father's presence. But he never understood the draw of the language and of the identity that merged with it. It didn't bother *him* when Americans who studied Russian spoke Russian, or when Russians chose to speak English. Over the years he just accepted his parents' quirk, like one accepts another person's pain without feeling it himself.

Greg went for the job interview, arriving ten minutes late, dressed in ripped jeans and a wrinkled t-shirt, at once desperate not to be hired and craving to be liked. The nursery school was in Midtown, on the ground floor of a modern high-rise. Hands in his pockets, he walked in, chewing mint gum to kill the smell of cigarettes. A middle-aged, sweeter-than-aspartame director wearing a thick layer of makeup met him beaming. Her name was Karen. In her office, Greg was shy and spoke little, giving curt, dumb answers.

"Do you like children?"

"Sure."

"Such a joy, aren't they? Have you worked with children before?"

"Not that I know of."

He saw her face getting closer to him, desperately trying to interpret each answer in his favor, pretending she had misheard. Greg felt a red wave of shame rolling over his face.

"No, I have never worked with children before," he said clearly. He would have got up and left at once, but that was not what people did; it required more audacity than he had.

"Do you have any little nephews or kids of your friends that you've babysat?"

"Nope."

"Why did you decide to interview for this job?" Karen persisted, her little piggy eyes getting shrewd. A legitimate question.

"I don't know," he mumbled. "My girlfriend is pregnant. I guess I thought I needed some experience with kids."

Giving an F answer again revived in him the painful sensation of failing tests in school. He didn't want the job, of course, but even so he couldn't bear rejection.

"Let's visit the classroom," Karen suggested brightly, appearing unfazed as she led him firmly out of her office. The hallway was decorated with kids' paintings, motley spots, smeared colors, primitive figures of men, and smiley faces. To his surprise, Greg found himself relaxing.

"This is our infant room," Karen cooed lovingly. Curiously, Greg looked through the glass at the little cribs and the little people in them. They seemed like a different species.

"This is our one-to-two-year class, Rabbits," Karen continued. "Next to it are Bears, two to three. Look at how sweet they are, how cheeky! And here is where we're headed. To the Tigers!" With each announcement Greg felt increasingly as though they were at a circus. Among the Tigers, he sat down on a low red chair next to a boy with hair yellow and thick like straw.

"Who are you?" the boy asked.

"I'm Greg," said Greg, extending his hand. "And you?"

The boy giggled, neither answering nor taking notice of Greg's hand. "Can you make a plane for me?" he asked instead.

"Sure, I can make a plane. Can you bring me some paper?"

Greg made a paper plane for the boy. Desperate to escape Karen's sickly sweet tentacles, he made more planes, and showed how they fly and how the motor sounds. Playing was easy. He was amazed that these small creatures understood him; in fact they listened to what he said with their little pink mouths open in rapture. Gathering around, they talked about Transformers and Power Rangers. They touched Greg curiously, gave him little punches, and soon hung on his arms like monkeys. Greg laughed, trying to free himself from so many plump clutching fingers, until the director poured her sweet voice into the middle of them and brought order. Greg stood up, hair tousled, sweating and still cracking up.

"You *are* good with kids!" she remarked.

He could see her attitude change. The shrewd cautiousness, the artificial plasticity relaxed a little. Inconceivably, he had won the battle. Greg was proud, a full booming joy filling his chest.

"I have two more applicants coming this week." Karen said. "I'll call you." But Greg knew at once he would get the job.

On the way home his joy trickled out. Who would want a job worth only thirty thousand and having ten-hour shifts? And yet he admitted it would be almost impossible to say no.

The director called him at the end of the week, her voice all cream and honey.

"Wonderful news! You got the job! I really marveled at how easily you found contact with the children. They loved you! Can you imagine, they asked me if you were coming back the next day! It was a tight call, given that you have no experience, but I decided to give you a chance. Congratulations! Are you happy?"

"Thanks. Sure I'm happy."

When he hung up, he was confused. Pride and disappointment clashed in him like two surging streams.

"What was that?" Eva asked.

"I just got a job at a nursery school," he said. He left out that his parents found him the job.

"You did? You got a job?" Eva hung on his neck, covering his face with wet kisses. "At a nursery school? You're a genius!"

"I don't know if I want it. Maybe I should call her and say I changed my mind."

"Of *course* you should take it!" Eva cried, stepping back and flailing her arms like a bird. "At least one of us will know how to change diapers!"

Diapers! Greg thought. *No way!*

And so Greg began his new daytime employment. Fearing the job wouldn't last, he held on to his shift at Luca's Lounge as well. The hardest part was getting up at seven in the morning. Once at the daycare he would play with the kids and learn the basics of instruction from the main teacher: how to issue time-outs, promote sharing, and use positive reinforcement. It seemed to be going well enough. But one Thursday, after a late shift at the bar, Greg couldn't force himself to get up. He called in sick, and Karen took it amiably and expressed concern. He stayed at home that day, and then the next as well, worried that if he came back too soon they would suspect he hadn't been sick at all. On Monday Eva furiously dragged him out of bed. Over the next weeks Greg was constantly exhausted. He did not play guitar. He had onsets of breathlessness each morning. Greg tried to ignore it, since it had no cause and no solution and therefore had to be his fault – or perhaps another face of *cowardice,* instilled in him by his father.

He liked being with the kids, but the initial enthusiasm waned and nothing else filled its place except for anxiety, exhaustion, and the meager paycheck he was handed every other Friday. One morning he got a coffee at a Starbucks and, reading the newspaper, forgot the time. He did not like being admonished for arriving at work half-an-hour late, his hands sweating and his chest tight. The next day he overslept and, not wanting to be told off for being late again, decided at the last moment to skip work altogether. As he turned onto Park Avenue, where he could not be captured and held accountable, bliss descended on him. He felt light and exhilarated, full of life again. Having a day for himself seemed a luxury, a forbidden pleasure that made the city sparkle with excitement. Greg wandered the streets, watching the cabs and street hustlers and women in office clothes, many of them in mini-skirts and high heels, and he sang aloud, oblivious to strangers' looks. The world was full of possibility. He walked up to Central Park, where he hadn't been in ages, fed the squirrels with the remainders of his sandwich and lay down on the young soft grass. Tender greens and blossoms of spring were all around him – the stolen moment was intoxicatingly sweet. He wasn't going back. Thinking about Karen, the aspartame director, made him dizzy. "I don't care!" he shouted into nowhere, watching a frightened crow curl her feet as she took off. Fresh baby grass gave off a wet earthly scent, and Greg breathed it in, filling his lungs with spring. Watching the sunspots and tree shadows, and feeling the brisk warm wind tousling his hair, he dozed off – his fears, like rain, soaked up by the soil.

The next morning he lied to Eva and said he was not feeling well. She gave him a quick physical and ordered him out of bed. Greg turned his back to her and put a pillow over his ear. Eva ripped the pillow away and threw it on the floor where it fell with a soft thump.

"Get *up*, damn it! Don't you see you're sabotaging yourself! You'll feel so much worse if you stay in bed!"

"I'm not going."

"Yes, you are! That's what I do. That's what *grown-ups* do. They go to work even when they don't feel like it."

"I'm not going. Just let me sleep."

Eva yelled, her face sharp and angry. Greg knew she wanted to call him a loser but was restraining herself. After she left, banging the door behind her, he couldn't sleep. The old sense of breathlessness came over him. He switched on the TV, drank a glass of milk. His anxiety grew, driving him out of his skin. I have an anxiety disorder, he decided. I can't work. I'll never be able to work. I never could because of this. The thought calmed him but also brought on sadness. Greg yielded to his melancholy willingly, disconnecting it from its cause but preserving its melody. He took out his guitar, struck the strings. Something was hidden in the jumbled sounds, something he could unearth and sculpt. He struck the strings again. Aha! – there, he had caught it! Patiently, as steadily as a metronome, he untangled the song and tried it out in his voice, throwing in meaningless words. The phone rang, and rang again, breaking his concentration. Greg ignored it. He worked, engulfed in inspiration. It was the best thing he had ever written, a jazzy twisted tune, too rich for his voice. A blockbuster.

After several hours of work Greg got up, stretched, rotated his tired wrists, and went to the bathroom. He had a hard-on. Watching his reflection in the mirror, his fine young face, his long boyish neck and sharp broad shoulders, he masturbated, imagining nothing in particular, the song still resonating obsessively in his ears. Later, he went out into the caressing warmth of May and bought cat food and milk, all the time thinking about his new lyrics.

I'm leaving you, he sang again and again. I'm leaving you, you. Your legs are yours, your tits are yours, forget the words. I don't love you, you. You are not mine, mine. The sun will shine, on you and me, broken apart. You are smart, I am smart. Apart. You are you, I am I, don't ask why, don't start ...

A *goodbye song.*

In the afternoon, shortly before Eva was due to come home, with chicken stewing on the stove and the table set, Greg took out his diary. The last entry had been made months ago. *Eva is pregnant*, he read. *Pack and run!* Greg scribbled the date and paused heavily, leaning on his arm.

I am an artist, he wrote. He put a thick, self-affirming exclamation point at the end. *Fuck work. Fuck convention.* The words were simple and yet meaningful and profound, making his face flush. Life was pulsating right here, within arm's reach. He could fly. He switched on his old record and danced, jumping, raising his knees up to his chin, laughing mindlessly and happily like a boy.

Thursday ended.

The next days brought emptiness and greater anxiety. Greg missed the kids. He cried remembering a kiss he got from little Jasmine. "See you tomorrow?" she had asked, swallowing her *s*s and *t*s. "Of course," he had replied, ultimately a broken promise. He found that he missed the structure and his paycheck, however meager – but there was no turning back. Karen called to leave increasingly angry messages which Greg erased before

Eva could get home. He burned bridge after bridge.

He avoided his parents as well. The sound of the phone ringing made him jump. He forced Eva to lie that he was not home when his mother called, which Eva eventually refused to do. It made him furious, the cold-bloodedness with which she handed him the phone, the caller ID showing Olga and Vladimir's number. When he pleadingly put his palms together, Eva gave him a contemptuous shrug and said into the receiver in a measured and clear voice:

"Oh hello Olga. Yes, he's here. Just a second! *Greg!*"

"Hi," Greg choked out. "Mom?"

"I was so worried. Where have you been?"

"Actually, at home," he answered in Russian, thanking God that Eva couldn't understand and fully witness his humiliation.

"Don't you work anymore?" Olga asked in a small, apologetic voice, from whose intonation he gathered she already knew and felt ashamed to ask, as if listening to his bleak apologies would make her an accomplice in his crime.

"I was sick, you know. And one can only miss so many days. Anyway I told you, it's not what I want to do. The pay is ridiculous."

"But it was a job," Olga whispered.

"I told you, I don't want you to find me jobs!" Greg yelled, jumping up from the sofa. It was easy to yell at his mother. "I don't need that! Stop treating me like an infant!" He hung up and rushed into the kitchen to gulp down some water.

In the hallway, Greg caught his reflection in the mirror, his eyes bulging, his mouth shapeless. Eva stood erect and still in front of him like a statue of justice, her scales weighing his sins against his virtues.

"Eva?" he called to her. "Eva, please. I love you."

Emotion stirred on her face, and Greg continued, encouraged, desperately craving her love.

"I'm afraid. Remember my panic attacks?"

Eva nodded.

"I go out and I'm afraid, all the time. Maybe I should say I'm anxious, because I don't know what I'm afraid of. I don't know what's happening. I liked that job, I did. I loved the kids. But I'm not like other people. I can't get up and go to work. I become nervous, jittery. I hate it. I can't breathe. I think I'm sick or something."

"You work at the bar," Eva said.

"I know. I guess because I know the place. I've been there forever. And it's at night. Drunken customers – I'm not afraid of them. Funny, I should be, with my father. But I'm not."

Greg took a step toward her, then another (like a merman walking on knives, he thought). Eva did not move away, and he pressed himself to her shapeless body, bending his knees to put his head on her chest. He felt her hands stroking his back. He just wanted to be held. He did not move, a prodigal son taken back into his mother's arms. Eva continued to stroke him, then put a hand on his crotch and, feeling his erection, took out his penis. Accepting her caress, he was suddenly so full of desire and yet so sad that only with silence could he express his gratitude. He came on her belly, putting a stain over the spot where his child was growing, quietly and inevitably.

Greg was nervous when the day of the screening arrived. He woke early. Eva was still asleep, her face peaceful and young, her shape round and beautiful under the sheets – like an icon of motherhood, remote and unknown to him. He could have liked her pregnant if they weren't already acquainted, he thought. Maybe he could survive it, after all. Without washing his face, Greg quickly got dressed and went out. It was bright outside, another hot day being born. He watched the green lawn with its brownish spots of withering August grass, the empty playground with its clock-tower, the joggers. Someone ate breakfast at one of the chess tables outside.

He was back by ten, carrying a brown bag with a chocolate croissant and an apple turnover from La Musette on Third Avenue, Eva's favorite bakery. He wanted to please her.

Eva stepped out of the shower, wet and furious in her cold, measured way.

"Where have you been?"

"I went for a walk. I brought you a croissant." He lifted the bag with a guilty smile.

"You haven't forgotten about the appointment, have you?"

"Of course not."

"We have to leave in ten minutes. Are you ready?"

"I guess so," he said, sheepishly glancing at his feet.

"You know, we're going to the *doctor*," Eva pronounced with poisonous slowness. "Why don't you wash your face and comb your hair, even if that's not what you usually do when you get up."

Greg obeyed, silently nursing his hurt.

"I went all the way to Third Avenue to get a croissant for you," he said when they walked out, his face clean, his hair combed. "Did you at least eat it?"

"Oh no! Sorry! I left it on the table! But I'll eat it when we get back. Anyway it's really not about croissants today. It's about the baby."

"Eva, please don't speak to me like I'm stupid all the time."

"Sometimes I think you are."

They arrived at Dr. Bisquit's office on time but estranged anew. In the cab, Greg had stolen glances at Eva's protruding profile, wistfully trying to revive the hopes and feelings of earlier that morning. Eva was irritable and curt behind her small talk. Greg kept to himself.

A red-faced jovial technician met them in the waiting area and gestured to them to follow her. Greg took Eva's hand

and got back a quick nervous squeeze. Eva was elsewhere. He walked along, swallowing his anguish and trying to understand. She was miles away from him. The baby was taking her already.

With a quick professional movement the technician applied gel to Eva's belly and switched on the ultrasound machine while Greg watched helplessly. Then she talked. Head, normal size, no hydrocephalus; heart, no problems; lungs, good; let's see the abdomen; liver's fine ... Greg listened to her droning voice and wondered about this plump middle-aged woman going about her business. Was she bored? Was she *hoping* to find abnormalities – a missing lung, a double heart, six toes – with an almost perverse excitement?

"*And,*" he heard her saying with cheer and pride. "No doubt about it! It's a boy!"

He felt Eva's eyes scanning his face. *No doubt*, the technician had said. *A boy*. Greg stood still. Back to square one. All those fantasies of little girls that had kept him going had been stripped away. Only the naked truth remained: he didn't want it.

On the way back, Eva asked,

"Were you disappointed?"

"Yes," Greg said, but did not explain.

9

Max's arrival changed things. Greg was displaced, replaced. Forced to serve this little screaming thing that he *had* to love. And he did – he loved and hated Max despite himself, silently suffering from the murderous fantasies that began almost immediately after Eva came home from the hospital, clutching the little shrieking bundle of his son to her breast:

Greg leaned out the window and lit a cigarette. "Don't smoke in the house!" Eva shouted with the sharpness that governed her attitude toward him nowadays. "It's bad for the baby!" Greg took a deep drag and then let the burning cigarette, the last he would smoke in their presence, fall into the naked crowns of maple trees and moist winter soil. Dizzy with smoke and fear, he saw his hands holding the baby out the window and then letting him fall. The image was so graphic that Greg shuddered in horror and disgust, shutting the window with a shattering shove.

"Are you crazy?" Eva cried. "You'll break the window!"

"We need window guards," Greg replied. "We have to inform the landlord."

He fixed a sandwich for Eva and boiled water to sterilize baby bottles. Then he asked in a quiet, friendly voice, "Do you need anything? I'm going out for a walk."

"No, thank you," Eva said, and he left, longing for something else, fleeing his alien family.

Outside he felt better. It was crisp and clear, a thin crust of ice shrinking the puddles of the morning rain, the sky dark, the buildings festive with their lights and busy expectations of a rapidly approaching Christmas. The holidays were coming, and with them Greg's own thirty-second birthday, just two weeks after the birth of his son. He crossed Fourteenth Street and went down Avenue A, shivering in his light grey coat, hiding his hands deep in the holey pockets, touching old things lost from last winter: dry bubble gum, a Blistex lipstick, a penny, someone's business card. Down the road, music was trickling out of crackly loudspeakers. *Jingle bells, jingle bells, jingle all the way...* He sang along, and was almost happy. On both sides of the street there were little Christmas stores selling cheap colorful garlands, blinking lights, frosted glass balls, red stockings with furry stripes, twinkling stars, snowflake ropes, cheery Santas, and nativity scenes with crudely made holy families. Christmas trees stood in rows like blind soldiers, little price tags hanging on their branches. Greg halted, lost in the tawdry glitter, and stuck his nose into one of the trees to sniff its fragrant needles. He loved Christmastime, that sole period in winter that held all of a year's magic: Christmas and the New Year with its special Russian festivities, the magic of wrapped presents, the old Russian songs his relatives would sing in soulful nostalgic voices...

Greg continued down the street to gaze into bars teeming with loud, careless life. He could walk in and order a drink and no one would know that a baby boy awaited him at home in a crib.

A woman passed him, brushing him with her shoulder. "Excuse me!" she cried bossily. She was pushing a stroller. Greg apologized and, feeling useless and foolish, stepped out of her way.

The memory of Eva giving birth came back to him, still fresh: her screaming, her pain, her swollen legs, her blood. Greg had suffered with her. He'd almost fainted. He'd had to escape it all again and again, hiding in the hallway where the other fathers happily paraded their newborns. And already then, through his compassion for Eva, he had a small voice in him saying *some babies don't make it.* It wasn't explicit. He didn't wish his baby dead, of course – just, maybe, in the great mystery of life, there's room for wonder... maybe somehow Eva would become whole again and the baby would vanish. Standing behind the door, confused and sweating, Greg had heard Eva's moans becoming sharper and more urgent. One frightened step at a time on the polished linoleum floor, he had returned to the birthing room, almost expecting his terrible thought to have been realized. Eva exhaled loudly with each contraction, her hair stuck to her forehead, her eyes bloodshot and wild. "Push!" Dr. Bisquit had shouted in a military staccato.

"I need anesthesia," Eva had cried and moaned and moaned and moaned.

"One, two, three: Push, push! Puuuuuuuush!" Greg had found himself straining his own belly.

"I see hair!" Dr. Bisquit yelled. Greg wanted to cover his ears and run away.

And then, all at once, the baby was there – red, screaming, and beautiful. Eva laughed and cried, the two emotions bound up in one, and very quietly held her baby to her chest. Greg timidly approached and kissed her sweaty forehead. It was a miracle that he had witnessed, a human being born from another. He cried with Eva and carefully held baby Max in his arms, supporting his neck as he'd been shown by the nurse, studying his son's face. The baby had shivered. The nurse had taken him away and placed him in a brightly lit glass box. There Max lay, flailing his little extremities and spreading his long red toes.

"My baby, my baby," Eva had muttered while Greg had stood by the glass box and watched, immersed in a conflicted bliss. At that moment, with unspoken solemnity he promised himself to love his son. Because Max was his son. His son.

Eva noticed that Greg was suddenly earnest and sad, looking for jobs online, the baby in his lap, going out for long, lonely walks when Eva took over. He quit smoking, to Eva's confusion (she had asked him to quit nine months ago – why now?). He also quit drinking, spending money, and smiling, or at least at home. They took turns feeding Max at night, but there was no more talk about "all services provided," and Greg made no attempts to touch Eva, as if *he* were the one afflicted by postpartum depression, leaving happiness to her, in something of a role reversal. Eva was grateful and concerned at the same time, but didn't delve into it. Max took all of her, and she watched the changes in Greg with her peripheral vision, with whatever energy she had left to be a girlfriend. She hoped that Greg was growing up. Part of growing up is sadness.

Eva lived, days and nights running together, in a circle of love and fear for her baby. Sometimes, in the first weeks, she would run to Max's crib with a sudden rush of love to discover him again, her tiny precious present, wrapped in a striped blanket. It was just her and her baby and the exalted unity of breastfeeding. Nothing else had order or meaning. Time, sleep, hunger, and consciousness itself were all disorderly and fragmented; Eva and Max moved through this chaos as in a dyadic cocoon in which there was only enough space for the two of them. Greg existed outside it. The company of others felt like a burden to Eva, puncturing the delicate balance within.

Greg's parents came often, bringing with them fussiness, fresh Brooklyn smells, and bags of healthy foods that did not fit into the fridge. Eva felt tense in their presence. She was breastfeeding. She was fat and wore ridiculous white t-shirts with flaps that opened at the breast.

Eva's mother Eleanor flew in from Paris with her imperial bejeweled heaviness, Petit Bateau overalls, sighs and wet kisses that left the imprints of her lipstick on Max's pimpled cheeks. She stayed two weeks, commandeering the living room, which displayed her silky oversized clothes, high-heeled shoes, encrusted belts, Louis Vuitton bags and jewelry that formed a shiny golden heap next to the computer's wireless mouse. The modest apartment acquired a different smell: of perfume, nylon, and the sweaty underarms of an overweight, elderly woman. Even after Eleanor's departure the smell lingered, sticking to surfaces as if to remind them of her large, guilt-inducing persona. By the end of her visit, even Max seemed to tire of her; he squirmed and cried in her arms and eventually at her mere appearance. Eleanor sulked, sighed and offered stale advice on how to handle "colicky babies." On the doorsteps, while the limo service waited downstairs and Greg triumphantly pushed her pink suitcases into the elevator, Eleanor broke down in sobs.

"Max!" she cried through hiccups of tears. "My little monkey! He's going to miss me. But I'll be back. I'll just squeeze that son of a bitch, Claude, and then I'll come back forever!"

Pressed against her mother's proud bosom, Eva wondered if she had been held like this when she herself was a baby. Their parting kiss was full of troubled affection.

As weeks passed, Eva became accustomed to Olga and Vladimir's presence. She learned to appreciate their occasionally pushy help and to cherish the free hours they gave her. Max in their care, Eva would walk out into the cool winter air and wander the streets, dazed and excited, amazed to see the world unchanged whereas she was so different, longing for Max and yet happy to move and breathe independently again. With her in-laws, Eva could share new and important things: lactation, patterns of sleep, milestones of baby development, the dozens of tiny dramas that happened over just a couple of days. She showed them daughterly respect, naturally becoming in their presence a sweet, deferential girl – to Greg's scoffing surprise. Vladimir loved to drone on about the nutritional value of the foods and of their importance for the growing human brain, misusing long scientific words filched from Russian health journals.

Eva nodded and did not argue. She knew he meant well.

One day, when Max had turned two months and she had just cut his blond curls, Eva rushed to open the door for her in-laws, a sandwich bag filled with Max's first shorn hair still in her hand. As the three of them locked in a quick, awkward embrace, Vladimir tapped Eva on the shoulder. "You are a good mother," he said significantly. Eva beamed – she had been accepted into the family.

Sometimes, Olga shared stories of child-rearing as it was done in Russia some thirty years ago, told in her unhurried low voice. Those foreign memories, conjured by the halting rhythm of her language, were as sweet and thick as Eva's own milk.

"Grisha did not take breast well, and my milk dried out," Olga recalled, her eyes misty and tranquil as they looked upon the past. "Every morning I went to milk kitchen to get milk for him."

"Milk kitchen?"

"Kind women who had a lot of milk would bring their milk to the kitchen for a little money so that other women could feed their babies. They said mother's milk was very important."

"At the same time in this country women bound their breasts because they believed formula was healthier," Eva laughed, and Olga shrugged at yet another confounding American eccentricity.

"If we stayed in Moscow, he'd be working now. Like everyone," Olga whispered wistfully.

"Or killed in the army!" Vladimir said. "Thank God we left in time!"

When three months had elapsed and it was time for Eva to return to work, Olga and Vladimir helped her find a babysitter. Galina was Russian – a modestly dressed woman in her late fifties with a soft, timid expression in her brown, deeply set eyes. During the interview she appeared shy. Maybe too shy,

Eva thought, holding Max protectively in her arms. Point for point Eva went through the list of recommended questions. Galina's English was good enough, but hesitant as she answered Eva in her soft voice, often pausing to find the right word. She had raised two kids of her own, then worked as a babysitter for five years, earning excellent references. She loved children. Eva had interviewed three potential nannies already, and they all said this. Eva needed more certainty. Greg joined them at the table, placing a hot cup of coffee in front of him. He greeted Galina and ran his finger over Max's cheek; Max opened his mouth wide and greedy like a bird.

"Can I ask?" Greg said, raising his hand. "How are you, mm, going to be with Max?"

Galina pressed her hands together and said with genuine feeling that tuned her voice deeper and clearer,

"I will love him like my own!"

10

In the months that followed, dizzy with tiredness and bitter with resentment, Greg frequently reminded himself of the moment when his son was born. He did his duty. He fed Max at night and rocked him in his arms when he cried. He quit smoking. He signed up for education courses at Baruch College. He applied for jobs to schools and nurseries.

At times, with Max sleeping in his lap, Greg thought he could get used to this life. He hoped it was all stress and sleeplessness that took Eva's affection so totally away from him. He hoped he was strong enough to live through it like other dads did. And then night would fall, and he would feel restless among the baby stuff; he would pace in the apartment and throw glances at Eva, wrapped up in her maternal love, and at his forgotten guitar. Eva was lost to him, he saw this clearly. Almost a year had passed and she was still absent. Even his parents deserted him. Even his mother. All his loved ones were escaping him, their love and hopes transferred onto his son.

Greg had to please. If he did better, more, maybe love would be given back to him.

He registered with a temp agency, which unexpectedly promptly placed him at PS 19 – a neighborhood school with lagging academics – as a classroom aide. During his first week he met Lora, a tough, petite blonde who worked as a music therapist attending to kids with behavioral problems. She had snake-like, unblinking eyes, blue and liquid like Lake Michigan, where she'd grown up, and her voice was so loud and bossy that initially Greg couldn't stand her. Then, in the classroom, boot-camp fashion, she made everyone sing –

first Greg, then the unruly kids under their care. Lora sang the beginning sounds and then Greg and the children had to continue inventing a song of their own. The exercise was based on a theory, developed by some guy on the West Coast, that uninhibited singing helps to enhance one's self-esteem and release tension. Greg found the theory bizarre but went along with it; Lora was his boss. He felt phobic and weak for the first few seconds, while his voice gathered strength. And then his song, the Goodbye Song, erupted from him and Lora gave him a long steady gaze that made him avert his eyes.

"You're really good!" she'd said and gestured to one of the boys to begin singing.

Half-listening to the boys' scratchy voices, Greg stood engrossed into his song, swept by nostalgia so piercing it brought tears to his eyes. The tune playing in his mind as though on a loop, Greg softly hummed, tapping its rhythm on a table surface. He could arrange the song differently, add drums, maybe a violin. Or a saxophone to make the jazzy, underwater part of it more sculpted.

When Lora invited him to lunch that day, Greg was convinced it was to scold him in some way or another. He felt uneasy with her, her every movement causing him awkwardness.

"Don't be so ..."

"So what?" Greg asked meekly, stepping a little behind her.

"So shy," she said finally. "I loved that song. Is it yours?"

"Yeah," he said cringing. "How did you know? Was it so amateurish?"

"No. Don't fish for compliments. I told you I loved it. If I'd heard it before, I would have known. Sing it again."

"What, here? Right now?"

"Why not?"

"I don't feel like singing right now," he mumbled.

Lora changed the topic. "Have you recorded it?"

Greg shook his head.

"Listen, I'll help you. I have connections. Really, I do. I don't bullshit," she looked at him pointedly. "Why're you so shy?"

"You make me shy. I don't know. I feel like you're about to scold me or something."

"Sounds like your conscience isn't clear. Do you like me?"

"I'll like you a lot if you help me record my song," Greg smiled after a moment's hesitation.

"You see, you found your lines pretty quickly. If you're shy because I'm a girl, don't be. I'm not looking for a boyfriend or anything. Just in case you were wondering."

They continued walking step in step, him next to her, dreams boiling over in his head. At lunch, Lora told him she was a professional singer, and about the band she sang with in LA before the group fell apart. The rest of the bandmembers got hooked on heroin and threw her out because she didn't get high and refused to lend them money for drugs.

"We were *this* close from the record label!" Lora said pinching her fingers together. "And I said, fuck it all, and came here."

The following Saturday they got together for a rehearsal. Greg called Nestor. On the subway to Williamsburg, Lora eyed Nestor suspiciously but refrained from making any rude remarks. Nestor flirted with her, oblivious to her attitude. It was his trademark, his secret way into women's hearts, Greg thought wearily. Nestor could manage an affair with Lora – Greg wouldn't be surprised.

They got off at Bedford Avenue and turned onto a dark deserted street close to the canal, wet wind biting their faces. A rat feasting on an overflowing garbage bin fled at their sight. The studio turned out to be a shabby dilapidated space neighboring a wholesale butcher and a U-Haul. It had a disturbing, booming acoustic. When they unloaded the instruments, Greg became nervous.

"Don't be scared, man!" shouted Nestor cheerfully. Greg

hushed him, blushing. He was still tuning up his guitar when Nestor was already wildly drumming away, and, stealing a glance at Lora, Greg saw her approving nods and felt a pang of jealousy. Nestor was a good drummer.

When Greg finally sang, Lora squinted.

"Your voice sucks," she declared. "There's no depth, no strength. You should take lessons."

"Are you trying to make me feel good?"

"Just telling the truth."

"That's so un-Californian," he remarked.

"Go ahead and joke. Now, let's try this!" she jumped up and took the mike from him.

"You do the guitar. I'll sing."

And Lora sang, transforming his song into a super hit, an absolute and total blockbuster that chilled his blood and gave him goose-bumps. They cheered and jumped onstage, and whistled and shrieked, and sang the "Goodbye Song" again and again.

"What else do you have?" Lora asked, when the wave of excitement had passed. "Sing, man! We're going to make it together! We'll be famous!"

Greg sang, liking his songs more than he ever had, moving his hips as he struck the chords and got carried away until Lora clapped her hands with the impatience of a film director.

"That's old. Second-hand. I've heard it a hundred times. You need to write new stuff."

"I want to cry," Greg whined, letting his arms down, the guitar hanging loose on his neck. "You just deflated me."

"C'mon! You're not a balloon. You have to learn to take criticism. If you can write one great song, you can write other great songs. Do you trust me?"

Greg nodded. Lora rose, stretching her short agile body.

"Next Saturday, same time," she said. "Bring me a new song. Write from your gut. Meanwhile, let's get drunk …"

Greg arrived home late, swaying as he entered the dark hallway. In the closet, he hung his coat next to Max's white snowsuit. He checked the crib. Max was sleeping peacefully, his lips parted in the dim night-light. Eva was awake, reading. When he appeared, she didn't look at him right away, taking her time. Then, slowly and heavily, her gaze shifted to his face.

"Are you drunk?"

"I had a couple of beers."

"Max has been running a fever. He just fell asleep. I gave him some Tylenol."

"I was rehearsing a song. It's a great song. I want to sing it for you. It'll make me famous."

Greg almost whispered these last words, feeling resistance from her. His face bore a silly, pleading expression.

"I'm very tired. I have to work tomorrow," Eva said slowly. "You're drunk."

"But it's a great song! It has nothing to do with me being drunk or sober," he said stubbornly, his tongue thick and heavy. *I am ridiculous*, he thought. He was furious at his tongue and at Eva. "It's okay, Greg. You'll sing it tomorrow. It won't run away, will it?"

Greg heard a raging rhythm begin to pulse in his head and set to work immediately, forgetting to wish Eva good night. He sat at his keyboard, earphones squashing his ears, until five in the morning, alternating his drumming anger with the peaceful melody of sleep, punctuated by the ticking of the clock and a soft repetition of words borrowed from a Russian lullaby his mother used to sing to him. At last, the rhythms found one another, and clashed and dissolved in the final words, spoken plainly without accompaniment: *And now, wake up! The sun has risen!*

It was almost eight when Eva got up. Drowsy with tiredness, she switched off the alarm clock and found her slippers under the bed. Greg emitted a loud snore; Eva turned around, giving him a hateful look. He had an absent, contented face, broadened by his supine position. The room faintly smelled of stale beer. "How about a little help?" she hissed. He didn't stir, and she shut the door behind her with a bang. Max lay in his crib behind a blue partition painted with clouds and a flying elephant. His cheeks were glowing. When she leaned over him, he opened his eyes. They were glazed and heavy.

"My dear boy," she whispered. "Do you want some milk? Please have some."

Max closed his eyes again. His arm was limp. Eva squeezed baby Tylenol into his mouth over his weak protests, spilling a little on a pillow, and wiped the drops off his face. Then she pulled a chair closer and sat down by his bed, watching him sleep.

On the living room table she spotted Greg's music notations, scribbled on sheets lying around in disorder. Seized by rage, she crumpled the sheets up and threw them on the floor. Then, obeying some instinctive fear, she gathered and smoothed them into a pile on the table. Max coughed again. Greg appeared at the door in his pink t-shirt and checkered boxer shorts.

"Hi!" he said and yawned. "I'll make you some coffee. You must be tired as hell. Or, you know what, just go to sleep. I'll watch Max. How's the cough?"

"Same. I called the pediatrician."

"I heard," he gave her his shy enchanting smile. "Do you want a coffee?"

Eva rose from her chair, shaking her head.

"Poor girl," Greg whispered, and she found herself in his arms, weeping like a fool.

"Go to sleep now. When you wake up, I'll sing you my song."

At eleven Galina arrived with an air of quiet competence. She boiled water and applied mustard plasters that she had bought on Brighton Beach to Max's back.

"Very good remedy," she said knowingly. "We always do it in Russia."

The plasters emitted a bitter but comforting smell which Eva liked. She helped take the plasters out of the hot water and stick them to Max's tiny back. While Eva prepared an antibiotic suspension, as ordered by the pediatrician, Galina watched quizzically.

"What is it, Galina?" Eva shook the bottle, screwed back the top and glanced in her direction. "Don't give him poison."

"Poison, Galina? It's antibiotics. This is what people take when they get bronchitis."

"It's no good for babies," Galina said. "Take him to Anna and Ben. They heal everything."

"Anna and Ben?" Eva repeated. "I know Anna. She read cards for me once."

Galina rarely expressed firm beliefs. Everything in her world was soft and tentative: her hands, her smiles, her footsteps. But what did Eva and Greg know of her life apart from its intersection with theirs? Only that so far she had kept her promise to love Max like her own.

"How do you know they can heal?"

"I go to them."

Eva looked up in surprise. Galina was fit and measured in her habits, ate healthily and never after seven, and jogged every morning on the ocean boardwalk in Brighton Beach where she lived. She was never sick and hadn't missed a single day of work.

"I have back pain." Like many people with insufficient language knowledge, Galina gesticulated and showed Eva with her hand where the pain was. "And also very nervous now."

Her son had just landed in rehab and refused to talk to her. She hadn't even known he was using drugs. What were drugs, anyway? They didn't have drugs in Russia.

"But I was told I shouldn't worry. And I feel in my heart it is very true."

"What else did they tell you?" Eva asked sarcastically.

Galina's expression became sad and confused.

"They said I have curse. I need to go fifteen sessions to heal, but they give no guarantee."

"What if they just want your money?"

"No, no, they helped many people. They cure severe illnesses." Galina shook her head. "Heart attack, diabetes, cirrhosis. Benjamin even cure AIDS."

"Galina …"

"You bring Max. I talk to Benjamin yesterday. He knows. He says babies don't get bronchitis."

Eva threw her hands in the air, exasperated.

"This is the most ridiculous thing! Who's the doctor here? Please, Galina, don't throw away your money on a bunch of charlatans!"

With stubborn politeness, Galina shook her head, and Eva did not pursue it any further. She felt like a grownup trying to persuade a child that Santa Claus doesn't exist.

In the evening, after she put Max to bed, Eva drank her tea alone. The mention of Anna stirred sadness in her. She remembered the time of the card-reading, of her and Greg's fresh and erotic love, of her high hopes and innocence broken by Anna's dark prophesy – and all that came afterward: Clair, Bill, Eva's first job. "Changes are coming," Anna had told her later, at the Thanksgiving party that occasioned Greg's humiliation. And changes did come, as they always do in life: Eva became pregnant. She had Max. Eva remembered telling Bill that her love for Greg was like love for a child. She had Max now and no longer knew whether she loved his father. Maybe already then, by stopping the pill, she meant to leave Greg while taking the best from him – their future son – in a passive-aggressive act of rejection and retention.

Greg came home after a shift at Luca's Lounge, and, looking at his hopeful face, Eva felt remorse. Of course, she loved him still. They had problems, but so did every couple she knew. She was irritated by his indolence. She was under stress working full-time and taking care of the baby. But he was a good father. He cared about her. It was life. Anna's prophecies were a sham.

They got into bed in silence, wearing their pajamas. Eva wished he would move toward her, give her a kiss. She sensed his tension and wondered whether he sensed hers. It had been a long time since they last had sex. Greg yawned, wrapping himself into the blanket.

"So tired!" he said – somewhat dramatically, Eva thought. *She* was the one who should be tired, working during the day and worrying about Max's fever at night.

"Good night," she whispered.

The Christmas tree still stood in their living room, glistening with decorations and releasing its drying pine smell. The presents were gone, their wrapping ecstatically ripped by Max and thrown away, the presents themselves already familiar members of their household. Motley shadows played on the wall: green-red-green-red. Eva got up to switch off the Christmas lights. It was late and dark. Sad and restless, she finally fell asleep.

Greg began talking about recording music again. Eva would nod and ask polite questions from time to time. To her, it was baby talk, easy to listen to and easy to dismiss. When Greg flew to LA in the spring, Eva was surprised and irritated. She needed his help with Max.

"It's important to me," he said. "I'm on my way to fame," he added and winked.

He left a CD of his songs for her on the dinner table. It had a red cover with a screaming man on it – Eva thought she recognized Nestor – and *Don't Bother!* scrawled diagonally across it in a yellow, Matisse-signature-like font. The band's name was *The*

Troubamours. Eva listened to the CD while she did the dishes, becoming irritated by the violent monotony of its rhythms, the recantation of sexual objects, puffy goodbyes, and, more than anything else, by the steely female singing voice: Lora's voice. So, that's how it sounds. She could understand why Greg was not attracted to Lora, or so he claimed. So much for jealousy. Yet she was jealous. Eva turned the CD cover over, ran over the song titles and fast-forwarded to one called *Eva's Song*. Here it was, Greg's voice singing the song he had composed for her almost three years ago, his deep baritone playfully hoarse – the simple, little sentimental tune with which it all had started. For a moment Eva felt tender; she sat down and wistfully replayed the song to hear Greg's voice again. I should be softer with him, she thought. I should take some interest in his music. At least, he did this.

On the weekend, while Greg was still in LA, Bill came by to see Eva and Max, curiously choosing this time when Greg wasn't around. He brought his cute girlfriend Grace, who smiled showing sharp little teeth and cooed to Max with such pure-seeming delight that Eva liked her. Even so, she felt a little guilty in her company.

"You want to hear Greg's CD?" Eva suggested.

Bill cracked his finger joints. "Let's hear it, Dr. Leigh!"

As they listened, Eva found she enjoyed the songs more. They were not any worse than what she heard on the radio.

"I like it," Bill declared finally. "It has potential. They need to get at least two good singing voices though, and a bass, and maybe something quirky, like harmonica. Or a saxophone."

Eva remembered his words, taking them as an expert's advice. She repeated them verbatim when Greg called the next day.

"I'm coming home tomorrow," Greg announced dejectedly. "You sound just like Luis."

"Who's Luis?"

"The agent. Anyway, we tried. And, by the way, I've been

to Lora's house in Santa Monica."

"Yes?"

"She's stinking rich and has totally crazy parents, something to do with movie production, of course. They're apparently quite influential people, but not on this occasion."

"It's okay. You just have to keep trying."

"I thought that if I came home with a victory in my pocket, all could be saved," he said, and Eva realized he was drunk.

"What could be saved?" she asked, alarmed.

"Never mind. See you tomorrow. Kiss Max."

When Greg came back, nothing changed. Habit sucked them right into where they had left off. For Eva, time passed in a haze of work, loving Max, and tired contentment, leaving little time for anything else, at once obliterating and elevating her. She was a working mother. These two words defined her. Greg continued to go to college, to temp as a classroom aide, and to take a shift at Luca's Lounge twice a week. They barely talked. There was no time. They had occasional arguments that were nothing out of the ordinary, not really, settling into a kind of a wordless routine that Eva knew was not uncommon among young parents. It was easy for her to accept because Max had become the love of her life, her baby, her sweetheart, her little pumpkin. She was happy.

11

One spring morning, Eva had a session with one of her young single patients, A. Eva was especially intrigued by A.'s case, not least because there were many similarities between A. and herself, which made Eva agonize over the particulars of psychic determinism. Like Eva, A. was an only child, with an absent father and a distant critical mother prone to fury. Like Eva, she was bookish and dreamy and had had a good education. And yet in this configuration, Eva was the doctor and A. her patient, seeking Eva's help in the tropes of work and love – the two areas, where, according to conventional psychiatric wisdom, one has to be reasonably successful in order to be called healthy. Eva listened and tried to understand and instill hope. She also prescribed medications, addressing the dichotomy of nature and nurture.

"I'm just unlovable. No matter how many sacrifices I make, I'm cursed," A. said.

"Maybe you make too many sacrifices," Eva suggested kindly.

"I thought you would say that. And you're right. It's my own fault. But that's how I feel: cursed. Maybe I am? I have a friend who goes to an old Arabic woman to read tarot cards. I wish I could go to her. Maybe she'd do a couple of those hocus-pocus things and make me well again!" A. bit her lip, afraid to show Eva her dissatisfaction with their lack of progress together.

"You want a magic cure. Unfortunately, therapy doesn't work like this. Do you feel disappointed?"

"Yes and no. I'd be frightened by an instant cure. It wouldn't feel real. But I'm so tired!" A. gave a high sob, like the squeal of a dog, and covered her face with both hands. "He said I look like an aging whore!" she whispered, and shuddered, horrified at what she had just said, as if Eva, too, might agree with A.'s latest lover. Offering her tissues, Eva watched with deep compassion; if A. had held on to this insult until the end of the session, she must have believed it true. None of her relationships had lasted longer than six months. A. blamed it on her low self-esteem. But low self-esteem is such a common affliction. Couldn't I claim the same? Eva thought.

Clearing her throat, Eva concluded the session with a soothing observation,

"You're going through hard times. But this is not going to destroy you. When we're young, everything seems a tragedy, but later on we learn that life goes in waves: high wave, low wave."

After work Eva walked to the VA building to pick up Max at his daycare.

Already Max was almost two-and-a-half. Time was passing so quickly. It seemed a mere few weeks ago that he had made his first steps and said his first words; more recently he had astonished her by marshaling his words into complete sentences.

At her sight, his face lit up.

"This is my mommy!" he announced and jumped into her arms. She picked him up, trying to kiss his plump cheek, but he rebelled, squirming out like a fish.

"Come, come with me!" he demanded. "I'll show you something!"

He led her to his Lego ship for dinosaur transport, and Eva felt the tiredness of the day lift little by little as she entered his fantastic state of mind. This transformation was among the most wonderful things about her experience of motherhood. Being with Max made her a child again.

On the playground, she played monster with Max and his friends, who giggled and teased her, scattering around. Then lightning cracked the sky, followed by heavy thunder, and immediately it poured. At seven-thirty, hungry, drenched and filled with the easy happiness of one another's company, they reached home. Greg was not there. Eva cooked noodles and fixed a cucumber tomato salad that Max loved.

"I want to watch *Charlie and the Chocolate Factory*!" Max whined, sipping apple juice from his Superman bottle. "I want to watch it now!"

"I'll just listen to this message, okay? Be quiet now."

Max wasn't quiet, as she knew he wouldn't be, and pressing the receiver to her ear she opened the DVD case and switched on the TV.

On the answering machine it was Greg. He's spent the night before at Nestor's, rehearsing late for an upcoming show at the Knitting Factory. "I know I should probably talk to you in person, and I will. But I felt I had to tell you ..."

She couldn't hear the rest because Max yelled, "Mommy! I want the movie!"

"I told you to be quiet, don't you understand? Or there will be no movie!" Eva shouted. Then, quieting down at the onset of his tears, she inserted the disc.

When Max settled down at the table, hot noodles steaming on his plate, a plush T-Rex tucked next to him in his seat, the movie playing, Eva replayed the message.

"I'm moving out," Greg's voice was saying, sounding remote and alien. "I feel it's best for us ...," he made a pause. "I'll call you. Okay. Good-bye. Tell Max I miss him."

She replayed the message again and again while a chorus of Oompa-Loompas sang in the living room, and Max eagerly giggled at the sight of the chocolate river. As Greg spoke, Eva kept thinking that he sounded drunk and tired, probably sitting on some strange woman's sofa, his long hair oily after last night's sex, his breath reeking of stale alcohol. Vividly she pictured him stepping into an unfamiliar bathroom, splashing cold water onto his face, and eyeing another woman's toothbrush. She imagined all those things he ought to be feeling: guilt, fatigue, insecurity. Conspicuously, the other woman was absent from the picture, probably gone to work. The fantasy was painful but faintly pleasant too. She wanted him to suffer.

When Greg called the next day, Eva was exhausted. All night she had lain awake, waiting for him to come in hunching his shoulders in expectation of her righteous wrath. He wouldn't have the guts to break the negative news. His way would be to pacify, to smile and hide until she confronted him; then, propped against the wall, he would confess.

"Did you get my message?" he asked.

Eva knew straight away she shouldn't provoke an argument, but, as frequently happened, it was precisely this awareness that made her do it, as if she had exculpated herself in advance by knowing it was wrong. Rage, mounted and stored during her long night and day of waiting, exploded from her. She could afford to yell carelessly. She didn't believe he was leaving. He couldn't exist without her.

"Do you know what you're doing?" she screamed. "Is this some kind of adolescent game? You have a son, for Christ's sake! Grow up!"

Greg, in contrast, spoke with chilling calmness, as if she indeed were done with, dead, a piece of trash to be disposed of.

"You're the only woman I couldn't make happy," he said, among other damning things. "You're too righteous. In fact, I don't think there's any point trying to talk about it anymore. It's like a ... never mind. I'll call you."

Eva felt the clasp of fury in her throat.

"You piece of *shit*! The only woman you couldn't make happy?! How did you even *try* to make me happy? Tell me that!"

It was easy for him to escape. He hung up.

Greg was an escapist. But he was also right: Eva was righteous. If he believed it, she had the right to act it out. And so she screamed into the beeping silence, *"Fuck you! I hate you!"*

Hitting the kitchen counter with her opened palm, Eva screamed wordlessly at the top of her lungs. She suffered from bouts of theatricality in private, imagining momentarily that it would squeeze out her anger; in the end, she felt ridiculous and empty. She paused to hear if she had woken up Max. The night was still. She tiptoed to his room and peeked in to make sure she wasn't needed and was allowed to be weak and cry. He breathed quietly in his yellow car-bed.

Eva returned to the kitchen and leaned on the windowsill. Max's cactus had stopped blooming. The soil in its pot had shrunken dry. Eva filled a glass and doused it, spilling water across the sill. Then she sobbed, fueling her agony with her memory of bits and pieces of the conversation.

"I'm sorry," Greg had said. "I just can't be with you anymore. You never cared about me or about my music. You're always unhappy."

"You can't say things like this, it's not fair. It's called character assassination."

"You got pregnant on purpose. Not that I don't love Max because I do but I never wanted to be a father. And I can't help resenting it."

Although it was true Eva wouldn't admit it, not only to him, but to anyone. She retaliated:

"I was drunk for God's sake, I forgot the pill! You lost your keys twice in the last six months! And how many times have you forgotten to feed the cat?"

"It's not like we had no options. Last time I checked Roe hasn't been overturned."

"You son of a bitch! Don't dare ever say it again! Do you wish him dead?"

"Please, Eva. I love Max. But I can't live like this anymore. I have to breathe, compose, *be*. I can't be locked up. Other people live like this, most of the world lives like this, I know, but *I* can't. I want my life back. Do you want me to go on pretending I'm happy?"

"You'll never be happy because you can't assume responsibility, not even for yourself! The only thing you do is dream, dream, dream. You don't ever *do* anything because you're afraid of the real world, because any moment reality can burst your dreams like a needle in a bubble. That's where all your anxieties and panic attacks come from!"

"Shut up! Just because you're a psychiatrist, you think you've got me all figured out? The truth is you don't know shit, because you never wanted to know. It's over!"

While they spoke Eva had poured herself some vodka from the fridge, more than she intended, but it didn't matter; this was misery with just cause. She threw ice cubes into it along with some cranberry juice and took a deep cold sip. A stack of dirty dishes sat in the sink. *It's over*, Greg had said, *I'm gone*. And yet he was still on the phone, waiting for her to say something. Suddenly Eva became insane with jealousy.

"So who is she? Your new benefactor?"

"Please, Eva!"

"Tell me right now!!!"

"Don't start on that, I never depended on you!"

A blatant lie. Eva said nothing.

"You *wanted* me to depend on you," Greg went on. "That's different! And like I said. You got pregnant on purpose."

"Huge psychological insights!" she retorted. "Pretty impressive for a slacker!"

Eva took another deep sip. In fact, there was some truth to what he was saying. She wasn't sure what would hurt more – his independence or his running away with a new girlfriend. It was so much easier to blame it all on his being a loser.

"I'm tired of being your pet," Greg said calmly.

"You egocentric swine. Why didn't you use a condom? Did you ever ask whether I minded taking the pill? You knew I was a smoker. You knew I was thirty years old. What was I supposed to do, just ignore all those warnings about heart problems and breast cancer? Because *you* didn't want to use a condom? No, let me finish! You! And you say you love Max?!"

"I always said you knew what you were doing," Greg muttered.

So that was it. He was right. She'd given herself away. She'd wanted the baby.

When Greg hung up Eva needed to keep talking. She dialed Robin's number and let it ring for a long time before she heard Robin's sleepy "hello." It was eleven. Eva was miserable and tipsy.

"Hi, I'm sorry to wake you up. Greg just broke up with me."

"Oh my God!"

"He says I didn't care about him enough because I didn't have an abortion, and he resents being a father."

"He didn't!"

"He did. And then he hung up."

"You mean you housed and fed him for years, and now you single-handedly take care of his son, and *you're* the unfair one?"

"Precisely," Eva said. She liked Robin's summary.

"Asshole is what he is," Robin concluded. Eva agreed.

"He used me up and dropped me," Eva said, choking on angry tears that sprang from her eyes as though from a fountain. Holding the phone to her ear, she walked to the mirror in the hallway and with morbid satisfaction watched the reflection of her wet, distorted face, her howling mouth looking like an overturned boat.

Back in her living room Eva put down the phone and edged deep into the sofa. She thought of their years together, of Bill and Clair, her pregnancy, her disillusionment with Greg's fantasies, her attempts to make it work. No, she decided, and then said out loud, to add credibility to her words, *I don't love you anymore!* She lived as well as she could. What did it all make her? Tolerant?

Righteous? Or just stupid? All three, she decided. The real question was in Greg's right to blame her. Who was *he* to make this judgment? He was an asshole. Robin said so. And when he comes back begging, Eva won't let him in. The circle was complete now, having come back to self-pity. He doesn't love me, Eva thought, he never did. He had never loved Max either.

The television bubbled noise in the background. Restlessly, Eva turned the volume up.

Avian Flu continues to spread through Asia and Europe with unprecedented speed. All birds have been slaughtered in Southern Italy; several confirmed cases have been registered in the south of France, Portugal, Spain, Romania, Russia and Uzbekistan. No human fatalities have been reported in Europe. The European Union's special committee is gathering in Luxembourg today to discuss measures to be taken against the sweeping disease as well as economic solutions to the devastation caused by the slaughter of poultry on the continent. No cases of human-to-human transmission have been registered so far, however experts are concerned it's only a matter of time for the virus to mutate. Worldwide, two thousand human casualties have been recorded. All of these cases concern people who have had direct contact with live or dead poultry. Our special correspondent from Luxembourg reports ...

Eva switched the television off and went into Max's room. He slept with his mouth slightly open, breathing quietly, a plush T-Rex under one arm, a teddy bear at his shoulder. Gently she removed the teddy bear and knelt to kiss his cheek. He was warm and smelled of milk. Overwhelmed with emotion, she abandoned herself to tears.

Despite a slight vodka-induced headache, Eva felt strangely calm the next morning, controlled in an elated way, her mind clear and her movements precise. Lying in his car-bed, Max burbled something about dinosaurs, airplanes, and Spiderman.

"There was a dinosaur, a green one and a red one, a Stegosaurus, and a T-Rex. Then the dragon came, and he ate him up, and he flew away because he was very hungry, and then the Batman came with the police car and shot him," Max chatted, gesticulating excitedly, his eyes wide.

"Wait, who ate whom? Whom did Batman save?" Eva asked laughing heartily.

"No, Mommy, listen to me, no interrupting!"

"Okay, I'm listening."

"The Spiderman came and the Batman came and they shot the dragon …"

Eva dressed him, still warm and sleepy, kissing his knees, hands and stomach, while he giggled and kicked her with his little feet in red Spiderman socks. She packed his lunch for the daycare, drank her morning coffee, and took a long hot shower. Then she combed her hair, applied her morning cream, ran a lipstick over her lips and got dressed herself: pants, shirt, jacket. She looked and felt good. A change was coming. Something big was happening in her life. She strode to work, pushing the stroller ahead with a sense of exhilaration.

"Where's daddy?" Max asked.

"He went away."

"On a plane?"

"I don't know," Eva replied earnestly, wondering where her pain had gone.

She would wonder for a long time.

12

Lora sniffed contemptuously and switched off the news. "What are you doing?" Greg cried. "I was watching!" "You're being duped along with the whole nation!" she said. "Whenever Bush has problems, his people try to get everyone all worked up over some nonsense, like this Bird Flu shit. It's a nation of fear. There's a good book by that title."

Greg gave her an unconvinced nod.

"C'mon! Cheer up! You're a free man now! You're not afraid of anything anymore!"

"I don't know," he mumbled. "I'm afraid of you."

"Ah. What if I made you rich and famous?"

"That would help."

"Or if I took off my shirt?"

Lora slipped off her t-shirt, opened her bra and lowered the cups a little, teasing Greg with a skewed smile. Greg disliked her lips: thin and wiggly like worms. But seeing her breasts, so full and fine, with pale pink nipples, brought on a rush of excitement he hadn't expected. He took a step forward and jumped on her, which he thought she would like. She did. She clutched him firmly in her short freckled arms. She bit his shoulder, and for a second he wanted to laugh, but decided to try enjoying it instead. Their copulation was forceful and quick, robbing him of desire he might have otherwise nourished a little longer. Lora was melodramatic, a shrieker, and in the middle of it all threw a fashion magazine on the floor, flailing her arms. It wasn't the best sex of his life, but for a couple of minutes before he came he felt ecstatic: powerful, rich, and famous.

"You're so hard! So big!" Lora moaned, biting his ear. The

124

sensation was painful and sudden, but also intensely pleasant. He wanted to hold onto it a while longer, but couldn't.

Afterward, sweaty and embarrassed, he apologized. "I'm usually not that fast."

"Don't worry, darling. Your days of oppression are over. Was she good in bed?"

"Who?"

"Who else?"

"I guess so," he said. "You have beautiful tits."

"Two surgeries. Nice job, huh? I was flat as a board before. Look, I'll show you the scars."

"No, thanks, it's fine," he said, laughing awkwardly and moving away.

"What? Does it shock you?"

Greg shook his head. He was tired. He wished she hadn't told him. He would never be able to look at her breasts the same way again.

"You're a bit of a prig, aren't you?" Lora watched him so closely with her blue, snake-like eyes that Greg felt dizzy. Her sharp elbow was pinned into his chest. She was smiling.

"I guess I am," he agreed lamely.

"Well good news, Mr. Prig! They're real!" Lora laughed triumphantly. "Touch them! See? Have you never touched fake boobs?"

He shook his head. "I don't know. Maybe I did. Why did you tell me about the surgeries then?"

"I was just joking. Being crazy. I'm crazy. Haven't you noticed?"

"I guess I have."

"You want a joint? I'm having one," she said, getting out of bed and marching proudly in front of the open window. He watched her. She had a firm white body. Like cheese, he'd thought when he touched it earlier: cold and a little sticky to the touch.

"I thought you didn't use drugs."

"A joint isn't a drug. It's a celebration stick," she said, lighting up. "And don't start telling me what to do in my own apartment. You're just a tenant."

"A pet," he muttered bitterly.

"No," she said, firmly taking his face into her palms, a joint stuck between her teeth. "A partner. A talented lazy son-of-a-bitch who needs to be pushed and exploited like a goldmine by a charming blond miner."

Greg smiled at that, flattered, and kissed her lips. She smoked with her bare back to him, filling the room with the sweet nauseating smell of marijuana, while he stared into the ceiling, jittery and craving the fame she promised him, believing and disbelieving her at once. He was desperate for her to switch off the light so he could curl up in bed and disappear into the privacy of darkness.

He thought of the comfort of his bed across town on the East Side, and of his things, folded into a suitcase now standing in Lora's living room in the Village. He thought about Max's green eyes, so like Eva's except for their innocence, and of his conversation with Eva that night. *I'll be back*, he thought. *I'll be back, rich and famous.* Greg suckled on this fantasy for a while. It would be his little secret; Lora didn't need to know. *A cool rock star.* It couldn't be too hard. He just had to discover its rhythm, get the feel. He'd mastered some basics already. He could handle agents without having a panic attack, perform in front of a large crowd, and not be destroyed by critics' reviews even when they weren't totally positive (although most of them were pretty good). He could even handle Lora. Almost. But Lora was a stranger, so cool and explosive at once; how could he sleep next to her?

That night, he screamed.

13

Weeks and months passed with increasing ease, which made Eva wonder about the meaning of her broken relationship. She had escaped the separation whole, taking nothing and leaving nothing to Greg. She remembered that last hurtful and drunk conversation with bewilderment, all its ups and downs and the tearing pain of abandonment, which so soon gave way to lightness. Over the first weeks Eva worried about her detachment, her indifference, and almost out of guilt tried to feel hurt again. Yet even then, she realized she was forcing it, blowing wind on the quiet water surface so the storm would not settle and she could continue playing her role of an angry abandoned girl.

Life changed little. Olga and Vladimir smoothed the transition, bathing Max in love and presents, and picking him up for weekend visits with Greg, who was still too afraid to show his face. They treated Eva like a daughter abandoned by a careless boyfriend whose name they dared not mention in her presence. Her mother Eleanor called from Paris every night, too, cursing at Greg, sighing and concluding their conversations with the grating reminder: "I told you so, remember? Mother knows best!"

When Greg finally did come, Eva was friendly and calm – to his surprised discomfort. For a few weeks, he continued to arrive at her door like a beaten dog, loaded with guilt and apprehension. He spoke fast and fidgeted like his father; his smiles were awkward. Sometimes he left CDs on the glass table with little Post-Its asking her to play his songs for Max during the week, which she did out of a sense of duty. Once, Greg took Max to a recording studio, as Eva gathered from

Max's jumbled stories about a big room with black boxes and singing into a "telephone."

She didn't ask questions, even though she was curious. With Greg it seemed safest to create a total partition. Take nothing, give nothing, feel nothing. From Max she knew he was living with a blonde named Lora – the band's singer. At this she felt jealous in a childish possessive way, as if Greg were her property.

Separation opened her up in an unexpected and wonderful way. She dreamed. She read. She signed up for drawing and painting courses at NYU. For a long time she wondered whether it was just the exhilaration of change. But as the weeks moved through the summer and rolled into fall, as days shortened and filled with rain, she decided it was permanent.

"You look good," Greg said one Saturday morning, sipping coffee while Max gathered his favorite toys (a Pokemon plane, a monster truck, a T-Rex) into his Superman backpack. They giggled nervously, like old lovers brushing over the surface of memories. Greg was looking at her with fresh and eager eyes. He still liked her, she could tell; she smiled shyly, withdrawing her glance. Greg was thinner than she remembered and on his forearm now wore a tattoo of two coiled blue lizards the size of a quarter. Otherwise, he seemed the same to her: tall, insecure, playful like a teenager. She glanced away from his tattoo, resisting curiosity.

"You look really good," he spoke again, encouraged by her silence.

"Thank you. I feel good."

Greg nodded, swallowing disappointment, and pulled his sleeve down, over his tattoo.

"Remember our talks of normalcy? I became confident all of a sudden. Maybe it's entering middle age, the fusion of personal and professional."

Greg gave a short laugh. "Sounds like I cured you!"

"Maybe you did," she answered earnestly. "I've thought about it. Maybe it was cure by disappointment. Disappointment with love."

Eva switched on the coffee machine, filling the kitchen with its contents' fresh aroma.

"Do you descale it regularly?" he asked.

"Never. You never showed me how."

"The instruction manual is under the sink. You should really do it once in a while."

Greg got up, putting his coat on.

"I'm moving to LA next month."

"Oh."

"Just wanted to tell you," Greg said, shifting his feet. After a heavy silence, he called,

"Hey Max, buddy! Are you ready?"

When Greg had moved to LA, Eva was sad. On the last day, Greg was crying. Max sat on his lap, confused, kissing Greg's hand. "Don't cry, daddy! I can draw a snake for you."

When Greg hugged Eva, she patted his back. "Good luck," she said, removing herself from him. And that was it. He was gone. No meaningful words, no rage, no forgiveness. What was she waiting for? She couldn't tell. All was over, and she was happy again, and yet there was an emptiness waiting to be filled with something she couldn't define.

The phone woke her. Eva glanced at her watch, wondering whether she should answer. It was midnight. Half-awake, she picked up.

"Eva! Switch on the radio!" Greg shouted into the phone. "105.5!"

"What happened?" she cried in panic.

"I want Max to hear it!" Greg yelled.

"Greg! It's midnight. He's sleeping."

"So what?" he cried. "It's my song! It's a huge success! Do you understand what's happening? My fucking song, the one I wrote in your apartment, is on the radio! I want my son to listen to it!"

Eva turned up the volume and walked toward Max's bedroom. Beat, another beat. Saxophone howling. Then, Lora's voice piercing through. *I'm leaving you, you. Tam-tatam-tam. Your legs are yours, your tits are yours, forget the words. Uuuu. I don't love you, you. You are not mine, mine. The sun will shine, on you and me, broken apart. Tam-ta-ta-tamtam You are smart, I am smart. Uuuu. Apart. You are you, I am I, don't ask why, don't start.* Saxophone howling. It was strange to hear the words, so obviously written by a man, delivered in a woman's voice.

"Eva! Eva! Are you there?"

"I'm here."

"Did you wake up Max?"

"Hey, your father's song is on the radio," she said, shaking Max's shoulder. She knew Greg was listening. "Wake up! Listen!"

Max stirred. Eva stroked his warm sleepy face, gliding her fingers over his cheeks and lips.

"I want to sleep!" Max said angrily, loud enough for Greg to hear his high raspy voice.

"Sorry," Greg said, suddenly deflated. "I'm sorry to wake you up. You know, it's three hours earlier here. I miss you!" He added this with feeling, and Eva didn't know whether he meant both of them or just Max, breathing quietly in his car-bed.

Thinking about Greg's success, his first, Eva couldn't sleep for a long time – perhaps because he had accomplished it without her. She was jealous, her reaction obvious to her now. She got up, splashed cold water into her face, and switched on the computer to google his name. Three hundred entries. She whistled. There it was: the song, the album, the interview.

"It's Lora who made it possible," she read. "She knew how to push me."

Lora knew how to push him. That was true. Barefoot and bare-chested, Greg was sitting on the sofa in their Santa Monica one bedroom with a view of the ocean. The sofa was new and smelled of leather. It crunched under Greg's bottom when he moved, and he fidgeted back and forth, catching the rhythm. He got up and fetched his guitar, inspired for a moment, but when the guitar landed on his lap, he was impotent. Stubbornly, he touched the strings and played a melody that he first vaguely and then distinctly recognized as the Moby song he'd heard recently in his car while driving to the studio. Inspiration fizzled. For a while, he continued shifting his weight and listening to the leather crackles. What was it he wanted to sing? He cursed and lit a cigarette. He wished Eva were there to tell him no smoking in the house. He was going to die of lung cancer.

Lora lay on the bed, wasted from too much pot and alcohol, mumbling half-consciously from time to time. Greg walked over, covered her, brought her water and a cold towel to put over her forehead. "Fucking worst headache of my life," she muttered, and he bent to kiss her, not even wincing at the smell of vomit on her mouth. Same old pet.

Jimmy, the petite bohemian saxophonist they'd hired, sat on a chair sniffing coke.

"I'm good, man! I'm high!" he cried, throwing his curly head back. "Have some," he offered amiably.

Greg sat down, leaning over the white powder, careful not to blow it away. He rolled a paper straw and drew in the perfect white lines, first through one nostril, then the other. His cigarette was still burning in the ashtray on the mahogany table by the window. He walked over to it slowly, awaiting the effects of the coke.

It was not his first time. The first time had been the best. He would have been happy anyway, back then, just after they had signed their contract.

To their celebratory dinner that night Lora had worn a dress, pink – a color he hated but had to admit looked gorgeous on her. She was the princess, glamorous, savvy, exploding with wit. He was the prince. Lora's parents, smartly dressed, trim and still vaguely sexy in an aging and confident way, smiled at them with patronizing adoration. Greg saw himself through their eyes: a cool New Yorker, full of Woody Allen-esque self-deprecating jokes, an ascending star with long blond hair to match their daughter's. A fabulous, unforgettable evening it was.

Coke was a star's privilege, one he accepted easily as part of the game – even in the presence of Lora's parents. He went to dinner with them high, so high he thought he could fly out and rise above Los Angeles in all its enormity, seeing its lights from above, embracing its skyscrapers, diving into the sea at will. Later, drunken to the point of unsteadiness, he went to the beach alone. He took off his clothes and ran, treading barefoot the soft sand, which still held the warmth of the day. He plunged into the ocean and swam for a long time, surrounded by stars and the half-moon hanging over his success. Engine cool and head clear, he stepped out, shivering. Stillness hung over him. It belonged to him, too. Power was everything. He was living. Life was wonderful.

Now, weeks later, Greg sighed and opened the window, letting in the disquiet of the ocean breeze. The coke wasn't working. Jimmy turned up the music, their music, and sat tapping the rhythm with his feet. Listening to his songs, Greg remembered his fans' faces on the days of the promotion tour, half-naked girls with their arms in the air, moving to the sound of his music, intoxicating him with love. He stood on stage, lit brightly, and ripped his shirt open, screaming into the mike: "I love you!" The sea of love cheered back, overcoming him like a huge sonic wave.

It had felt overdue, like an awakening after a prolonged guilty sleep. Time itself became compressed and now emerged in his memory in the flickering bright images of a TV ad. He lived. And then he died. Now, he couldn't write. He was tired; the coke sucked the life out of him in huge powerful gulps. He had to sleep again.

The business of *The Troubamours* moved along in white impeccable offices to which Lora dragged him occasionally. It was she who'd made it all possible. He didn't even object to his tiny 5% share. He accepted it gratefully. Like a pet.

"Congratulations!" she said condescendingly. "You paid the rent!"

When someone made him aware of the injustice, he suffered voicelessly; he had no rights. His hurt and envy seemed as intense at times as his high. He calculated the profits. He hoped to become a #1 hit on the radio; that would bring in money. He spent hours on the Internet watching their sales. He acted rich even though he wasn't. He sent Eva ten thousand dollars with a small, stupid note, the memory of which now made him wince. "I am king," it said. For some reason, he thought it cool when he wrote it. He'd been high, probably. He bought a Jaguar – black, shiny, and fast. He drove it with Nestor, then, when Nestor went back to New York, alone along the coastal roads, taking in the expanse of the water and the brown burnt-out hills. He dreamed. He played deafeningly loud music. He bought a real Persian carpet and sophisticated loudspeakers. He bought cool clothes. He sang at clubs. He acquired fans. He did coke. And he slept.

Now, all he felt from the coke was the numbness in his throat and his own heartbeat, driving him into rage. He counted Lora's profits again and again. He saw her naked with Jimmy, her laughing brazen eyes gripping his, Greg's. Just yesterday.

"You want to join in?" Jimmy asked in a dreamy voice.

"No, thanks."

"Don't be so touchy!" Lora teased. "Come. We're having a great time. Dive in!"

Greg shook his head.

"I never promised you faithfulness. Wives are boring. I thought you knew that by now, after all that time with your live-in psychiatrist."

"*This* is boring," Greg had said, walking out.

Now, burning with anger, Greg stood in his usual place against the window, his hair stirred by the wind, his throat numb, his fists clenched. His anger had had a delayed quality. It had mounted over twenty-four hours. And the fucking coke didn't work.

"Hey man!" Jimmy called, as if reading his mind. "I'm sorry for what happened last night. She wasn't that great anyway."

Greg took a step toward him, then another, his face grim.

"Are you crazy?" Jimmy yelled, shielding himself with an elbow.

Greg struck him ineptly in the shoulder, his strength sapped by fear of his own rage. But after he felt Jimmy's flesh under his knuckles, a dour satisfaction settled in him. His tribute to coolness.

"Serves you right," Greg muttered and went back to the window. He wanted to feel the wind on his face again, but he was afraid Jimmy might stab him in the back.

"I'm sorry man," Jimmy whined, remaining seated, his nose red. "She wanted to. I thought it wasn't kosher myself, to tell you the truth."

Another pet, Greg realized, and somehow it seemed funny. He gave a guttural, full-chested laugh, and with an odd combination of conspiracy and contempt offered the bewildered Jimmy a high-five.

Later, alone, Greg lay on the couch and day-dreamed

of his refuge: of his little Max, and of Eva. Of his mother's devoted and anxious face. All of these blessings hundreds of miles away. Then he wept until sleep took him into a jungle of bare-armed girls cheering him onstage.

14

Eva's patient A. was dating again. In fact she had been happy for so long that Eva had almost begun to expect the bad news. Now here it was: A. had had a fight with her boyfriend, the same kind of fight she always created, from the repetition-compulsion of jealousy and feeling unloved. During the session, Eva and A. explored past conflicts and the ways in which A.'s feelings emerged and transformed into irrational beliefs. Then, breaking away from the psychodynamic approach, Eva gave her some advice.

"Speak to him. Tell him all these things you've just told me. It might seem embarrassing, but he'll understand. Or at least he should. That would be genuine bravery."

Eva could hardly believe her own words: the advice was carved out for herself.

After school, Eva played Greg's CD for Max. It wasn't for little kids. She had to explain words like *tits* to him – and worse. *I need love, love, love. Give me love, love, love. Forget the baby. The baby is sleeping. Give me your love. Now.*

"Is daddy very lonely?" Max asked.

"I don't know."

"Why did daddy write this song?"

"I don't know, dear. You should ask him."

"Because if he is lonely, he can come back to us."

Eva put Max to bed, made up a tale about a firefly and a worm who stole the firefly's lamp, and then sang him a lullaby. When Max was asleep and his grip on her fingers softened, she tiptoed back to the living room. The CD was quiet, finished. Eva thought of A. and the advice she had given her. Then she dialed Greg's number. He answered immediately.

"Hi, it's me," she said.

"Oh, hi!" he said eagerly. Eva was pleased but didn't let him hear it.

"I thought you'd have a secretary by now," she laughed.

"Not yet!" he laughed with her. "How are you?"

"I'm good. Max has just started reading. I'm sure you know from your mom."

"Yeah. He's going to be really brainy. Like you. A doctor."

Eva paused, then spoke softly and intimately.

"Listen. I'm calling to apologize."

"For what? I'm the one who should apologize."

"What you've done is great," she continued. "Very few people achieve fame. I'm sorry I never took your music seriously and … and that I called you a loser. We're proud of you. Max and me too."

"Oh, it's nothing. I'm still a loser. Did you receive the check?"

Eva was silent. Immediately Greg wished he hadn't asked about the money just then.

"Yes, I got it. Thank you," she said. "But I'm not calling because of the money. I thought a lot about your success and my attitude toward you, and it's been a burden for me. For a long time – since the release of your record, to be precise – I've lived with the realization that by being with you, and by being who I am, I denied you success. I wasn't supportive. I didn't believe in you."

"And now? Do you believe in me?"

"Now you don't need me anymore. All I can do is apologize for past mistakes."

"If it were so easy, Eva," he sighed. "Maybe the congratulation I waited for most was yours. You know how it is. You're the psychiatrist."

"Well," Eva continued tentatively, her voice lucid and soft. "It's heartfelt. Congratulations."

When Eva hung up, she was proud of herself, and flattered, but also disturbed. Did he want her back?

Winter came and went. In the spring, Eva took Max to visit his grandmother in France.

They walked around Paris, Eleanor waddling behind Max and getting out of breath, speaking strange words like *Huguenots*, *Invalides*, and *Quasimodo*, which he repeated with fascination over the dinner table. Curiously and gratefully, Eva watched her mother and her son develop a loud affection for one another, a relentless alternation of quarrels and hugs. At night, Max fast asleep in a tented baroque bed, mother and daughter talked in the kitchen.

"Good thing you dropped that son-of-a-bitch," Eleanor said, her cheeks red with rouge and wine. "Not that I didn't like him; he was kind of sexy. But it's time to find a nice young doctor for you! Or have you met another shit-head?"

Eva laughed and shook her head.

The lawsuit with Claude was coming to a close; Eleanor was winning the case. Her mood was brighter, her pains gone, her appetite more voracious than ever. She burst with uncharacteristic generosity, taking Eva out for elegant meals and buying her bright, feminine clothes, "to change her style." The day before her own departure Eva asked her mother whether she would be staying in Paris.

Eleanor winked. "I may not spend my old years alone after all..."

"Is he French?" Eva asked, laughing.

"No more romantic mistakes, darling! The French are horrible!"

"So who is he? Tell me."

Her mother raised a long pink nail to her lips.

"Sh-sh! His name's John. I'll say no more. Old people are superstitious!"

Saying goodbye Eva realized she had forgiven her mother. *Finally*, she thought, *I'm a true grown up. Maybe now I'll be happy. Forever.*

Spring became summer, and summer autumn. Eva worked and loved her son, buoyed on by the flow of routine. Life was simple. She came to her office at nine. She treated her patients, taught her students, and conducted her research. She published two articles in prominent psychiatric journals and was promoted to Associate Professor. The late afternoons she spent in playgrounds, talking with other moms about schools and play-dates; the evenings she gave over to playing hide-and-seek, doing puzzles, and reading with Max. In her free time, when Galina came to baby-sit, or when Max spent time at his grandparents', Eva took long walks, read at a nearby café, and consoled Robin, who was divorcing Dan. Life was humble.

One sunny day in October, Eva woke up at dawn to the chirping of birds and it occurred to her that she hadn't given a thought to Greg in many days. *The King of Courts*, Anna had predicted. *You'll be happy with the King of Courts.*

"Well where is he?" Eva said aloud to herself. "I'm ready!"

After rehab Greg stayed with Lora's parents. They were nice enough, but old and uptight. Around them he had to be respectful and starched, neither too caring nor too cool – balances alien to Greg. The couple's benevolent presence diminished him. Among gilded rooms, antique furniture, and dark pictures of old masters he felt small and lost: a little thief, a little loser. He overcompensated with subservience, always offering coffee or a blanket to Lora's mother, Dominique. "We have servants, Greg, haven't you noticed?" She said this with a slight arch on her eyebrows. Her face was a mask, smooth and yet aged in an unnerving way. All the same, Greg was grateful for the roof over his head. It wouldn't be for long; in rehab he'd written a couple of good songs. The studio recording was scheduled for November, and in two days he was going live again. He was worried about Lora's voice. Too much smoking and drinking, he told her. She did not take it kindly. But that didn't matter. He was leaving LA.

As time went by, especially in the empty months at rehab, his longing for Max and Eva transformed into an ache greater than any he'd ever known. He didn't need Lora anymore – of this he felt convinced. He didn't need LA, either. Most of the music business took place in New York. He'd rent a sunny loft with high windows and lots of space; for Max he'd install a little play-gym like the one he saw at his lawyers' house. He'd beg Eva to come back to him. He'd buy flowers and write songs for her: brilliant songs the whole world would hear. He'd never be unfaithful again. And she'd come back to him, smiling shyly with her beautiful green eyes; he'd make her coffee, they'd sit for hours just holding hands, and at night make love, like they used to …

Restless and optimistic, he waited for the concert. He would be elevated by the cheering crowd once again, the inebriating joy of performing spinning him up to the heights of his talent. He would be successful; he had to be. Success was his ticket home.

Halloween. In the parlor downstairs, Lora was having another fight with her mother. Every time they argued Greg cringed inside.

"Darling," Dominique was saying, haughtily sweet. "I don't want you to go out tonight."

"I don't care what you want."

"Darling, this virus news makes me nervous. We need to be careful."

"What virus news? What are you talking about?"

"The Avian Flu. If you're going to live in my house, I want you to be prudent."

"Jesus Christ," Lora groaned. "I've lived alone in fucking

New York City! I'm an adult. I don't need you telling me how to live my life. If you don't want me to live here, I'll move in with Vicky, or camp out on the beach. But I'll tell you one thing: No matter where I am I'm not going to fall for this Republican fucking farce of a health alert ..."

"Darling," Dominique interrupted. "All I'm asking for is prudence. Your father will talk to you and to Greg as well."

Greg knew how it would end. It was certain now that Lora was going to the party, just to spite her mother; no one could stop her. An hour later he walked down the marble stairs stealthily, hoping Dominique wouldn't notice. A monk holding a candle in a heavily framed Italian painting watched his progress. The monk's face and hand gleamed yellow; the rest of his robed body blended into the picture's dark background. Greg liked the painting. He liked the house, too. He wished he could apologize for Lora and stay, watching TV and drinking beer.

Instead, he let her drive the two of them to Malibu, to a mansion belonging to an actress who was filming elsewhere while her children hosted a celebrity masquerade. Greg had dressed up as John Lennon – it was easy; all he needed were little round glasses and a tied-dyed t-shirt. Lora was going as Cicciolina in a naked suit.

"What do you think?" she asked, wiggling her large plastic butt.

"It looks stupid. Why don't you just go naked?"

"Oh shut up! I'm so tired of you!"

They drove in silence. The dislike was mutual. On the way to the party Greg remembered his last phone conversation with Max ("Look, daddy!" Max had cried in his sweet, bossy voice. "Mommy got me a big snake!" "I can't see it on the phone," Greg had said. "But I'm coming home soon." "Tomorrow?" "No, not tomorrow, maybe in a week. I have a show tomorrow. I'm going to sing a song for you because I love you so much...") Closing his eyes, Greg hummed the song now, rocking back and forth. It was good. It was really good. Maybe even his best yet ...

"Ahhh!" Lora shrieked, battering the steering wheel with her fists. "Stop! It drives me mad!"

They drove through a heavy automated gate, past palm trees lining the road. Large candles shaped like pumpkins flickered in a sunken garden, in carved gazebos and on fountain ledges. One could see the expanse of the faraway ocean and the crescent moon's reflection on the water. When they entered the house through a large, spider-web-decorated door, the party was well underway. Servants in skeleton suits served champagne and appetizers. Greg soon found himself the center of attention. Acutely embarrassed, a weird smile on his lips, he answered questions about his recording plans. He craved coke.

After a loud announcement that he'd been in rehab Lora broke away to talk to a costume-less man with a mature face and looming eyebrows. Greg drank champagne and made small talk with a struggling actress dressed as Maria Callas. Talk turned to the Avian Flu news, and, bored, Greg drifted away, toward the oysters. A stranger touched his elbow – the man Lora had been talking to. "So," he said to Greg. "You're Greg Spassky. I love Don't bother."

"Thanks."

"Tony Brown." They shook hands. Tony's was warm and confident, Greg's sweaty; reflexively he wiped his palm on his jeans. Tony didn't seem to notice. He conversed easily with Greg, with genuine interest, and Greg decided that he liked him. After a couple of drinks they went out to the garden.

Encouraged by Tony's eyes, which were shining and warm, and his rich mellow voice, Greg talked about Eva, Max, music, the fright of success, and his coke addiction. Then, embarrassed at having said too much, he stopped, waiting for Tony to talk. Tony spoke willingly. He was a producer for Columbia Pictures; he mentioned this modestly, passingly.

His parents had died when he was young. He struggled as a student. The beginning of his career had been a disaster – one failure after another, perpetuated by his own former drug and alcohol habits – it had taken him years to break the cycle. "Although one is never completely free from the past," Tony said. "It haunts you, especially in hard times." Greg agreed.

The night was clear. It was chilly, but Greg and Tony stayed in the garden, on a bench in a gazebo, pumpkin candles gently lighting their faces. From the house came the sound of music mingling with laughter, from the coast the low crashing of waves on a cliff. With drunken gratefulness, Greg spoke about the deep depression that had followed his cocaine period, of his experience at rehab and of his dreams of returning to New York. When Tony's warm hands stroked his hair and Greg felt moist lips touching his own, he wasn't shocked.

"Have you been with a man before?" Tony asked tenderly, his cheek brushing Greg's.

"Once," Greg said. "I played a gay policeman in a movie, in New York. The director was gay." He wanted to add that he still loved Eva and still planned to go back to New York soon, but didn't.

"Did you like it?"

"It was okay," Greg laughed. "It was, what's the word? Intense, kind of a little violent. I loved the whole world then. Actually, I loved Eva, but somehow, it made me love everyone else too. I don't mean I was promiscuous. Just happy."

"And then? What happened?"

"I don't know. Life happened. Eva and I had a son, Max. It was unexpected. And I left. You got kids?"

"Two. They're adults now."

"What about their mother?"

Tony laughed, throwing his head back. "It was a long time ago."

Greg nodded, suddenly nervous.

"I'd like to see you again," Tony said. He gave Greg a card from his pocket. "Call me."

They returned to the party. Greg shivered, still feeling Tony's kiss on his lips, remembering his slightly sour breath and the viscosity of his saliva.

In the house he poured himself a glass of wine to wash the sensation down. Feeling lighter and dizzier with alcohol he danced and played the piano, urged by his hosts. Lora joined him and sang along, holding a vodka bottle like a mike in her hand. A crowd gathered around them, clapping and beaming with admiration. The recollection of the odd but not entirely unpleasant encounter in the garden began to buoy Greg, who in his state of drunken revelry took it for a positive sign: a sign of promise, of unexpected change, of chance encounters that redirect life toward newer, bolder, and more ambitious goals, previously unimagined. Along with the alcohol and the adoration of fans surrounding the piano, everyone clapping and pronouncing their belief in him and his future, made Greg feel he deserved Eva and Max after all, and that the very next day was the time to say or do whatever necessary to be with them again, to proceed in life a perfect, harmonious, happy trio.

And then dozens, or maybe hundreds, of cell phones came alive in an insistent, cacophonic chorus of panic, and the nightmare began.

15

In Hong Kong people are dying in enormous quantities. Corpses are piling up and being thrown into the sea. Those who can afford to are trying to escape. Others hide in their homes. Streets all around the city are jammed with cars. Hospitals are overrun with patients lying in the hallways and at the entrances to the emergency rooms where desperate relatives leave them to be picked up ...

According to city healthcare officials, New York is taking every possible precaution against the disease. All flights have been suspended. Quarantine stations are being set up for potential carriers already within city limits. The symptoms are basically the same as those experienced with the common flu: chills, muscle aches, high fever, sore throat, diarrhea and vomiting in some cases, headaches, and a cough that can result in spitting up blood. However in the case of Avian Flu, these symptoms get progressively worse very quickly, sometimes within a single day, and up to thirty percent of the afflicted die swiftly from multiple organ failure.

Although the chance of the pandemic spreading to the U.S. is high, Americans are advised not to panic. Wash your hands frequently. Avoid crowded places. Stock up on nonperishable foods and water. Get batteries and candles in case of an electricity fallout. The drug Tamiflu may be an effective cure although this still remains to be proven on a large scale. It will be dispensed to anyone who contracts the Flu as well as to all healthcare workers at pharmacies and hospitals in the event the pandemic spreads. There is no vaccine ...

Anna switched channels and watched the Halloween parade on NY1 for while. A red-cheeked young reporter yelled into the microphone through the noise of music and cheer,

This is an amazing crowd, Barry! By our estimates this is the largest parade in the history of Halloween in New York City ever. And we didn't even know whether permission for the parade would be issued this year! I think it's a pretty good indication of the people's state of mind. They're hopeful! They want to celebrate! And they do!

On screen, big floating animals crept through the sky, men in large colorful wigs and tight glinting dresses danced, orchestras marched. The predominant theme, however, were death and horror masks, which Anna watched with aversion. A bad omen, she said, shaking her head.

For the past couple of years, when reading cards for her clients, Anna had noticed a dark and disconcerting pattern: a Joker would pop up on top of problematic card combinations. She had been waiting for a calamity, had even given it a name: The Joker. But didn't Ben dissuade her? As recently as yesterday, when she had told him about Vladimir stocking up on food?

"As your spiritual prowess increases," he said, "you'll be able to look far into the future. Yes, the world will come to an end one day, as all living matter is condemned to death. But it's not going to happen tomorrow. Think about it and spread the cards for yourself."

Anna did, the same evening. Her spread was good. There was no Joker.

Someone banged on Anna's door. Over the radio she could hear thuds and cursing in the hallway – men's voices, muffled, arguing about something. Her heart jumped in her chest. Benjamin was not yet home, and this worried her; it was nearly nine. She had already called his cell phone several times, and left him as many messages in a tiny, childish voice that she had for their life together as if a more forceful tone might offend their delicate happiness.

"Who's there?" she shouted.

"Nestor! I need your help."

"I'm sleeping. Come back tomorrow."

She'd seen Nestor last week. He used to be a drummer in Greg's band, a tattooed playboy with needle-marks on his forearms and soft, caressing eyes. "Do you use drugs?" she'd asked sternly, and he'd said no but looked up at her like people do when they lie. He had joint pains that recently had become so severe he failed to show up for a gig last Sunday. A "gig"? she'd asked. A show, he explained, laughing. She did not like the way he laughed. It was lowly and somehow violent. He had an edge about him, as though he could unexpectedly do something creepy. She treated him nevertheless, and pocketed eighty dollars for the first consultation and treatment. That night, she called Olga ostensibly to chat about this and that, trying to find out if Greg and Nestor were close and what Olga thought about their friendship. When Olga volunteered her opinion – that Nestor was a "shady character" – Anna agreed. And she had resolved not to see him again. However, he called her the next day, ecstatic and full of gratitude, telling her how much better he felt, and despite herself she was glad and proud, and agreed to see him again the following week. This week. And so, here he was, banging on her door. She should have trusted her intuition more. She should have known better.

"Let me in or I'll break the door! I'm sick! And there's a sick man here!"

"I'm calling the police!" Anna shouted, horrified.

"Bitch!" she heard, and then more footsteps.

She called 911 and waited inside her apartment for the police to arrive. When the officers came she opened the door to find Benjamin, her Benjamin, lying on her doorstep. "Oh my God," she cried, "What have they done to him?" She kneeled next to her husband on the dirty floor. His forehead was slightly swollen, but there was no blood. He breathed unevenly, rarely, with his belly surging up when he did, and he was unconscious.

"Ben? Sweetie?" she tried, in her small voice. The policeman tactfully stepped back, averting his face from her prostrated body, from her breasts hanging loose out of the bathrobe, from her wide arthritic knees on the cold stone of the staircase.

The ambulance took a long time to come. Trying to concentrate, Anna straightened her back and attempted to measure Ben's aura. They used to practice on each other when she was learning her technique, and she knew his aura, its form and colors and consistency, better than anyone's. "I'll help you, honey, just hold on, okay?" she whispered, leaning over him. His aura was not the color of death (pale yellow) but dark purple with lighter spots and stripes, indicating bad distress.

"Can we move him into the apartment?" Anna asked, encouraged.

"Can't move him," said the policeman, shaking his head. "He might have internal bleeding, or a skull fracture. A health professional has got to call the shots."

"Well, where are they?" she raised her voice impatiently, wiping sweat off her forehead.

"What do you want? It's Halloween."

She returned to her healing movements, almost physically sensing the progress in Ben's body. His respirations became smoother, his cheeks and lips rosier. When the ambulance arrived, Ben was coming back to consciousness.

"Don't take him. He's going to be fine. I'll take care of him," Anna pleaded, but a red-faced man with strong arms moved her aside. Armed with a stethoscope, a thermometer, and a blood pressure cuff, he inspected Ben and, over Anna's protests, took him to the hospital. She insisted on going as well. As they rode, jumping on the bumps and speeding with the siren on, Anna listened to their conversations and radio calls. The scraps of sentences she overheard made her fear surge. "You're busy today," she ventured timidly.

A tall paramedic with mountains of muscles protruding from underneath his scrubs shot her a significant glance.

"Flu?" she continued.

"Maybe," he shrugged.

"I know it's the Bird Flu," Anna said quietly, staring at the second paramedic in a yarmulke. He attempted to deny it but she talked over him. She could see him as a boy playing in a backyard with his little brother, and then lying in bed, pale and emaciated.

"You had an illness as a child, you were very sick. Your lung and sex chakras are damaged, I can see, they have a different light. I don't know how many are going to survive this but you should go back to your family, lock the doors and stay out of harm's way."

"Are you a psychic or what?"

"I am a healer."

"Why don't you heal your husband if you're a healer?"

"That's what I was doing when you arrived. Please let us out. I can take care of him. You have enough to do today as it is."

"What about my chakras?" the muscular man asked, studying her through the rearview mirror with his small bright eyes.

"You're healthy, but too gentle. Don't fight your anger. These are going to be trying times. Anger is good if used properly. Many people don't know it."

Both paramedics burst out laughing, punching each other playfully on the shoulders.

"Lady, all due respect, don't make dire predictions. You know, it's Halloween today," the muscular paramedic said. "And, just to let you know, I'm not as gentle as I seem."

The car bumped and turned; Ben groaned on his stretcher. She saw his forehead chakra pulsating bright red and put her palm on it. "I love you, honey, I love you," she whispered, her eyes filling with tears. "Please, let us out!" she pleaded again. Ben opened his eyes and attempted to talk, but all she could hear were garbled sounds. The car came to a halt, the doors squeaked and flung open, letting in the cold November air.

Ben was triaged. An attentive young doctor asked Anna many questions, and after answering them she waited, her panic mounting while Ben was sent for a CAT scan. The ER was filling up. Patients arrived in their Halloween costumes, their Death masks cast off and replaced by blue hospital gowns. "Diversion!" a nurse barked into a phone that would not stop ringing.

This is how it starts, thought Anna.

At last the young doctor returned. Anna jumped up, but he motioned her to sit and settled next to her into a floor-mounted chair.

"Your husband had a stroke. He might not be able to speak or walk for a while."

"Someone assaulted him!" she said. "He'll be okay."

"His life is not in danger right now but he's in need of treatment. He has to stay in the hospital for a couple of days."

"I need to take him home right now. Don't you see what's happening? The Black Death is here, the Bird Flu!" she clutched at the lapels of the doctor's lab coat, pulling him closer.

"I'm sorry," the doctor said, rising and pushing her fingers away. "Your husband has to stay here for a couple of days. Surely you want him to get better?"

"NO!!" Anna screamed. "Let him go! I'll take him home with me!"

The nursing staff approached her and gave her a pill with a little plastic cup of water. She had to see a psychiatrist, they informed her. Anna did not resist anymore and sat limply in the chair waiting for the pill to work. Quickly she felt relaxed, tired and detached in a way she didn't like. Ben was somewhere out of her sight but it seemed okay to her now, for she had lost the will to act.

The ER was in a state of nervous excitement. Eva could see it in the way her colleagues tightened the surgical masks over their faces, in the jerky movements of nurses, in everyone's eyes gleaming with fear and in the startle of her colleagues when their beepers went off. The always quiet ER director spoke even slower than usual and in a hushed voice that faded into a whisper now and then, only the wrinkles on his forehead betraying his worry.

"Do you think it's the Avian Flu?" Eva asked, speaking for a group of four doctors standing at the door and waiting for him to emerge from the resuscitation room. "I have a little son, you know," she added hastily. He considered her words, slowly taking off his gloves.

"Everyone has a life. Before we get word of confirmed cases there is nothing I can do. We're all in the same boat. Wash your hands, wear the gloves, wear the mask. That's all I can say."

Escorted by a nurse Eva went into the waiting area.

"Hi, I'm Dr. Leigh; the staff asked me to see you. I'm a psychiatrist," she said, automatically extending her hand to a hunched seated woman. The woman appeared listless, not in the least agitated, as Eva had been told. She was dressed in a bathrobe, and her salt-and-pepper hair was unkempt, sticking out of her bun.

"Anna?" Eva cried when the woman lifted her face.

"Oh my God, Eva!"

"What happened? Why are you here?" Eva said, considering her options. She was not supposed to treat acquaintances but there was no other psychiatrist on call.

"Someone assaulted Ben, so I called 911. They say it's stroke, but it's fate. Why else would I see you here tonight? The Joker is here, the Bird Flu. I saw it in your cards. Now please, let us go, Ben won't survive here. I told the young man-doctor. I was maybe too forceful and he didn't like it, but now you can tell him I'm fine." Anna fussily tidied her hair.

"I talked to Dr. Stern. He told me your husband had a stroke and needs treatment. It would be unwise to discharge him now. Do you know what would happen if we let him go?"

"I'll take care of him! I know his energy, I helped him regain his consciousness. Ask the paramedics, he was unconscious."

"Maybe you could first tell me your concerns about the Bird Flu?" Eva asked, moving deeper into the chair. Anna looked at her in disbelief, impatiently clapping her hands.

"My dear, don't tell me you aren't worried! I see your aura, the red circles at your temples and around your belly. You're stressed. You should go home and take care of your little boy and of yourself. The Black Death is upon us."

"So far the pandemic has not spread to the United States. The airports are shut down, and the railways and roads blocked. Not a single case has been reported in the boroughs." Eva spoke in a soothing voice, though her words did little to reassure even herself.

"Look: the sick are all around you. They'll be dead tomorrow. Then, it'll be too late for Ben. He could help when everyone starts dying. I'm sorry about you and Grigory. He should have stayed with his family." Anna said all of this in one breath, making Eva wince.

"Please, don't worry about me," Eva said firmly and proceeded to the structured psychiatric interview. Anna had odd beliefs in ghosts, auras and her healing abilities, but was otherwise healthy, with no noteworthy psychiatric symptoms. "You can go home now," Eva said swiftly, rising and extending her hand. "Your husband will have to stay here tonight. I'm sorry."

Anna remained in her seat, holding onto Eva's hand.

"Regarding the Avian Flu," Eva continued after a second's hesitation, "As I already said, there are no confirmed cases in the United States. But of course that doesn't mean we shouldn't take precautions. Make sure to wash your hands often and avoid crowded places. Now goodbye."

Anna got up early and watched the sun rise through the grille of her window bars. Yellow maple leaves whirled a violent dance in the gusts of wind and then fell despondently to the ground, stripping the year naked. The gray sky grew lighter, the cheery pink that Anna hoped for obscured by the clouds. Light rain began to drum on the air conditioner outside. Anna sipped the second cup of her morning coffee. A local radio station gave news of catastrophe. The pandemic had been given a green card on American soil, the news of thousands of cases in six different states confirmed by dawn Eastern Standard Time. How many years have they lived in this neighborhood? Anna tried to remember. Must be fifteen. Reflecting back on her life with Ben, all she felt was gratitude. She was ablaze with life every single day of those years. There was so much to do and learn, and everything was in its place, safe and right under Ben's firm guidance. And who cared now about past disappointments? He was hers, he was in danger, and she had to get him back. She had a mission again, maybe her last one.

Anna put the coffee mug into the sink and glanced at her watch. Five to seven. Time to get going. Vladimir was already pulling the car to the roadside. Muffling herself up into a hooded raincoat, Anna emerged into the wind and rain and the raging pandemic.

"Hi," she said. "Thanks for coming."

"Sure," Vladimir answered gloomily.

Anna had a hard time squeezing through the crowd of the sick and coughing, all of them pushing their way into the emergency room, but signing Ben out of the hospital proved easier than she expected. He'd never been transferred to the floor he was destined for, as there were no beds available. Ben was fully conscious now and his vital signs were stable.

153

Most importantly, no one had the time or energy to argue. Fear and chaos ruled. "Give him these medications for a week," a harried doctor muttered, handing Anna a stapled bag and walking away without saying goodbye. A couple of steps away, he coughed, then stole a glance around to see whether anyone had noticed.

Vladimir waited for Anna on the sidewalk covering his nose with a handkerchief as if fighting a bad smell. His Toyota's radio loudly blared Russian news. Anna walked slowly, Ben leaning heavily on her neck and shoulders. Ben was smiling and emitting garbled sounds that were full of joy and excitement. Like a big toddler, she thought tenderly. She sweated and panted but grinned all the same. Vladimir opened the back door and helped put Ben on the seat.

"Are you sure it's not the Flu?" he whispered into her ear.

"It's a stroke, they say. That's what the CAT scan showed. He'll be okay." She seated herself next to her husband. "We're the two happiest people in New York City, do you know that, dear?" she said to Ben.

She opened her handbag, took out some hand disinfectant and lovingly rubbed their four hands with it, his and hers. Ben giggled weakly.

16

It all seemed surreal, surely not to apply to Eva. The cough, the rapid demise were meant for others, surely not for doctors, and the deaths of her colleagues were viewed at the hospital as news exaggerated by fear, and then ignored, pushed out of the consciousness. Tired and craving company, Eva picked up the phone. She still had her friends. They were there. They weren't sick. Weren't they?

Eva called Robin first. There was no answer, and for a long time she sat still with the phone on her lap. Next, she dialed Bill and reached him on the first try, her heart jumping with joy. He sounded anxious for news, a nervous kind of energy bubbling in his voice.

"How are you?" she asked, feeling the hopeless inadequacy of her question.

"Fine. Oh my God, I'm so happy you called. It just can't be happening, can it, this surreal nightmare? How are *you*? Have you heard from anyone else?"

"I'm okay, under the circumstances," Eva sighed. "It's crazy at the hospital."

They had no more words. It was just fight or flight, hope and fear without thinking, from the gut. Ruminations were the privilege of the healthy. Eva talked about what was happening matter-of-factly, like an observer of some awful African calamity, painting herself a hero among heroes – she realized before too long. She recounted the extreme efforts being made at the hospital, the numbers of the dead, the politics of the horror. She described intubations and treating DTs and her dealings with grieving families. As she went on, she strained to find words other than *Bird Flu*, and yet those two words seemed to encapsulate it all.

Of herself she could not talk, afraid to awake the terror sleeping inside.

"And how's Grace?" Eva heard herself asking.

"Still cruising. She never came back from vacation. Smart." Bill was quiet for a moment. "We can't leave, can we, Eva? Isn't it claustrophobic? Knowing we can't leave?"

Uncertainly Eva hummed assent. Bill continued. "I never thought about it like that. I actually barely ever left the city. Now, what bothers me most is the fact that I can't escape. It's a prison. Do you feel the same way?"

An acute sense of loneliness overcame Eva again. "Yes," she said.

"Can I come for dinner?" he asked, as if reading her thoughts. "Tonight? Can I come over? I'll bring a pizza."

Bill arrived at Eva's apartment that evening wearing a breathing mask. Standing close and greeting him, she remembered his sharp smell and was overcome by awkwardness. He pulled his mask down. They looked at each other expectantly. It had been a long time since she last had sex. A quick exciting sensation in the bottom of her belly made her step back.

"Marvelous!" Bill said, and they chuckled, still standing and looking into each other's eyes.

"Let's drink," she offered, turning into the kitchen. "Let's get drunk, like old times."

Bill fell into a chair with a loud sigh of relief, took his boots off, and drummed his fingertips on the table. Suddenly excited, he jumped up again, crying eagerly,

"Yeah! Let's celebrate! Should I put the pizza into the oven?"

"No, no, sit," said Eva, waving him to stay where he was, her nose peeking into the fridge in search of something perishable she wouldn't regret sharing indulgently with a stranger.

"I'll play some music."

"Not too loud, Max is sleeping."

Bill moved around, rummaging through her CDs, humming, drumming, bringing noise and merry excitement into her living room. With the first sounds of music Eva became more cheerful, hospitality winning its battle with fear. She took out cheddar cubes and a tomato, which she washed and sliced, licking the juice off the knife and arranging the slices on the plate. While strewing salt and rotating the pepper mill over the fruit she found herself dancing to Goran Bregovic's *Get The Money*. She was infected with his excitement. Suffering didn't exist. She was an actress on the world's arena of death.

Eva opened a bottle of Chivas Regal and poured it into the motley, triangle-shaped glasses she had bought in Paris last year on the Rue de Seine. The song ended, and with it her joy trickled out. She stared at the glasses, the plate with cheese and sliced tomato still in her hands.

"I'll be right back," Eva said to Bill, placing the plate in front of him. "I'll call my mother."

Eleanor was excited and bubbling about returning to journalism and writing up an eyewitness report of mass graves in Paris. "Mom," Eva said, weighing her words. "It's the same everywhere: in Hong-Kong, in New York, all around the globe. You have to get out of the city if you can. Think of Hurricane Katrina. This is going to be a thousand times worse."

Eleanor yelled angrily into the phone. "Why do you always criticize me? You used to accuse me of negativity; now I'm being positive and you're still complaining. Why?"

"You have to get out of the city," Eva repeated firmly, realizing this was the way she talked to her patients now, with dry competence intersecting the possibility of discussion. Mother sighed.

"John wants to take me to a little village in the South of France tomorrow."

"Good!"

"I don't know if I want to go. This is my place."

"Trust me, you will want to go soon enough, only it won't be possible later. Go!"

Her mother was silent for a long time.

"Mom? Are you still there? Hello?"

Through the crackling of the connection Eva discerned a sob, distant and hushed.

"Mom?" Eva repeated.

"I don't want to die alone," Eleanor said, voicing Eva's own horror.

Back in his kitchen chair, Bill was watching her intently.

"I know, mom," Eva said, softening. "I have to go now. I'll call you again in a bit."

Eva's blue glass was almost empty.

"To life!" Bill said. "Life's great!"

Galina coughed in her sleep, just a slight tender cough, nothing dramatic, but which nevertheless made Eva jump up from her chair.

"Who is that?" Bill said frowning.

"It's Max's nanny. She's staying over."

Galina was asleep in Max's room, afraid to go back to her crowded apartment where her long-hated Polish roommate had developed a nasty cough. When Galina had asked to stay two days ago, Eva was torn. She wasn't sure she trusted Galina to say honestly whether she had been exposed. Now, Eva recalled the request with renewed suspicion, panic hammering in her temples.

"What is it?" Bill asked anxiously, adding, "Did you hear her cough?"

She had. This was what they all feared: a cough. The first messenger of death.

"I can't have her sleeping in his room. What do you think?" Eva whispered hastily.

"I wouldn't."

"I'll put a mask on her." Eva rose decidedly, picked a mask from the drawer where she held a stack of them and marched into Max's room.

Galina and Max were both soundly asleep in the blue darkness of a night lamp, and, listening to their calm breathing, Eva felt a healing quietness descend. Her suspicions turned foggy and unreal. She kneeled and took Max's hand. He stirred in his sleep. She touched his full cheek with her lips and put her head down on the mattress between his side and his plush T-Rex. Her body became heavy and she dozed off for what seemed only a second.

"Eva?"

She turned to see Bill's dark silhouette against the living room right and rose to her feet. "I'm sorry, I just dozed off." Walking out she still held a mask in her hand. She felt dizzy and sleepy, the light making her squint.

"You didn't put a mask on her," he noted.

"She doesn't need it, not today. She was breathing like a baby."

"It was quiet, wasn't it?" he said. "Blessedly quiet."

Eva smiled. "It must help in such times to be religious. Have you ever prayed?"

"When I was very little my grandfather locked me up in a potato barn because I was a spoiled city kid who didn't listen well. Sitting there I prayed that my grandpa would die and go to hell. He had a stroke a week later and I always felt I was responsible. I still do. Never prayed again."

"I pray. I never used to, but I do now," she confessed. "For Max."

They walked to the table and sat down again, sipping more whisky with downcast eyes, as if the significance of the moment demanded a respectful silence.

"I still love you," Bill said quietly and put his glass on the table. "Maybe it's a stupid time to confess, but who knows if there will be another chance. If we live, will you marry me?"

They embraced. The pathos of the moment did not touch her, and she desperately wished she could respond in the same key, with a pure heart. She didn't think him ridiculous. The way he had said it made the matters of life and marriage connected by an illogical leap. *If we live I will marry you. If I marry you I will live.*

"I will," she promised, superstitiously. "Will you love Max?" she asked, for credibility's sake.

"I will," Bill said eagerly.

They fell silent again, Bill stroking her hair, Eva curiously rubbing his hairy chest between the buttons. He still had that strong smell, acrid and virile like the curls on his chest.

"I have to tell you something," he said huskily.

He gently pushed her away. They were seated again. The clock chimed two in the morning.

"I never went to the hospital."

She opened her eyes wide.

"I never did. They paged me and left a thousand messages asking me to report, and I pretended I was with Grace on vacation and couldn't get back. I guess they think I'm dead." He chuckled softly but didn't seem amused and looked at her worriedly. She waited.

"I don't even know why I went into medicine. You know how it is. Your father is a doctor, your grandfather is a doctor, and then one day you find yourself studying anatomy and wondering, what the hell am I doing dissecting corpses? You know me, I'm not a coward. But the Flu raised the existential questions. It was, like, BOOM! You could be dead, man! I looked into myself with clarity. I don't want to be a doctor. I never wanted to."

He breathed audibly, and Eva thought, *You're pathetic. No one wants to be a doctor during the worst pandemic ever.*

"So what have you been doing?" she asked, more reproachfully than she intended.

"I took pictures. I walked the streets hiding behind my

mask, photographed the Flu and felt ludicrously safe doing it. Here is a piece of wisdom: a photographer has to hide his face. This explains why I never felt comfortable doing portraits in the past. It actually felt dangerous before. To observe people you have to be prepared to be observed yourself. I suppose I never was an alpha-male," he said with a forced chuckle.

Eva nodded. *No. You are not an alpha male,* she thought, this time with a glimmer of compassion.

"It's important to block out the emotions when recording the suffering of others. I loved my mask. So safe, so anonymous, so much space in which to discover myself! It did feel like a great liberation. I wonder whether women wearing burkas feel freer than the actually free ones. I'm drunk, I know, but do you know how great it feels just to sit here, to be with you?"

His eyes became moist and she saw his chin contracting. He took her by the shoulders and roughly pulled her closer, sobbing into her neck and shoulder, scratching her with his stubble.

"I'll run you a bath," she said, freeing herself from his embrace.

"Do I stink?" He wiped his eyes with the back of his hand.

"Yes. I'll wash you."

She ran a bath, speculating on the risks of public water use as she rolled up her sleeves. Could it transmit the virus? What if someone who was sick drowned in a reservoir? Max's rubber shark fell into the water, and Eva tenderly put it back. His big foam plastic numbers stuck to the wall in disarray. A pirate ship rested on a shelf, three little whales piled on the windowsill. My little boy, she gasped, engulfed by the naked knowledge of death lurking behind the corner. My dear little boy. On her way back, Eva stopped to listen to the sounds from Max's room and returned, reassured by Max's slight snoring and Galina's measured breath.

Bill seemed desperate. "I didn't do a good job explaining.

When people started dying around me, I was afraid. It hit me that I was mortal, too. Then I walked out and took pictures. You'll cry when you see them. No childish crap anymore, no imitations. I've realized medicine is not my calling. I know it sounds corny, but big moments call for corny sayings. That's why we're so cynical, aren't we, because nothing tragic has ever happened to us. Until now. Comfortable people get cynical. Why're you looking at me like that?"

Eva, drunk and tired, and at last quiet, wasn't aware of looking at him in any specific way. "You're right. It's hard to be honest," she mumbled.

He continued, "It's courageous to hide, can you understand that? It's so much easier to run in a pack, which is ultimately only about managing the fear. Dying is not an emotion or a driving force. Fear is. To escape fear soldiers take up their guns upon command and march and die fearless because they're together and there's someone giving orders. I have no one. I'm alone. I have everyone to fear. I must be who I am and not who I've been pretending to be out of conformity or laziness." He was swaggering again, his eyes glazed.

Eva took a big sip of whisky, coughed, and exploded into his complacent face. "That's sophistry, Jacobs! You want to sell yourself as a hero? Fine. I'll tell you what I think. It's courageous to discover who you are and to live accordingly. But it's cowardly to avoid your duties when the time comes for them."

"Don't you see? This Flu is devastating. My little personal effort as a doctor would be a drop in the ocean. I've decided that *I* will not die. *I* have the power to make this decision."

"The *power*?"

"Knowing who I am. The ability to strategize. Most people are like animals. They move with the flow, unable to think for themselves. I'm not a coward. I've got the guts to know what I want and choose my own way."

"You and Sinatra," Eva mocked.

"You're just annoyed because *you* went to the hospital. And I'm sure you had your good reasons. You felt it was the right thing to do. Right?"

"Of course. Because dying as well as helping are not about statistics. It's an individual business. Even if a hundred million people died today but I saved one life, it was worth the effort."

"For you. That's your point of view."

"For me," she agreed. "And for that person who would have died without me. What I resent is your narcissism. We're all stupid, we all go with the flow and deserve to die, while you think you're so fucking sophisticated and above us all that you choose your own way, which is to hide in your apartment, and then you're not even able to say: 'Okay, I was afraid, I was a coward.'"

"Okay, I was a coward, I admit. I'm sorry if I offended you."

"It's not about me," she said tiredly. "Why did you come? I mean, that's also risking your life."

"I wanted to see you. I was lonely," he said. "Everything's so horrifying. I stuff my pockets with napkins and gloves and iodide solution. I don't take elevators anymore. I took the stairs to you, to the 10th floor, sweating like a pig in my mask. Do you take elevators?"

She shook her head. They yawned in unison. The whiskey bottle was half-empty.

"The bath must be full by now," Bill remarked, listening to the sound of running water.

"I don't judge you," Eva offered softly, conclusively. "I understand."

She took his head in her hands and put it on her lap, straightening out his oily hair. He had the smell of death on him. Or did she just imagine it?

"Do you, really? Understand?"

"I do. Let's bathe."

17

en didn't get better over the next couple of days. Anna sat by his bedside, lost and kind, holding his hand and talking to him the way one talks to a baby. It was hard to get him to the bathroom. He often giggled and then cried, joy and misery mixing together, and she was never sure if he understood what she was saying. She talked anyway, more for her own sake: about the Bird Flu pandemic, the Joker in her spreads, and about her plans for the day, so he wouldn't feel abandoned if she stepped out. She made a trip to the store and, after much pushing and hours on her feet, returned with three cans of tuna and two toast packages tinged on the edges with mildew, her feet hurting and her spirits low. Her trip to the pharmacy the next day was unsuccessful. After five hours of standing on line she was told by the pharmacist that there was no more Tamiflu in stock, but he could get her some if she paid a thousand dollars. She prayed for patience, and for her and Ben's health, as she climbed the stairs to her apartment. Ben lay on the floor, having collapsed on his way to the bathroom. As she changed him, lovingly, discreetly, he stroked her arm, and she turned to kiss him. He reacted with a moan of surprise and looked at her, for the first time alert and alarmed. Putting a smile on her face, she said bravely: "I got some food, darling!"

Several times their own patients came to call for treatment and each time, from behind the door, Anna said, "My husband just had a stroke. I'm sorry, but we can't help right now." And it worked. They went away. For good, she hoped. But they returned, again and again, ringing and knocking, night and day, waking her. Three days after the pandemic was declared official Anna wrote up a sign informing visitors of her husband's illness and of her unavailability and posted it on the door. Holding Ben's waist in her arms she called, "Ben, Ben! Come back, I need you now!" He didn't respond, didn't even stir in his deep, neurologically impaired sleep, and she practiced her meditation to find her balance, and asked God for guidance until sleep relieved her temporarily of this waking nightmare.

The next day she made a calculation of their food supplies and realized they would starve if she didn't try to find more. But something held her back, as if she had been paralyzed as well. The fear of what waited beyond the door of the apartment made her unable to move or think, and so she sat, motionless, sweating and breathing noisily. Nestor's face, with its soft but shady eyes, flashed in her mind. She heard his voice threatening to break in.

Over four days Ben had remained the same, refusing her attempts to get him out of bed and do exercises. Instead, he pointed at the TV so she would switch it on and lay giggling, crying and mumbling unclear words, his reactions unrelated to the content, which became increasingly just one: Bird Flu. Together they watched footage of crowds pushing into hospitals, pharmacies, and stores; piles of corpses, now an everyday horror; and fires. The whole world began to look alike: New York, Paris, Prague, Rome, Moscow, Beijing, Delhi. Every major metropolitan area was experiencing food and water shortages. Looting and crime were rampant. Celebrities advocated health and safety initiatives, calling for order alongside federal, state, and city officials. A famous TV host coughed violently, covering his livid face with both hands. Anna watched how he pulled on his suspenders, trying to conceal his panic: "And here is a piece of advice in case I'm not here tomorrow: love yourself, love your neighbor, and never ever forget to wash your hands ..."

Anna felt that with Ben's health and reasoning gone, her own healing powers had begun to ebb. Twice on the evening of the sixth day she attempted to read Ben's aura and couldn't see anything at all.

"Ben, I can't see it anymore," she said, looking deep into his pale clueless eyes. "Please, you have to come back. I'm losing my gift."

But all he said was "AMMM," and then burped and smiled his new, innocent toddler's smile. Anna brought some water and the pills Dr. Stern told her to give him. The day was waning, the last rays of sunshine slanting over the rooftops. She prayed and meditated. Memories of their last vacation came to her, the pink castle at Disneyland, the glittering parade, Ben eating ice-cream and philosophizing on the unfortunate folly of haunted houses. She was startled out of her reveries by the phone's shrill ring.

"It's me, Vladimir. Olga is sick. The hospital won't take her, no beds left. Please help us."

"I can't treat it. Did you call Eva?"

"I talked to her yesterday, she's at work now. She said to give her water, Motrin and Tamiflu, but Olga is getting worse. She keeps shivering under three blankets. Please, Anna."

Anna got dressed hastily, choosing warm and comfortable clothes. She realized that she hadn't had anything to eat that day, and ran to the kitchen to make some cereal for Ben and herself. Then she switched the TV on for Ben, left his breakfast and a cup of sweet tea on the night table, and kissed his forehead. In her agitation, she tried to grasp the significance of the moment. She had a premonition they might not see each other again. When he opened his eyes, she said soothingly: "I have to run some errands, darling, but I'll be back soon." She stepped outside. Someone's body lay in the hallway one flight down. His arm was thrust back in an unnatural position. Anna's breath quickening, she looked closer, recognizing the tattoos. "Nestor," she whispered with a mixture of repulsion and relief. At least he can't harm us now, she thought fighting the uninvited nausea. The body did not yet smell.

When the first reports of Avian Flu, still unconfirmed and largely debated, had emerged in Hong Kong, Vladimir did what his father couldn't during the blockading of Leningrad: he started stockpiling food, bringing loads of it up into the apartment over Olga's loud protests.

"You are turning the house into storage!" she exclaimed. "The whole place reeks of sausages! What's the point?! If we need something, just go down to the store and get it!"

"If people are hungry, they will find their way into the store," he reasoned back in a steady drone that drove her insane.

"We are in America now!" she yelled.

"America will not feed you. In America, you have to feed yourself," he retorted, and carried up more and more boxes: sugar, candy, vitamins, dry milk, cookies, dry rye bread, fruit bars and loads of rice that he stacked along the walls, first in the closet he had cleaned out for this purpose, then in the guest room.

He brought up protein powder for athletes, and juices, and flower, and salt, and gallons after gallons of water. He drove his van to Ikea and then built an elaborate shelving system – turning the guest room, save its small library, into a huge storage space filled with food up to the ceiling.

"You can feed a whole regiment for a year!" Olga said desperately.

"If my father could have done it, he would not have died …" Vladimir started, but Olga interrupted him. "Your father is long dead!"

A moment later, more softly, she said: "I told Eva what you're doing."

"Did you?"

"I did. She says you are still trying to save your father; it's a kind of defense, this hoarding. She says it happens sometimes when people get older."

"Well," he said, thinking it over. "Maybe I've gone a little overboard. Or maybe not."

The next day he installed a steel door with a deadbolt and a shock absorber. These cost a thousand dollars.

"You are out of your mind!" Olga screamed.

"Why don't you call Eva. For another diagnosis."

"Oh yes, I will!" she snapped, hands on her hips.

"Time will show!" he retorted angrily.

With the first reports of the Flu, Vladimir knew that his stocking up on food would pay off handsomely. But right now, he wished he hadn't been right. His Olga was nearly lost to him.

In his car, Anna said: "Nestor died. His body is in the staircase in our building. Would nobody want to claim it?"

"He was a junkie," Vladimir replied dismissively. "They say there is a service, a car gathering the dead and bringing them to the morgues. We'll call from home."

"How are you?"

"Tired. Olga's parents are gone. She found them in bed, peaceful as if asleep. I got the coffins, paid three thousand bucks for the funeral, then dug the grave myself, the bastards refused to touch the bodies. But the priest came and sang at a distance." He sighed. "You know, we wanted to take Max with us because of Eva's job, and then Olga fell sick. Since yesterday she's been coughing so hard I thought it would rip her throat apart. And then the shaking."

"I'm sorry about your in-laws. Have you heard from LA?" Anna did not mention Greg's name out of superstition.

"I called yesterday. His girlfriend's parents howled something into the phone and hung up. I kept dialing but they didn't pick up again. I wish he'd call. This is what's killing Olga."

There were few cars in sight, just garbage and stray dogs roaming the streets.

"So empty!" Anna remarked.

"Everyone who could leave left. The others hide, like you

and me."

They took the Brooklyn Bridge. The military post at the road let them drive unchecked. Many buildings stood unlit, forming black rectangles against the sky.

"Why haven't you left?"

"Waited and waited," he said, impatiently waving his hand. "Waited for Max, then to reach Greg, then they closed the city, as if it would help. Where could we go, anyway?"

The bedroom was lit by a small nightlight that cast bizarre shadows. Olga lay on her cozy bed with embroidered pillows under a heap of blankets. She didn't move but seemed to notice that someone entered and emitted a rasping sound. Vladimir ran fussily to the kitchen, tripping over something that fell on the floor with a clank, and returned with a sponge that he applied to her forehead and lips. Her face was small and wrinkled as a newborn's, sweaty hair stuck to her forehead. Framed black and white photographs of her deceased parents hung on the wall above her. They sat on a beach towel holding hands: her mother wore a summer skirt and a white blouse with a little bow, and was kneeling; her father sat in waist-high swimming pants, his legs crossed; both were shyly smiling, the pale expanse of the sea gleaming behind them. Olga's bedside table was crammed with cups and medicine bottles, a thermometer and an open pack of Tamiflu. Anna approached cautiously and bent over her, seeking to make eye contact. Olga's eyes wandered and stopped, steadily scanning Anna's face, a shadow of recognition passing over them.

"You," she mouthed.

Anna was suddenly engulfed by an intense pity and collapsed, sobbing. Vladimir sat opposite to her, helpless, tired, his arms hanging along his wiry body.

"It's okay," Anna said, composing herself. "It's good to cry. You've been very good friends of mine. Dear friends. I just wanted to say it. Now, let's see what I can do."

She got up, feeling light and dizzy.

"I see your heart, Olga. It's strong and red. It's fighting. I want you to know it. You have to fight now. Your extremities are dry, they need water. Let's see, your energy paths are blocked in the chest and abdomen. Turn on your back, I'll even them out."

Olga turned, gasped for air, and started coughing, jerking like a wooden doll pulled by invisible strings. The phone rang.

"It's Eva!" Vladimir announced. "No, she is worse. The hospital had no beds. I've been calling you all day. I brought Anna. I can't give her the pills, she won't drink anything."

"You have to force water into her, any way you want, even if you have to sit with her for hours giving it drop by drop! Vladimir, are you listening? It's her only chance, do you understand?"

Vladimir was listening.

"I know what to do!" Eva shouted breathlessly, "Give her a high enema, water is absorbed from the bowels too. Give her Gatorade to drink. Don't wrap her in blankets if she's hot; give her ice instead. Give her Motrin. Don't force her to eat. And continue with the Tamiflu."

Eva's advice seemed useless to him. Most of all he was resentful. Eva didn't do a thing for them, nothing to help find Olga a hospital bed.

"How are you?" Eva continued desperately, trying to break through Vladimir's apathy.

"Fine, thank you," he said.

"Are you wearing a mask? You have to wash your hands."

"Thank you for your advice. I have to attend to Olga now, she's coughing."

He hung up and made a calculation in his head. If he didn't wear a mask, then maybe they could die together. At Olga's bedside Anna sat quietly with her head lowered. Mourning, he thought. He repeated to her Eva's advice word for word.

"Yes, yes, yes," Anna muttered, jumping up as if someone had given her a weapon. "She's right, that's what we're going to do. Where's the enema?"

And so she took over, bursting with the nervous energy of hope, as if Olga's case represented her and everyone else's personal salvation – as if only by saving her could she also save Ben, and herself, and Vladimir, and the whole world of this pain and misery. Vladimir watched, first trying to be helpful and lend a hand, then more and more detached, already grieving his wife. Watching him, Anna wanted to yell *Wake up! She's not dead yet!* Finally, she took him by the hand and led him to the sofa in the living room. "Sleep now," she said kindly, covering him with a robe.

Returning to her fervent duty, Anna gave Olga another enema and then held her head, pouring water drop by drop into her parched mouth, patiently waiting for the cough to subside. She called Eva to find out how many enemas she should give and what Gatorade was and got a recipe for salted and sweetened water instead. She pulverized Motrin, Tylenol, and Tamiflu and forced it into Olga's mouth bit by bit. Around four in the morning Olga's temperature fell to 102, and Anna, exhausted but happy, dozed off in an armchair. Before she closed her eyes, she saw a framed photo above her head: Max on a swing, showing his little teeth with gaps between them, his face wearing a wide happy smile, his hair flying.

"A good omen," she sighed aloud.

18

anessa May tore Eva from a dream she could no longer remember. She sat up in bed rubbing her eyes. Bill opened his eyes for a second, smiled sleepily and turned on his side, putting a pillow over his head. Eva had a hangover. Like a somnambulist, she wandered into the kitchen and swallowed Ibuprofen with a glass of sour and fizzing orange juice she hadn't the heart to throw away. The presence of Bill in her bed was disquieting, as if she had committed adultery and was going to be punished – or in fact was being already being punished: by guilt, her headache, and her fear of going out. Or worse. Or worse. Had she put their very existence at risk by letting this happen? She winced, remembering Bill's confession of love. Greg's face came to her mind for a second, a wave of nostalgia flooding her. Gazing out the window, she listened to someone's screams and, trying to make out the words, realized with sudden clarity that she was afraid.

Max awoke and appeared in his pajamas at the doorstep of the room he shared with Galina.

"Mama! Look! I have a truck! It can fly."

"Good morning pumpkin!" Eva answered as brightly as she could, her heart softening.

"Are we going to school today?"

"No, school is closed."

"Why?"

"I told you, Max. What did I tell you?"

She had answered this question a hundred times already in the past four days.

"That there is a virus. Is it still there?"

"Yes, pumpkin."

"Is it big?"

"No, it's very-very small."

"But if it's small, why can't we go? I want to go with you."

"Because it can infect you and you can get sick."

Eva picked him up in her arms, and he circled his legs around her, not letting her put him down. He kissed her, and she fought tears as she kissed the back of his neck. She thought of the physicians who hadn't shown up for work yesterday. Her fingers ached with cold although it was warm inside and so far everything was still functioning: water, heat, electricity. She rubbed her palms on Max's back, overflowing with love and homesickness as if she, too, were going to disappear today like those doctors of whom she tried not to think. Galina stepped out soundlessly, barefoot. She had large, expressive feet with long toes that gripped the floor firmly, like a Rodin sculpture's. Why had Eva never noticed that before?

"Mama has to go to work," Galina said softly. "But she will come back soon."

"Galina will stay with you, and Bill will be here too," Eva added.

"I don't want Bill! I don't want Galina! I want to throw them out into the garbage! I want my mommy!" Max was always saying he wanted to break something and throw it into the garbage.

Eva unclenched his little fingers with tender impatience, "I'll come back and we'll play Monster, I promise," she said, gathering all her strength in trying not to break down.

"She'll come back and play Monster with you," Galina echoed, and with surprise and gratitude Eva saw tears running down Galina's cheeks. Ska came out too and stood watching them, trying to comprehend with her feline mind what life had in store.

This overwhelming sense of personal tragedy was new to Eva. It made it impossible to cross her doorstep without wondering whether she would be coming back. The feeling was exhilarating and awful at the same time, her perceptions painfully intense and colorful. Her mood fluctuated between heroic and miserable. Out on the street she felt better, her fright abated. Fresh autumn wind blew into her face. The weather was mild and moist. Eva quickened her pace, anxiety driving her forward. Something big was happening, changing and ending human lives, and there was just one way to survive: by walking on.

She passed the Oval and the soccer field and entered the 20th Street Loop on her usual way to work. Two men in civilian clothes were sealing off the exit with broad yellow tape. When she approached, her head held high and her arms swinging, one of them gestured for her to stop.

"Key!" he called out like a guard from a medieval fairy tale.

"Here," she said, showing her apartment keys. "I'm a doctor."

"Good luck!" he winked. He didn't wear a mask. His face was amiable and cleanly shaven with a small cut on his chin and a patch of shaving cream stuck behind his ear. "Be careful of looters!" he warned when she was several feet away.

"Wear a mask!" she cried back, waving good-bye.

Her route was short: she had to cross 20th Street and Peter Cooper Village, then 23rd Street to the building of the Manhattan VA. There were no stores nearby, just apartment houses, and she was grateful for the relative safety of being away from the main looting sites. In Peter Cooper she had to show her keys again, this time to an aging local activist with a wandering eye whom she remembered gathering signatures for democratic elections the year before. She nodded at him in recognition, but he just waggled with his agile fingers, "Move, for God's sake!"

Eva reached 23rd Street and craned her neck, trying to ascertain the condition of the crowd in front of the VA and counting the ambulances. It was like reading tea-leaves in an irrational and childish hope that it was all over and that the pandemic had ended as precipitously as it had begun.

The automatic doors stood wide open. Paramedics loaded patients on stretchers from the ambulances parked at the entrance. Patients streamed toward the doors, forming a many-headed crowd slowly squeezing in. There was a special entrance for healthcare workers but no one adhered to it, pushing in with the desperation of the condemned. It was a swarm of sick and dying. An old woman fell, but no one bent down to help her up. They just walked over her, one by one, pale, weak, coughing. Eva noticed that the crowd was smaller and sicker, with no children and few relatives willing to tease the death. She went up the ramp slowly, tightening her mask as she moved. A male nurse with whom she had worked yesterday but whose name she could not remember approached from First Avenue. Eva greeted him with the small joy of recognition. He squeezed her elbow and said, almost chivalrously, "Shall we?" Rounding his large palms in front of his mouth like a megaphone, he then announced, dispassionately and urgently, "All patients please step aside from the left entrance door! You are hindering the doctors on duty! I repeat: all patients please free the left entrance door!"

Patients obeyed, some of them turning around and looking for the doctor, as if hoping to be saved right there and then. They moved grudgingly, lining up along the wall into a narrow corridor through which Eva, the nurse, and the paramedics carrying a stretcher squeezed into the hospital. Patients coughed, doubling over and not bothering to cover their mouths. Someone pulled at the nurse's sleeve, rasping, "Doctor, doctor!" Inside, no one was X-raying the visitors' bags per usual procedure. The two security guards on duty, masked and gloved, stood at a distance to the crowd, shouting and directing patients forward into a makeshift ER in the wide, brightly lit lobby.

As on the day before, Eva was assigned to the third floor's general medicine unit. The nurse held the door to the staircase for her, his large, square-shaped head bent like a bull's.

"I'm sorry, I forgot your name," she said, walking in.

"Benji. And yours?"

"Dr. Leigh," she said extending her hand. "You can call me Eva."

"That wouldn't be good," he remarked, shaking his head.

"Why?"

"That would mean we've given up. It's not professional."

Eva smiled uneasily, halting before the door to the unit and automatically unbuttoning her coat.

Inside, it smelled of blood, excrement, and fear.

At the start of the pandemic, hours after chaos had broken out, everyone had been summoned to a staff meeting. The chiefs of the departments, nursing, social work supervisors, and administrators had set about deciding how best to organize the personnel, how to deal with the patients already registered and how to redistribute resources. General decisions were made concerning the mobilization of residents, retired physicians, and medical students. Shifts would have to be as long as necessary. Questions about compensation were left unanswered aside from promises of food and preferential medical treatment for healthcare workers. Dr. Kardinal, the chairman of psychiatry, was overly articulate and ended up chopping up the issue of psychiatric patients along the lines proposed by surgery: discharging all psychiatric patients and freeing the beds for Flu victims. All psychiatric treatment was suspended indefinitely except in "acute situations," which had not been defined. Dr. Atkinson, an elderly internist widely respected for his knowledge and integrity, had raised his hand. "What do we do about delirium tremens, cases of which are bound to surface, if our psychiatric resources are inaccessible?"

"As I said," Kardinal retorted in his smooth way that suggested thoughtfulness, respect for the opponent and yet somewhere, hidden between the lines, his intellectual superiority. "psychiatrists will be made available for any acute problems related to psychiatry. However, right now we have to establish and address priorities. And I would propose our top priority be the Flu."

"Physicians untrained in the subtle differences are not going to be able to distinguish between DTs and the Flu. We need to ensure that specialists are on hand at all times."

"These are technical details that I'm afraid are going to have to be left to the discretion and applied knowledge of the physicians in question."

"But we can treat DT!" Atkinson shouted, half rising from his chair. "We *know* how to do that. We *don't* know how to treat the Flu! We're going to lose lives unnecessarily!"

"While your concerns are legitimate, we cannot waste time on arguing the details of each condition. Please consider it the end of the discussion."

Eva turned to her seat neighbor to whisper, "This is going to be a disaster."

Her neighbor had looked at her, annoyed, "Actually, I do think the Flu is the priority."

"Yes," Eva had hurried to defend herself. "So do I. But we can treat withdrawal." Her neighbor had ignored her and Eva had let it go. Everyone was rising, a sea of white coats nervously broaching the ominous, unknown adventure.

The Starbucks stand in front of the auditorium was empty and shut. With sudden hunger Eva remembered the huge scones they used to sell. Behind a glass door leading into an inner garden that, in happier times, accommodated goldfish, al fresco luncheons, and cigarette breaks, she discerned the silhouettes of people in the dark, a sole cigarette being lit. It oddly comforted her to see that there were still smokers taking refuge out there; it seemed to represent continuity.

Later, Eva stood in line for the day's assignment, listening to her stomach rumble and waiting for her name to be called.

"Dr. Leigh!" she heard, trembling as if it were her sentence.

Like those whose names had been called before hers, she answered in a high-strung voice.

"Yes?"

"You are assigned to the third floor internal medicine unit under the supervision of Dr. Firbas, anesthesiology."

That day Eva forgot about food for her family – the food that was still available. Hours went by, hours and more hours, even when she thought she couldn't go on anymore. She saw people die, just like that – people who only the day before had enjoyed perfect health. At first she tried to absorb the tragedies, to find the time to talk to the affected families, but soon there were neither kindness nor energy left and she shifted into autopilot, her limbs still working but her compassion shut off. At ten in the evening she had her first break.

In an unused treatment room she leaned heavily against the wall. She was alone; it was strange and wonderful. The room was white and windowless and contained a table with instruments, a scale, blood pressure cuffs and stethoscopes hanging from an IV rack, a growth chart on the wall, surgical gauzes and alcohol swabs on a tray. It was a sterile, purifying environment, quiet and remote like an uninhibited island in the middle of a crumbling urban empire. Eva had an overwhelming desire to sleep. A Chekhov story came to mind: it was about a seven-year-old maid who had to clean and cook and take care of her madam's colicky baby – until one night, sick with exhaustion, the little girl pressed a pillow to the baby's face and at last was able to sleep. Eva sank into a couch. She hadn't slept in thirty-seven hours. She lay down (just for a second, she thought) and closed her eyes.

Her dreams were a kaleidoscope of victims dying on her, always through some fault of hers. She became covered in sweat. The faces she had tried to block out during the day – those of the dead and their mourners alike – swam up in front of her. Ugly, hollow and nauseating, the fear she felt was unlike any of the fears she had known until then. Senseless loss and helplessness drove her insane. She remembered the prayers, of patients and staff alike, divided by the dread of contamination into their separate corners. A hospital priest clutching a Bible to his chest, walked around talking about the end of the world until he, too, collapsed at the end of the day, blood on his mouth. And the children! Ever since Max had been born, Eva couldn't bear to watch movies where children were hurt. Now it was happening all around her. *Not Max! Not my Max ...!* Eva woke abruptly, opening her eyes ...

Through the chink in the door she could see the medication room, the nursing station and the hallway. Healthcare workers walked by carrying bags with energy boosters to take home. Eva saw Benji look around and then open a drawer to take out several cans of Ensure, which he hid methodically in his backpack. His black forehead, coated with sweat, reflected the light of the lamp like a concave mirror. Eva let him do it. She would be smart to do the same. When he'd finished his stealing she gathered her strength and rose, empty of food and longing for her son.

19

Anna forgot to draw the curtains that night and woke up dreaming in intense red. A sunbeam reached her face and she opened her eyes, squinting. Her back was stiff from sleeping in a chair and she stretched herself, then ran to check on Olga. She approached, taking her hand tentatively, feeling for a pulse. Olga's hand was warm and full, and her pulse, though rapid, was nothing compared to the disappearing thread it had been yesterday. Full of hope, Anna touched her peaceful face, its wrinkles softened now that the suffering had subsided, its eyelids slightly trembling. The room was quiet, its fading wallpaper saturated with sun. Vladimir, cowering at the door, watched, pale and tense, his face creased by pillow folds.

"Come," Anna invited him. "Don't look like that. She'll need you today."

Together they took her temperature, which hovered just above normal. Olga stirred, opened her eyes, and smiled weakly at the two faces above her. They beamed back, crying out simultaneously: "Thank God! You're better!" Propped up by Vladimir, she drank water and took her medicine. After a violent and prolonged coughing fit, Olga lay back and slept.

They had their morning coffee, Anna cheerful as a butterfly, Vladimir grumpy and exhausted despite his relief. Wind moved the curtains and a sun-stream cast a road of light from the window to the hallway. It all seemed so normal: the table covered with lace, pots and pans hanging on the walls, a stack of clean china and blooming geraniums on the sill with their bitter, familiar smell. Anna closed her eyes, giving herself in to the homely comfort. Warm honey-colored bliss flowed through her meridians, divine golden energy filling her. She smiled.

"You know, when we first met, I had a crush on you," Vladimir offered out of the blue.

Anna shook her head. "I was not much to look at. A bluestocking. Only Ben liked me."

"You were different. Spirited."

Anna's cheeks flushed easily. She shook her head, throwing her hair, now out of its bun and streaming over her shoulders.

"You have hair like a witch," Vladimir blundered. "Why don't you color it?"

"Ben likes salt-and-pepper." Anna paused. "Will you drive me home?" she said then, suddenly edgy. "Ben's waiting, I need to change and feed him."

"Please don't leave her! Maybe I just go and bring him here?" Vladimir pleaded. "Isn't it much better? We could be all together. It's too hard for you to lift him anyway. You need a man."

"I don't know, Vladimir. I think he'd better be at home."

"Please! We're going to die without you. Please ..." Vladimir's chin trembled slightly and Anna thought he might start crying, but he didn't. She imagined him as a boy. That's exactly how his chin would have trembled then, she thought. She nodded, and Vladimir took up her hand and kissed it in the old-fashioned way. Like his parents and grandparents used to do. They burst out laughing, and he added light-heartedly, holding his sides,

"I've never done that before!"

As they left the house Vladimir attached a hand-printed sign to the entrance of his shop. *CONTAMINATED*, it read.

Nestor's body was not in the staircase when Anna walked up, her heart quickening. She failed to insert the key on the first try, her hand trembling with anxiety. The elation of Olga's improvement was forgotten; only her guilt remained. *How could I have left him here for all these hours, so helpless and lonely?* She burst into the apartment, Vladimir running after her, through the hallway with its dark coats and old closets, through the spare living room with its dust and disarray of the last days, to where the TV unrelentingly talked of death.

Ben was cold when she touched him. Cold and still smiling.

Anna stood beside him for a long time. She did not cry. Vladimir, his fussiness revived, ran around, offering her tea and vodka and condolences she was not able to accept. She could not feel her own body.

"So, that's it," she whispered repeatedly.

And then: "No one will come to the funeral."

Vladimir held her awkwardly. Her body felt as unbending as steel.

"We need you," he whispered. "Olga needs you."

They carried the body downstairs. A long-time neighbor opened the door only to shut it immediately at the sight of death.

"I left him!" she screamed, collapsing and letting Ben's body fall next to her. Vladimir, quiet and persistent, wrapped his arms around Ben's chest and dragged him on his own. "Just one more flight," he muttered while Ben's wooden feet jumped, hitting the steps with their naked, bluish heels. Motionless, Anna watched how Ben's body obediently bounced down, one step at a time.

Olga was unchanged when they arrived, her fever still around 101. Her cough had turned productive; on the tissues around the bed they saw sputum tinged with blood. She was still too weak to get up by herself. "It's good if she's coughing up," Eva had said on the phone, so Vladimir didn't worry.

"Ben died," Anna said quietly. Olga closed her eyes.

They carried his body into the community garden

where several neighbors from the surrounding houses were digging graves for their loved ones. Anna's eyes glided over the playground, deserted and eerie under the bright sun. "He wanted to be burned," she said evenly. With the help of the neighbors they sawed some branches off the trees, splashed gas on them and made a fire on the open space next to a slide. Anna felt she had to say something but words deserted her, and she watched silently how Ben's body caught fire. One moment, she had an impulse to run to him and save his dear hand. The stench of the smoking flesh was awful; those watching stepped back and to the side, out of the wind. Vladimir threw in more twigs to keep the fire going. From a distant corner a ragged panhandler cried, "November barbecue, ha?" and limped away. Vladimir yelled angrily, but Anna wasn't offended. The tramp's punishment was on its way.

After Vladimir left to attend to Olga, Anna stayed alone, watching and remembering, but mostly just vegetating in a state of shock. It was cold, and she stamped her feet and approached the fire. She felt better when Ben ceased to be recognizable.

When it was over she gathered Ben's ashes, his bones still preserved but fragile and falling apart in her hands, and put them into a green vase that Vladimir had given her. She picked through every single bit with her bare fingers until her fingertips bled and lost sensation from the cold and scraping. Then she sealed the top with plastic wrap and, pressing the vase to her chest, carried it back to the house.

"Where do you want to put it?" Vladimir asked cautiously.

"Under my couch," she said.

Although the smell of his burning body hadn't left her nostrils all evening, it became unbearable when she went to bed. She was still awake, turning on her left side, tormented by the stench and wondering whether it wasn't the urn that emitted it, when she heard his voice.

"Ben?" she asked sitting up.

You shouldn't have barbecued me.

"I love you so much! I didn't mean to desert you! I didn't want to! Please forgive me!"

The voice said nothing more. The smell faded shortly after.

"Forgive me!" Anna screamed into the dark silence. Vladimir's head emerged from the door.

"Are you okay? I'll give you a sleeping pill."

Vladimir shuffled toward her in his slippers, his white t-shirt gleaming in the dark. "It will be okay, everything will be fine, you're just tired, you didn't do anything wrong ..." He stroked her hair.

"*You* killed him," Anna whispered coldly. "You lured me away."

"I'm sorry, Anna. I'm so sorry," he said, continuing to stroke her hand, softly and fatherly, giving her a pill and water, which she obediently swallowed. Then she prayed. Vladimir stayed with her until she fell into a deep, dreamless sleep.

The next day Olga was able to get up and, aided by Vladimir's caring hands, walk to the bathroom and sit up in bed. Anna read Pushkin to her, first *Eugene Onegin,* parts of which they could both recite from memory, then *Feast at the Time of Plague,* vaguely yearning for answers but instinctively rejecting Pushkin's hedonistic solution. They drank sweet black tea and Anna cried about Ben, and herself, and all the suffering that was yet to come. She didn't mention Ben's ghost. Maybe Vladimir was right and it was nothing but a nightmare. From time to time pangs of pain accompanied her memory of the smell and she felt like screaming and pulling out her hair, like grieving women have done since ancient times. She tried to distract herself with reading, cooking, and caring for Olga. She attempted to assess Olga's aura, but her gift was gone. She was blank as a slate, unbearably blank. Only action could save her now. She suffered in her voluntary prison, filled with food, apathy, and memories.

Seated in the kitchen that night, Vladimir switched on an old record of a Russian bard Okudjava they used to love back home. The song was of Georgia, grapes, and love. Vladimir and Anna listened and ate their supper in silence, Anna barely touching hers.

"Are you afraid?" Vladimir said.

"Of what?"

"Death."

Anna shook her head, "I wish I were dead."

He continued as if he hadn't heard this. "*I'm* afraid. Eva said, wash your hands, wear a mask. I didn't do it. I was waiting to go with Olga. Would you read cards for me?"

"I could, before," Anna made a vague gesture toward the past. "I could see the calamity coming, all these Jokers in the cards. But Ben said I shouldn't worry, and I didn't. Now I wish the Joker would take me too."

"What's going to happen to us? Where is Greg? Will Max live?"

Anna shook her head again. "I don't know."

That night she had another vision: Ben's hand, burning. *You'll burn, too*, his voice warned her, hatefully, sending a current down her spine.

20

Robin appeared at Eva's side out of the blue. No one asked questions. Their supervisor, Firbas, gave Robin a short list of instructions and a sympathetic shoulder punch. When they had a moment alone, Eva was too afraid to ask about Robin's son.

"Spencer's with Dan. In the Catskills," Robin said curtly, averting her eyes.

"I called you. You didn't pick up. I thought …" Eva didn't finish.

"I'm fine. I came because I needed to do something. I wanted to be somewhere familiar." Reflexively, Robin bit her nail. Her eyes were dull, her red hair shaggy. Tracing Eva's glance she quickly put her hand away like a little girl.

"It's good to be together," Eva said. "We'll be okay. Just wear your gloves. Always. And don't bite your nails without a pre-op level disinfection."

Their medical training became reduced to barbaric simplicity and inefficiency, to what medicine had been for centuries – until a hundred years ago, with the revolutionary birth of bacteriology, hygiene, antibiotic treatment, immunology and genetics. Psychiatric problems proliferated too. Eva saw several types of conversion disorder for the first time in her career. Hysterical paralysis. Hysterical blindness. She saw people screaming, cursing, and lashing out. The emotional upheaval of the Flu had made it hard for her to distinguish between pathology and health until finally she stopped trying to tease them apart and concentrated her efforts on minimizing any and all suffering. After the initial shock of what was happening, Eva developed an angry determination that surprised even her. She was caught in a hurricane of activity that subsided only when she was at home. At the hospital, acting on her own instincts, she found that priorities sorted themselves out quite easily. She made decisions and relayed tasks without the hidden guilt that had ruled her relationships with others prior to the outbreak.

Robin, on the other hand, seemed broken, the sunny side of her nature imprisoned by fear. A deep vertical crease that Eva had never noticed before divided her friend's eyebrows. At work, Robin passively shadowed Eva and Firbas as well as a radiology resident named Taylor.

There was a severe shortage of nurses, and Eva initiated the practice of self-administering medication for patients experiencing alcohol withdrawal whenever possible. She and Robin left the pills and printouts of dosing schedules next to the patients' beds along with instructions to yell for personnel if their self-counted pulse exceeded 150 or if they broke out in severe sweat, had seizures, or hallucinated. Of course, everyone yelled, and rarely did any of the overwhelmed staff members answer their calls, but that was to be expected. Initiative felt liberating. Emboldened by her success, she began to isolate addiction patients, creating *de facto* a detox ward. She wouldn't realize how much controversy this would ignite until several days later.

"I'll report you!" shouted Taylor, the radiology resident. "You'll lose your license when this is over!" Taylor had a long, beak-like nose that made him look like an angry ostrich in a mask. Strain and insomnia had left a spider-web of thin red veins in his eyes and Eva wanted to comfort him. She too was tired. She understood so well.

"Don't you see, I'm here just like you," she said in conciliatory tone.

"Just drop the junkies and do what you're told to! The Flu is the priority here!"

"We can't treat the Flu!" she yelled back. "Sure, we can

give them fluids and Motrin, but that's it. Those we *can* save, why don't we save them?"

Taylor bellowed, sticking his nose out, his big belly trembling. Veins bulged in his neck. "You're just afraid to come near the Flu! It's easy to treat junkies! We're working a double load because of you! *We're* the ones who get exposed!"

"Excuse me, but I go near Flu patients just as much as you do! And for your knowledge, psychiatric patients die too! It's not like alcohol is a Flu vaccine!" Eva stepped toward Taylor. She itched to strike him in the face. She could understand how people become physical.

Suddenly Firbas was there, taking them by the shoulders.

"Enough politics," he said firmly. "We're all heroes."

He stayed with his arms holding them apart until their bodies relaxed and lost interest in fighting. Eva felt herself flush with anger and embarrassment.

"Good!" said Firbas. "I never want to see this again. Get to work."

Mr. Rodriguez lay on a cot between two beds in Room 20, among the other alcoholics going through withdrawal. The room reeked of sweat, blood, and excrement. Robin, masked and dressed in a stained lab coat, hammered a nail into the wall above his head so she could hang his IV fluids. His young, clear face was twisting into a baby's grimaces. He was mumbling in Spanish something about calling his mom.

"Where is home?" Robin asked tenderly, patting his big tattooed arm in search of a vein. That forgotten intonation startled Eva, and she turned around and listened in even though she didn't understand. "Puerto Rico?"

Mr. Rodriguez was absent, lost in his hallucinations. Watching him Eva was worried. He needs a CAT scan. He needs to be washed. He lay in a pool of urine, as everyone did.

There was no way to change the sheet. There *were* no clean sheets, no laundry personnel.

"It's going to be okay," Robin said with the same tenderness she used to speak to baby Spencer.

"Mama, mama!" he shrieked back.

Robin squatted next to Mr. Rodriguez, lost in her reveries, and though it was a struggle Eva did not interrupt her. Robin was slow, unbearably slow. In the time it took Eva to care for twenty patients, Robin managed five.

"You have to pace yourself, Robin," Firbas had told her just that morning. "I know we're swamped, but please try. Try to learn from Eva. We need to be more efficient."

"I'll try. But you know what? I stay here after she goes home, and I do my best."

"I know, but unstable patients decompensate quickly if not attended to right away, and someone has to do it, not in twelve hours but right now," he said kindly, squeezing her arm. "I know you can do it!"

In the stinking hallway full of crumpled sheets covered with feces, soiled paper towels, and dirty footprints, Robin cried, the mask on her face blown in and out by her gaping mouth.

"Hey!" Eva said, putting an arm around her. "It's okay."

"How do you do it?"

"What?"

"Be efficient."

"I just do it. I block out the emotions. I don't comfort anyone because there's no time for it. I set the priorities. I don't spend too much time on hopeless cases. I know what you think: that it's heartless. But efficiency is crucial; otherwise nothing gets done. And in fact if I didn't *have* to be dispassionate, I couldn't survive."

"I couldn't do it without the compassion," Robin said. "What's the point?"

"It's not really that I'm not compassionate, Robin," Eva said quietly. "It's just that I can't let one patient die because I took thirty minutes to comfort another one. I guess it's my way of being compassionate."

"I miss Spencer," Robin said, the crease between her eyebrows deepening.

Mr. Rodriguez was nursed and discharged by Robin only to be re-admitted the same evening with broken ribs and a fever. He expired a couple of hours later, probably of the Flu, but maybe from internal bleeding or hypothermia. No one could say for sure. Lab services weren't functioning anymore. Robin witnessed him die.

"Mr. Rodriguez just died," she said blankly when she met Eva in the hallway.

Eva nodded. "You did what you could."

Eva had five patients die that morning alone. No doubt, it was tragic, but this is what they did day and night: trying and losing, being helpless, tagging dead bodies. Eva was marginally aware of being bossy but someone had to lead. The more will she exerted, the less initiative Robin seemed to have, hushed by Eva's energy. It didn't use to be this way. Robin used to be funny and tough.

"I can't sleep," Robin said with a distorted face.

Eva heard it and yet blocked it out like she blocked out all the suffering around her. Heroes were not allowed feelings. If she started contemplating her weaknesses now, she would break down. She turned away.

It was warm out, and drizzling, raindrops and yellow leaves falling all around. Gusts of wind blew from all directions, stirring trash and foliage together. Garbage overflowed in the streets. Eva saw a rat, then two. Otherwise the streets were deserted. How long before their electricity would fail? A masked couple passed her. She recognized the parents of one of Max's playground friends.

"Hi," the man said. "How's your son?"

Eva did not like questions about Max nowadays. Telling people he was well seemed to invite illness. Overcoming her hesitancy, she said,

"He's fine. He's upstairs with the nanny."

"Jamie is sick," the man continued. "She is at the hospital. You're a doctor, aren't you?"

Eva nodded.

"Do you think we did the right thing?" the little girl's mother asked in a voice nasal from crying.

"Yes, absolutely."

"We wanted to stay with her but they wouldn't let us," the woman went on, breaking into fresh sobs, breathing hard under her mask.

"It's okay, Jenny, it's okay," the man said, leading her away, his hand on her back.

Eva turned into the darkening alley that led to her building. A rusting old excavator stood at the corner of the nearby basketball court, abandoned, its shovel still full of stones, road works suspended. Heaps of fallen foliage covered the broken pavement. Eva's thoughts were with Max, her heart aching to see him.

"Eva! Eva, wait!" Bill appeared out of nowhere and strode toward her with a victorious smile. "I got us milk and honey and three apple turnovers with minimum mold! Yahoo!" he raised his bag above his head.

Eva nodded weakly.

"Aren't you glad to see me?" Bill asked, taking her elbow. "What happened?"

"The neighbors' daughter is sick," Eva said quietly. "Let's take the elevator. I have to see Max now."

Max sat on her lap, and Eva held him tightly, smelling his hair. It smelled of bread. A homey, cozy smell. She wished he would stay on her knees, but he slid away, madly jumping around and tugging on her and Bill's sleeves.

"He needs exercise," Eva said. She wished she could take him out.

"Mommy! I want to go to the playground. Please."

"Max, you know there's a very bad virus out there. It's not safe to go out."

"But I want to," he screamed and kicked his legs and slapped her arm. She held him, ready to threaten him with a time out, but then remembered the neighbors' little dying girl and softened.

"Okay, I'll go with you, but you have to promise you'll wear a mask and gloves. And you absolutely cannot touch your face or put anything into your mouth. Do you understand?"

When she put a mask on him, he squirmed and said again, "I don't want it!"

"We can't go out if you don't wear it! If you won't you can get sick and die. But you can't die because I love you so much."

"Let's take a ball?" he asked through the mask.

The playground was dry and deserted, strewn with old brown and yellow leaves. An old woman was sitting on a bench as they approached, afflicted by a hacking cough. "Someone help," she whispered. Eva went by, turning Max's face away.

"Mommy! Is she sick?"

"Yes."

"Is she going to die?"

"I don't know. Don't speak so loud."

"Why?"

"She could hear you and get upset."

"Mommy! There's no one here. Where are the children?"

"At home, I think. Everybody's afraid to go out."

"Are they dead?"

"No, Max, they're just hiding."

"Like daddy?"

"Sort of. Do you want to play soccer?"

They played for a while, running and laughing mutedly through their masks. It felt good to be out in the fresh air and to move. Dusk was approaching quickly.

"Five more minutes!" she shouted at Max.

"No, seven more minutes!" he yelled back, catching the ball. Then he fell. His mask slipped off, and before Eva could reach him, Max was rubbing his nose and eyes with dirty gloves.

"No! No! Don't do it!" she screamed, horrified, and threw herself on top of him, taking his hands away from his face and re-adjusting his mask. He was crying.

"Mommy, do you love me?"

"Of course, I love you more than anyone in the whole world."

On the way back they saw the old woman again. She was reclining on the bench, still coughing weakly, sweat dripping from her forehead. Eva tried to look elsewhere but something made her glance at her. Their eyes met.

"Help me," rasped the woman.

"I'm sorry, I can't," Eva said, pressing Max's hand in hers and pulling him on. "I'll call an ambulance."

When they got home the television was on.

Fellow New Yorkers!, the mayor was saying. *We urge everyone to protect our pharmacies. Tamiflu cannot be delivered unless there are pharmacies available to dispense it. Medication will be continued to be given out free of charge to anyone in need, but only by trained medical personnel on designated sites. Lootings and killings make this task increasingly difficult. We urge the public to form local National Guard brigades. Masks, food, and medical care will be provided to every volunteer guard at pharmacies, banks, and hospitals. You can register at the following locations: Battery Park, City Hall, Union Square, Times Square, Bryant Park, Lincoln Center ...*

"Insane," Bill said. "This is worse than Hurricane Katrina. Why don't they ever learn? Where is our emergency food? Are they going to let us starve?"

Galina looked distraught.

"What's the matter?" Eva asked her finally.

"Dana is dead. I cannot go back. Everyone is get sick. My son in Tver don't pick up phone."

"Maybe the phone's not working?"

"It's working. What I do?"

"You can stay here for now. We just need more food. The food that Vladimir brought a week ago is almost finished. We also have to boil and store water while there's still gas. Otherwise, it's fine. You can stay with Max while I'm at work."

"You should not work," Galina said, shaking her head in disapproval.

"I have to," Eva said, falling into a chair and extending her legs. "Someone has to."

Ska rubbed her head against her calves, meowing.

Galina straightened her back.

"Cat has to go," she said determinedly.

"Her name is Ska, Galina," Eva snapped with guilty defensiveness, called to address an issue she had avoided so far. "And she's staying. We have enough cat food to feed her for a week."

"Cat food is good food," Galina continued with respectful obstinacy. "When I come to this country I and my friend eat cat food for six months! My friend cure her stomach ulcer," she rubbed her belly. "Cat food is good food and cheap! A cat has to go."

"She's not *a* cat, Galina! She's *our* cat. Max's cat. Please, I don't want to hear about it anymore!"

In her room, after she carefully closed the door, Eva checked her Tamiflu supply: two packs, one for Max, one for her. This, she decided, she would not share. She wrapped the medicine into her underwear and hid it in a drawer. Then the phone rang, and nervously Eva picked up.

Greg.

21

In Santa Monica the early days of the Flu were not that bad. Whether it was the weather – sunny, breezy and untroubled – or something else, Greg didn't know. Nothing depended on him; it felt like a vacation. There was the beach, endless in both directions, the ocean, and the adventure. People buzzed around, stocking up on food and water and forming long twisting lines under the clear sky. Exhilaration and fear trembled in the rich salty air. Blue and green masks on so many faces created a carnival-like feeling. People continued to tan, surf, and swim. Masked joggers ran along the wave strip.

Nights and days, Greg wandered through the city. The pier had been sealed off by the police on November first. Its Ferris wheel stood still towering over Santa Monica like a huge sculpture. Local youths climbed through the cordons and into the amusement park and cheered, drinking beer and throwing bottles into the ocean. Fishermen came at dawn and stayed all day, salting and drying their catches on strings in the sun. Illegal vendors cruised the streets selling food and camping equipment. Greg bought a sleeping bag on a whim. Stores and restaurants closed, one after another. At his favorite café he drank his last cappuccino and helped the owner board up the shop, which they did exchanging morbid jokes. The Third Street Promenade looked ghostly at dusk, its iron dinosaurs darkly guarding the future, the fountains dry. Greg listened to preachers standing under lanterns among the herds of ragged homeless, forecasting the end of the world. He passed by street musicians who continued to play guitars and sing although no one dropped money into their cases.

Three days into the pandemic, the city emptied overnight. Only the elderly crawled out of their holes to the soup kitchens, fearfully looking over their shoulders. Looting began. Teenagers with gold chains around their necks drove Porsche 911 Cabrios and played loud music in the wind, their arms wrapped around their girlfriends' shoulders. Greg saw Rolls-Royce Phantoms and Bentleys stolen from auto-salons, their number plates shamelessly blank. Reality had cracked; actions no longer had consequences. Criminal dreamers finally lived the life of Hollywood stars. Greg watched them wistfully, almost wishing he had the courage or foolishness to do the same. On Venice Beach, with the last of his money, after six months of abstinence, Greg bought coke. The high was almost as good as the first time. On the beaches, among stars, sand and water, life went on into the early morning hours, reckless and youthful.

Then Lora got sick.

At the first signs of malaise Lora was quarantined in the small guest room in the basement. It happened naturally that Greg was the one to care for her. Greg was handed a mask. His carefree beach adventure was over. All day he watched TV, drank soda, ate whatever was left for him, and looked at Lora, who did nothing but sweat, moan, and wriggle in bed. How could her own mother not want to be by her side? He didn't see Dominique caring for her the way his own mother cared for Greg – the sea of love he enjoyed as a child when he was sick, full of songs and kisses and bedtime stories, and the smells of boiled potatoes whose steam his mother made him inhale, covering him with a heavy towel – but then again, Lora was a nasty adult. Maybe, when she was a little girl, with blond locks of hair and sky-blue innocent eyes, it was different. He gave Lora Ibuprofen as instructed, and water to drink; he worried about her and feared getting sick himself. But he didn't panic.

People don't *really* die of the Flu. Or do they?

Lora's mother came down a couple of times. It was easier to talk to her when she wore a mask that concealed her face.

"How is she?" she asked Greg.

"The same. I wanted to ask you," he suddenly became uncomfortable.

"Yes?"

"When she was a little girl, did you ever, mmhh, did she ever get sick like this?"

"I don't know. Why are you asking?"

"Just wondering," he said, feeling like an idiot.

"I told her not to go. It's the virus."

They sat in silence.

"Should we bring her to the hospital?"

They drove to the hospital in two separate cars – because Greg had already been exposed, he was told. With Lora lying limp and wheezing on the backseat, their album playing loud, Greg drove her Sedan in a state of bewilderment. The roads were empty and clean like the phantom streets of Universal Studios. His sense of freedom had long evaporated and been replaced by a nauseating fear. As he followed Lora's parents' car to St. Jones Hospital he thought of his mother, and of Eva and Max. He tried to call from his cell phone but the service was busy all the time. Or was he too afraid to call? He concentrated on the road. His songs sounded shallow and boisterous. He wished he had Andrea Bocelli to listen to. He wished he had coke.

With the others, they waited in line. It was hot. Lora hung on Greg's arms, gaping for air and coughing up blood. He wanted to get away. He was tired. He needed to get a coffee, to escape, even if only for a second.

"I can't hold her anymore," he said.

"What?" Lora's dad asked distractedly. They were elsewhere, all this time, Greg could see it. He wished he could escape too, to the hidden places, like rain forests where no human had ever set foot and even sunlight had trouble penetrating.

"I can't hold her anymore! And I'm thirsty," he said louder.

"We don't have any water," Dominique replied, and he understood by her inflection that they didn't have any water for him.

His shoulders and arms ached. He laid Lora down on the naked raw pavement like the others were doing with their sick around him. The sun was shining into her sweaty face and she covered her eyes with a helpless gesture. She was shivering.

"Don't do that!" they shouted at him in unison. "Fetch a blanket!"

Greg straightened, shaking his tired arms. "Why don't *you* fetch a blanket?" he mumbled in a low voice, still leaving space for reconciliation.

"You are her boyfriend, aren't you?" Dominique asked, raising those thin eyebrows.

Greg wanted to shout that Jimmy had been her boyfriend until recently, but that would have been mean.

"And you're her mother," he pronounced quietly, raising his eyes.

Lora's father elbowed his way into the ER. Soon, a nurse came out, paramedics following, and Lora was wheeled into the hospital over the loud protests of the crowd. It was still a time when connections and money mattered. Mournfully, they followed the stretcher with their eyes. Only one blood relative was allowed in, but Lora's parents stood still, holding hands. Greg could feel they hated his presence.

The news of her death arrived by phone early the next morning.

"You surely understand our grief, Greg," Dominique said in the parlor. "Do you have anywhere to stay?"

Greg nodded and walked down to the basement, still full of Lora's things, to pack his bag. There was her cell phone, her pink lipstick, and her hairbrush, still holding blond twisted hairs in its bristles. Her pink toothbrush was stuck into the holder next to his. Greg wished he could be sentimental. He wanted to write a song about despair and leaving, and death, but music escaped him. He felt cold and empty.

Back in the parlor, packed and ready to leave, he called his other friends in LA. Rings trickled into nothingness, interrupted by the mechanical voices of answering machines. He always left the same message, "It's Greg, Lora is dead, I need a place to stay." A couple of times the phone was picked up, and in fearful tones he was told, "Sorry, I can't. Take care." That was friendly. Once he heard, "Sorry, wrong number." It was undoubtedly the voice of his lawyer's wife, but what difference did it make? In the end, he even called Jimmy. Jimmy was chatty, talking fast and choking on words, nonplussed by Greg's news. He was smart. He had lots of food. When push came to shove, he'd be the one to survive. "So, can I come over?" Greg interrupted, getting impatient. "Oh, no, man! Are you kidding? You've been exposed, right? I mean, I'm sorry, but I plan to live." Greg put down the phone. He was through his list. Fleetingly, he thought of calling Tony, but dropped the idea as ridiculous. "Don't need another humiliation!" he told himself, slamming the phone on the table. It's what Eva would have said.

No one came out to wish him goodbye. He left dragging his sleeping bag behind him.

In the car Greg cried for a long time. The Sedan shook slightly with each bout of tears, sending a little plush panda swinging back and forth under the rearview mirror. He started the engine, switched on the music, and drove aimlessly, trying to work out a plan. The tank was half-full; he couldn't get very far. He couldn't get to New York. He was alone. Even Lora had left him. For a second he felt acute anger at her desertion and at bringing him into this situation: into this city, into her parents' house, into this lonely desperation. He pushed the accelerator.

There were few cars around, and he sped up, the wind hitting his face, tearing his eyes. *What does it mean that I've been exposed*? he thought with mounting panic. *Am I going to die?*

He parked his car on an observation point on a cliff over the ocean. Pulling on a sweater, he stepped out. His knees were trembling. He looked around, the wind blowing his long hair into his face. The ocean was quiet and dark, the air fresh and sparkling. A boat sailed toward the horizon. Greg took out his guitar and sat on the stony ground, crossing his legs. Then he sang, wordlessly, into the darkening lonely ocean, the saddest song of his life.

22

"Eva? Thank God! How is Max?" Greg shouted through crackles of static.

"Fine, we're fine so far. How are you? Where are you?"

"I'm stuck in Santa Monica, homeless. Lora died two days ago. The cops got my car. Have you heard from my parents?"

"Your mom had a bad cough but she seems OK."

Eva heard screams and cursing in the background, and Greg shouted in the phone,

"I have to go now! Miss you! Take care of Max!"

She shouted back: "Take care!" but already he had hung up. Greg, she thought. That was all, no sadness, no agony, no pity. She felt tired and concerned by her detachment.

"Do you think there's something wrong with me?" she asked Bill when they sat down to eat. "My emotions are drying up. Sometimes it's like I'm pretending to feel something while I don't feel anything at all. I can make myself cry but it's superficial."

"It's a stress reaction," Bill offered. "It's good. We've been programmed to be less emotional in emergency situations. It also means a stronger immune system, hopefully. What did Greg say?"

"His girlfriend died. He's homeless. His mother is probably dying too. He didn't talk about his girlfriend, didn't cry. I understand it so well. I just care about Max, only him. What if that's going to disappear as well? My love for him."

Max, dressed in pajamas, appeared in the door holding Ska in his arms.

"Mommy, Ska's asking if she can sleep with me. She's afraid."

"Of course, dear, of course," she said, getting up to kiss him. "Are you ready for a lullaby?"

Galina watched them quietly, pressing her lips together.

When Max had fallen asleep with Ska curled up next to him, Eva and Bill listened to the news. There were three channels still broadcasting: CNN, Fox, and PBS, which increasingly took the crude form of a newspaper page projected onto the screen. International reports were scarce; Eva browsed the Internet for information. The French had managed to distribute Tamiflu nationwide, although its effect on thwarting the pandemic was not yet clear. There were general descriptions of chaos in Paris. People were hiding on top of the Eiffel Tower and freezing to death. When Eva dialed her mother, it took an hour to get through the busy signal; the international connections were overwhelmed or failing. And when the call did go through, Eleanor did not answer.

At the hospital, Robin often stayed behind, working late. She developed a soft spot for Firbas; it began with that first rough and manly punch on her shoulder during her inauguration. Around him, Robin came alive, often asking unnecessary questions, standing close to him, waiting for his kind hands to touch her, hoping his lab coat would brush against hers. On her face she often wore an adolescent look, eyes glinting with adoration.

During the afternoon of November ninth, Robin disappeared. She did not answer Eva's and Taylor's pages. When she finally returned two hours later Taylor almost jumped at her throat. "Where have you been?" he screamed, brandishing his pager in front of her nose.

Robin stood still and spoke robotically, her gaze resting somewhere in the middle of Taylor's chest. "I assisted in surgery. Did some real work, instead of treating junkies."

Taylor took a threatening step toward Robin. His eyes were bloodshot.

"Calm down, Taylor," Eva said quietly.

"Surgery called me for a consult and then ordered me to assist with a short procedure. Do some real work, like you say."

"Who cares what Surgery ordered you to do? *This* is your unit!" Taylor demanded.

"Just leave me alone."

"It's called envy," Eva remarked. And then, her voice louder, she launched a little speech meant for Taylor but directed at Robin. "*We* do something real, Robin! *We* continue treating patients. *We* use our medical-psychiatric knowledge, not the mantra every layman is now capable of: 'IV fluids plus Tamiflu plus Tylenol.' It's bullshit. Useless bullshit. Anyone who believes that *we* have a reduced exposure to the Flu is an ignorant asshole. If we wanted safety we'd hide at home. It's just fear and stress. Whoever gave you orders to work in another unit was just trying to punish you. And you were stupid to stay, because Taylor and I had a lot more work to do."

"He said he'd report me."

"Bullshit! He's not your boss. Firbas is our boss!" Taylor yelled and Eva nodded enthusiastically, putting her arm around his waist, aping Firbas.

"Alcohol withdrawal is serious," Eva said. "If you don't treat it, that's it, the patient is gone. We don't want people to die if they can be saved. There's too much death around as it is."

Taylor's body was stiff against her hand. Robin was quiet. Eva looked at them, victorious, her eyes tearing with emotion. This is how it comes to people, the sense of purpose, the heroism, she thought. Finally, she was *feeling*. "Okay. Let's get back to work!" she said brightly. But when she'd entered the hallway she noticed that Taylor and Robin had hung back behind the partially closed door.

"She's full of shit," Taylor was saying. "Why does she talk in slogans? Does she think we're stupid or what?"

Eva walked back in, ignoring the anguished expression on Taylor's face.

"You're right, Taylor. I guess that wasn't necessary," she said dryly. "Now, let's get back to work. Please?"

Food did not arrive that day, and everyone was engrossed in theories as to why (The truck was robbed. The driver refused to drive to the hospital. They're out of gas. There're no drivers left.) Eva tried to block out anything she couldn't control. Together with other staff she went to the basement to gather whatever could be found in the dimly lit kitchen area: sachets of sugar, dry creamer, salt, packaged milk, breakfast cereal boxes, a little bottle of orange juice that she drank on the spot plus another that she stuffed into her backpack. The kitchen supervisor moved his large body around, trying to keep things in order with his magnanimous red face and husky smoker's voice. He had a fondness for Eva that she used to find exasperating, but when he took her aside that day and handed her three cans of applesauce she cried with gratitude.

"I know you have a little boy. I remember," he said and winked at her, and for the first time she didn't find it distasteful.

"Thank you," she whispered. "Thank you Harry."

Back on the floor with its stench and disorder, her backpack wrapped in plastic to avoid contamination, she proceeded to the office area where she kept her things, stepping around patients lying along the walls in the hallway, and around pools of urine and crumpled sheets stained with blood and feces. As she approached she heard soft instrumental music from Robin's room. The door was unlocked, and, silently stepping, she peeked around it. Behind the recess in the wall, on the brown hospital chair, she saw Robin's unnaturally white bottom rolling and dimpling on Firbas' lap. Firbas's spindly freckled legs stuck out to the middle of the room, his pants and shoes pinning his feet together. His white, turned out underwear was stained yellow. Their masks were on. She heard Robin let out a moan and jumped back before she was discovered. At the door Eva hesitated and then shut it loud enough for them to know they had been seen.

The scene disturbed her in a morbid, almost necrophiliac way. Carnal blasphemy, she thought, her superstitions waking up. Copulating in the middle of death. She was sickened. And she was scared for them, so human, so ugly – scared for Robin's heavy ass jumping on Firbas's lap and for Firbas' spider-thin, ridiculously long legs curving up and down. They begged for punishment.

Eva walked back to the ward. One of the patients in the hallway appeared stiff, and, bending down to him, she knew by the color of his skin that he was dead. She checked his pulse, pressing her gloved fingers into his neck. *He died while they fucked*, she thought, and immediately wondered if Robin had made up the story about the surgery consult. Robin did not deserve love. She needed to grow up. The Flu had no space for love games.

Wake up! Eva wanted to shout. *Move! Work! Survive!*

23

The morning announced itself with a loud rattle downstairs.

"They're breaking into the grocery store," Vladimir said, raising his finger as if lecturing someone, his pale eyes wildly triumphant over the mask. Anna and Olga continued looking at him, frightened like two little birds with pupils so large they seemed to occupy the whole iris.

"I told you it would happen. Now, what would we do without food?"

"Should we call the police?" Olga suggested, realizing how stupid the suggestion was as soon as she spoke.

"Everyone for himself now!" Vladimir continued with the same agitated pride, and tightened his mask. He wore the mask continuously now, not even taking it off to sleep, and demanded the same from the women.

"The virus is in the house!" he repeated, giving Olga, who continued to cough, a stern look, his reddish eyebrows frightening and converged into deep creases over his nose. He instituted an iron discipline of handling the dishes, wearing gloves, talking aloud and listening to the radio. He couldn't yell anymore, afraid of being heard by the neighbors, and wordlessness drove him into silent rages erupting several times a day.

Olga, still weak and recuperating, shuffled back to the kitchen to pick up dirty dishes and dropped a plate into the sink with a loud clank.

"I'm sorry!" she squeaked. "It slipped."

Vladimir tiptoed to her and squeezed her arm so hard

that she writhed in pain, tears running down her cheeks. Anna helplessly stood nearby.

"Please," she whispered, "Let her go!"

Vladimir turned around. His face was so full of hatred that Anna fell silent and took a step back, collapsing into a chair.

He was everywhere, like a watchdog following them, controlling and finding fault with everything they did. Sometimes he felt guilt. Then he became fidgety and gave both of them quick embraces, cautious not to come too close. "This is a war situation," he would say, his quick eyes running from Anna's to Olga's face. "I'm going to take care of you, but you have to remember: I'm the general, and you're the soldiers. No war has been won without discipline." And he fidgeted, and smiled, and ran to the bathroom to wash his hands after he had touched them. His hand-washing became so frequent that he developed excoriations that wouldn't heal because of the rubber gloves he wore around the clock. He took to sleeping alone in a sleeping bag in the corner of their bedroom, away from Olga's cough; he even erected a makeshift partition between them out of old winter clothes and bedsheets hanging on a dryer. To soften their steps, he took down the old Arabic carpet from the wall and spread it in the hallway.

Anna hadn't slept in days, drifting away for what seemed a couple of moments, then waking up with a startle. Ben hadn't appeared anymore, but the smell of his burning body still taunted her. She longed to bury his ashes.

That night, plagued with insomnia, Anna tiptoed to the kitchen and flung the window open, only to let in the unbearable stench of decomposing corpses. Hastily shutting the window, she stepped back. Vladimir was eyeing her from the hallway, his eyes glinting in the dark. Anna froze.

"I'm sorry," she muttered in a thread-thin voice. "I needed the air."

Vladimir sat down on a chair heavily, pulling down his

mask.

"Sit," he said, gesturing to the empty chair. Anna sat on the edge, straight and rigid, expecting a remonstration, but Vladimir stayed silent and after a while got up to fetch some whisky from the kitchen cabinet.

"Do you want some?"

Anna nodded.

"Can't sleep either, you know," he said. She knew this; she had heard him tossing and turning in his sleeping bag while she lay still in her own bed, eavesdropping. Sometimes he would whisper to himself, but she could never make out what he said. Now, he looked so cozy with his tousled hair and soft, tired face, in his worn training pants and an old tattered sweater that for the first time in a week Anna wanted to forgive him, to let the pain out.

Handing her the whisky, he pressed her hand and she saw his eyes tearing.

"It's all fear, Annushka. Thank you for sitting here with me. The hatred! It's like hunger. It's worse, I can't even die from it. All the hatred!" He sighed hiding his face into his arm. "I can't help it, do you understand?"

"You know," Anna said. "Ben used to hit me."

Vladimir raised his eyes at her.

"I never told anyone."

"So tell me, Annushka," he said tenderly, squeezing her hand.

Anna did, starting from the beginning.

They got married in City Hall. It was early May, with trees still blossoming and a cloudless sky, promising them years of happiness together. Ben didn't want any witnesses or a celebration. "God is watching, and so are demons," he said mysteriously. Anna listened and tried to learn. At home, in his one-bedroom apartment on the Lower East Side, where he grew up and where his parents had lived and died, he burned incense, lit candles, and put pink drapes over the furniture for their first night together. He cooked a vegetarian dish with green beans, onions, garlic, ginger, and cilantro. Alcohol was forbidden.

"Demons are looking for cracks in the aura to slip in. Alcohol is a demon's natural entry."

Anna agreed with everything Ben said, and he liked it: her softness, and her eager expectation of wonder. She was used to loud, merry weddings with champagne and vodka, juicy meat dishes, dancing and kissing – but this was the life she had chosen. She was thirty-six and longed for a baby more than anything else.

She was not sure she liked the taste of their wedding dinner, for she had never tried Indian food before, but somehow its spices held promise for her. After dinner Ben recited his poetry and told her wonderful stories about healing. Pointing at a dry flower on the wall he told her about a little girl burned to her bones, Gladys. "A nice name, don't you think? A sweet little girl she was, burned so badly her bones went black. No one believed she'd survive. I lived in their house for weeks working with her energy, helping her grow new skin and muscle. When she began talking again, she asked for a flower. Her father wanted to give me all his money. I just said, send me flowers, so that I know she's well. She's married now, a real beauty, and still sending me flowers."

Anna talked little, enchanted by his world. Ben did not ask her about her own life.

"You're my inspiration," he confessed, his freckles dancing in the candlelight, his voice soft and sweet. "You have such a light soul. Healing makes me too heavy to write poetry, but you're like a fairy blown my way. My grace, my flower! Yes, tender flower!" He took her face gently into his big soft hands. She smiled, touched and incredulous at the same time, looking at herself in search of those qualities she knew nothing about.

"I'm not beautiful," she whispered.

"You're luminous. You're heavenly!"

She gave a tiny embarrassed laugh and flushed to the roots of her then-black hair.

The sun set, its disc smoothly rolling through the purple clouds, behind the urban horizon, and a blue darkness embraced the city. A warm wind rattled the blinds, mixing with calming rhythms of Kitaro. Benjamin rose and stretched his arms toward the disappearing light, bowing deep into the ground.

"Thank you for the light and the wisdom and the glory of this day. Thank you for uniting me with my only other, my love and grace, Anna." He spoke in a throaty, otherworldly voice, his eyes closed. Anna watched timidly until he pulled her to him and made her do the same.

"Thank you ..." she began awkwardly.

"No to me! To the sun! Speak to him, he hears you! Louder!"

"Thank you, sun, for a wonderful day!" she managed, and Ben jumped around her like a boy, exclaiming: "That was so pure!"

As night approached Anna was nervous about what was to come. She had not had sex with anyone in many years, not since her boyfriend was killed in Afghanistan, and Ben hadn't touched her in their nine months of courtship, which she had taken as a sign of romantic timidity.

"Good night, my love!" he said tenderly, rising from the table. "You're about to enter the most wonderful adventure of your life. Be fresh and positive, you're about to become a healer!"

She kissed him on the cheek he presented to her and mumbled "good night," not yet quite sure what his little speech meant. In the bathroom she took a long hot shower, scraping her body until her skin crunched under her fingers, and shaved her legs, armpits, and bikini strip with a razor she'd bought the previous day for this purpose. She dried herself, rubbed body lotion into her hot pink skin, pulled on a starched white nightgown, and emerged barefoot, her wet hair scented and streaming over her shoulders, her belly full of nervous anticipation. The light was already off and she entered the bedroom cautiously, waiting for her eyes to get used to the dark. Ben slept on the couch by the window, curled up under a blanket. The other, open sofa lay empty, dressed in pink sheets, readied for her.

Hesitantly, Anna approached her new husband:

"Ben?"

He didn't respond, and she lay down alone on the cold bedding, bitter disappointment burning inside her, tears running spilling onto her face. *He said I was beautiful*, she remembered, and sobbed silently. *I want a baby*. She cried for a long time, until sleep finally took her.

The next day Ben rose cheerful and singing. He brought Anna a toasted bagel with cream cheese for breakfast, and a cup of sweet-smelling tea, and gently rubbed her cheek. She felt better. Surely it was something mystical, she decided, some special tradition to avoid intimacy on one's wedding day.

They marked the sunrise with a bow and a greeting and did some stretching exercises, Anna embarrassed by being less flexible than Ben. Ben was amazingly lithe. He could fold his body in two, touching his forehead with his toes. He could put his foot behind his neck and bend backwards like an acrobat.

"Just breathe right," he advised. "The rest will come with practice." And Anna breathed with her belly, like he showed her, awestruck before him.

Two patients were scheduled for the afternoon, and Ben gave her his first lecture that day. It would become their morning routine for the next year.

"Greet the patient cordially, always shake hands. Even if you don't know if you can help with a particular disease, never refuse a patient. Remember, the patient came to you, and that, by itself, makes you a healer. It is trust, and trust is gold. Remember that you help the patient heal himself. You are the facilitator, the transmitter of the great cosmic energy. It's not you that heals, the healing happens through you. Work with your hands laid on patient's body. You will learn to differentiate the energies with time, you will read the aura like a great mystery book, all in time."

Anna listened and took notes in her orderly round handwriting.

Mrs. Robinson was a newcomer. Ben pressed her hand with both of his, smiling. His slight natural stoop disappeared. He was luminous. He introduced Anna, putting his hand around her shoulders, and she felt a surge of warmth and reassurance, and an erotic longing she wouldn't admit to. She yielded to his embrace, proud to be standing next to him as a healer. Ben listened to Mrs. Robinson's complaints, of which there were many, including nervousness, sweating, frequent urination, dizziness, and depression. He told her to undress to her underwear and lie on the couch. She was a tiny, frightened woman with pelvic bones sticking out, prominent ribs and hanging breasts. The couch she lay on was the same one on which Ben slept, now covered with a clean sheet and looking semi-professional. He studied Mrs. Robinson's chakras and measured her aura and ran his palm just over her body, without touching her. He hummed as he did it, letting one remark escape his lips before he could catch it: "Looks like a curse." Raising his eyes to the patient, he reassured her, "No need to worry just now." Later, Benjamin poured oil in his palms and glided his hands over Mrs. Robinson's skin, her husband watching him suspiciously. At times Ben was overcome by a deep cough. Covering his mouth he muttered: "Bad blockage, black energies!" Catching himself again, he turned to the patient to explain: "Energy currents are akin to blasts of wind. When energy is toxic it causes me to cough. But we are going to work on it, that's why you're here, right?" Ben motioned Anna to switch on the music, and she pushed the *play* button on an old tape recorder. Ben invited the husband to sit for the first time, and Mr. Robinson walked to the black leather chair in the corner and sank down, noisily shifting in the seat. Ben covered the patient with a towel up to her chin and gave her a bright smile. Then he sat on the sofa, Anna next to him, and turned his attention to Mr. Robinson.

"As I said, I detect some energy blockages in your wife," he stated firmly yet amiably. "What it means is that there are certain meridians, highways of energy, if you like, where a congestion could happen if the side streets are being affected by disease. Your wife has several of those. When I feel them, I cough. Your wife has diabetes and pyelonephritis, which cause frequent urination and easy tiredness. Her aura is thin in several segments and has a very particular configuration of a mushroom, which occurs when someone had experienced a curse. Such a configuration presupposes to different kinds of cancer – in her case, to breast, lung, and ovarian cancer, as well as to blood cancer, which is associated with high sugars. I suggest I start treatment without delay. Your wife might experience some lightheadedness and surges of emotions today, even crying spells. This is totally normal. Tomorrow she will feel healthier and lighter. But the benefits of one treatment will not last. She has to come three times weekly for the first month, then we'll see."

"How are you feeling?" he asked, leaning to Mrs. Robinson with his open, boyish smile.

"Okay," she replied uncertainly and smiled back.

"Good, that's what I want to hear! Ready to get started?" Ben glanced at her, then at her husband.

"Yes!" Mrs. Robinson said, louder and more determined

this time, before her husband could interject. Ben turned the music louder and uncovered the patient, throwing the towel on the sofa. Anna folded it, watching him attentively.

"Relax now, let your energy fly, be light as a feather and free as the wind!" He spoke with his eyes half-closed, his body languid. He connected his fingers as if in prayer but with his palms apart. Then he gestured for Anna to fetch a wooden pot where he mixed massage oil with eucalyptus extract, sending its fresh and spicy smell into the air. Now he massaged the same lines he worked on before, his work interrupted only by spells of his coughing.

"That will clean your meridians," he explained, opening his eyes and studying her with the same reassuring, boyish smile. She lay still and relaxed. Mr. Robinson remained motionless in his chair, looking tired. After he was done, Ben wiped Mrs. Robinson dry with a towel.

"You can get dressed now," he said. "We did great work today. Do you feel lighter now?"

She nodded, her face dazed and excited, and Anna, rising and catching a glimpse of herself in the mirror, found the same expression on her own face.

"I feel cleansed," Mrs. Robinson said, and Ben beamed.

Another appointment was scheduled, Ben sternly leafing through his calendar to find a free window. "Lucky you!" he said finally. "I have Wednesday at five free."

Mr. Robinson uncertainly opened his wallet and Ben joked about how much lower his fees are than traditional doctors'.

"You sure you don't want your own checkup?" Ben asked, taking Mr. Robinson's cash.

"I'm fine, thanks," Mr. Robinson answered curtly, leading his wife to the door.

Another patient came at seven for her fifteenth treatment. Like Mrs. Robinson, she was in her fifties, and also suffered from anxiety. She was loud and talkative, and yet eager and subservient, and praising Ben time and again. "You are my savior!" she said at the end of the session, wrinkles folding all over her face in a grotesque mosaic of delight.

When she left, Anna said, "She seems *too* happy."

Ben became angry. Seating Anna down like a little girl, he rebuked her. "You must appreciate your patients' gratitude. Without it you'll never become a healer." He remained in a sour mood for the rest of the evening and went to bed early. Anna didn't dare call out to him that night; instead she stayed up in the living room reading. She didn't cry.

A month went by. They still had no sex, Ben acting innocently, as if unaware of her expectations. Anna wondered whether he even thought about sex or was aware of his marital duties. When night came, after their cheerful bows to the sun, she often felt bitter and betrayed, and increasingly guilty. She knew not of what. She longed to have a baby and was beginning to think it might never happen. In the mornings her resentment was gone, as if someone had healed her wounds overnight, and she reflected on the goodness of the sun, of her strange celibate contentment, and of Ben's spiritual prowess, which made her happy. She learned to read energy with her hands, to mix oils, and to administer healing massages. She learned aura shapes. Studying came to her easily, unlike during her university years, when she used to be terrified of exams. Ben interpreted this as a sign of her healing talent. She was grateful for his faith in her.

Anna rarely saw friends. Isolation, Ben declared, was necessary to the development of healing skills during one's apprenticeship. Anna accepted this. She was partaking in a miracle, after all.

Mrs. Robinson continued to come and was feeling better. Her husband stopped accompanying her, until, about a month after her treatments had begun, he came in her stead. When Anna opened the door, she knew something unpleasant was bound to happen. Mr. Robinson entered buffalo-like, his head lowered, exposing a shiny wide forehead with receding hair. His eyes were bulging.

"Where is he?" he demanded, and Anna tiptoed to the bedroom.

Ben stood in the middle of the room, distressed as she had never seen him.

"Charlatan! Liar!" Mr. Robinson shouted, advancing into the room uninvited.

"Easy, take it easy," Ben hissed in a calm but threatening way.

"Let's make it easy for both of us. You give me my money back, and I'll just go. It makes exactly nine hundred and sixty dollars," Mr. Robinson said. He was overbearing, large and solid compared to Ben's delicate frame.

"I'll tell you what I didn't tell your wife out of respect to your marriage. *You* are her curse. *You*!" Ben pointed a finger at Mr. Robinson.

"No, I'll tell *you* what. You give me my money back or I go to the police and report you. You diagnosed my wife with diabetes and pyelonephritis, didn't you? Well, we went to a *real* doctor, and her laboratory results show no indication whatsoever of either! You exploited my wife! She *trusted* you!"

"I *healed* her! She doesn't have it because I took care of it! Why didn't you let her come and talk to me herself? This is just a misunderstanding."

"Misunderstanding! Yeah, right! You people will do anything to milk the money. It's only money you're after, isn't it?"

"She wanted to come, didn't she?" Ben asked this gently and retreated, giving his opponent the entire space of the room in which to falter.

"Who the hell cares what she wanted!" Mr. Robinson cried, but Anna could see that he no longer was certain of his words. It was clear that Mrs. Robinson had wanted to come today.

"Be kinder with her. She is a good woman. There is so

much suffering in the world."

At this moment Anna became conscious of how much she loved Ben. With tears in her eyes, she stood still, overcome by bliss. She admired the wisdom of his words and this dramatic turnaround, accomplished solely by his spirit. She desired him. She wanted to have a baby more than ever. Waking up from the stupor of happiness, she accompanied Mr. Robinson to the door, feeling goose bumps on her skin and wetness in her eyes. Mr. Robinson left, grumbling and beaten.

Back in the living room Anna found Ben clutching his head with both hands. She embraced his shoulders and said, "I love you."

He gave her a tortured look, "I love you too."

"You were so strong," she continued, in a search of a better phrase. "I'm so proud of you!"

"I need some fresh air," Ben said, rising from the chair and picking up his jacket. "Back in an hour. Don't forget your sun salute!"

"I won't!"

For the first time Anna bowed to the sun alone. Her prayer to the reddening sky felt like a confession. Something in her became free that day. *This must be my spiritual awakening*, she thought and laughed in a pure expression of happiness.

After the sun salute she called Olga but could find no words to describe her rapture. The Robinson story sounded banal in her retelling; in the end Olga said, "Wait, but did she have diabetes or not?" Anna didn't know what to say. During the awkward pause that followed she realized with sadness that her only real spiritual connection was Ben. Only he understood her.

Olga changed the topic. "Are you trying?"

"Trying what?"

"To have a baby!"

"Oh, that. Well, believe it or not, we haven't had sex yet," Anna ventured brightly. "But we're happy together," she rushed to add.

"Are you kidding me?! Is he impotent?"

"I don't know, I think it's something spiritual. I don't know myself."

"What do you mean, you don't know? You mean you didn't try to..." Olga didn't finish.

"No," Anna admitted, and all became clear to her now. Her own ineptitude explained everything.

"You're not a teenager, Anna. You can touch him too. Take initiative if you want a baby. You don't have all the time in the world." Olga's advice seemed so obvious that Anna couldn't understand why she hadn't thought of it sooner herself.

That night Anna sang in the shower. She shaved and put on her starched white nightgown. When she stepped into the dark bedroom Ben appeared to be fast asleep, lying with his back to her on the couch.

Anna approached him thinking of her love and of the wonderful revelation she experienced earlier that day. She sat down softly on the edge of the couch and kissed his shoulder, whispering tender words. She stroked his fair hair, and his cheek, and then his back, putting her hand underneath the blanket. She moved closer, pressing her body against his, and reached around him to stroke his chest. He wore pajamas, and, suddenly hot and panting, she yearned for his skin. She threw aside the blanket and reached into his pants, running her fingers over his buttocks toward the heat of his loin. Suddenly, Ben jerked and punched Anna with his elbow, knocking her off the couch. She fell, clutching her belly. Lying on the floor she saw him bolt up and move toward her, briskly and menacingly. She was still in a daze and too caught by surprise to defend herself. Ben grabbed her by the collar, ripping its soft fabric and punching her in the face. She fell on her back with a groan, shielding her throbbing cheekbone with both hands, her nightgown sliding up and exposing her legs. Frantically she pulled it down and scrambled backwards, away from his fury.

"You're a disgrace! A whore! A dirty whore!" he shouted, his voice high and wild, ripping through the night. "Never ever make me do it to you again!"

Anna nearly toppled over trying to get up, her foot caught in the nightgown.

"Don't you dare touch me again!" Ben hissed, advancing toward her.

Anna ran to the bathroom and turned the lock with shaky hands. For a long time she sat on the edge of the bathtub, continuing to shake uncontrollably, her knees weak, queasiness rising up her throat. Her cheekbone throbbed, but she was almost glad she was in pain. She felt she would have passed out or died otherwise. When she felt strong enough, she got up and glanced into the mirror. Her eye and left cheek were swollen. She splashed ice-cold water into her face, wincing. Hurt, fear and humiliation mixed together, and she was unable to think or reason, just sob. Tears came spasmodically, explosively, beginning with huge loud hiccups and followed by bittersweet waves. When her tears finally dried up she felt only one emotion: horror. Anna was physically, utterly afraid like never before in her life. She had decided to spend the night on the bathroom floor, but then Ben knocked on the door with dry, decisive taps and ordered: "Anna! Get out of there!"

She trembled and did not respond.

"Get out of there. I am not going to hit you again."

Anna put on her bathrobe and obeyed. Her face was swollen and puffy. Not for a second did she think of leaving Ben. She felt no anger, just horror and nameless guilt.

"Sit down," he gestured. The light was on, and everything in the living room appeared ordinary and unchanged, which gave her some feeling of normalcy.

"I apologize for hitting you. I shouldn't have done it. I want to tell you where it's coming from. I feel violated. Do you know how rape victims feel? Well, it's something like that. Violation at the hands of someone you love. Do you understand?" Ben spoke sternly but paternally.

Anna nodded, although she wasn't quite sure she did understand. Something was wrong with what he said, but at that confused moment she was too afraid to see it.

"I want you to promise me that you will never do it again. Do I have your word? Anna?"

She swallowed and touched her aching cheek.

"Anna!"

"I will never do it again," she said and cried anew, tears running down her cheeks. She hid her face in her hands.

"That's good, that's my girl." Ben stroked her hair and kissed her wet salty fingers. She pulled away involuntarily and immediately froze, afraid to provoke more anger. She wanted to be good.

Squeezing her hand, he whispered, "It's okay, it's going to be fine."

As she yielded to his hands, accepting his caresses, her tears returned.

"What is it?" he asked, gently disentangling her hair.

"I wanted a baby," she replied meekly, looking into the floor.

"A baby?" Ben was startled. "Why didn't you tell me before? I thought you knew."

Anna glanced at him uncomprehendingly. "Knew?"

"You can't have a baby. You're infertile. And whole. That makes you a healer."

She didn't question him on the source of his knowledge.

"I thought you had enough power by now to know it yourself," he remarked, and she shook her head. So that was the explanation. She suddenly felt empty, tired, and strangely relieved.

"In any case," Ben continued, "I don't engage in sex. Sex has the same effect as drugs and alcohol. All holy people are abstinent. I don't pretend to be holy, by the way; you just saw how I lost my temper … But that was his curse."

"Whose curse?"

"Mr. Robinson's. I had to block the curse. But some of it infected me. Couldn't stop coughing outside. Will have to do more cleansing tomorrow. This work takes a toll."

"Oh dear!" Anna said empathetically.

"So now you know that sex is not for us. There's no higher reward than enlightenment, but the way to enlightenment is thorny. Do you think you can walk the walk with me?"

"I will try," Anna whispered.

"Good night, my love!" he said, kissing her forehead.

Anna switched off the light in the living room and leaned out of the window. The night was pitch-dark and the summer air fragrant. She breathed it in, and then slowly exhaled, relaxing her muscles. "He is good," she whispered to the absent sun, and felt at peace. "He is wise. He knew. It wasn't his fault that he hit me. I will never do it again."

Vladimir sat still. The candle flickered on the table.

"I never told anyone," Anna said quietly. "Now it's too late. He lied to me. I could have had a baby. Mrs. Robinson never had diabetes. You never had cancer. I don't know why I believed him. All these years."

Vladimir was crying.

"That's okay. I was happy as it was. I just wish he would leave me alone now."

"I'm not a bad person. I just want to live," Vladimir uttered desperately, raising his wet eyes to her. "Please forgive me."

Anna's eyes were glassy and remote. "I wish I could cry," she said.

"Have another drink," Vladimir offered, wiping his eyes on his sleeve. "Maybe that will help."

24

A black woman lying on a makeshift bed was drifting in and out of consciousness. She sometimes coughed, but weakly, apathetically, while her life hung on the shallow wheezes of her breaths. Firbas approached in wrinkled blue scrubs, his face pale and puffy and the rims of his eye red from sleeplessness.

"She's a goner," he said, shining a flashlight into her eyes. They contracted as they should have, and Eva suppressed her wish to argue with his conclusion. Half an hour later, the woman was slowly suffocating. Helpless, Eva watched her turn bluer by the second. Shallow peaks of breaths rose alternately in her chest and abdomen. Her pulse was so fast Eva could not count it.

"Maybe it's an asthma attack?" Eva asked.

"Maybe, also. She got Prednisone, and Theophylline, and Albuterol, and the whole mix, with zilch effect. With a fever of 104 that can't be brought down it won't matter. Do you want to intubate her? I won't be here for much longer."

"Yeah, you have to get some rest. But you'll be coming back later?" Eva asked hopefully.

"Like Lazarus, like Lazarus," he murmured.

"What do you mean? Are you getting sick?"

"Don't worry. Just keep your mask on and learn the procedure."

She obeyed. Being a psychiatrist she didn't know how to intubate, but somehow the procedure, which she had witnessed a hundred times in the past week, seemed easy to do. As she inserted the tube into the trachea, holding the patient's chin tilted back to ease the process, she wondered where her performance anxiety had gone. This wasn't like during her internship; here, she could only help. Firbas gently guided her through the next steps.

A teenage boy was brought in by his father, his ruffled golden hair covering half his pale face, his blue lips slightly pursed, as if in surprise at what had happened to him. His father put him on the floor and kneeled beside him while Eva shone a light into the boy's dilated pupils. "Wake up, Dylan," he said, pressing his son's hand so hard his knuckles turned white. He had the massive red hands of a construction worker, freckled all over, with coarse red hair right up to the distant finger joints. Eva rose and stepped aside. The father's knees were shaking when he got up to follow her. He smelled of alcohol.

"I'm sorry, there's nothing we can do," she said.

He continued looking at her pleadingly, then yelled, his eyes whitening with fury, "Then call a real doctor!"

Firbas materialized between them and halted the man with an extended arm.

"We are sorry for your loss," Firbas said firmly. "Your son has died of the Flu. Now take care of yourself. Wash your hands and wear a mask please."

The man left. They heard him coughing at the door. There was no Tamiflu left to offer him. Eva returned to the woman on the respirator. Her eyes were blank, staring into the unknown.

The loudspeakers crackled and announced: *All medical personnel please proceed to the ground floor for mandatory vaccination.* Eva picked up her bag.

"Aren't you coming?" she asked Firbas.

"I'll attend to the patients," he said. There was no medical staff left on their makeshift ward, which held fifteen mattresses. Benji hadn't shown for work that day. Robin and Taylor were out disposing of corpses.

Eva crossed the hall and turned left to join the thin stream of people, all of them robed and masked, looking like an uncanny Halloween procession. They weren't many. Eva had expected to fight a crowd, to have to elbow her way through to the potential cure, but it wasn't necessary. Everyone stayed civilized. She even heard laughter around her, and it rang eerily in her ears.

"This is the vaccine that killed half of NYU," someone joked.

"We're probably better off without it," someone else put in.

The door to Max's daycare was open. Of course, they have to make use of the space, Eva reasoned, but nevertheless she felt as though Max were somehow being endangered by extension.

"My son used to come to this daycare," she said to the next person in line.

"Pray for him," the woman said with nauseating sweetness.

"He's fine!" Eva shouted, taking a step back. People turned around curiously.

"Then pray more," the woman murmured stubbornly. "Jesus loves you."

"Jesus has been dead for a long-long time!" someone interjected with a chuckle.

Eva peered into the daycare. On the wall to her left she noticed a photo of the children's field trip to the Central Park Zoo. Max, dressed in an orange t-shirt with two plastic lizards sewn inside a pocket on his chest, looked serious and tall, holding hands with his friend Christopher. The dark silhouette of a sea lion was visible on a stone behind them.

Down the hall were cubbies with a photo of each child attached to the folder on top.

"Here! This is my son!" Eva cried to no one in particular, breaking away from the line. People moved to let her through.

"He looks like you!" the Jesus lady said.

"You think so? He actually does. You want to see?" she asked, pulling down her mask.

The lady stepped back, frightened.

"Put it on! Put it on!" people hissed at her, and she did, breathing hard.

Two stocky red-faced women gave out the shots. No one bothered to ask the usual questions about allergies and medical history. Eva was done in twenty minutes. The stocky woman smiled at her through her mask, her eyes disappearing into fans of wrinkles at their corners, and leaning toward her, Eva whispered, seized by jittery hope:

"Can I have a dose for my son? He used to come to this day care." As if that mattered.

"Sorry," the woman shook her head.

When Eva returned to the ward, Firbas was sitting on the floor blissfully smiling, holding a broken Morphine ampoule in his hand, a sling and syringe beside him.

"What are you doing?" Eva cried.

"Just a cough suppressant to get me through the day," he said woozily. "Don't report me."

Eva dreamed. Strangers were seated at tables in a brightly lit room resembling McDonald's, separated from her by yellow tape. They were eating French fries with ketchup, chomping and licking their fingers. Her table was empty, sparkling with its green polish, and she got up to demand her portion. Firbas, in a white coat, a stethoscope dangling around his neck, informed her severely that she wasn't allowed fries because of her high cholesterol. Desperately she tried to explain that there had been a mistake in her blood results; she knew this, she was a doctor herself. Then it occurred to her that Firbas was dying. Was she dying as well? Was she already dead?

When she awoke she was sweating, her mouth full of saliva,

her stomach rumbling. She gripped for Bill. He wasn't there, but his sheets were still warm. She listened for the sound of running water, assuming he'd gone to the bathroom. After a while she heard the sound of a flush, and embraced her full body pillow to drift, comforted, back to sleep.

Meanwhile, in the bathroom, Bill was stuffing cheese crackers into his mouth, three at a time, chewing at a desperate speed, as soundlessly as possible, softening them with tap water that he drank from cupped palms. He was careful not to leave any crumbs. He didn't feel particularly guilty. It was more the gnawing obsession with food that he'd developed in recent days, even when he wasn't hungry, that made him uncomfortable – and the necessity to keep it hidden. Eva wouldn't notice, but Galina would. He was sure that she counted every little cracker in the house. "I hate the bitch," he mumbled and splashed cold water onto his face, then ran his moist hand over the edge of the sink to gather crumbs in case there were any. "Time to sleep," he told himself, then dried his hands and unlocked the door. Galina was standing outside like a ghost.

"Oh my God!" he exclaimed. "Sorry! You scared me, I didn't see you!"

She didn't respond, just walked past him into the bathroom, closing the door behind her.

"Bitch!" he muttered through his teeth and tiptoed into the bedroom. All was quiet, and he sighed with relief, laying his head on a pillow. He couldn't fall asleep for a long time, turning, thinking of Grace and crackers and death. For a while he tried to meditate, breathing slowly with long expirations. When he turned on his stomach, he felt Eva's hand lightly stroking his back.

"Can't sleep?" she asked.

She embraced his shoulders. He had the impulse to push her away, but he didn't.

"Good night," he said instead.

"Good night," she answered kindly, and he pulled her closer, regretting his irritation. He felt almost grateful, as though she'd forgiven him for the stolen crackers. They kissed, pressing their bodies against one another, and Eva smelled the crackers on his breath. They said good night again and Bill fell asleep like a comforted baby, fed and held by his mother. Lying next to him, her hand on his chest, she didn't feel any anger, just pity. If it were Galina and not Bill who stole the crackers, she would have exploded. It was unjust, but that's how it was. Eva closed her eyes.

Later that night Eva was woken by a metallic bang. Barefoot, she tiptoed to the living room, past Max's room, halting for a second to listen in. All was quiet. The light in the kitchen was on. As Eva quietly approached, her hungry nose discerned the smell of canned meat, causing a flow of saliva that she had to swallow before taking another step.

Bent over the kitchen counter, Galina was devouring cat food with a big spoon. Ska stood nearby, watching her intently, and gave a loud meow.

For ten days Stuyvesant Town had been quarantined by the settlement's National Guard activists, a resolution passed by the residents' committee on the Oval. From her neighbor Anthony, an ex-cop and chess enthusiast, Eva heard gossip of guards attacking residents but dismissed this as alarmist. Still, as she went out the following morning the situation suddenly seemed real and disquieting, piercing the oppressive silence of the Oval with a sense of danger. Eva felt weary, sweating under layers of clothes and wondering whether she was getting sick as well, after so many days of fear and exposure. And yet she dragged herself out of the house to the hospital. *Why? Why?* she asked herself, walking down the dark staircase. There was no ready answer. As she stepped forward, she played an imaginary discussion with Bill in her head, something she had done frequently, often without being fully aware of it. Was she just keeping herself sane by working, and keeping Max safe by some mystical, wishful, and counterintuitive way? Why not just turn around and go home, where Max was waiting for her with two fighting strangers? Why bother with this desperate work? Ten floors down and out amid the desolate landscape that had once been her happy community, among the clutter and the stink of garbage, she didn't turn back. *Are you a hero? Are you?* The inner voice inquired this ironically, with Bill's intonations.

Disquiet propelled her forward along the street, around the fountain that was not working any longer, housing the corpse of a dog who'd maybe been looking for water, and further along the green soccer field where a Brazilian guy who'd once been a professional player used to train local kids in the summer. Eva remembered him as a wiry, handsome man with a sculpted face. Now, he and his little son Guy, just a year older than Max, lay dead somewhere in the common grave.

I'm doing it for Max, she whispered, stubbornly. If I turned back, that's it, I would be hiding, a prisoner of Avian Flu listening to Bill bickering with Galina, death breaking out through them, breaking them, and me too. Bickering about crackers, how ridiculous! The unbearable task of consoling Max, that too; she couldn't bear it. She had to work. What else could she do?

Eva halted for a second and looked around as if in search of an answer. Nothing but garbage, emptiness, puddles here and there, and death hidden inside the identical redbrick houses.

As she crossed the 20th Street loop two men armed with clubs stopped her.

"Guards," they announced curtly, with the anonymous voices that official occupations often bestow. "Do you live here?"

Knowing the procedure, Eva showed her keys in silence.

"If you leave now, we won't let you back in," the fat man warned.

"I'm a doctor, I work at the VA."

"A doctor?" the other asked in a eunuch's voice, surprisingly high for his tall stature. Eva saw him shifting from one foot to the other, hesitating. "Come with me!" he ordered her. He must have someone dying at home, she thought anxiously. And he won't let me go until the resolution, he won't feed me, and I'll never see Max again.

"Where are you taking her?" the fat guard interjected before she could reply.

"I need to be at work!" Eva cried.

"You're coming with me now," the tall guard said and grabbed her arm awkwardly, like a kid pretending. She could read fear in his eyes, and it gave her confidence to bluff.

"Do you have a sick relative at home?" she asked compassionately, like a snake, sensing she was betraying his secret. "It's best to bring her to the hospital. There would be nothing I could do at home, we would need ..."

"I don't have anyone at home!" he snapped, interrupting her, but Eva knew by his reaction that he was lying. Guards are not allowed to have sick family members, she guessed. If the other guard found out, he would lose his job. She made her face blank, keeping up the survival game. He'll never let me go, she thought again, panicking as she glanced into his watery blue eyes.

"Wait a second!" the fat guard started, poisoned with suspicion.

"She should serve the community." the eunuch-voiced guard said defensively and stepped back.

"Cut out the bullshit. Where do you want to take her?"

Heart thumping, Eva watched the fat guard's menacing eyes now directed at his companion. Then she ran. She heard their steps behind her and stumbled; already falling, she felt the grip of a hand tightening around her arm and lifting her back into the air. Her thoughts were of death. Convinced she would die instantly, she raised her eyes to the sky to catch her last glimpse.

"Stop, I told you!" She heard this through the waves of her own breathing and looked up, trembling and defeated.

"I have to go to the hospital. Please let me go," she said faintly.

"You'll come with me to his place. Then I'll let you go. And don't you run again!" the fat guard said. She had to concentrate hard in order to understand him.

Her legs leaden, she followed meekly behind the two men. In silence, they reached 20 Stuyvesant Oval. She regained her composure somewhat, becoming conscious of how much the trembling in her knees bothered her.

"I'm telling you, there's no one there," the thin guard insisted without passion, more as a mantra to stay calm. They took the staircase to the second floor, and the thin guard fumbled guiltily, searching for the keys.

"Do you need help?"

The tall guard helplessly lifted his face to his companion. His mouth was slightly open. They entered the apartment, the fat guard pushing his comrade in the back. In the kitchen Eva spotted three cans of tuna and a bottle of beer and instinctively turned away, as if she had discovered the evidence of a crime. Following the guards down the hall, Eva watched their heavy, mud-covered boots carrying the square, animal strength of their calves. The basic masculinity of their boots frightened her. *Please don't let them rape me,* she thought, fighting horror. *I love you Max!*

A young pale woman was lying in the bedroom. Eva moved to take her pulse. A tissue covered in blood lay cramped next to the pillow. The woman's hoarse breathing was the only sound. The room stank of urine.

"Holy shit!" the fat guard cried, and pushed Eva to the

exit.

"You can go now!" he barked. "Go!"

"Man I swear! She's my sister! ..." Eva heard this as she sprinted out on the tips of her shoes – as if the clatter of her heels might change her fate. Already at the door, her hand on the doorknob, she turned, dashed into the kitchen and seized the tuna cans, the beer, and the bag of rice standing in the sink, then flew out the door which closed behind her with a shuttering bang. Breathlessly, she raced around the Oval toward home.

The last words she heard upon leaving the apartment slowly took form and meaning. They came back to her when she hid in the cool darkness of her own building's entryway, halting to catch her breath. "Kill her," the deep voice had said, while the eunuch's voice repeated pleadingly, "She's my sister, man! My sister!"

Kill her, or I'll kill you!

Eva peered out the door. No one had followed her. She went up one flight of stairs and collapsed on the top step, sobbing.

In 20 Stuyvesant Oval, the thin guard was pressing a pillow to his lover's face.

When Eva reached the tenth floor, she heard Bill and Galina arguing again. Their bodiless voices were full of hatred. She entered softly, catching them by surprise, and was pleased to see that her presence silenced them back into reason.

"What happened?" they asked simultaneously. Their faces were suddenly innocent, like those of high school kids caught by the principal drinking beer.

Eva held out her bag.

"Food," she said.

Max was sitting in the corner playing with cars. He said "Mommy" when she walked in but didn't approach her. His eyes were sad and remote.

"Please don't argue in front of him," Eva said.

"Did you hear?"

"It was hard not to. You were loud."

"I was just saying that if she wants to eat she should get off her ass and go and get food rather than stealing food from a child," Bill said defensively, still standing.

"He think if he sleep with you I should die. He want my death. He don't care for Max. He eat applesauce today, and he steal crackers last night, I find little pieces!" Galina said, raising her voice. Max continued mechanically moving his cars left and right, his back turned to them. Eva knew he understood but refused to acknowledge them.

"Shut up both of you!" she screamed, jumping up abruptly, the chair falling behind her. "Shut up! I said not in front of him! You can both go to hell! This is my house! Enough of this shit!" Her neck veins were bulging and her face turned livid. She hit the glass table with her open palm. "Enough is enough!"

Bill picked up the chair and with a stroking movement seated Eva back.

"I'm sorry," he said uneasily.

She burst out crying, covering her face tightly with both palms, overwhelmed with rage, fear and loneliness. *I took that woman's pulse, I shouldn't touch my face*, she thought, and with childish stubbornness decided that it didn't matter; she wanted to die. Bill continued to stroke her hair, helped her out of her coat, and untwined her scarf.

"It's okay, I'm sorry," he repeated.

"I'm sorry too. I shouldn't have said that." She spoke through tears. Max's hair brushed against her cheek a minute later.

"Why are you crying, mama? Are you going to die too?"

"No, I'm just upset, darling. We're going to live!" she exclaimed with pathos. She grinned at Max but didn't touch him, cognizant of her dirty hands.

"That's my gal!" Bill laughed and bent down to kiss her

forehead. Galina continued to stand apart defiantly.

"Galina, I'm sorry for what I've said. Could you please bring me some hand disinfectant?"

Galina silently moved to the bathroom, returning a moment later with a cup full of disinfectant, which she handed to Eva with the same vacant expression on her face.

"I don't need so much," Eva said, surprised. Galina patiently waited for Eva to rub her hands, then removed the cup and left the room.

"So what happened?" Bill asked, shrugging his shoulders in Galina's direction.

"The guard didn't let me out. But he gave me food," she said, trying to sound natural.

Galina returned, listening eagerly, her eyes big and mournful.

"Gave you food?" Bill repeated with astonishment, putting the bag on the table and peering in. "Tuna. Beer. Where did he get it?"

"I didn't ask, just took it and ran," she said.

"You think they're getting food supplies?"

"I don't think so."

"But why did he give you food?"

"I don't know. How should I know? Maybe he stole it from someone and shared out of guilt?"

"Yeah, right, out of guilt," Bill said and laughed. She laughed too, looking at Max, who joined in with a small giggle. Eva turned to Galina, still feeling bad for her outburst.

"He is a man," Galina said laconically, pointing at Bill. "He should get food, not you."

"Where's that guard? Maybe if I'm lucky he'll share with me too," Bill said genially.

"I'd be surprised," Eva replied, shrugging her shoulders.

Galina cooked a quarter of the rice and mixed it with a can of tuna. Max stood next to her asking every couple of minutes whether it was ready. Ska meowed non-stop, circling around Galina's feet and clawing them.

"Take away a cat!" Galina yelled and kicked Ska away. Ska turned over and recoiled, arching her back and hissing.

"I said take away a cat!" Galina urgently yelled again.

"Take it easy," Bill said rising. "She's hungry." He picked up Ska, holding her under her belly, took a piece of cheese from the table and locked the cat in the bathroom.

"Cat has to go. Enough mouse to catch outside," Galina stated loudly, stirring the food in the pot, her eyes on her cooking.

Eva was quiet and after a while Bill remarked,

"She's right."

When Galina tasted the mix to check if there was enough salt, Max pulled on her skirt.

"I caught you! You took my food!" he declared, echoing Bill.

Galina silently stared at Eva and Bill, who were waiting at the set table. Her expression was full of reproach. Bill turned away.

"It's okay, Galina," Eva said while Max continued whining and demanding his portion.

Galina served the meal in punishing silence. They ate passionately, lost in savoring the food, their taste buds acute and fresh like never before.

"I need to lie down now," Eva said, wiping her mouth with a napkin. *It's still so civilized,* she thought. *The worst is yet to come.*

"Galina, please make sure that all the pots are filled with boiled water," she added on her way to the bedroom.

Bill appeared at her bedside a minute later, fully dressed, wearing a fur hat that made him look like a savage Kazakh. "What happened really?"

"I told you."

"Are you all right?"

"I'm fine."

"I'm going out now. Should I hide from the guards?"

"Yes. They won't let you back in. Be careful."

"Are they armed?"

"With clubs. I didn't see any guns."

"Come on, give me a kiss!" Bill looked scared and brazen at the same time. She kissed him on the lips, then pulled him closer and kissed him again, wet and hard until his stubble hurt her lips. If she kissed him long enough he'd come back with food. So many simple acts had turned into rituals and obsessions in the past two weeks. And if something happens to him today? If he doesn't come back? She withdrew her lips from his.

When he was gone, she closed her eyes. A while later, Max climbed into her bed.

"Mommy! I want a tale about the stupid T-Rex!"

Eva adjusted her blanket, drew air and started in a warm, homey voice:

"Once upon a time there lived a stupid T-Rex in the jungle. A giant fly Tsetse flew by and bit him on his back. Tsetse flies were huge at that prehistoric time, as big as your bed, and could even bite through a T-Rex's skin, which was very thick. Our T-Rex was looking for something to scratch his back on because his arms were too short to reach behind. After a while, he came upon three boughs sticking out of a bush. Perfect for scratching! But as soon as he neared them, they let out a horrible howl and stabbed him really hard, because those weren't boughs at all. What were they, pumpkin?"

"Triceratops!"

"Right, a Triceratops eating leaves in the jungle. Our stupid T-Rex yelled and ran away as fast as he could. He ran for a long time before he came upon a beautiful glade with huge red flowers growing on it and decided to have a rest. But as soon as he lay down, he heard feet stampeding toward him, and saw that the flowers had feet and were about to attack him."

"Stegosaurus!" Max yelled.

"That's right. Those were a Stegosaurus, whose back plates gleamed red to scare away predators, but stupid T-Rex didn't know that. Well, before they could trample him, he ran away again. Panting and tired, he decided to have a nap under a big naked tree. But when he came closer, the tree lifted a huge root and yanked him out of the jungle."

"It wasn't a root! It was a Brachiosaurus' tail!"

"And the stupid T-Rex never went to the jungle again because he decided it was jinxed. Boughs, flowers, and a tree had attacked him. He wasn't going there again! And everyone lived happily thereafter."

"The story is funny. Why are you crying, mama?"

"I feel like a stupid T-Rex."

"But you're not! T-Rex is big!"

25

Once the door had shut behind him, Bill slipped on his gloves and unhurriedly leaned on the wall, listening into the dark. Far away someone cried for help. Otherwise it was silent. "All dead?" he wondered aloud, his low voice booming and echoing in the staircase.

Outside, his courage faltered somewhat. He was on his own now, exposed to the unseen danger. Yet it also sharpened his senses. The wind was fresh and humid. He breathed deeply, enjoying the urgent smell of the late fall, and raised his arms, stretching toward the grey, unfriendly sky. There was no one in sight. He chose the route Eva must have taken on her way to work, bending down when crossing the roads, calculating the best ways to stay unseen. He hoped the guards were not watching the area from windows. In the deep pocket of his coat he held a kitchen knife wrapped in tissue.

On the Oval he saw the lonely figure of a man, and from the apparent purposelessness of his movements assumed it was a guard. He ran through the grass to soften his steps and hid behind a fountain. While peeking out, he noticed three human bodies on the other side, huddled close together as if they had chosen to die in each other's arms. The corpse of a dog lay stiffly on its side in the fountain, its fur bleak and shaggy, sharp ribs showing through. All this left Bill unmoved. It was much more benign than what he had imagined.

When the guard was at a safe distance and his back turned to Bill, Bill ran toward the soccer field and hid behind a bench, which offered a good overview and shielded him from sight. He felt reckless now, and strangely, nervously joyful. He waited for a while, then ventured toward a garbage truck abandoned on the path leading to the 20th Street Loop. The truck smelled of dead bodies. Bill moved behind an excavator that was blocking the road. The smell appeared stronger there, and, wondering where it came from, Bill peered out. At a distance of about twenty feet there was a pit. "Where the bodies go," Bill murmured. *And yet they didn't kill her. Just raped her and let her go. But she didn't tell me.* He rushed further down the street. The exit was sealed by yellow tape. No one was in sight, and Bill ducked under the tape and jogged to First Avenue freely, no longer hiding.

The stores and delis had all been looted and now stood barren and ugly, emptied of their flowers and goods. Under the iron, half-lifted gate of a bagel bakery a pair of still legs stuck out from the darkness. Of Gristedes there was just its sign left, blue and cheerful letters ignorant of the destruction inside. Huge, zigzag-shaped holes gaped in the windows of Petite Abeille, the kids-friendly Belgian restaurant where Eva used to take Max. Its tables stood overturned and its chairs were missing legs, but the Belgian flag with its black, yellow, and red stripes still hung over the shattered bar. Two men were at work smashing the gate of an adjacent carpet store, using axes and hammers that they probably got in Town and Village Hardware next door.

A fire truck and three ambulances swished by, sirens off. A group of teenagers trying to break into a Jeep Cherokee parked in the middle of the road stopped for a second and stepped aside to let the service cars pass. Someone honked desperately from inside the car. The last honk, long like a howl, was silenced by a hammer that sent an elaborate spider web through the car's windshield. A bicyclist wheeled by, looking stiffly ahead of him, as if nothing were happening. There was no other traffic for a while. Several shots fired close by and Bill instinctively ducked his head. The sense of danger was stronger now, weighing on his steps.

He proceeded hiding behind phone booths and building recesses. On his way he passed a Radio Shack, the Stuyvesant

Town Leasing Office, and a toy store, all more or less intact. Swiftly, like a rat, he crossed 19th Street, taking cover in the shade of half-naked trees. On the other side someone was shouting inside a burglarized Ameritel store. Bill quickened his pace to remain unseen.

Blockbuster, its doors wide open, seemed remarkably preserved. Cautiously, Bill stepped in. As expected, the chocolates, chips, and soda were gone, but Bill rummaged around for a while nevertheless, hoping something might have been dropped or forgotten. Movie titles cried out to him from the shelves; he smiled wryly at *Apocalypse Now*. He shoved a couple of kids' DVDs into his backpack for Max and moved on.

The blue, shabby buildings of Beth Israel Medical Center opened themselves to his view. People peered down from the safety of balconies in residents' housing. Some held cameras. At the sight of the hospital Bill felt a pang of guilt. An ambulance turned into the 16th Street ER entrance.

A bum was picking through a heap of decayed vegetables outside Elm Drugs Store. He was unmasked and had a long, shaggy beard. The door to the store stood open. Stepping closer, Bill took out his camera and took several snapshots, including of the bum and of the hospital's onlookers. Hearing voices inside the store, Bill stopped, listening. There appeared to be several men and a woman talking. The voices sounded ordinary, unhurried. They must have done it many times, Bill thought: raided stores. The idea of joining them seemed not out of the question, perhaps because a woman was involved, or because they didn't bother to harass the homeless man. He peeked inside.

"There must be more fucking food somewhere," a man's voice said.

"Don't break the window, you idiot!"

"Yeah, the cops may come," the woman agreed.

"And what if it makes me feel good?"

They laughed, and Bill laughed with them, stepping forward. They stiffened, their smiles suddenly gone.

"What're you looking for?"

"Food," he said in his most charming voice. "Any luck?"

"We don't share," a tall scrawny man answered gloomily. They were two men and the woman, who appeared older. None wore masks.

"Did you look in Radio Shack?" Bill asked. "It's still untouched."

"What, are we going to eat radios?"

They sniggered. Bill laughed with them.

"I could eat anything right now!" he said in what he hoped was an ingratiating way.

"Show us your face," the tall man ordered. Bill took it for a step toward friendship and pulled down his mask. The man scrutinized him mockingly, the others adapting his attitude.

"Now come to me and I kiss you! I have a big flu in my mouth!" the short dark guy said, and everyone cackled again.

"No, thank you," Bill said, nonchalantly pulling his mask into place.

He walked out and bent over a crate with vegetables outside. The bum moved to give him space. None of the vegetables appeared edible, but Bill nevertheless turned over a couple of onions with the tip of his shoe. Then, with pleasure, he squashed a brown half-liquid apple.

"You! Come here for a sec!"

He turned and walked back into the store.

"See that shelf over there? Check it out, take the ladder. Put your bag over here."

Bill knew they were interested in his bag and let them have it. He climbed the ladder unhurriedly, aware of being watched and sure there was nothing to be had. Then he saw two boxes stacked close to a wall, and more further down the aisle.

"Bingo!" he cried. "Unless they're full of radios..."

"Shrek 2!?" the gawky tall man said, throwing Bill's looted DVDs on the floor and turning his bag upside down. A coin fell out and rolled on the floor.

"Heads, you're in, tails you're out," the man said. The woman nodded. They bent over the coin, Bill watching them from above.

"You're in," he announced. "Get those boxes down here."

The box was light when Bill lifted it and held it out for the man to take. It was ripped apart instantly.

"Napkins, man, fucking napkins!" The man kicked it aside.

There was a shout on the street, followed by curses and bangs. Bill turned to look but his view was obscured by the wall. The woman was sent to check things out and returned waving reassuringly. They heard a squeal like a wild cat's, and then it was quiet again. A car started up somewhere and sped by, screeching its tires.

"Boys having fun!" the dark man mused aloud, peeking out and shaking his head. No one else paid attention.

"More napkins," Bill said, throwing the second box on the ground, and then the third. He climbed down and moved the ladder to the right. The next box was heavier. When he lowered it, something rattled inside.

"Light bulbs, can you believe it?" the gawky man giggled through his teeth. "Hey you, you eat light bulbs?"

Bill took another box and read on the side "Sea salt."

"Salt! Do we need salt?" he asked innocently, knowing right away that he needed it.

"You stupid, man! Who needs salt? Nothing more?"

"No, that's it."

"Bring it down anyway, maybe it's not salt."

The box was ripped open revealing eight blue sea salt containers inside. Bill got down. The gawky man climbed the ladder up. "Just checking if you forgot anything."

They checked out the other side, sending Bill up the ladder again.

"Bingo!" he cried, spotting a can of black olives at the end of the shelf. He stepped higher, stretching and breathing hard, but still couldn't reach. "Give me a stick or something, I'll get it!"

They fetched an umbrella for him, and after a short fight, almost losing his balance once, he rolled the can to the edge. The gawky man caught it in both hands.

"Olives! You lucky bastard!" the man said.

"You see, I told you we'd find something!" the woman cried. She had a pleasant nasal voice.

"We'd share," the gawky man remarked nonchalantly. "But there's no can opener."

The woman nodded and took a step back from Bill. The men watched him, defiantly squaring their shoulders, their eyes small and cold.

"Well, then, thanks for the company," Bill said, keeping a careful balance, maintaining his dignity while avoiding a fight. He almost expected to be beaten and humiliated, just for fun. They didn't move, and he walked out, picking his bag up on the way.

"Your salt!" the dark guy called to him.

"Thanks," Bill replied, turning back to gather the salt under the men's stares. All of a sudden he felt heavy and tired. The joke wasn't so funny in the end. He just hoped they wouldn't strike him on his head for the anarchistic delight of lawlessness, its crown rapture being murder.

The sun came out. The bum continued to sift trash. Bill walked quickly past and then halted to decide which way to turn. The jeep was gone. Someone's body lay in the middle of the street. Bill took a picture. Terror and innocence were imprinted on the murdered man's yellow, middle-aged face, his hazel eyes golden in the sunlight, his pupils large and still. A snake of blood divided his face in two. There was an unbearable silence in his posture: his left arm trapped behind its body, legs flexed at the knees in an inverted V, the pose so uncomfortable-looking that Bill felt an urge to free the body's arm and lay its legs straight. Resisting the impulse, Bill moved aside and took another shot. Making the body presentable would be comfort for the living, not for the dead, he decided, just as closing a corpse's eyes is comforting to those afraid to see them open. They should see him like he is, ugly and frightening. Maybe that will deter another murder.

Bill continued down the street taking pictures. It wasn't his neighborhood, and the desolation wasn't personal to him; he wasn't attached to any of these places. He hadn't jogged among these red-brick houses with green window frames; he hadn't been friendly with the waiters of these wrecked cafés and restaurants; he hadn't rented movies at this Blockbuster. Death and destruction have little meaning when they hold no roots in memory. The street was empty now except for some activity in front of the hospital. Ambulances moved soundlessly in and out of the drive. Otherwise, there was no one in sight.

The wind picked up, clearing away the clouds. It was sunny and cold. Bill's jittery joy returned. He felt like a journalist on a mission, the reality surrounding him so close and yet so remote, as if all the emotions he was supposed to feel were attached to the digital images captured by his camera. Images to contemplate later, while sitting comfortably in an armchair and drinking coffee in front of the TV.

He heard a bang. Farther down the road, men were breaking the windows of Citibank. Bill hid in the gaping entrance of an Italian bistro. Two more bangs followed and then an alarm sounded, shrill and piercing. Bill looked around. The bistro smelled faintly of breadcrumbs and mold. The shutters were closed and it was quite dark in contrast with the bright sunlight outside.

When his eyes had accustomed to the darkness, Bill walked

behind the counter. A broken bottle of raspberry marmalade lay on the floor, dry and dark like blood, the label of its shattered bottle its only identification. Bill picked out a plastic spoon from a utensil rack mounted on the wall and scrubbed the marmalade from the floor, eating it and spitting out the pieces of glass. He checked the drawers. They were empty. The alarm at the bank continued to ring annoyingly. He walked back to the entrance and opened a cabinet that ran along the front wall, stepping over pieces of glass that cracked soundlessly under his feet, drowned out by the noise of the alarm. A black, rounded shape in the depth of the closet caught his interest, and he bent down to pull it out. It was a large travel bag, stuffed to bursting; he lifted it and put it on the floor. Oblivious to the glass shards under his knees, Bill unzipped the bag with suddenly tremulous hands. A jar of peanut butter was the first thing he saw. Immediately he zipped the bag shut, afraid to spook his luck and afraid that the café's owner might be standing behind him, ready to whack him with an iron rod. Holding the bag, Bill reached the exit, cautiously peering out. At the far horizon of First Avenue he spotted a car. *Police!*, he thought with alarm, and hurried away, dragging his new bag between his legs. A couple of times something sharp and heavy inside hit his shins but he barely paid attention to the pain, consumed by the frenzy of escape. He reached the corner and jumped behind it just as the police car reached the bank and braked abruptly. He heard shots, someone shouting. He continued to run forward, bending deep to the ground, deeper with every shot, each sounding close enough to have been aimed at him. Finally, he fell into a half-frozen ditch, lying on top of the bag with his stomach. No one was around when he gathered the courage to peek out. He exhaled and leaned back. It was quiet and safe in this spot, and for a second he thought of burying his treasure right here in the ground. But someone might be watching him above, from a window, and anyway he had no shovel with which to break the frozen earth.

After catching his breath he ventured out, his panic

growing by the minute, affecting his strength and coordination. Now that he had food, his task ceased to be amusing. Now he had something to lose.

The First Avenue loop lay before him, another yellow tape sealing off the entrance just thirty feet ahead. He crouched underneath, his heart beating wildly. *Almost there!* he urged himself on.

Seeing no one, he moved quickly and silently, over grass wherever possible. The sun was still high and shining brightly and he watched his short, quirky shadow with apprehension. He passed along a huge basketball playground with its two high showers that made him think of gas chambers; here he halted, in front of the expanse of the central Oval, where it was impossible to stay unseen. He wished he knew the area better. He would walk through backyards.

How on earth did I manage to cross the Oval the first time? he thought, frozen by hesitation. He almost decided to run for it, which would be the quickest way to get to the house, but then remembered the corpses lying on the grass. It seemed like a bad sign, and he chose the way along the park instead. The playground, with its little fire trucks, cars and mock clock tower, stood empty, blanketed by fallen foliage. Like a rat, he sneaked by. An old woman's body lay on a bench, a walking cane still clutched in her hand.

The call came out of nowhere; his heart missed a beat. He felt nauseated and hollow for a split second before turning around.

"Hey you! Stop!"

He saw the guard's beard and mask. Instinctively, Bill clutched the knife in his pocket. The man was heavy-set, his bulky belly rounding his coat. *He can't run*, Bill determined with a flash-like clarity. *He has no weapon.*

"One more step and I'll eat you alive, motherfucker!" Bill bellowed in a cold, deafening voice.

The man stopped in his tracks.

Bill had a sudden impulse to chase him, to beat him up, to tread him with his boots for all the fear Bill had had to endure. He stepped toward the guard.

"Boo!" he yelled and watched with satisfaction how the fat man trotted away, swaying from side to side.

That's how they break windows, Bill thought, already in front of Eva's house. This discovery seemed groundbreaking to him, and he gaped with excitement. He was an alpha male. As he entered the house and started up the stairs, his elation grew.

"I'm a hero!" he cried, and then announced it again at the doorstep of the apartment.

Eva hung on his neck a second later, Max tugged at his sleeve and Galina hugged his shoulders, smiling as widely as if he were her son materialized from Tver.

He talked non-stop, recounting the story of his adventure while Eva and Galina gazed at the bag in wonder, hypnotized by the sight of food now laid out on the glass dinner table. Peanut butter, golden and fragrant; a whole stack of fruit bars falling out on the floor; a huge pack of cheese; ten chocolate bars; three thick dry sausages; a can of cream cheese; M&M's; dried cranberries, cashews, sunflower seeds and sesame crunches, all in large see-through packages; Kavli crispbread; raisins; dry milk; cereal; beans; rice; sugar and a bottle of Remy Martin.

"Wow!!!" Eva cried, clapping her hands. "It's the catch of the year!"

Max clapped too, a chunk of chocolate in his mouth. They sat down, brought out plates and grew quiet for a moment, each calculating in their heads how long the food would last.

"Let us count portions!" Galina exclaimed with thrifty enthusiasm, taking a notepad down.

"No, c'mon, stop it!" Bill said, easing into his chair with an air of tired vanity. "Let's eat and let's drink. This might be our last time to have fun!"

Galina opened her mouth to retort, her face tense again, but said nothing. Instead she brought out the little motley glasses.

"To life!" Bill proposed succinctly and grandly. They clinked and drank the cognac down.

"Never tasted cognac before," Bill said. "It's not bad, what do you think?"

The women nodded, their mouths stuffed with pieces of Kavli and dry sausage.

Bill dipped a spoon into peanut butter and smeared it on the thick slice of cheese Galina had handed to him, swallowing it all in one piece.

"That's marvelous!" he beamed, ripping the cashews open. "I wonder why cognac is the rappers' drink? We should change that! After it's all over."

He took another sip. Max ate, stuffing his mouth with cashews and chocolate, oblivious to his surroundings, and Bill bent down and kissed his head in a rush of affection.

"Can you bring me ice cream?" Max asked hopefully, lifting his face to Bill.

"Sure. What kind do you like?"

"Soft vanilla ice cream," Max said dreamily, and everyone laughed. Max proudly looked around and bit into a chocolate bar, smearing his nose and chin brown.

"Where's Ska, by the way?" asked Bill.

"Hunting mice," Eva said, smiling at Max, her face painfully, impenetrably composed. "Cats have to go hunting sometimes."

Max pitched in enthusiastically, "She is going to catch a rat. Big like this," he said, jumping up and widely opening his arms. "Like a T-Rex!"

Bill laughed benevolently. "Yeah, buddy, Ska might."

"A very-very-very big rat!" Max repeated, his repetitions rising in a rapid crescendo.

Bill recounted his adventure again, adding glorifying details on the way.

"You are man!" said Galina, already tipsy, raising her glass.

"Oh, thank you," he answered graciously, clinking his with hers. She smiled, shaking her hair off her forehead with a youthful coquettishness. Eva noticed that she had put on some lipstick.

"No, I am a man!" Max cried.

"Imagine that," Bill continued. "There comes this sack of a guy, belly hanging down to the knees, the man can't even run, and tells me to give him the bag or die. So I face him and yell: I'll eat you alive, you motherfucker!"

"Like a wolf!" Max drawled excitedly, and Bill squeezed his little hand in rapture.

"Listen! That's Freud in action! I told him about the red cap and a wolf last night, and became a wolf today! That's how the unconscious works!" he cried. "You saved me Max! You *are* a man!"

While Max was beaming, Eva observed Galina's changed face.

"But they eat people. They say it all the time on radio."

"Galina, please! It's not true!" Eva cried, gesturing with her eyes in Max's direction.

"Who?" asked Max excitedly. "The wolves?"

"Yes, wolves can attack people if they're very hungry, but only in the forest. There're no wolves here, pumpkin."

"Where are they? In the radio?"

Half a bottle of cognac, half of the cheese, four fruit bars, crackers, a whole sausage and a can of tuna later they went to sleep, drunk and heavy. Galina stayed in the kitchen, hovering over the food and counting the remains.

"I ate too much," Eva said in the bedroom, undressing.

"Me too," Bill agreed.

"I feel so sad. With all this food! How can I feel sad?

Shouldn't I feel happy now?"

"Me too. It's because the feast is over. Nothing more to celebrate."

"I think it's because of Ska," she whispered, eyes tearing. "Poor thing. She could have eaten with us now."

"You had no choice," Bill said. "Are you going to work tomorrow?"

"I don't know. I really must."

"Let's make love? We'll feel better," Bill suggested tenderly, moving closer to her.

They were half-undressed when Max's appearance interrupted them. Eva pulled her t-shirt down, her nipples still erect, and asked in a thin, breathy voice,

"What is it, Max?"

"I want to sleep with you. I'm afraid of the wolves."

"There're no wolves here."

"There're wolves in my room! In the radio!"

The radio was on. Galina lay on a couch in the living room, lipstick smeared around her lips, crying.

26

reg had met Randy and Booger on the beach. They were drunk enough to have lost their fear, or careless, or just kind. They gave him grilled fish sprinkled "for taste" with sea water, and whisky that they drank from the bottle. Booger was big and black, with dirty dreadlocks and a Jamaican accent. Randy was a blond ex-marine with gaping teeth, bad temper and reeking breath. His right hand was missing three fingers. From too much booze his nose was big and purple with deep dirty pores like a mushroom. Both loved the Lord.

It had been Greg's idea to break into the Santa Monica aquarium. With a round pink stone they found on the beach, Randy broke the glass door, stuck his hand in and unlocked it from the inside with the quick competence of a crook. It was dark. Like an altar boy, Greg walked around with a candle, wishing he had taken a flashlight out of the car before the cops seized it from him.

The sea creatures moved in their tanks, turning their blind alien eyes to catch a glimpse of Greg. Funny that they were still alive, he thought. Someone must be feeding them. He felt momentary remorse for taking their lives. In one tank he saw a large octopus. Greg had loved biology when he was a kid growing up in Coney Island. His father used to take him to New York Aquarium nearby, and then to the amusement park next door when the weather was nice. The ocean was different in New York: more severe, grey, windy, especially at this time of the year. Holding his candle to the glass, Greg studied the creature. It must have been old, older than Greg.

"What are you skulking around there?" Randy yelled in a

husky voice strained by his days as a marine.

"I found an octopus. A real old one."

"I hope it tastes good!" Booger said approaching, smacking his lips. He rolled up his sleeves.

"Be careful with it, it's strong. Maybe you better kill it first," Greg warned. "Octopus-wrestling was a sport in the sixties, didn't you know?"

No response. Booger submerged one of his arms. "Octopus is very smart," Greg warned, holding the candle over the tank. "It can change its color to hide." The octopus recoiled at Booger's touch and retreated to the far side of the tank. "It might shoot ink at you," Greg added.

"If it's so smart, ask him to come out nicely!"

The octopus did not shoot ink. After a long and comic chase, it leaped out onto the floor with a loud wet thump. Greg left Booger and Randy to chase it on the ground. He listened into the dark. There was a faint noise coming from an adjacent room like a dry leaf scraping the ground. Stepping quietly, his heart beating wild, Greg entered a lecture room. It looked empty. Folding chairs stood in dense rows of no more than fifteen. The only place to hide was behind a column opposite a ceiling-high tank holding seahorses. Stepping forward, Greg peered behind the column. A small grey-haired woman squatted on the floor, covering her face with her hands. She was shivering. Hesitantly, Greg put his hand forward and stroked her shoulder. She lifted her head and he quickly pressed a finger to his lips.

"Where are you, goddamn it, white boy?" Randy shouted.

Greg waved his hands up and down, motioning for the lady to be quiet.

"Just looking," he answered cheerfully. "Nothing in here."

"I killed the bastard!" Booger yelped gleefully.

Greg retreated. The woman watched him pleadingly, her face slowly darkening as the candle moved away until he could no longer see her large fearful eyes. For some reason he assumed she had no family and lived a solitary life devoted to these odd creatures of the sea. He wished he'd apologized to her in some way, promised to make amends in the end. When he had the money, if ever he would, he'd repair the damage and make a donation to the aquarium. The old woman would smile and in gratitude shake his hand. Maybe then, Greg and Max and Eva and Greg's parents would survive.

Back in the aquarium's lobby Greg said loudly, so the lady would hear: "Don't touch the moray eel, they have sharp teeth! And let's get out of here! We've had enough for today."

"There'll be nothing left by tomorrow! Not a piece of seaweed! Trust the old man!"

They got an octopus, a huge crab, a nautilus, three tiger sharks and two moray eels, one of which ripped a piece of flesh out of Booger's hand.

"I told you, they're hungry and dangerous!" Greg said inspecting the wound.

"You is our brain!" said Booger, glowing with satisfaction and indifferent to pain.

On the beach they made a fire. The octopus was large indeed, one of the largest Greg had seen live. Inside his flesh he had something like a carapace.

"It's a male," Greg said, ruefully biting into the chewy flesh.

After the feast Randy became belligerent, demanding that Greg share his sleeping bag.

"I'm gonna fuck your fucking fuck! I'm gonna shoot a bi-ig hole between your fucking eyes!" he yelled. "You with me, sport?" he barked to Booger. "You with me, fucking nigger?"

Booger rose to his feet towering over Greg with his massive thoughtfulness.

"Randy is my brother. You have to share."

Greg wished again that the stupid police hadn't taken his car. Even without gas it was a clean hiding place, his private cave with leather seats. He was sick and tired of sand getting everywhere, into his clothes, his eyes, his nose. He was sick of Randy with his bellicosity and alcoholism and of Booger with his stoic stupidity.

"Randy," Greg said firmly. "I think you need a drink."

"I sure as hell do!"

"How about this? I go and get you a drink and you just rest here and wait for me. Okay?"

"Wait, you! How're you gonna get me a drink?" Randy yelled suspiciously. Greg walked off without turning. The white boy is hiding treasures in his pants, Randy was probably saying now. It didn't matter. They wouldn't run after him. It was a closed chapter.

Greg walked slowly, throwing sand with the tip of his shoes, leaving his sleeping bag and his company behind. He thought of the aquarium and the woman trembling inside. He hoped she would have the sense to leave. He knew Booger and Randy would be back in the morning.

Greg walked in the direction of Marina Del Rey. His path lay through Venice Beach. Shops and bike rentals stood open and drifters amused themselves by riding idly around on stolen wheels, dressed in looted t-shirts with sexy or political slogans on them, exchanging light-hearted laughs. The tourists had gone and all the cafés were boarded up, but still the place buzzed with life. Lights, lamps, and fires burned here and there. Shadowy figures moaned and rubbed against one another on benches and beside trees. Shivering swimmers raided dark shops for colorful towels patterned with stars and fish. People slept in pull-carts. Alcohol and drugs were bartered on the corners in exchange for jewelry or food. Brawls erupted occasionally, sometimes accompanied by gunshots. Occupied with their prioritized protection of "high value targets" such as banks, pharmacies, and hospitals, police were nowhere to be seen.

"Welcome to Baghdad!" Greg heard a radio joke wryly. A

group of young girls sitting around the boom box giggled and clapped. On the beach side of the street a crowd of local kids were playing ball under the scant light of a lantern, yelling with hysterical cheer.

Greg would have walked along the water, but the sky was clouded, obscuring the moon, and he feared darkness more than human hands. He walked at a pace that wouldn't arouse suspicion, neither too fast nor too slow. No one could know who he was in the dark. No one could know he'd been exposed. One of the bike rental shops stood open just ahead of him, a weak bulb dangling from its doorframe. Greg approached cautiously and peered into the dim space, feeling handlebars with his fingers. The shop was dusty and smelled of crude oil and rusted metal. As his eyes accustomed to the darkness Greg made out some ten to fifteen bikes standing before him in a row.

"Welcome to Skeleton's Grove!" a grating voice startled Greg. "How can I help you?"

"I'm looking for a bike," Greg laughed nervously.

"Go ahead."

He just wanted a bike, a regular bike, he told the man. A rusty one with a wide seat and high handlebars, no speeds, was wheeled out and displayed under the dirty bulb. Good enough. Greg squeezed its tires between his fingers and then straightened, studying the man's face, which he could now see. It was thoroughly wrinkled, and long blond strands fell into its deep-set, glinting eyes. The man was short but sturdy, had sensual lips, and wore a silver cross and a shark's tooth around his neck. Greg thought there was a strong physical resemblance between the guy and himself. Or maybe it was just the hair …

"I think we look alike," he spoke up finally. "I mean, you could almost be my father."

The guy chuckled and didn't answer, just removed a strand of hair from his cheek and looked at Greg expectantly.

"So that's it?" Greg asked.

"What do you think this is, Christmas?"

"Jesus, sorry. I don't really know how things work here..."

"You never been to a store before? You some kinda Borat, or what? Fresh from Kazakhstan?"

"New York, actually ..."

"Well New York ain't Communist. In fact it's fuckin' expensive, as I remember."

"I don't have any money. Sorry. Wasn't thinking." Greg made for the door.

The man put a hand on his shoulder.

"Take some advice. *Son.*" The man punctuated this word by giving Greg's shoulder a fierce squeeze. "There're a lot of assholes out here. Don't cheat 'em: you'd make for a nice soup. Now take the fuckin' bike and get out of here. Anyone asks where you got it, say you're runnin' an errand for Rudolph-the-Rhinoceros."

Rudolph-the-Rhinoceros! Greg hopped on the bike and took off before the guy could change his mind, then shook his head and laughed breathlessly, racing down the beach. Wind flew into his face while the beacons of streetlamps and bonfires faded in his wake. Greg slowed, straining to discern the road, and thought of Eva's soft voice reading Max a story about a rhinoceros caught in Africa and brought to a big city on a whale's back. Rupert, that rhinoceros was called, he was pretty sure. Rupert and Rudolph. Rudolph the Red-Nosed Rhinoceros ... He longed for Max, to tell his son his own rhinoceros story, to watch his eyes droop and his little head sink into the pillow as he fell asleep. The lights of Venice Beach were invisible to Greg now, and although he had scored himself a free bike he still had nowhere to go. The shore had become enveloped by a thick tropical blackness. Greg braked, dismounted, and, slowly wheeling his bike beside him, wept for his life.

27

Eva woke at dawn, grey morning light striping the closed blinds. Her winter coat formed a thick fold under her leg and she moved to straighten it out. The heating had failed two days earlier and it was cold. She had heard on the radio that the house would stay warm as long as the windows were closed. Galina must have opened the windows while I was at work, she thought wearily. She turned over. Bill was asleep, his fur collar sticking out. Lazily, she got up to find her slippers and go to the bathroom.

The door was half-open, revealing Galina's trim, broad-boned body, totally naked. She didn't seem to feel the cold. Leaning close to the mirror, she muttered something to herself quietly in Russian, baring her teeth as she studied her reflection. Unaware of Eva, she stretched yoga-style, exposing her wide, horse-like ribcage and lithe muscles, and took something from a shelf. Then she shook the bottle of hand disinfectant, turned it upside down, and squeezed a voluminous stream of its clear mass onto her shoulders. Shuddering, she rubbed it into her flesh – into her stomach and her breasts, which were weighed down by age and motherhood, and into her legs, all the while humming with satisfaction. As the alcohol evaporated, goose bumps raised on Galina's skin, visible in the gray morning light.

"Galina!" Eva said. "What are you doing?"

Galina was startled; her look turned at once suspicious and polite. She yanked a towel off a hook and covered herself before speaking.

"You see what I am doing," she said. "Do you not see?"

"But this is a waste of the disinfectant! It's not going to

help you if you do that! It's for disinfecting our hands! It won't protect the rest of you from the disease!"

"You don't bring me the medicine!" Galina shouted with a wild, trapped expression.

"I can't give you the medicine because I don't have it!" Eva said with exasperation. She took a step forward, toward the light switch.

"Don't come close to me! You have the virus!" Galina shrieked, jumping back. Eva flipped the switch again and again. Galina said something more but Eva didn't hear her.

"There's no light," Eva stated quietly. "They've turned off the lights."

Hurriedly, she went to the living room, trying all the switches. Nothing.

"There's no fucking light!" she yelled, running into the bedroom and jumping on the bed. "Bill! Bill! Wake up! They've turned off the lights!"

Bill sat up, his eyes heavy and red, his hair tousled, looking ridiculous in her grandmother's fur coat. Like a drag queen after a night of wild partying.

"There's no light," she repeated desperately, her heart sinking.

Bill put his heavy arms around her, suffocating her in the fur. It smelled of the naphthalene that her grandma had kept in her closets to ward off moths – a nostalgic smell that revived in Eva memories of afternoon tea, cookies, and cards games at night.

"Think of the Amish!" Bill said nonchalantly. "It's not the end of the world. We'll survive."

"This smell," she said. "I love it. It makes me want to cry."

"Are you kidding? If I survive this, I'll have two smells to hate until the end of my days: naphthalene and hand disinfectant."

"Galina is crazy," Eva said, righting herself and looking at Bill with alarm. "I just saw her in the bathroom, naked, rubbing herself all over with disinfectant."

"She's been doing it since they turned off the heat," he said. "And she talks to herself all the time."

"I can't trust her with Max anymore."

"I've been watching her. She's actually good with him, really kind. It's just partial insanity, like in a delusional disorder."

"Maybe I shouldn't go to work," Eva uttered softly, thinking aloud more than asking for Bill's opinion.

"Really? Don't! Of course! Don't go! You've done enough! It will be such a relief not to be locked up alone with that crazy woman all day long!" Bill said this excitedly, bouncing on the bed like a big furry monkey.

Eva walked into Max's room fearfully, as she did each morning, and squatted next to his car-bed to put a hand on his forehead. He slept quietly, his pink mouth slightly open, his white snowsuit zipped to the neck. She smelled him, brushing her lips against his cheek. Although he had lost some weight his cheeks were still plump.

"My dear boy," she whispered.

Max stirred, opened his eyes, and immediately locked his arms around her neck.

"Mommy?"

"Yes?"

"I dreamed about daddy. Is he coming back?"

"I hope so, Max."

"Daddy that plays music," he said. "That has a guitar. And sings into the phone. It comes out really loud!"

Eva gathered him up into her arms and smelled urine. He was all wet, his snowsuit soaked though. She would have to wash it in cold water.

"Max!" she said carrying him to the bathroom. "You peed in bed."

He captured her nose with his strong little fingers and she laughed out loud, freeing herself from his grip. In the hallway, she stopped dead in her tracks.

"Oh shit, holy shit!" Eva said.

"What shit, mommy?"

"Don't repeat stupid things, Max," she said. "There's no water."

"Why not?"

"Because they switched off the electricity. The water pump runs on electricity, and now it's not operating. Let's see if there's water in the kitchen."

She put him down. His urine left a dark spot in the front of her green cashmere coat.

"I'm cold! Pick me up!" he demanded, stretching up his arms.

She picked him up and let him turn the faucet in the kitchen. It hissed, let out yellow drops, and went dead.

"Oh my God, oh my God," Eva said.

"Water pump is cool!" Max exclaimed with fascination. "It's like a big-big crane!"

"Galina!" Eva called frantically, walking back to the bathroom with Max still in her arms.

Galina emerged fully dressed, looking shy and beaten.

"Did you fill up the buckets with boiled water as I asked you?"

Galina lifted her head, her eyes wide and uncomprehending.

"Did you?" Eva raised her voice through Max's whining. "Max, be quiet, will you?" she shouted at him.

"I did. But Max play with water," Galina said, gesturing in his direction.

"What do you mean? We have no water? None at all?" Eva cried, leaving weeping Max behind and striding to the bathroom. The bathroom smelled of Galina's feces. The toilet tank was empty. A plastic bucket that in good times was used for washing the floors lay overturned in the yellowish bathtub behind the curtain. Eva picked it up and threw it against the wall with furious desperation.

"Fuck! Fuck!" she yelled, kicking the wall. A dusty shampoo bottle fell on the floor and rolled under the sink.

Eva came out possessed by a quiet fury that made her steps slow and her face grave.

"Galina," she said. "Will you please sit down? We need to talk."

Galina obeyed, perching on the edge of a chair, her eyelids hanging deep.

"There are rules in this house, and I want you to follow them. Do you understand me?"

Galina nodded, her eyes fixed on the floor.

"I asked you several times to keep boiled water in the house. How did it happen that you haven't done it?"

Bill shuffled in wearing his boots and still wrapped in furs. A black sable swayed above his knees. "Can I join you?" he said presumptuously, already seated. "What's up?"

Max appeared with a Lego tower. "Mommy! Look! I made you a pump tower," he cried.

"I do it," Galina mumbled, and then turned to Max. "I told you not to play with water! Now you see your mommy's unhappy."

Eva jumped up and seized Max by the shoulders, turning him to face Galina.

"Look at him, for God's sake!" she shouted. "He's three!" Max's tower fell into pieces on the ground but he remained where his mother stood him, wearing a perplexed stare.

"Do you know how many days you can survive without food?" Eva went on. "Take a guess."

Galina shrugged her shoulders.

"About two or three weeks. Now tell me how long can you survive without water?"

Galina edged further off her chair. She was trembling.

"Three *days*," Eva seethed. "For children it's less."

"I will go if you want," Galina said miserably.

"Stop pretending to be a victim!" Bill said abruptly.

Eva nodded. "Bill is right. The least you could do right now is apologize."

The corners of Galina's mouth hung down, and for the first time Eva noticed that the skin on her cheeks and neck was pale and flabby. She's lost weight. All of them had. Except Bill.

"I go and fill water now?" Galina said, half rising.

"What?! You don't get it?" Bill said incredulously. Galina stubbornly turned away from him and he let Eva speak.

"Galina, the lights are off. There's no electricity and so the water pump is not working."

"There is water," Galina jumped up with a fussy eagerness to please. "Here! Here! Come!"

In the kitchen, on the windowsill, was a one-gallon pot filled with water, plus a half-empty kettle on the stove.

"That's it?" Eva asked, Bill skeptically assessing their water stores from behind her shoulder. "Okay. I'm going!" Eva hurried to the hallway, picking up her backpack.

"I thought you were staying!" Bill said.

"I'm going to the hospital to get our water!" she shrieked.

In a half-run Eva crossed Stuyvesant Town and Peter Cooper Village through the chilly grey mist, clutching a pocketknife. The guards had been gone for several days. Approaching the hospital she saw lights and exhaled with relief. The emergency generator was rumbling loudly. Inside, in the hallway leading to the nursing station, Eva noticed that there were far fewer patients on the floor.

"Benji!" she called out, spotting him.

"Dr. Leigh! Thank God!" he cried. "Are you all right?"

Eva nodded, unbuttoning her coat.

"Your family's OK?" he continued, squinting uncomfortably.

"Yes, everyone is fine," she said. "Except there's no water. Did you know?"

"Of course. The whole city is black. Except for the fires. Look over there, across the street – someone trying to stay warm. Do you want a coffee?"

"Coffee!" Eva repeated dreamily. She felt like Cinderella setting her eyes on a golden carriage. "Yes. Coffee and water."

Benji left and Eva sat back, savoring a moment of solitude before what was bound to be a long and difficult day. The floor felt strangely empty and quiet and Eva wondered where the others were, Robin and Firbas and Taylor. When Benji returned she accepted the hot paper cup from his hands and put her nose into its steaming aroma.

"Ah!" she sighed.

"Sorry, no sugar. Here's a Splenda if you want. And my last creamer."

She took a sip, burning her tongue.

"So your family is fine," he said, sitting on the nursing station table.

Eva looked up, surprised. Something was off.

"Are you mad at me for coming late?"

"No, no," he said. "I understand. I was just worried, that's all. Drink, drink!"

She took a sip of cold water and poured some of it into her coffee to cool it.

"It's delicious! Delicious!" she said smiling. "Where is everyone?"

"Taylor's in the treatment room."

"What about Robin?" Eva took another sip.

"Eva ..."

Eva froze, the coffee cup an inch from her lips.

"Robin died this morning, about an hour ago. And Firbas too. Yesterday."

When Benji opened the door to the training room and she saw Robin's body covered with a stained sheet she felt numb. *They couldn't even find a clean sheet*, was all she could think.

Robin's boots poked out, dirt and dry leaves stuck to the rubber grids on their soles. Taylor sat nearby on a round rotating stool, his arms crossed on his chest, clasping his shoulders with his hands.

He nodded hello and cleared his throat.

The treatment room with its white sterile odors of iodide, alcohol and camphor, its tile floor, and steely surgical instruments on a tray, the room that offered Eva comfort when she wanted to escape the Flu, housed Robin now. Eva approached slowly and rubbed the sheet covering Robin between her gloved fingers.

"You can look at her," Taylor said. Eva didn't move.

Taylor lifted the sheet from Robin's face and Eva saw its forever frozen reproach, its inverted blue mouth, rigor mortis having claimed its features. Robin's red hair was still lively, its red curls splayed on the white paper. In fact only her hair seemed real – her hair and her hands, which Taylor had arranged one on top of the other, on her belly. The rest was a wax imitation, a nauseating copy borrowed from a horror museum. Eva didn't feel anything, only dizziness, increasing dizziness. Must be the coffee, she thought as the room began to rotate around her, causing a wave of queasiness …

"Eva? … Eva?"

When she opened her eyes she was on the floor, Taylor's stool next to her head. Benji and Taylor were leaning over her.

"What happened?" she asked.

"You fainted," Taylor said calmly. "You must be dehydrated. Here, drink," he gave her a cup of water. Feeling its plastic sides cave in her trembling grip she sipped obediently.

"More," he ordered, and she obeyed again.

"How're you feeling?"

"Okay."

"She died from an overdose," Taylor said. Eva looked at him blankly, finding it difficult to absorb this information.

264

"I mean, she *was* sick," he continued. "She stayed in the hospital overnight. She was coughing." Eva nodded. "But I guess she didn't want to suffer the slow suffocation."

They fell silent.

"She and Firbas ..." Eva said.

Taylor said nothing. Benji nodded.

"I was a bad friend," she said instead of finishing.

"Stop talking nonsense," Taylor said with kind impatience. "She left this for you."

He fumbled in his pocket. "Here," he said, handing over a folded slip of paper. The note was written on a piece of call stationary. Eva sat motionless, breathing loudly.

"It's my fault," she muttered again. "I wasn't a good friend."

"I'll read it for you," Taylor said. Benji put a hand on Eva's arm.

Eva, my dear friend, Taylor read. *you are not here. I am worried about you. I hope you are fine and Max is healthy. Tell Spencer and my mother that I love them. Going to a better place. Robin.*

Eva took the note and re-read it through a glaze of tears. The mask made it impossible to cry, tears and nasal discharge running and staying inside. She howled, only vaguely aware of the men respectfully silent beside her.

"I'm so sorry Robin!" she cried repeatedly, each exclamation triggering new tears. She slipped her mask off and grabbed a tissue to blow her nose. Taylor restrained her, forcing the mask back onto her face.

"Are you insane? Put your goddamn mask on!"

Eva sat back, frightened and quieted.

"She was sick! Think about your son," he added, admonishing her.

"Thank you," she said.

For the rest of the day Eva worked. Hanging IVs and taking patients' blood pressure, she thought of Max. She was saving him with every little act she performed here. There were fewer patients around. Many of the newly admitted, when re-hydrated and warmed up, showed signs of recovery. Around two in the afternoon she packed her backpack with six bags of glucose solution and filled her thermos with hot coffee.

"Taylor," she said. "I have to bring some water home. I'll be back."

"Okay," he said, and then, with a sly smile, "Have you noticed, the wind is changing?"

She wasn't surprised that he phrased it like this. She understood.

"I'm discharging a patient today," he whispered gleefully. They exchanged smiles.

"She could have lived," Eva said then, her smile fading.

"There'll be time to mourn later," Taylor spoke wisely. "Bring water to your son."

28

va couldn't sleep. She thought about the dangers that plagued everyone day and night and about people eating people. She remembered Robin. Max cuddled next to her, his dear body pressing on her arm. She could not see his face in the dark. Bill emitted measured snores. His night noises used to hypnotize her like the ticking of a clock before Robin died, before the electricity no longer worked. Eva turned over and thought of her mother, whom she hoped was eating cheese and drinking wine and healthily losing weight in the fresh, French sea breeze. She thought of Greg, homeless in Santa Monica. She turned and tossed and straightened out the thick folds of her coat under her body – until dawn, when sleep mercifully enveloped her for a couple of hours before her Swatch beeped its shallow electronic alarm and it was time to get up for work.

Eva became apathetic. Her fervor was gone, and her thoughts turned to death more and more, balanced only by the presence of Max. She wanted to escape. She was tired and hungry. Every day the kind kitchen supervisor at the hospital gave her two cups of applesauce: one for her, one for Max. Benji brought her coffee. She was grateful. Sometimes a truck would arrive with food, and, sitting aside listlessly, she let Benji and Taylor wrestle out her portion. As if all of it were happening on a screen, she watched people shouting, struggling over food. Touching her body, she felt bones, bones, bones. She cut an additional hole into her belt. She was weak. Her gut screamed hunger, and yet, when there was food to eat, she had to force herself, her stomach having become a knot that resisted food with stubborn queasiness.

The Flu seemed to plateau, and yet, through the darkness of her mood, Eva refused to be optimistic. "Yes," she agreed with Taylor, sipping bitter, unsweetened coffee. "There're fewer patients. But that's probably because people don't believe they can be saved anymore."

"Eva!" Taylor cried. "Enough pessimism! Open your eyes! We actually *discharged* two Flu patients today!"

Benji walked by carrying an industrial-size bottle of bleach. He flashed Eva a quick bouncy smile and disappeared into the conference room. Benji's mother had died the day after Robin's overdose and he had taken to sleeping in the hospital since, in a little room in the basement underneath the Emergency Room, which was heated. He never told Eva about his mother's death. She found out from the nurses. Eva understood. He worked to survive, not to be pitied. She had been doing the same, although it became more and more difficult by the day.

A few minutes later Benji joined Taylor and Eva with a cup of milky coffee.

"Where did you get milk?" Taylor cried.

"A favor for a favor," Benji smiled mysteriously. "But this is all I got," he added, telling Eva with his eyes that he was sorry, he had none for her to take home.

"Well it must've come from somewhere!" Taylor continued.

"Where does the kitchen supervisor get Eva's applesauce? Where do I get my coffee?" Benji laughed.

"Yeah, good question!" Taylor agreed. "Where *do* you get your coffee?"

"*I*," Benji whispered, leaning in conspiratorially, "am the only surviving heir to the Starbucks Empire!" he winked. "Shhhh!"

Eva laughed, cheered for a moment.

At home, the feeling of relative normalcy they'd enjoyed in the beginning slowly evaporated. The forced seclusion, the cold, the lack of electricity and water, the intensifying stench in the house, the danger of going out and trying to procure food, the informational vacuum, Galina's gradual derangement, Max's nightmares ...: this was their new world.

At home Eva relied on a portable radio she used to keep in her office, powered by a supply of Costco batteries. In the evenings she and Bill stayed glued to the news, which was full of desperate stories and reports of doubtful wonder-remedies such as smearing masks with garlic, drinking urine, taking loads of aspirin or eating dogs' fat. A lot of talk was devoted to looting, although even looting seemed to be in decline, with burglars either dead or afraid of contamination. Cannibalism was another popular subject, frightening Galina into a stupor.

"Galina, it's their job to make up sensational news! You don't even go outside, so don't worry about it." Eva repeated and repeated these words to no avail.

Galina hadn't left the apartment in weeks, not once since the pandemic started. She retained her melodic bearing, cooked, and was kind to Max, but she'd shied away from Eva in recent days. She talked to herself constantly, supplying both sides of the dialogue. Sometimes, catching a glance of Galina's moving lips, Eva wondered whether the woman wasn't hallucinating.

Although dominated by sensationalist scares, the news did give some reassurances. The government was mobilizing the army. The President was well. Steps were being taken to ensure food and water delivery to urban centers. Scientists were making progress with a vaccine. But Eva and Bill did not fully believe it. Though they hoped for resolution they did not hold their breath.

"Misery hates company," Bill remarked with a giggle and switched off the radio. "Why don't we save our batteries?"

"I want to listen," Galina said in a surly voice and turned the radio back on with an intense look that shut Bill up.

The radio host was interviewing a police officer from the 13th Precinct. *We got a big problem with hoarding,* the officer was saying. *Just the other day, my partner and I had to break into an apartment because its neighbors were complaining of the stench.*

"Who cares," said Bill. "Everywhere stinks!"

"Quiet!" Galina cried furiously, pressing a finger to her lips.

Once inside we saw flies everywhere, and stocks and stocks of food, as if the poor dead guy had cleaned out half a grocery store: dozens of rotting chicken, cheese, butter, milk. The whole family was dead, and I kept thinking there're all these other families out there dying from hunger, instead. This city is full of food. If only it was distributed properly. This is what I love about being in the police force. There's discipline, everyone and everything is accountable, and we don't have to starve. I mean, it's not like we're feasting every night, but we have enough to survive...

"Of course you do!" Bill spat at the radio. "Grab a gun, break into a couple of apartments, take the food. *I'd* like to be a police officer!"

"Don't be so cynical, Bill," Eva remarked quietly. "The police also have to handle decomposing corpses and bring sick people to the hospitals." Momentarily humbled, Bill was silent.

Max wet his bed several times a week even though Eva tried to wake him up at night and force him to use his potty. After the power failed, she allowed him to sleep in her bed between her and Bill. Max accepted Bill more and more, even taking to calling him daddy. The first time Eva heard it she had to resist a cross impulse to reprimand him. It upset her that Max forgot Greg so easily. *Would he forget me too, if I died?* she wondered.

After work Eva avoided Max's embraces until she'd disinfected herself and put the day's clothes into a plastic bag and changed, shivering in the cold. Then she kissed and fed him, devouring him with her eyes. The more he ate, the happier she was.

"Oh, mama, don't kiss him too much," Galina said half-jokingly, half-accusingly.

"He needs me."

"He doesn't understand. He is a baby."

"I'm not a baby!" Max screamed, lifting his head and pointing at Galina. "You're a baby!"

"He understands everything," Eva said calmly.

Fully dressed, looking ready to go out and take a train to a happier place, they sat around by the flickering candlelight, their faces mysterious like shadows. Absorbed, Max watched the flame moving, licking the air.

"This is how it was in prehistoric times, Max," Bill said softly. "People lived in caves and sat around a fire. Fire was sacred because it gave light and warmth and frightened away wild animals."

"Dinosaurs!" Max cried jumping down from Eva's lap. "I'll be a T-Rex. ROOWWRR!"

"Okay. I'm Batman," Bill said.

"No, I'm Batman!"

"I thought you were a T-Rex!"

Eva giggled with them, forgetting herself. Max kept her alive. He gave them all illusionary moments of happiness and invincibility.

"If it weren't for Max I'd go crazy," Bill said, breathing hard after one evening's wrestling match. Max pulled at his coat's sleeve yelling: "More, daddy, more!"

"It's so true!" Eva agreed, her eyes moist with emotion. "If someone is saving us, it's Max."

"Hey buddy, once it's all over, you'll get a medal!" Bill said, slapping Max's palm.

"Today?"

"I don't think it's going to be today, but one of these

days."

"I want my medal now!" Max demanded.

"Do you even know what it is? A medal?"

"Can you eat it?" Max asked, a sweet and puzzled expression on his face.

"No," Bill laughed heartily. "But it's still good. While we wait for it, why don't we play Monster?"

When the door closed behind Eva, Bill played Monster with Max as promised, growling and walking in large steps, his knees bent and fingers crooked like claws, his voice deep.

"Where's that little boy?"

Max was hiding under the table.

"I'm gonna catch that yummy little boy!" Bill growled.

"No! No! Freeze!" Max yelled, putting out his hand.

Bill froze, bending forward uncomfortably.

"RRRRR!" Max shouted, jumping on Bill's back.

Galina stayed in Max's room, her and Bill's tactic for avoiding conflict.

"Daddy! Look, daddy! The birdies are sitting on the applesauce!" Max pointed at the window.

Eva was keeping their supply of applesauce in a plastic bag outside the window, "for the black day." Looking out, Bill noticed two meager-looking pigeons clawing the bag and pecking it with their beaks. "Yeah, looks like those birdies are hungry!" he said cheerfully. "Thanks for telling me, buddy. Let's save the applesauce, OK?"

"Yeah!" Max cried enthusiastically. "Let's save it and eat it up!"

From behind the door, growing fidgety, Galina listened to the rustling outside the window, the bag being pulled in accompanied by Max's excited comments.

"One, two, three, four, five, seven," Max counted.

"No, not seven, count again."

"Eight!" Max cried.

"How much is eight take away two?" Bill urged him.

"I don't know. Are we going to eat it now? Can you open it for me, daddy?"

Galina heard more rustling, then slurping and cries of gratification. When it became too much for her to bear she burst into the living room, appearing in front of them in all her hot, disheveled fury, her tangled hair sticking every which way, her mask bulging. Bill and Max sat shoulder to shoulder on a bench, gulping the applesauce with big plastic spoons, an expression of utmost pleasure written on their faces. Their masks rested high on their foreheads.

"You steal food!" Galina hissed, rushing toward them.

Max laughed, not comprehending the thrust of Galina's emotion, as often happened. "Galina! Look! We saved applesauce from the birdies!"

"*You!*" she cried pointing to Bill. "You teach him to steal!"

"Relax," Bill answered, shooting her a contemptuous glance. "Max was hungry."

"You! You!" she shouted, coming closer and still pointing.

"You, you!" he repeated, mocking her in a high voice. "*You* live because I bring you food, risking my fucking life! So shut up and get lost!"

"You steal! I know! I find pieces. You think you hide but I find them. I will tell Eva!"

"Oh? You'll tell her, will you?" Bill gave a derisive chuckle. "You know what? Why don't you go out and get some food yourself before we continue this conversation? Then you'll have earned your right to talk."

"I …! I …!"

"What? You're afraid, huh? Then don't stink around!"

"Yeah!" Max shouted. "You stink butt!"

"Max!" Bill admonished him, stunned. "*You* can't say it. It's not nice. Say sorry."

"No. You say sorry too."

"I know what you do," Galina uttered quietly, her eyes

becoming suspicious slits. "I know how you get food."

Bill studied her with contempt.

"You're crazy," he said. "You don't know anything."

"I know," she repeated with a distorted face. "I know a lot. Now I go and get food too."

She walked out stiffly and locked herself in Max's room.

"Go and tell her she shouldn't go anywhere," Bill whispered into Max's ear, regretting the whole conversation. The lady was obviously crazy. Eva wouldn't like this little development.

Max banged on the door. "Galina! Daddy says don't go!"

Galina didn't answer. After a couple of minutes she emerged fully dressed, a green knitted cap slid low on her eyebrows, leaving just her eyes exposed. She reeked of disinfectant.

"I don't talk to you," she told Max coldly. "You say stink butt."

"Sorry!" Max cried desperately, pulling at her coat. "I said sorry!"

"Don't pull!" she said abruptly, walking toward the door.

Bill watched quietly. *Let her go,* he thought. *She should go and try. It will do her good. A reality check. Fresh air, a little exercise...*

"Be careful," he said, giving her a friendly wave. "Good luck!"

Galina shot him a gloomy glance and crossed herself, murmuring something in Russian. With her head lowered she went out the door, ignoring Max's calls.

Downstairs, Galina slid out the door swiftly like a shadow and crouched treading the frozen ground with her four extremities, surveying the landscape. Not much had changed from the healthy times, no corpses in sight – in fact, no one in sight at all. It gave her courage, and walking upright again, she set out on her journey. She didn't know where she was going or how to go about getting food; there was just the suspicious hurt driving her forward, her hatred of Bill and his hidden deeds that landed food on their table. She saw blood trailing behind him. She saw Max succumbing to his influence, fed by unclean food, nurtured by dirty hands.

She passed a flagpole. A squirrel rushed into the bushes looking well fed and happy.

Maybe there is no Flu? she wondered, her heart as loud as thunder in the ringing silence.

She walked in the direction of Avenue B, passing cars parked intermittently along the curb, all of them vandalized. There was no traffic on 14th Street. The streetlights were dark. The corner diner and the deli on the other side had their iron gates demolished and sprayed with graffiti. A pack of dirty dogs appeared from around the corner, three Rottweilers and a German shepherd among them, and Galina froze, waiting for them to pass. When they disappeared she made the sign of the cross and congratulated herself on her use of the disinfectant, which evidently numbed dogs' senses. For a while she stood still, shielded by evergreen bushes that in Russia she had seen only once, on her honeymoon in Krim.

The emptiness and absence of noise were surprising and vaguely frightening. To distract herself from her fear she tried to think of her hometown of Tver.

On the outskirts of Tver it was quiet in her wooden house with the fretted windows she painted green and red every spring. No sirens, rarely any cars in sight, just grass rippling in the wind, branches creaking, grasshoppers chirping and frogs croaking on the lake in summer. Autumn brought rain and leaf-falls, tragic smells of decaying nature; winter: snow and long evenings at home in front of the TV. But it was spring and summer that Galina remembered most. She had a little garden where she grew peonies, gladioli, flags and lilies, and, on a different bed, vegetables: potatoes, carrots, cabbage, and beets. Toiling in the garden was what she loved best, digging into the pungent soil, planting and watering and even weeding, though it gave her a stiff back and chafed fingers. Mornings Galina would take a bruised yellow bus to work, riding for an hour on a bumpy road through a grey town, its scant lights flickering here and there, the ride making her carsick. At work she would wash and scrub dimpled aluminum pots and trays in the factory's dirty kitchen, breathing in smells of soap, rancid sunflower oil, and burnt food. At five in the afternoon, rush hour, her feet heavy and aching, she would take the same bus back, pressed against strangers who sometimes touched her private parts with an expression of stony boredom so that Galina never knew who to blame. Nauseatingly aroused, she would get out a stop early and buy groceries at a local store that smelled of fish and rotten vegetables; then, laden with heavy bags whose handles cut into her palms, she would walk home to her kindly mother, her passive husband and their two sons. Her sons' childhood faces she had trouble recalling now. They'd grown so quickly into tall, pimple-faced youths full of dirty secrets and rough words. Everything changed about them: the way they smelled, the geometry of their bodies, their voices; only their taste for food remained the same: Kolya didn't eat fried onions, Dima hated fish, both loved mayonnaise, which as little boys they used to lick from their fingers out of the jar. In the evenings, if the weather were mild, Galina would drink sweet Chinese tea on a wooden bench in the garden, where Masha, her neighbor, sometimes joined her for a conversation. There they would sit among Galina's flowers talking about gardening, husbands, illnesses and children, and watching the empty street, the field, the cemetery on the hill, and the smoking chimneys of a factory on the horizon.

Like Tver, New York was dark and quiet now. Galina closed her eyes and opened them again. It was so still she could hear herself breathing. The sun came out, clouds segregated by abrupt gusts of wind. Unwilling to cross the street and be caught in the hostile emptiness of the neighborhood, she continued along 14th Street on the Stuyvesant side, with its trees and green grass hidden under fallen leaves and emitting the tranquil odors of fall. There was a supermarket she knew on the way, and trees to hide behind if someone came. Maybe the store had a pharmacy; she couldn't remember. Maybe she could even get the medicine there. Maybe someone was just too sick and dropped it on the floor; then she would find it. She wouldn't be afraid to look in someone's bag either, or even to search the pockets. She didn't have the medicine. No one told her the Flu was coming. Eva didn't. She needed the medicine. She would disinfect the bag and her hands, and then she would take the medicine and sleep quietly for the first time in weeks.

Galina walked on, hiding behind bare poplars, silently cursing the sun that shone on New York and praying for deliverance. Here was the corner with the grocery store on it, her destination. To prepare herself, she stopped and said a quick prayer. Then, with her heart full of hope, she walked on, continuing to dream: maybe there was a cake she could take home for Max, a chocolate cake, the kind he liked. There was broken glass on the pavement and empty crates in front of the store, but she carried on, undeterred.

When Galina approached and peeked inside, she saw dirt, ripped food packages, crumpled paper and plastic, broken flower pots with their soil spilled out and plants wilted and dry, crooked dusty shelves, newspapers, and tabloids strewn on the floor. She walked in, her steps slow. The freezer's doors had been slid open; there was nothing inside. On the floor in the corner of the dairy compartment she saw several grains of buckwheat, which she carefully scooped into her palm and then hid in her pocket. A rat dashed by. There was an unpleasant odor coming from the side of the store where they used to sell rotisserie chicken.

Meticulously, Galina inspected every corner. There was nothing. Nothing at all. Still, people forgot things, oversaw them. Others were looking for food; she needed medicine. But she saw now that this store did not have a pharmacy. It was, after all, only a food store. She could try the Rite Aid across the road. There was still the uninspected area where the smell came from, and she walked up three stairs, circled around the section that used to contain fruits and vegetables, all empty, and turned to the deli department. Holding her breath, she approached the counter and peeked inside, standing on her toes.

"AGHHR!" she exclaimed, jumping back. Death was lying on the floor, in a huge white mask with empty sockets and a round screaming mouth. The body was covered by a black robe. A raw arm half-eaten by maggots and moths stuck out. *A child's arm*, Galina decided; *a boy's*. Her stomach contracted powerfully and then, a second later, contracted again when she saw a rat dart by. *Come*, she heard distinctly, a command in her own voice. She felt a forceful pull backwards that almost threw her over, back to where death lay. *Come!* She vomited into her mask and then choked on the bitterness of her own bile.

Galina ran out, stumbling, her mouth watery, saliva and vomit wetting the mask. She touched its rough fabric with her tongue and embraced a poplar's trunk with her whole body, ripping her latex gloves on the bark. She shook with a coarse tremor that, she imagined, only the tree could stop. Bark scratched her forehead. *Come to me, my sweetie!*, she heard again, the devil's whisper turning into a high-pitched howl. *Kiss the ground, repent*, she heard another voice, piercing her to the core. *The White Angel*, she whispered to herself. *The White Angel.*

She pulled her mask down and crouched on her knees to where the tree's brown roots stuck out of the wet, fragrant earth, and pressed her lips to the ground. With zealous devotion she rocked up and down, kissed her cross, pressed it into the soil, kissed it again, said a prayer.

"She's eating," a voice said behind her, and before she could turn around she felt a kick in her ribs. She rolled to her side, heavy like a sack, the cross still pressed to her lips.

"She ain't got nothing!" another voice said. A big meaningless face emerged in front of her. She squeezed her eyes shut, whispering her prayer. Someone's hands went over her body, took off her mask. The stranger coughed into her face, tiny droplets of saliva falling on her bare cheeks and on the cross she had been kissing.

"Fuck her," she heard again, not opening her eyes, not reacting. Another kick turned her over onto her belly. Her face lay close to a root. She could see the bark's intricate design, its folds and ripples. She felt no pain. Soon, all was still again, no people, no voices, just her, an elderly woman lying on the wet November ground. Galina turned her head, found her cross again. *Judgment Day,* she whispered serenely, collecting her weak and still trembling body, taking one step, then another. After several minutes she reached the garden fence, and, holding on to it, brought herself back to Stuyvesant Town, empty-handed.

29

Bill came home pale and exhausted, covered in soot, sporting a cut on his arm. He retrieved two plastic bottles filled with dark liquid from his backpack and, like a statement, thumped them on the table. Their labels were ripped off. Galina crouched in the corner, the radio murmuring in front of her. When Eva sat down next to her and leaned forward to turn up the volume, Galina recoiled, tightening her mask.

"Look, mommy! Fire!" Max yelled joyfully, and Eva, who was on the brink of a cross remark, got up. A flame surged on one of the upper floors of a neighboring house. With fright and fascination they watched sparks and pieces of broken glass tumbling down as the flame grew, licking the brick wall.

"Are they keeping away wild animals?" Max asked.

"No, buddy, they're just trying to get warm and got burned themselves," Eva explained wearily. "Let's hope no one tries that in our building."

Late that evening someone screamed in the hallway and banged on their door, asking for help. They didn't even get up; Bill just shouted "Go away!" Most likely they were looters. Galina froze and murmured something into the wall in front of her, oblivious to being observed. Then she took out her cross and fervently kissed it several times through her mask.

"Galina!" Eva said. "Who are you talking to?"

Galina turned guiltily. "I not talking."

"I heard you talking. I'm worried about you. Do you hear someone who isn't here?"

"No, no! I—just lonely, talking, thinking."

Galina was lonely. She was probably worried about her son in Russia, about her mother, and about her other son, somewhere in upstate New York. Eva was too busy surviving. She never once asked what troubled Galina, implicitly expecting gratitude for the shelter she gave her.

"Are you thinking about your children?" Eva asked. Galina gave her a blank stare.

"Children? No."

"Aren't you worried about them?"

"I don't know. I cannot change situation. I do not know where they are."

Eva let it go and leaned back, closing her eyes. Maybe that's how people survived. Out of sight, out of mind, she thought and smiled bitterly. It was time to sleep.

"Bill?" she said, getting into bed and searching for his hand in the dark. Max was already asleep between them. "Galina talks to herself all the time, have you noticed?"

"At least she stopped bathing in our disinfectant. Good night."

Galina woke up early. She'd been sleeping badly, especially since Max had relocated to his mother's bed, but there was something else that morning that bothered her, like a slowly mounting pressure. When she opened her dry, inflamed eyes to the darkness she became aware of a thread-thin voice demanding her attention. For a second she mistook it for Max, talking in his sleep. *Look for it. It's here,* she heard. She got up, seized the flashlight and tiptoed to the living room, listening to her unseen guide. It knew where the medicine was. She turned around, aiming her flashlight randomly, allowing intuition to lead her – as in the past when she'd chosen lottery numbers, hoping for a miracle. The light fell on the blue dishware cabinet. Galina had searched its drawers before, but there was still a chance. People oversee things all the time. She'd find the medicine and fall asleep like a baby.

She opened the drawers one by one. Here was the Swatch collection – she'd looked there already, even took everything out and sifted through it a couple of days ago. Unless, of course, it'd been put in there since. Empty jewelry boxes, coins. Paper, glue, scissors, Post-Its, envelopes, a screwdriver. Photo paper, photos, videotapes. Phone books.

Footsteps! Someone was coming! Galina crouched down and switched off her flashlight, holding it awkwardly against her stomach.

The White Angel was silent.

"What are you doing?" Eva asked, unpleasantly surprised.

Galina said nothing, looking at her like a guilty dog. Eva came closer and surveyed the room with her own flashlight.

"Did you eat food?" Eva continued accusingly.

Galina shook her head and sank down in a chair. Eva harshly shone the light into her face and saw that she was soundlessly weeping, her shoulders rhythmically jumping up and down.

"What were you looking for?" Eva insisted, suddenly furious. This woman ate her food, slept and shat in her house; she deserved to know.

"Anything to help," Galina said. "You are doctor. Why don't you bring me medication so I don't die when I get sick?"

"I told you, Galina, we have no medication in the hospital. I've told you a thousand times."

"That cannot be," Galina said firmly. "They say medication is in hospitals."

"Where? On the radio? They don't know shit! Come with me to work tomorrow and see for yourself."

Bill emerged wrapped in his black sable. Pulling out a chair, he sat opposite to Galina, making his face mockingly severe. "So? Misbehaving again?"

"She was going through the drawers," Eva said matter-of-factly.

"We've been through this before," Bill analyzed. "Or is it déjà-vu? Did you take food?"

"She was looking for medication."

"If we see you going through Eva's things again, you will have to leave," Bill delivered in a measured voice. He was serious now. "Do you understand that?"

Galina gave a series of short jerking nods, her face like a stone.

"Go to sleep now," Eva urged Galina with a helpless wave. She knew she wouldn't have the heart to set her out of the house. They would just have to endure one another until the end, whatever that would be.

Eva went to the bathroom, where she urinated into the stinking bowl, then closed the lid. Since the electricity had been cut off they defecated like dogs into plastic bags cut into pieces to last longer. The bags were thrown out first into the chute, then, when the chute was full, out the window – as everyone did. Luckily, there were still ample quantities of baby wipes to wipe their bottoms. Eva dipped her hands into the iodide solution, shook them vigorously, and dried them with paper towel, of which there were only two rolls left.

Galina's room was closed when Eva came out of the bathroom. She could hear Galina mumbling and shuffling her feet inside. Then the radio started in a low murmur, static breaking through here and there, and all went quiet except for the usual sounds from outside, hushed by closed windows: neighbors' hacking coughs, dogs barking, wind singing in the branches. Eva stepped forward, the parquet wood creaking under her feet. Although she couldn't understand the words from the radio, the voice delivering them was cheerful. Maybe that's how they always sounded: meaninglessly upbeat. She heard Galina's shuffling again and suddenly the door flew open into her face.

"Listen, listen!" Galina cried, unruffled by finding Eva behind her door. Excitedly she thrust the radio into Eva's arms.

Eva accepted it and sat down on the sofa, pleased that Galina sat next to her again. To save its batteries she switched off her flashlight, which landed them into total darkness. Someone screamed outside like a frightened animal, and both women leaned closer to the radio, listening intently. A nasal, brainy voice narrated with fast-paced serenity:

Unfortunately, we've encountered problems with the production of the vaccine. The scope of he Flu caused the closure of some pharmaceutical factories. So we have had to put our heads together with government officials. Our solution has been army involvement.

Dr. Lanstead, how much time do you estimate is needed to produce and distribute the vaccine to the population? This was asked in the upbeat female voice Eva had heard from behind the door.

No more than a couple weeks. The other thing to keep in mind is that when the virus goes through its hosts it becomes attenuated, or diluted. Every one of us who gets it makes it weaker by the sheer fact of our struggle – just like when you dissolve a drop of paint in a pool of water. Our observations in the hospital wards suggest that after weeks of deadly combat we're now winning the battle. Patients everywhere, from Seattle to Florida, are getting well. The real disaster is not the Flu anymore. It's the desperate situations in many of our urban areas: lacking access to clean water and food. Maybe the most important message I have is this: If you got the Flu and survived, you have nothing to fear. That's it: you've had it; you're immune. Step forward, help wherever you can. Don't hide. Go out, get food and water for your family, help a stranger on the street. You can make a difference.

Eva got up and switched on her flashlight, squinting.

"It's really true," she said, turning to Galina. "It's ending."

30

Anna refused to eat. Vladimir peered helplessly into her pale, hardened face, into her eyes with their red rims, a burning agony deaf to his words. She was mute all day again, sitting by the window and staring at the drawn curtain, at its hunter scenes printed on green fabric. Her silence made him angry, and he even shouted once, forgetting to whisper, "Speak! I am talking to you!" Olga led him away, taking him firmly by the elbow.

"I wish I didn't bring her here!"

"She saved me," Olga reminded him.

"Who knows. Maybe you'd have recovered on your own," he said hesitantly. "If only she would start talking or eating. It's like living with a mummy, it drives me insane! I do everything I can. People die every day now. I give her food and shelter. Is this what you call gratitude?"

The shouts and pleas started again, people scraping at their door, asking for food. Vladimir grew quiet, afraid to be heard.

"Please, Vladimir," someone begged. "Open up! It's Tirso!"

Tirso was an illegal Mexican who'd worked at Papa's Deli for the past five years, a short amiable guy with spiky hair. Olga and Vladimir knew his family well, his wife and three kids.

"I know you're there! Please help me! My mother is dead. My kids have nothing to eat!"

"Let's help him, just this once," Olga whispered.

"Are you insane? You let one of them in, and the whole city will come tomorrow. Now, every man for himself! I don't want to hear about it anymore!" he hissed, afraid to shout, and this hiss was more horrible than any shouting. Olga sat down to knit, persuading herself that he was right. Vladimir was drunk again, alcohol fumes filling the close room.

Anna watched, quietly, and went to her room without a word. The smell returned, and she winced, trying to fight it off. Olga silently joined her, sighing and picking up her knitting.

"Don't be mad at him," she said after what seemed a long time.

"I want to leave," Anna said suddenly, in a rasping dry voice, startling Olga. She hadn't uttered a word in two days.

"Where would you go now? You will die," Olga said, leaning toward her.

"I want to die. I can't stand it any longer."

"Please don't go."

"I can't help you any more," Anna said robotically.

"Where is my son?" Olga cried, tugging at her sleeve. "Tell me, I want to know. Can you read cards for him? Is he dead?"

"I don't know. I'll go in the morning. Maybe then I'll have peace."

"Anna!" Olga called with a surge of emotion. "Anna, we've been friends for how many years? We have to keep together to survive. You'll die out there."

"I want to die," Anna repeated placidly.

"You're mourning Ben. That's why you want to die. But I'm here. I'm your friend and I care about you. Do you think I'm not mourning? My parents are dead. I covered their bodies with sheets. I washed them and dressed them and put them into coffins. I dug the grave myself. Do you think it's easy for me to be locked up in these four walls thinking of my boy? Do you think it was easy to get well? I got well for Grisha, to be here when he returns."

"I'll leave in the morning."

At night she lit a candle and packed her belongings into a backpack she found in the closet. Into the bottom of the backpack she put some food: chocolate, protein mix, and fruit bars. Vladimir appeared silently and stood in the doorway watching her. She noticed him but didn't stop.

"What are you doing, for Christ's sake?" he asked finally, hands on his hips.

"I'm leaving tomorrow."

"I told you," Olga whispered appearing at his side.

"You're crazy!" he cried. Anna didn't reply.

"Once you leave here, you can't come back, do you understand that? Why do you think we are locked up here like three little mice? There is Flu on the streets, have you forgotten? Speak to me!"

"I know," she said and smiled for the first time.

"There's no water or food. You're going to freeze to death if the virus doesn't kill you."

"I know."

"There're gangs of hungry and desperate people outside who are going to take your food first and then kill you."

Anna shrugged her shoulders and went to the bathroom to get her toothbrush. Vladimir followed on her heels.

"I'm not opening this door for you. They're going to torture you and you're going to tell them where you got the food, and then they'll come here for us."

"I'll leave the food then," she said, unzipping her backpack.

"Don't be a fool! There is nowhere to go!"

"I still have my apartment."

"I'm not letting you out."

"It's okay, Vladimir," she said bitterly. "I promise to never come back. I give you my word."

"I told you, I'm not letting you out. You're out of your mind."

"Then, I'll scream and tell them that you have food here, lots of food!"

Vladimir retreated, desperately fuming and at a loss for words.

Anna got up quietly the next morning as the sun rose. For the first time since Ben's death she did the sun salute, silently greeting the day obscured by the curtains. It felt good. She'd gotten three hours of sleep and was glad of it. Peace waited for her outside. She just had to step out.

She put the urn into the backpack, empty now that there was no food. She heard Olga and Vladimir waking up, turning and whispering to one another. She went to the kitchen. Through the slits in the drawn curtains she could see the sunny late autumn waiting for her outside. She poured water into a cup and added five tablespoons of a protein mix she liked for its raspberry flavor. It was going to be all her food for today. She wasn't hungry but forced herself to gulp it down. Olga came in shuffling, her face full of painful worry. She held Anna's backpack in her hands.

"Are you sure?" she asked, but didn't wait for the answer that was obvious. "I put some food in there."

Anna nodded, "Thank you."

Vladimir entered without his mask on. He'd grown a long, reddish stubble that made him look old and sinister. Flatly, he said: "I wanted to bind you up with rope like they do in nut-houses but she wouldn't let me. So I guess you're on your own now." He shifted from one leg to another as if he needed to urinate.

"Olga gave me some food," Anna pointed to the backpack.

"You'll need it," he said.

"Thank you for everything."

"No, thank you. What do they say, farewell my concubine? What is it, a concubine, anyway?"

"I don't know," Anna said.

Olga gave her a long, silent embrace. She was crying.

Vladimir pulled his mask back on, cautiously unlocked the door and peered out. The stench of a decomposing body filled the hallway.

"You can still change your mind," he offered.

Anna waved and took her first step out, the green urn in the backpack under her arm. A short run downstairs and she was on the street. The fresh cold air blew on her face. It was good, almost unbearably good, to be outside. The sun had come out and hid behind heavy, low-hanging clouds. Anna looked around. The street was deserted. The iron gate to Papa's Deli was open and the windows shattered. All of the groceries were gone, not even a bottle of vinegar or detergent left on the wrecked shelves, just a film of dust that was days old. The smashed cashier lay on its side, drawers open. Here, too, she could smell death, coming from somewhere in the back, by the bathroom. Anna remembered Tirso asking for food for his kids. She didn't go in.

She saw a video store, a café, two bars, a row of gray silent houses, all of them crushed, devastated and dull on the clouded November morning, reminding her of an urban landscape from a science fiction movie she'd watched years ago. It was chilly with frost, shrinking the few puddles on the street, wind rustling the table covers inside the café. Black motionless shapes lay on the ground to the right. A stray dog, the only moving creature in her sight, approached sniffing at one of them, and Anna hurried to turn away. Excrement and garbage lay on the ground, scattered on the empty walkway, long-deserted by pedestrians. A few cars stood gloomily, their windows shattered, glass lying around them, their gas caps ajar. Anna guessed that someone must have taken their fuel to warm up or burn bodies. Ben's smell came back to her momentarily.

The air was crisp, and Anna breathed and breathed and couldn't get enough of it after the staleness of Vladimir's apartment. She had no plan and went first to where Vladimir said his car was parked. Although she didn't drive she thought she might risk it in this void of a world in which the rules of safety no longer applied. She turned into a side street lined with chestnut trees. The trees reminded her of the alley in Moscow where she used to live, of her big apartment house with a green, shaded courtyard where bed-sheets hung drying on strings tied to tree trunks. One block up she found Vladimir's car, a blue Toyota Camry. The doors were bent, the fuel gone. Still, she leaned in, the keys jingling in her pocket not necessary, and brushed aside some pieces of glass to sit down on the driver's seat. "Where now?" she asked aloud, her voice resonating in the emptiness. After a while, getting cold, she climbed out.

The wind was getting stronger. It smelled of the ocean. Drawing the scent deeply through her nostrils, she knew with certainty that that was where she wanted to go. Soon she arrived at the Bay Ridge Parkway. An ambulance siren howled in the distance. It came from the shore, where, still far away from her, lay the great volume of the ocean. When she heard a car driving by, she hid behind an abandoned fire-truck parked curbside. After it passed, she kept walking. A child cried somewhere. A dog barked. The now-familiar sound of a death wagon with its dry explosive siren sending, at regular intervals, three short shrieks into the air, howled ahead of her, heading for Steiner's Funeral Home half a block away. Anna hid from it. Two masked men dressed in bright orange suits jumped out of the refrigeration truck that read *New York Coroner* on the side and hurled corpses onto a cart. When the cart was full they rolled it up the ramp of the truck and unloaded stiff bodies that tumbled onto the metal floor with heavy thumps. The men shoved them back to make space for the others that came and came without end. A wave of nausea rising in her throat, Anna didn't wait for them to finish and walked further down the street to where the ocean lay. She felt strangely exposed, a walking anomaly among the dead and hiding.

The Shore Road was cleaner and friendlier, its benches empty. With sadness Anna recalled that there used to be many joggers here at this time of the morning. She crossed under the silent highway bridge and reached the ocean. The shoreline was full of the dead, waves tugging them back and forth like a cat playing with a dead mouse. They didn't smell, these salty bodies, now the property of the sea. The clouds hung low and grave, their round wavy bellies stretching wide and deep into the horizon above the grey rippling water. The sound of the waves comforted Anna, relieving her of the booming silence of the streets. She was still clutching her urn.

"Funny how I almost forgot about you, Ben!"

She thought of scattering his ashes toward the water, but the wind blew her way, and, remembering Ben's smell, she shuddered. Like a discus-thrower, she swung her arm and hurled the green vase, still sealed with plastic wrap, beyond the shore. She didn't hear a splash. Suddenly Ben was gone, consumed by the ocean.

"So long," she whispered, saying goodbye to the memories, to their life together and to the awful smell she hoped would never return to haunt her. She almost waited for an answer, but no answer came. Focusing on the roar of the surf, she closed her eyes. The wind stirred, burning her cheeks with its wet kisses. She shivered and turned up her collar, wrapped her scarf tighter around her neck. Her fingers felt numb in her leather gloves, and longingly she thought of her furry mittens hidden away in a drawer, on Stanton Street.

"Home!" she said out loud and started along the coast toward the north, where somewhere, far away, home awaited her.

For a long time Anna walked through the unchanging scenery of desolation. Sometimes cars passed and sirens announced that life still existed elsewhere. She ceased heeding fear and didn't hide any longer. On her way, she avoided subway stations, repelled by the smell of decomposing bodies and the sight of rats getting fat on human cadavers.

She still did not see a living soul. As hours passed by, Anna lost the feeling of her body and her movements became mechanical. Close to the end of Shore Road she took Bay Ridge Avenue and turned onto Fourth Avenue, so lively in her memory, so barren now. Anna stayed on it for a long time, passing Sunset Park and finally arriving at Greenwood Cemetery. The cemetery was full of fresh graves and lined with corpses lying on paths between tombstones, eerie in their white wrappings, fluttering in the wind. There, she discerned a faraway group of people bending over a tomb and the lonely figure of a man walking slowly among the graves and swinging his hands in the air.

When Anna glanced at her watch it was four in the afternoon. It seemed bizarre that in this ghostly city brought to its knees by the Flu time still calmly moved the hands on her watch, working even when no one looked at it any longer. Light rain began to fall, turning the pavement black. Anna's feet were tired and blistered, and, despite her quilted boots, she couldn't feel her toes. Her back ached unbearably under the weight of the backpack. She was hungry, the unfamiliar worm of appetite wriggling in her belly. And yet she was glad to endure it. It felt good just to *be* – to feel hungry, tired, and in pain again, longing for her mittens.

Around five Anna turned down a side street and hid in a black SUV where she was invisible and sheltered from the drizzling rain and winds, which were picking up. She took off her gloves and with stiff fingers unzipped the backpack, squeezing it between her knees. There were two bottles of water, a bunch of plastic cups and cookies – in fact there was all the stuff she had chosen for herself the night before. She grabbed a chocolate chip cookie and ate it so quickly that she almost missed out on the taste, and yet it was the most heavenly meal she had ever had. She gulped water straight from the bottle, then poured some into a cup and added a bit of protein mix for nutrition. She sat for a long time, content, almost happy, drunk on food. Then she dozed off. When she woke up, she was shivering. The street was pitch-dark. She got out of the car and stretched her limbs. The rain kept falling in a monotonous drone. It was seven o'clock, and she knew she wouldn't find her way home in the dark. She had to try to find an alternative shelter.

Park Slope looked like a war zone, its life and colors gone, its neon lights dark, cafés and restaurants wrecked. The houses stood like gloomy tombstones of happier times. It took Anna a long time to find Carroll Street. Her old friend Tina's house appeared dark and forbidding. Overcoming a bad premonition, Anna walked up its stairs and pressed her ear to the door, hoping for an indication of life inside. After what seemed an impossibly long time in the rain, she was rewarded. Someone talked; she heard footsteps. Anna knocked on the door frantically, disturbing the quiet of the night. The door opened. A tall man pulled her inside by the lapels.

No one will cry for me, was her only thought before a heavy blow on the head delivered her into darkness.

31

For hours Eva lay in bed in the dark, listening to the sounds outside: shouting and banging, muffled sirens of death wagons, dogs barking and wind whirling, brushing dry maple leaves against the window panes – leaves that during the day looked like big lifeless birds. She made her calculations, which divested her of her hope beat by beat, number by number. Seven dead, one discharged two days ago. Four dead, none discharged or getting better yesterday. Five dead, two getting better, or not getting worse (which could change) today. The temperature dropped and, despite her cashmere coat, Eva could not get warm. Was it hunger? Was it the end? Lying in her bed she thought of death and of her dear little boy whom she could not protect. Twice in the past week they had visitors. Thank God there was Bill to step up to the door and frighten them away.

Sometime after midnight they were awoken by banging at the door again. Bill bolted out of bed. Eva lingered behind, coaxing Max to stay in bed with a few tenderly whispered words. Max listened to her and lay down, immediately falling back asleep despite the racket. When Eva ran out, Bill was at the door, pressing his lips against the narrow space along the frame. He held a serrated kitchen knife in his fist while Galina clutched her flashlight like a weapon.

"I have a gun, motherfucker! I swear to God I'll shoot you now and then eat your tender flesh!" Bill threatened this in an awful, grinding voice, and then they all stood quietly, whispering and waiting for the footsteps to retreat.

Later, lying in bed again, Eva listened to the wind. Its sound, loud and boundless like the looters, startled her. The wind was staging moaning attacks on her desolate neighborhood, making trees creak and her heart jump and squeeze. In the early morning hours there was thunder. A blue flash of lightning lit Max's shape under the blanket, along with Eva's narrow hand, its veins running across it like rising rivers.

"It's alright," Bill spoke from the dark while the first raindrops fell on the air conditioner outside. "It's just thunder. Sleep."

"We have to gather water," she muttered. "Rainwater is safe to drink."

She got up, fetched the dusty bucket from the bathtub, wiped it clean and ran to the window. The drumming of the rain was intensifying. She pushed the window open and stuck out her arm. "Rain!" she cried excitedly. The bucket did not fit through the widow guards, and Eva shouted, running around wild, seized by trembling joy, "Rain! Rain! Fetch the glasses!"

Eva, Bill and Galina gathered by the window, their flashlights shining upwards and reflecting in the dark glass and back on their excited faces. Glasses, cups, mugs, and vases were brought in, feet running back and forth to the kitchen for more containers, arms thrust out into the rain to arrange receptacles on the air conditioner. Later, they stood shoulder to shoulder, breathing in the moist fragrant air, raindrops on their cheeks, on their hair, their arms numb, their vessels filling up and getting heavier. The glasses were brought in, poured into the yellow bucket, then placed outside again. Bill stuck out an umbrella, opened it, turned it upside down. Just when the rain started filling it up, a strong gust of wind blew the umbrella against the wall's brick corner, Bill desperately squeezing its pole with both hands, his arms bruising against the guards. They watched the spires bend, and turn upwards, Bill yelling and cursing all the way. The wind changed direction, and Bill let the umbrella go, spilling the water and smashing two glasses on the air-conditioner. The umbrella whirled down like a wounded duck, its rainbow colors disappearing in the crowns of the trees, where their weak flashlights no longer reached.

The rich heavy rain continued all through the night, the bucket and their biggest pots and pans steadily filling up. Eva left the task to her companions. The drumming outside calmed her. She lay down by Max's warm body and gratefully fell into a deep, untroubled sleep.

In the morning, the bucket and pots and pans were full, the rain stopped. The storm had broken several branches off the trees but also brought warmer weather. Eva and Bill opened the apartment's windows wide, letting in the fresh scented air, its warmth and mollifying humidity.

Galina was drenched and looked feverish and excited. Bill placed the yellow bucket in the middle of the dining table. Max was still asleep. He slept a lot nowadays, deprived of light and stimulation. They sat around the table, serving the water with a ladle unused since the start of the Flu, drinking and talking about the rain, the looters, and the fires in hushed voices.

Galina said that visitors came during the days as well, when Eva was at work; Eva listened to the details of their attempts to break in. Bill nonchalantly hummed to himself, savoring his water and chewing a piece of dry sausage leftover from his successful escapade ten days earlier.

"If Bill not here, they break in. We need big metal thing to lock door," Galina was saying.

"A bolt?"

"A bolt," Galina nodded.

"If someone comes when I am away," Bill advised, spitting out the salami's skin, "take a drill out of the closet. It operates on batteries, and it's an awesome weapon. As you know from horror movies."

"Horror movies," Galina repeated blankly.

"They know there's a child here," Eva said and fell silent, unsure of what exactly she wanted to say, her breath seized by the shadow of horror that could be waiting behind the door at any time. Max woke up, came out in his snowsuit looking like an angel, his eyes still dreamy, his movements sluggish and clumsy.

"Hi buddy!" Bill said. "You missed the rain. It rained all night. Want some rainwater? It's delicious. Here," he gave Max some water in the cup. Max drank quietly.

"Do you want some juice, Max?" Eva asked.

"No, thank you!" Galina answered in a loud and strange voice, making both Eva and Bill glance at her in surprise.

"When it rains, all snakes and alligators come out!" Max said.

He was gone into his room, carrying a yellow truck loaded with plastic reptiles; then he went back into the bedroom, where, in the corner, he gathered more and more of his toys moved from the room now occupied by Galina.

"Mommy, I pooped!" Eva heard him yell a minute later. She rushed to his potty and cleaned his bottom with wet wipes, then pulled up his snowsuit and zipped it to his chin. It had yellow circles in the bottom and around the legs from dried urine.

"My hands are freezing," he complained. He was pale and listless in a fidgety, whiny way. His hair stuck out funnily from his blue knitted hat. He was so small, so small and vulnerable. Eva wanted to kiss him. Instead, she straightened and said lovingly but firmly, "We have to wash our hands now," knowing she had to fight with him to get it done.

"I don't want to!" Max cried. "This water's too cold! And it's dirty!"

"It's not dirty. It's yellow because of iodide. Iodide kills infection," Eva explained patiently.

"Someone peed into it."

"Did you?" she asked, laughing.

"Galina said I should pee into a cup and drink it."

"What? When?" Eva asked, stepping back with a frown.

"Yesterday. She says people do it all the time."

"Did you?"

"No. It's disgusting! I put it there," he gestured at the basin with the iodide solution.

"Okay, Max. Now, wash your hands."

"But I don't want to!!"

Eva yelled at him, losing her temper, until he asked, clutching at her thighs,

"Mommy, you don't love me anymore?"

They cried together and he allowed his hands to be washed.

32

By the time Greg approached the marina he was exhausted. Water splashed under his feet as he wheeled his bicycle along on the pier's planks, careful not to stumble. Dark masts squeaked around him in the wind. The ocean lay around him, vast and terrible and greedy. Boats like black bodies rocked on the rough water, banging against the docks. Greg hadn't expected to find so many boats unclaimed. *If I had a boat*, he thought wistfully, *I'd have sailed away from here days ago.*

He chose a graceful sailboat with two high masts. Not too small, not too big (*Who am I,* Greg smiled to himself grimly, *Goldilocks?*), it was maybe thirty feet long, just cozy enough to curl up in for the night. But as he hoisted his precious bicycle aboard, he was overcome by doubts. Surely the deck would be too cold and windy without a sleeping bag? He tried the door to the cabin and gratefully found it unlocked. Indoors, he lit his dwindling candle, cupping its flame with his palm. He stood in a tiny kitchen. Items lay on the floor in disarray: toilet paper rolls, towels, and a plastic bottle with black peppercorns rattling inside. The cabinets stood empty, their doors swaying and groaning to the rocking movements of the boat. Greg descended a short flight of stairs to enter the sleeping cabin, which looked surprisingly neat.

He stabilized his candle on the steely table screwed to the wall. There was a stack of sailing magazines in a basket under the table and a simple white lamp on the wall. He tried the switch. It didn't work. The beds were made. Blankets lay on the floor. He lifted them, shivering in anticipation of rest and warmth, and put them on the little couch to his right while he arranged pillows and sheets he found in a cubby under the bed. Then he locked the door with a simple push-in lock that would deter no self-respecting burglar, took off his shoes, and lay back. Heaven. The day had been a success after all, he decided, adjusting his head on his pillows. The boat's rocking and squeaking along with the sounds of waves splashing on the boat's hull emptied his mind and relaxed his body. He fell asleep like a baby, smiling, his mouth slightly open.

He dreamed of the Santa Monica Aquarium, where he hoped one day to take Max. He and his son were admiring a huge octopus that looked more like a giant squid. It was a special day, the day of a rare octopus-wrestling competition, and to Max's delight Greg's number was drawn. A massive crowd materialized to hiss and whistle him on. Suddenly he was in an underwater ring, terribly alone, squinting at projector-lamps shining blindingly into his face. The public's shouting became unbearably loud. The octopus slithered toward him. Confusingly, someone began to shout, *Hit him! Hit him!* and through the water Greg felt a burning blow to his arm, and, shrieking in pain, was pulled from his bed ...

33

The sun came out. Bill, tousled and looking grey, played with Max at catching sunbeams in a mirror. Eva sat with a cup of rainwater, chewing crackers. Galina came out of the kitchen and leaned against the doorframe, watching Eva intently. Eva turned to her, swallowed.

"Did you give Max urine to drink?" she asked, anger rising to her throat.

Galina nodded.

"What on earth do you imagine you're doing? This is my son! *My* son! You are never, ever to do it again! Do you get that?" Eva got up from her chair. "Why did you do it? Why?" she took a step toward Galina. She would throw her out. She would. It was on the tip of her tongue.

"They say on the radio. They say it is good. Urinotherapy. It give you strength with infection," Galina muttered back with a lost expression.

"You are never, *never* to tell my son to drink urine!" Eva yelled. "Do you hear me? You're crazy! I tolerate a lot. You don't fill the buckets, I swallow it. You go through my things, I swallow it. But this I will not tolerate!" Eva hit the table, breaking crackers.

"I will not, I will not, I am sorry."

Eva sat down, her back to Galina, picked up the cracker pieces and stuffed them into her mouth, then drank some more of the water, forcing it down. *I have to eat,* she thought, *I have to eat no matter what.* Galina continued to stand behind her. Eva felt her burning gaze on her back. "What is it?" Eva asked, not turning around. Galina approached, her hands together, fingers interlocked.

"I have to talk to you alone," Galina whispered.

They walked to the bedroom together, Eva sensing Galina's tension, and sat down by the desk, right behind the dresser where Tamiflu was hidden in the third drawer, among Eva's underwear. She had checked on it yesterday. It was still there. Instinctively, Eva moved her chair so it would obscure the dresser from Galina's view.

"I'm listening," Eva said through an unwitting quickening of her heart, striving to keep calm.

Galina leaned forward, her eyes big above the green of the mask.

"Pomegranate juice," Galina said significantly.

"What about it?"

"I tasted it. Did you taste it?"

"No," Eva shook her head. "What's wrong with it?"

"I think he add blood to it," Galina whispered. "Wait! I bring it to you," she cried, rushing out.

Eva waited helplessly, considering her options. She was tired, so tired. She listened to Max laughing in the living room, chasing sunbeams. His joy distracted her for a second. Then she sighed, just like her mother did, the same deep, heaving sound escaping her lungs.

Galina returned, sat on the edge of a chair and placed a plastic cup half-filled with dark-red fluid in front of her.

"You taste it and tell me."

Eva picked up the cup and drank from it. The juice was sweet and sour and deliciously refreshing. She put the cup back on the table.

"You think there's blood in this juice, Galina?"

"You felt it too?" Galina asked excitedly.

"Was the seal on the juice bottle broken when you opened it?"

"No, but he got it in, I don't know how."

"Who is he?"

"Your friend."

"Bill?"

"He drink people blood. He get food from people. He get juice, and you see, juice is red like blood. You hear him talking at the door at night? He is not pretend. He kill people. People eat people. They say on the radio."

Eva looked into Galina's eyes, deeper and deeper, their glances locking in insanity. She could shout and tell her she was crazy. It wouldn't help. She thought of the cold and night and of poor Ska. For the second time in one morning she considered throwing Galina out.

"I think this juice is fine," Eva spoke evenly. "Do you think you could be mistaken, Galina?"

"You think it's fine to drink? You give it to Max?"

"I certainly will. There's no blood in this juice."

"I think I am maybe crazy, sometimes," Galina said. "You think he is good man?"

"I am sure he's a good man," Eva said, relief tearing her voice.

Galina nodded, her head lowered, obscuring her expression.

"How's your sleep?"

"No good," Galina answered shaking her head. "No sleep."

"I can't sleep either," Eva shared with a little smile.

"You afraid of him," Galina stated quietly, chilling Eva's blood.

"No, Galina, I'm not!" she said. "I have to get ready for work now."

Galina smiled and walked out in her earthly graceful gait.

Eva swallowed. There was a bitter taste in her mouth, a taste of fear, she thought. In the living room Bill was showing Max how two mirrors reflecting each other made a never-ending corridor.

"Mommy, look, if a bug gets into the mirror, it can go all the way to Paris," Max cried proudly. "Look! Look here!"

Eva bent to him, looked in the mirror and kissed his hair. "That's really cool, Max," she said. "I used to do it too when I was a little girl."

Her reflection was ghastly, thin, the cheekbones sculpting a dark shadow beneath them. Automatically, she brushed back her hair and made a beautiful face, lifting her chin.

"You have a beautiful mommy," Bill said kindly, and Eva touched his shoulder with gratitude. It's been a long time since they exchanged any words of this kind. She laughed at herself.

"Vanity is not curable," she said.

"If we turn into bugs we can go to the island. It's called S-Town," Max said.

"What's an S-Town? Stuyvesant Town?"

"S-Town," Max asserted stubbornly. "I'll show you."

He went to his room, tramping his boots.

"Listen," Eva said quietly so Max wouldn't hear. "Galina thinks you added blood to the juice."

Bill nodded and Eva continued.

"I'm going to get an antipsychotic from the hospital. I'll tell her it's for the Flu. I can't trust her with Max anymore. You have to keep an eye on both of them. Will you?"

"Let her go," Bill said, his voice rusty and irritated. He cleared his throat. Eva put a finger to her mouth, and he whispered urgently, "Let her go!"

"I can't. She's not a cat."

"Okay," he said, placing the mirror on the table, reflective surface down. "But if she's dead when you come back it'll be because I strangled her."

Max returned with a piece of play-dough cracked on the outside.

"Mommy," he said. "I'm thirsty."

Their stores of apple juice had lasted only two weeks. Galina kept diluting it with glucose solution until he refused to touch it.

"There's the pomegranate juice I got yesterday," Bill said coldly, eying Galina, who stood at the kitchen door. "Why don't you give it to him?"

"I offer," Galina answered firmly. "If he don't drink, he not thirsty."

"Let's open it! It's a great antioxidant," Eva explained enthusiastically, as if Max knew this word. She poured some into an orange paper cup with a T-Rex painted on it, a leftover from last year's birthday party. *Max's fourth birthday is in a month*, Eva thought suddenly, her throat tight.

"I want my sippy cup!" Max cried, stomping his foot on the floor.

Eva squatted in front of him. "Max! Look at me, Max!"

He hit her shoulder with his open palm, angry tears running down his face.

"Max," she said quietly, holding his arms. "As soon as we can wash your sippy cup you'll get it. Okay? Now, let's pretend it's a sippy cup. It's even got a T-Rex on it, have you noticed?"

Crabbily, he stole a glance at the cup.

"Okay," he agreed uncertainly, accepting the drink. With tenderness she watched how eagerly he emptied it out.

"Yuck!" he said, wrinkling his nose. Then: "Can I have some more?"

Eva glanced around. Galina had hidden in Max's room.

"I have to go, Max," Eva whispered tenderly, taking his hands into hers. "Promise to listen to Bill. Promise?"

He nodded. "Mommy! Is that old woman still there?"

"What old woman?"

"On the bench?"

"She is. Why?"

"Is she sleeping on the bench?"

"She is, pumpkin."

"I don't want to go outside. I am afraid of her."

The hospital operated on an emergency generator, and had running water, which, because of the fear of spilled sewages, they boiled in huge tin tanks or cured with bleach. During the first few days of power failure the whole hospital had been light and warm, but this changed after about a week, leaving only the ER and critical care units supplied with heat and electricity. The wards were cold. The staff kept patients warm with blankets, sweaters and unused coats brought from their own homes.

Only half of Eva's ward was occupied now; its dark hallways lit with tiny blue emergency lights stood empty and every patient had a proper bed. They were seeing more recoveries, even Eva had to admit this. Dr. Lanstead was right. From Seattle to Florida, he said. How did he know, she wondered? *From Seattle to Florida*, she whispered, hanging IVs and disinfecting her hands and counting pulses. Five of her patients, virtually unresponsive yesterday, were getting better. It gave her hope – still uncertain and flickering, but deserving of its name.

Food was hard to procure, and that day, as on all days when the truck bearing hospital supplies did not come, Eva had to steal meager portions from the bedsides of dead patients and rely on pity from the nurses in charge of meal distribution. During her lunch break she went through disposed-of food, looking for pieces still wrapped in plastic, or scraps that could be disinfected. She found a couple of crackers, a piece of plastic-wrapped toast, two orange juices and an old egg with a cracked shell, which in the end she discarded after agonizing hesitation. The catch was not bad but she felt no joy. Something was wrong with her legs. She felt heavy, unbearably heavy. She wanted to sleep, to disappear into the row of Max's mirrors, into S-Town.

Toward the end of the day, she got some Zyprexa for Galina out of the cast-off medication box. The bottle still bore the name of the person it had originally been prescribed for, a Jeremy Rosen. Where was Jeremy Rosen now? Where was

Greg? Where was Eva's mother?

It's Thanksgiving today, Eva remembered abruptly. This made her sad.

The sun had set and the city drowned in menacing darkness. The warm wind continued. Eva could hear its howls as it circled around the tall and lonely hospital building. When she came out, she unbuttoned her coat and felt lighter under the massage of the powerful airstream. The clouds were low and graceful, with dark rims around them against the violet sky, floating in fast motion like in a scene from *Kooyanisquatsi*. Eva thought again of the vaccine and hopeful statistics. Maybe they would survive. It had been nearly a month, and they were still alive, all of them. She wondered what the world would look like when it was over, and sighed from all the warmth and hope and trembling in the air, wishing she could sit on one of the benches and watch the squirrels chase one another, unaware of death.

On the staircase in her building Eva's fatigue returned. Almost upstairs, she stumbled and dropped her flashlight. It rolled down with loud, echoing bangs, causing her to freeze in fear. Looters could appear any time, steal her keys and force their way into her apartment. For a while Eva listened, holding on to the wall. She heard the wind and her own breath, then also mice squealing and rustling in the chute, growing plentiful on human detritus.

I'll go in, she decided, resuming her climb, *and I'll change, and I'll go to bed, right away, now...* Throwing around a last glance, Eva took out her key.

34

Bill opened the door for her, his face grim. Something was wrong.

"Galina," he said.

Eva was heavy, so heavy. She couldn't deal with this and she had to deal with it.

"What's wrong with her?"

"She's coughing blood. I told her to stay in Max's room and use his potty if she needs to. At this point I don't think she can get up."

"Where's Max?"

"Sleeping in our room."

"Why is he sleeping so early? Is he sick too?" Eva cried, jumping up.

"He's okay. He didn't have a nap," Bill explained, watching her as she strode to the bedroom. On her way she passed Max's room. The door was closed.

"Wait, you have to disinfect first," Bill called to her.

Eva obeyed, retreating to the bathroom and going through her ritual of change. She packed her work clothes into the plastic bag, swiped it with disinfectant, and washed her hands in a freezing iodide solution. Then she pulled on her home clothes, a t-shirt and blue pants she used to wear to the gym, a sweater, and a Patagonia jacket. Turning the doorknob with her cold, yellow-stained fingers, she rushed into her bedroom. It was dark, and she ran the flashlight twice over the bed surface before she saw Max's round cheek sticking out from behind a pillow. Eva pressed her lips to his forehead. His breath was even. She kissed him over and over, and he sleepily pushed her away, then embraced her neck.

"My love," she said. "My little boy."

"Mommy, is Galina still sick?" he asked, opening his eyes. Eva nodded.

"Is she going to die? I don't want her to die. I love her."

"No, she'll be okay, Max."

"Why?"

"Because I'm a doctor, and I'm going to treat her."

"Are you going to stick her with a needle?"

"I don't think so."

"You're good, mommy," Max said. "Don't leave."

"I have to go treat Galina."

"I'll treat her too."

"You can't go. You're not a doctor. Only doctors can go in. Otherwise you might get sick."

Bill walked in, closed the door behind him and leaned on the door.

"Daddy!" Max called excitedly, sitting up in bed. "Mommy is going to make Galina live!"

"I know," Bill said. "Your mommy is great."

"Go treat her, mommy!" Max cried and turned to Bill. "Will you build a train with me?"

"Okay. I can build a very fast train!" Bill's muffled voice responded with sincere enthusiasm, giving Eva the courage to make two steps forward and open the door to Galina's room, a bottle of disinfectant and a First Aid bag tucked under her arm and a stethoscope around her neck.

Inside, Max's old room smelled of death. Galina breathed noisily. Kneeling next to her Eva shone her light on Galina's face, struggling to interpret its color. The flashlight offered too much contrast, and Eva readjusted it, turning the head to de-focus the beam.

"Hi!" said Galina with raspy cheerfulness. "I am not sick. I healthy in the morning."

"I'll take your temperature."

"Oh, no, I am fine."

Galina was burning hot, and even without the stethoscope Eva could hear fluid in her breath.

"You're not fine," Eva replied softly. "You're sick."

Galina propped herself on her elbow, trembling with the effort.

"I go. I go now."

"You need care. You can't go anywhere."

"I am fine. It is rain. I can go. I make Max sick. I am grateful. Thank you. I go now," she said, each short sentence making her gape for air.

Maybe it wasn't the Flu. Eva put the stethoscope on Galina's hot back. Her lungs were thick with fluid, like porous sponges. Eva kept listening in, hoping to hear a pattern different from what she had been hearing at the hospital for the past four weeks. Bad news must have reflected on her face because when she removed the stethoscope Galina asked, "Flu?"

Eva nodded. Galina coughed, and Eva waited patiently until the attack subsided. Galina's crumpled napkin was stained with pink foam.

"I don't want to die," Galina mouthed up to the ceiling.

Eva knew that soon she would not be able to speak, and that reason would mercifully abandon her. Her body would keep dying for a day, maybe two, until it was all over. Then, Bill would wrap her into a sheet and carry her down on his shoulders and leave her to be picked up by a death wagon. Her body would decompose quickly if the weather stayed warm. No chance for her sons to see her again.

"I'll be back," Eva said, reassuringly patting Galina's hand.

"Help me."

Eva disinfected, put her instruments aside, and sat down on a couch in the living room, her head in her hands. Maybe she was catching it too. Why else were her feet so heavy? There was no way to get Galina to the hospital. Maybe she should just die. There would be no more exposure, no more insanity. She could ask Bill to carry her out right now. Eva got up and walked to the bedroom. Bill's voice was reading *Hansel and Gretel*. A father sends his children away so wolves will eat them. Why would a tale so macabre be read to children for generations? Eva stood behind the door for a while, listening, shifting her heavy legs. When the children had found the candy house, she walked back to the living room, overwhelmed by pity and helplessness.

She had Tamiflu. A pack of children's powder for Max and a pack containing fourteen capsules – a weeklong dosage for one adult – for herself. Now, with Galina down with the Flu, the chance of them getting sick, despite all precautions, was very high. She couldn't share her dose. Yet she had to share it. Eva knew what Bill would say: *Let Galina go.* She wished she had someone whom she could turn to for advice. Suddenly it seemed that the only person who could help her was Max. Only he, with his innocence and simple child's wisdom, could tell her what to do. She strode back to the bedroom and opened the door.

The flashlight shone into the ceiling, lighting up the scene of Max lying quietly on Bill's belly, Bill's hands around his back.

"I can find a way out of the forest!" Max said. "Because I'm very smart."

"I need your help, Max. Listen carefully," Eva said calmly, aware of Bill's intent gaze. "If you had just one magic potion, just one!" she raised one finger.

"One," he repeated.

"Yes, just one potion that might cure you of the Flu, would you share it with Galina or keep it all for yourself in case you got sick too?"

Looking at Max Eva could see that he didn't follow.

"Would you risk giving away some of your magic cure to Galina and maybe save her?"

"Don't give it to her!" Bill cried forcefully into her face. She could feel his breath on her ear. "Don't!"

"Max? Max, what would you do?" Eva continued desperately, gesturing Bill to step away.

Max pulled at the blanket with both hands and yelled angrily, "But I don't want to die!"

The next moment his anger left him, and he collapsed on the bed, his little body shuddering with tears. Eva put her arm around him, holding him tight. "You won't die! You won't! It was just a stupid question! I promise!" Bill stood nearby, shaking his head reproachfully.

Max embraced Eva and they sat still for a while, rocking. What had she been thinking? She used to rock him like this when he was a baby, pressing him to her body until, pacified, he would fall asleep ... How could she have been so careless with her words?

"My baby, my little pumpkin, my sweet little boy," she murmured. "I'm so sorry. You're so little, I completely forgot. It was just a stupid thing I said. I love you so much." Max made small cat-like sounds, clutching her tight. Bill sat next to Eva.

"It's growing long," he said, tenderly running his hand through her hair. "And you've got white hairs on your temples. They're new."

Eva nodded.

"You know, I don't have it either," he said. "Tamiflu. I don't have it."

"I'm going to give her at least one of my pills," Eva said tiredly.

Bill moved away, his face unreadable.

"Well what do you want me to do?" she cried desperately. "Watch her die? What can I do?"

"Let her drink urine!"

Eva turned away.

"You don't understand!" he said.

"No, *you* don't understand!" she yelled, and Max joined her, making a face and roaring at Bill, shouting nonsense objections. Bill waved his hands, calling them both to quiet down.

"Tamiflu is excreted in urine unchanged," he said softly. Max was still shouting and Bill had to repeat himself. "Just one pill, as you said. One pill isn't going to cure anyone if it's allowed to pass through the system just once. But if she takes it and then drinks her own urine ..."

Eva continued to look at him blankly.

"Read the connotation."

Eva opened her dresser drawer and took out the medication, which was still in the pharmacy's paper bag, and slowly unwrapped it. Bill stood over her. Max whined for attention, but they ignored him. Paper rustled under Eva's fingers. *Over ninety percent of Tamiflu is excreted in the urine*, it said. There was no mention of unchanged. Bill put his hand on Eva's shoulder.

"Why're you crying?" he asked.

Eva could say nothing.

"Am I a genius or am I a genius?" he asked.

So Galina had a chance after all. Eva took out a pill. It was a long capsule, half white, half yellow. Back in Galina's room, Eva approached her brightly.

"Ready to fight?" she asked, just like Firbas would have done.

Galina stared. Breathing harshly, she swallowed down Eva's sacrifice and lay back on her pillow to sleep. Just like she dreamed all these weeks.

35

Anna woke up. It was still pitch-black and she assumed morning was yet to come. She moved her legs and her arms cautiously; stiff as they were, they seemed to be unbroken. She ran her fingers over her forehead. There was blood stuck in her hair. Her head throbbed violently, but she was able to gather herself and crawl to the entrance of a room nearby.

"Hello!" There was no answer. Wind through the broken window was flapping the blinds. Feeling around with her hands, she grabbed the leg of a chair in front of her and slowly pulled herself up. She was in a kitchen. She rested her head on the table, enduring pain and nausea that periodically made her retch and, shivering in the draught, waited for morning.

The night was long. In time, agonizing from pain and cold, her nausea unbearable, Anna forced herself to look for a proper place to lie down. It was still dark. She remembered that the year was moving toward the solstice – "hell's potluck," Ben used to call it. She rose and proceeded along the hallway, holding on to the wall. Her fingers felt the glassy cold of a mirror and, sweeping through dust, toppled something that might have been a framed photo. She remembered her friend's large fleshy face, and her sweet twin daughters, always dressed the same. Where were they now? Anna stopped, her stomach rising to her throat. A few steps further she stumbled over a threshold, got on her knees and crawled, groping around. She found a bed just as she was about to pass out. Something hard was on it; Anna desperately pulled on the sheet. A body fell toward her. Anna leaned back to avoid contact. Inch by inch she crawled onto the bed from the other side, seizing the blankets and wrapping herself tight. There she lay like a caterpillar until she drifted into a deep black sleep.

It was light when Anna awoke. Her first thought was of the corpse lying next to her, and she drew air into her nostrils but couldn't smell it. Her headache had abated somewhat, and, slowly, she propped herself up. It was a man's body, big boots protruding from the sheets, dark hair on a massive head. Anna put her feet down, taking care not to move too briskly and upset her healing head, and kneeled next to her friend's husband. "Rob! What happened, my dear?" she mumbled, gazing at his yellow skin. A drop of blood at his mouth was all she could see, and the terrible pallor of death. She removed the sheet that covered him. "Oh dear! Where are Tina and the girls?"

She went searching. The first floor was empty. There was a bicycle in the hallway. Her backpack was gone, as she expected it would be. "I'll manage," she mumbled, climbing the stairs. The upper floor was flooded with sun and also completely empty. No Tina, no girls, no death. Things on the table were untouched. There was a photo of the whole family on vacation: Rob, robust and smiling; the girls giggling, entwining their thin, tanned arms; Tina embracing them all. Impulsively, Anna flung the closet open. If they had left, the closet would be empty. Clothes hung there quietly, withholding answers.

She was hungry. In the kitchen she found rice in one of the cabinets and emitted a joyful cry. Why didn't the boys take it, she wondered. It was simple, of course. No water. No gas. Or is there gas? No, no gas. Of course not. But she could chew the rice. She put a handful in her mouth, hard white stones sucking saliva from her tongue and too tough to break. She packed the rice into a plastic bag she found under the sink, still grinding a couple of grains. She was thirsty, but there was no water. She opened more drawers.

Medication bottles were there, and she took four tablets of Motrin, pocketing the rest along with blood pressure pills and Imodium for stomach discomfort. Who knows, maybe someone down the road will need them? She found chewing gum and chomped it vigorously, enjoying the sweet flow of saliva. Behind the refrigerator, in the grime, were two sachets of sugar. She ripped them, careful not to spill a crystal, and sucked the contents immediately. Coffee beans had been left in the freezer and she chewed up a couple of them too, the taste of sugar still in her mouth. In the hall she found mittens and a scarf that she wrapped around her neck and shoulders. She found some stale rusty water in the toilet bowl and drank it with pleasure. She was still too sick for the road, and, after weighing hunger against headache, decided to stay another day. As she lay in bed with Rob at her side like a scary wax puppet, she remembered that it was her birthday. The thought left her unmoved. She exerted herself as little as possible, mainly staying in bed to keep warm, drifting in and out of sleep.

The next morning Anna was still lightheaded but her headache was better. The sky remained clear and she watched the sunrise greet her with a purple canvas of hope. In one of the closets she found a ladybug backpack that belonged to one of Tina's girls. She loosened the straps to fit her shoulders and unzipped it. Oh, wonder, a crumbled cookie in the side pocket! Anna ate it avidly, then filled the backpack with rice, coffee, and medicine. "Bye, Rob," she whispered, glancing at him one last time. There was a bicycle in the breezeway and she wheeled this out with her.

Anna felt safer with a bike; she would at least have a chance if someone were to chase her. Ten minutes into her ride, she noticed a shadow and heard footsteps in her direction. She quickened her pace, desperately pedaling away. Wheezing from the effort, her heart fluttering in her ears, she became queasy, and, barely able to squeeze the brakes, she fainted, trapping one leg under a wheel.

Returning to consciousness Anna saw a woman's face above her. Her eyes were kind above her mask. Warm steady hands helped her up. She saw a red cross on the woman's arm.

"I'm not going to hurt you," the woman said.

Anna sobbed, abandoning herself to the woman's care.

"I'm thirsty," Anna said. "Give me water!"

She was led to a big building housing a makeshift hospital, into a room on the second floor where a group of medical workers sat around a gas stove talking. Someone fastened a mask on her face. She drank hot sweet tea from a thermos and was given bread, which she chewed slowly, following the directions of the kind woman. Then she cried again in bittersweet sobs rising from her belly like waves, unable to stop.

"So warm," she whispered.

The woman brought in a doctor. He shone a light into Anna's eyes, inspected her head, listened to her lungs and her heart and asked her whether she had lost feeling anywhere in her body.

"Healthy!" he pronounced at last, his dark eyes sparkling with joy. "The first healthy patient in ages. You'll be up in no time," he continued. "It's probably just a concussion and dehydration. Where do you live?"

Anna told him her old address.

"Ah!" he said cheerfully. "We're neighbors! I'll give you a lift in the ambulance this evening?"

Anna thanked Dr. Khanna and stayed in the stove-warmed room until night fell, sitting by the fire and listening to the healthcare workers. Although medical supplies were generally low, the storied vaccine had finally reached New York. The epidemic was in decline. Rumor was that Con Edison was going to start supplying power again, and city officials appeared more organized in their efforts to bring in food and water.

In the ambulance, on the way into Manhattan, the doctor was quiet.

"You must be very tired," Anna said timidly.

"Exhausted. Do you have anyone at home?"

"No, my husband died. Of a stroke," she rushed to add. "And you?"

"My wife died two weeks ago, overnight."

"My name's Permeet," Dr. Khanna said.

Anna nodded, saying nothing. He already knew her name.

"You should help us, you know. Volunteer at the hospital. Do you have any medical experience?"

"I used to be a healer."

"That's it then," Permeet said, laughing softly. "The job's yours. By the way: It's late and dark. Why don't you stay with me tonight and in the morning we'll go to work? I'll take you to your apartment at lunchtime, to make sure it's safe."

Anna agreed. Permeet asked the ambulance driver to drop them off at the corner. They found their way up the stairs of his building with a flashlight, and in the apartment he lit a candle.

"I hope you don't mind," he said then, his voice deepening slightly. "I only have one bed."

Anna said nothing. She felt nothing. When they had lain together for a few minutes, without touching, Permeet moved closer, and embraced her shoulders. How old was he, Anna wondered. Thirty-five, at most? She felt his erection. She helped him unbutton her pants. When he came he cried "Mama!" and then, quietly, remorsefully, "I'm sorry. Thank you." Anna embraced him silently.

36

Greg screamed, shielding himself from the blows.

"Stop it, you idiot! I know him!"

Greg opened his eyes. Three faces were bent over him. Suffocating from the pain in his arm and shoulder, he groaned.

"It's okay, relax," the lips said quietly. He saw thick looming eyebrows. Greg knew the owner of those eyebrows, but he couldn't remember his name. A second later, when he shut his eyes again, it came to him. The nice man, the gay man … from the party, Halloween. *Tony*. That was it. Through an ache he could barely endure Greg listened to the argument above him.

"Let's throw him overboard."

"Don't be ridiculous. I know him!"

"We'll give him a life jacket to satisfy your scruples, it's not far to shore."

A burly, dark-skinned man took Greg by the lapels. Greg stared at him helplessly.

"Where's the food?" the man demanded.

Greg shook his head, "I don't know."

"We have to get rid of him!" the man cried then. "He may be sick!"

"Then it's too late. Anyway I told you, I know him. It's OK."

"What's his name?"

"Greg."

"Greg what?"

"Greg Spassky. You know the radio hit, how does it go …? *Hm, hm, hm-hm...*"

The burly man searched Greg's pockets and was annoyed to find Greg's wallet with the driving license intact. "Greg

Spassky, born December 4th, 1969. New York driving license," he said.

Greg summoned a moan. "I think you broke my arm …" He'd read somewhere that when a limb breaks one feels a snapping sensation in the bone. He didn't think he'd felt that, but still, the pain was agonizing. Tony and the mean guy left him alone and retreated back upstairs. Greg was grateful, free to moan and cry. The keel grated underneath the boat while the boat rocked back and forth over the rough sea. Greg propped himself against a wall. He looked through a black window, listening to waves crushing against the hull. It was still night. He knew he wouldn't be able to swim, even with a life jacket.

Tony returned.

"How's your arm?" he asked.

"It hurts."

"Let me see." Tony straightened and rotated it over Greg's loud cries.

"I think you'll be fine. Take this. It's Ibuprofen; it will help you a bit with the pain. Drink some more, go on. Okay, that's good. Now tell me, do you feel sick?"

"No."

"Take this too. It's Tamiflu. Have you been exposed?"

"No," Greg lied.

Tony watched him intently. "You know, you screamed like hell."

Greg winced, "Well, it hurt."

"No, you screamed in your sleep. Were you having a nightmare?"

"I have sleep terrors sometimes. Please don't throw me overboard. I can't swim."

Tony shook his head. "Did you know it was my boat?"

"No," Greg said. "I had no idea. I was just looking for a place to sleep."

The pain slowly subsided, but only when Greg didn't move

his arm. The young burly man and a woman came down and observed him from a distance, their faces masked.

"Let me introduce you," Tony said brightly. "This is my son Brian. And this is his wife, Gloria."

Greg and the couple exchanged short nods.

Greg's arm was placed in a makeshift sling. He was fed, given a sleeping pill, and allowed to rest. When he woke up, the sailboat had docked and generous bright light shone into the cabin.

37

In the morning Anna got up at sunrise. Permeet was still sleeping, his face young and innocent. She tiptoed out. She used the bedpan as directed, detecting the smell of his sperm, and then awkwardly poured her urine out, spilling a little on the windowsill. She drank a can of Red Bull and ate three madeleine cookies that she found in the kitchen. Feeling full and peaceful, she looked around the apartment. The living room was spacious and held almost no furniture: a white loveseat with a low round back, a giant plasma TV, a library consisting of overlapping bookcases that could be rolled along to reveal the row behind, a low oval glass table and several boxes scattered on the rug. A framed picture of a smiling woman in a sari hung on the wall. *His mother,* she thought.

Where was home, now so close by? Anna went to the window, hoping to catch a glimpse of a street name. The sky was clouded, the street empty. A dead cat lay in the middle of the road. Second Avenue, she read, her heart fluttering with recognition. Yes, of course, she knew this place! Nearby was a Russian café with an outside terrace painted green; she had been there with Olga and Vladimir once. Moving to her right for a better glimpse, she discovered a half-open box on the floor. The box was full of jewelry of all kinds: pearls, gold, and diamonds; necklaces and earrings; countless rings – a sparkling multitude silently staring back at her. She kneeled and picked up a handful, letting them fall back with a dull tinkle.

"Take what you want," Permeet said from behind her.

"Oh!" Anna said, startled. "No. But thank you."

"It's not like *I* killed them," he added irritably.

"I know," Anna said, feeling hollow. She looked at him differently, sizing him up. This was a man who took jewelry off the dead. Did she blame him? She didn't, and yet her trust and gratitude toward him suffered. *Swindler*, she thought.

"I don't feel well yet," Anna said then. "I better go home now."

"I understand," Permeet nodded, his face grave. His beeper went off.

"Does your phone work?" Anna asked hopefully.

He shook his head. "No, the beeper is an emergency network, the staff keeps it running."

They descended the stairs in silence.

"Bye," she said waving awkwardly. "Thanks for everything."

Permeet raised his palm and turned away, in the direction of the approaching car.

Home was just three blocks away.

The door to Anna's apartment looked like a notice board. Post-Its and other missives covered its surface, all of them desperate, ending with exclamation points and begging Anna and Ben for their help. *Derek is sick ... Mother died ... Will come back at 9pm ... Please help!* Anna's lips moved automatically as she read. She picked up a thick yellow envelope from the floor and pulled out a card featuring a heart with a smile drawn into its center: *"To my savior,"* it read. And underneath: *"Ben, only you can help Wyatt now!!! Please call ASAP: 212-420-3450. Your most loyal patient, Val."*

It must have been their patients who broke into the apartment and defaced the walls, scrawling *help* and, later, when it was clear Anna and Ben had abandoned them: *Traitors!* Their patients had urinated and defecated in the corners, opened closets in search of food, and then lay down to die on her floor. Anna counted three corpses in the living room alone. The stench made it hard to breathe. There was a steady buzz of flies feeding on the dead.

Anna fled, not bothering to identify those who'd stolen her home. She fled and spat and retched on the staircase, feeling only hatred and horror and the howling misery of homelessness.

"No home," she whispered to herself, half-blindly, slowly wandering down the street. It was not just her physical home she had lost but the very promise of refuge and warmth that had kept her going until now.

Mechanically, Anna crossed Houston and walked up First Avenue to where she knew she wouldn't be alone: Permeet. On her way, she tried not to look around and not to remember. Her neighborhood, like her home, had been mutilated and abused. The streets, strewn with corpses, feces, garbage and broken glass, were ominously still.

Anna had to knock for a long time before Permeet, in sleepy disbelief, let her in. "You!"

She walked in wordlessly, not glancing up at him, just pressing his fingers for a second in a gesture of gratitude, and went straight to his bed, curling into a fetal position.

"What happened?"

"Bodies at home," she whispered. "Death. Bad air."

"Healer, don't be afraid. Bodies are just rotten meat," he said, lifting her chin with his fingertips, lighting her face with a candle. Her glance fell on his hand and she suddenly noticed how sturdy it was. A violent, potent hand. Not at all like Ben's.

"It was a death ward."

"The whole world is a death ward," he said, furrowing his forehead.

38

Galina convalesced with speed and a cheerfulness that were almost odd. Her new self was entertaining and flirtatious. She stopped wearing her mask and painted her cracked lips with scarlet lipstick. She smeared rouge on her dirty face so that flocks of dry skin fell off here and there onto the soiled shoulders of her coat. The rouge colored the scales dark red, and they hung like cancerous growths all over her face. She sprayed herself with Eva's perfume and painted her nails. She sent Bill smacking air kisses, spreading her fingers like a flower. She wanted to celebrate, Galina explained, and asked to look through Eva's clothes for "something more festive." At their belated Thanksgiving dinner, consisting of dry crackers and peanut butter, Galina wore high heels and Eva's orange woolen dress pulled over her jeans and sweater. The dress embraced her bulky shape awkwardly, stretching over each fold and protrusion. Holding the flashlight this way and that, Galina admired herself, wriggling her hips in front of the mirror.

"I am beautiful!" she sang, rouge glowing on her cheeks like two continents on fire.

Eva and Bill exchanged glances and smiled amused, smug smiles of the healthy and superior. If they were appalled at all, they didn't show it. What did it matter if she were a little more exuberant than they thought she ought to be? She was alive.

"If *I* had survived the Flu, I'd eat my socks," Bill said, and they all laughed because it was pleasant to laugh together for a change, even if Galina laughed longer and louder than anyone else, pressing Bill's hands and apologizing for her onetime ungratefulness.

"I cannot get sick anymore?" she asked from time to time, making frightened eyes, and they answered kindly, with a small shade of envy,

"No, Galina, you're immune. You can't get the Flu anymore."

Galina jubilated, tapping her feet, squealing and weeping with joy, loud and unrestrained like a toddler, while Bill and Eva watched her, moved as one is moved by a happy end.

"I want to say from heart!" Galina cried, her red-coral necklace and earrings rattling. "You save me. Okay. I am almost family. I take care of Max. Very good care! But you not only save me. You save other people. Strangers, and homeless, and bad people and good people, and that make you hero. You are hero! You are my hero! And what save me too is urine therapy. You laugh about me, I know. I know, but I am not angry. You can laugh. Russian saying is, good laugh is last laugh. I drink urine, I get healthy. I never feel so good in my life. I am totally different woman now. I tell you truth!" she leaned toward Eva, her lipstick smeared, peanut butter stuck to her molars. "I promise God to drink urine every single day of my life!"

Bill solemnly raised his paper cup, its cartoon T-Rex teeth gleaming in the candlelight. "To urine! Happy Thanksgiving!"

"Galina," Eva said, encouraged by Galina's praise. "I'm just curious: when you talked to yourself before you became ill, did you actually hear anyone talking back to you?"

"I totally different person now!" Galina repeated, shaking her index finger in the air. "You do not see? You will see! You will hear about Galina Sadikova, God willing!"

"That wasn't my question, Galina," Eva said softly. "Who talked to you?"

"People talk to me because I can hear things. But holy things are hush-hush! No talking!" she pressed her finger to her lips, her red nails locking scarlet lips in a sign of a cross.

"She's manic, Dr. Leigh," Bill stated, getting into the

bed. Eva didn't answer. Max was sleeping cozily under her blanket.

That night Galina sang an endless string of songs to the same deaf melody of excitement, hour in and hour out until Eva got up.

"You are very loud Galina. I have to work tomorrow."

"I tell you secret!" Galina said, still in high heels and the orange dress. The room smelled of burnt paper.

"Are you burning something?" Eva asked, surveying the room with her flashlight. The candle was burning on Max's red square table. "Do you mind if I take the candle?"

Galina fetched the candle with quick inspiration and brought it to Eva's face, so close that Eva felt the heat touch her nose.

"You my hero," she said. "Drink urine and be happy!"

Overnight, the emergency generator failed. In the morning, approaching the VA, Eva was numbed with disbelief at the sight of a gray lifeless mass that was the hospital building, all its lights extinguished. Jittery, she walked through the black frame of the door. A handful of personnel gathered in the lobby for a spontaneous meeting and Eva rushed toward them with nervous hopefulness. They were so close to the end. Surely it was a mistake; the lights would come back on in no time.

Eva stood at the fringe of the group, all of them familiar faces by now. Dr. Greenich was speaking. "The maintenance guy, what's his name, Nick, yes, Nick, we can't locate him."

"When did it happen?"

"Three, maybe four in the morning."

"What happened?" someone yelled, approaching them angrily, as if they were to blame for the power failure. Eva recognized Christopher Leach. She forgot the name of his department, remembering only that it was something heroic and interventional. Trauma surgery? Stretching her neck, she forced herself through the crowd, joining in Leach's question.

"What happened?"

"The generator failed, obviously. We're not sure why."

"Let's go down there! I mean, ten MDs will be able to figure out how to fix the generator!"

"Let's not get agitated, please," Dr. Greenich remarked somewhat contemptuously in his trembling, intellectual voice that sounded absurd among the chaos. Eva pitied him for a moment. "I, personally, was trained to treat people and I plan to stick by it. If someone has expertise with machinery, I welcome that person to take on this task. Otherwise, let's see what we can do as physicians."

Nasally, a tall stooping physician put in: "Maybe there's no fuel, you know; it's been so many days. My in-laws used to have a generator. It was diesel-powered, a primitive thing, really. I mean if you can handle a car motor … it's not rocket science …"

"On my way here, I passed Beth Israel," a young redheaded resident added. "They have light. They have more light now than we had a week ago."

"So let's go to Beth Israel and ask them for fuel!" Leach said.

"Why don't we stick to our responsibilities?" Dr. Greenich sighed irritably.

Eva felt the pull of fear and chaos around her. People talked over Greenich. Everything was falling apart. Eva stepped into the middle of the crowd, others making room for her to pass. She felt a surge of power, exhilarating and yet cold, devoid of self-consciousness and ripe with impersonal wisdom. She raised both her palms up, patiently calling for silence.

"We need a plan," she said calmly. "Let's set priorities. Since we don't know what the problem is, we have to: one," she bent her thumb, "continue treating patients, and two," she bent her index finger, "try to restore the generator. So why don't you," she pointed to the tall physician who'd mentioned his in-laws, "try to take care of the generator. Meanwhile, we need water. Water!" she repeated this in a calm, strong voice.

"We have enough fluids for at least a day," Dr. Greenich croaked.

"We need water," Eva repeated firmly. "In case the generator is gone for good."

"And how should we get it? Dig a well?" Taylor chimed in. Eva nodded, but only to acknowledge his presence.

"We put vessels on the roof to gather rainwater and we fetch more from the East River." She waved her hand eastward in a broad, generous gesture.

"The East River is full of shit and sewage and floating corpses!" someone cried.

Eva felt glances on her face and blushed. *I am a messenger*, she thought, suppressing her stirring, uncertain self.

"I know," she said slowly. "But we don't have a choice. We'll bleach it."

After sunset, everyone's low spirits and fear returned, and there was nothing Eva could do. It was dark and quiet in the hospital rooms, the silence disturbed only by the sounds of the sick, which took on a booming, unreal quality that triumphed over hope. With Eva's vision dulling, sounds and smells acquired an ominous presence. She could feel bodies turning and squelching on layers of feces and urine, drenched in sweat and emitting fetid oily odors. Patients coughed and wheezed in a cacophony like that of gigantic sick toads, and Eva knew that her wish to run and hide could be cured only by electricity. She turned on her flashlight and madly shone its beam into the faces of those who bore the horrible smells and sounds. She could do nothing. She could only quench their thirst if she had water. *Water*, the sick cried, again and again. Eva ripped open bags containing intravenous fluids and allowed them to drink from the nozzle on the plastic, one after another. They needed water to drink, to get well, to wash. Max needed water. The previous night Eva had dreamed of getting clean fresh water from a well, so much of it that she had laughed, splashed, and kicked around in joy until she woke up. "I've never even seen a well," she told Bill. "It's not the well, it's the idea of water," he said. "A Plato-Jungian thing, the archetypal memory."

"Let's just all go to BI," Taylor said. "What's the point?"

They deliberated in the darkness. Strictly speaking there was no point. There weren't even flashlights available. No lights, except for tiny medical lights used for neuro-exams and flashlights brought from home by the staff, Eva among them. Not even candles. When the sun set they became the blind caring for the sick. There was no point. Taylor was right.

"We can't transfer the patients," Greenich said tiredly. "What do we do?"

"They're short of staff too. Let's just go, BI, St Vincent's, whatever."

"We can't leave the patients," Eva said. Her voice quivered. She felt her authority slip away. She took a deep, full breath. "The night will not last forever." Her voice was full and bouncy now, like a plastic bag filled with water.

"I'm useless here, don't you get it?" someone shouted at her. She didn't bother trying to recognize him.

"We'll wait until the morning," Eva suggested evenly. "If you don't need to rest, go to BI and work, but be back in time. Otherwise, go to sleep. We all need rest. I'm leaving now."

Dead silence followed. She knew it was the wrong thing to say.

"I have a little son at home. He's three," she added quietly. "I can't stay."

"Of course she can't," someone spoke out of hostile blackness. "She just likes giving orders."

"At least leave us your flashlight, will you?" Leach asked.

Her moment of power had passed. She felt her heavy aching legs again.

"I'm sorry, I can't stay," Eva repeated. "See you in the morning."

Exhausted, she left the hospital. Shuffling her feet on the uneven pavement, she moved home through the moonless night, the spot of her flashlight unbearably lonely. Nights used to be red before, electric light saturating the air over the city. She once saw it from a plane. Was it on her way home from Paris? Where was her mother? Where was Greg?

Eva hoped for rain. Only rain could save them.

The next morning the generator was still out. Buckets and huge kitchen pots waited for rain on the roof. In the hospital lobby, among leathery benches and dark TV screens, plastic bags lay piled on a cart, filled with fetid river water yet to be bleached. Eva had heard there was a human tooth in one of them. She remembered water bombs she used to make for Max in the summertime. Once she had made dozens and stored them in the bathtub, their red, blue, yellow, and green bodies heavily rolling around her feet when she showered. Max smacked them on the dry pavement with the excited giggle of a deranged warrior, leaving motley rubber shreds scattered around. It must have been in August, Eva recalled. Last August seemed an eternity in the past.

They closed the hospital for admissions. With a thick red marker Eva helped color a big sign re-directing patients to Beth Israel. As she left the building that night the sign was fluttering in the wind like a scull-and-bones flag. *Stop!*, it said. *As of Nov. 29th VA Hospital is closed due to power failure. Please proceed to Beth Israel at Sixteenth St. and First Ave.* "Please" seemed ridiculous and misplaced, a correct word from orderly times, a waste of the word really, but Eva put it in anyway. She couldn't see the sign now, just heard the sounds of the fabric flapping against glass. Entering Stuyvesant Town, Eva placed her hand on the bag containing glucose solution that was bound to her waist. She could feel the water shaking against her belly with each step. Three more bags lay in her backpack. She was not sure why she bound that one bag to her body. Maybe it was a tribute to the goddess of water, to save them all from thirst, illness and insanity.

"Drink urine and be happy," Eva repeated, walking up the stairs, thinking of Galina. The water bag on her belly warmed up, soft and gurgly like her stomach. A mouse scurried away, frightened by her flashlight. The familiar stench on the staircase seemed almost welcoming. She was home now, whole and safe, carrying water for Max. She unlocked the door.

"Don't come close to me!" Galina yelped, her mascara running. "You did it!"

Eva blinked, startled. Galina was still dressed in Eva's dress. A string of Eva's pearls dangled on her neck. Her eyes were wild. Her lips were scarlet and scary.

Bill ran out of Max's room tousled and red-eyed.

"Shut up Galina! Eva, Max's running a fever. I think she infected him."

Galina stood by the door with a crazy smile quivering on her mouth. Eva saw it through the film of her fog. It felt like a fragment of a dream, and yet, for the first time in weeks, she was shaken alive. Something screamed in her with a pitiful, piercing force. Max was screaming through her – or maybe it was she who screamed, she didn't know. She found herself in Max's room holding her boy's hot and limp body, pressing his burning forehead to her face, kissing his eyes.

"Mommy's here now, mommy's here," she whispered again and again like a spell.

"Mommy," he said. "I'm thirsty."

"I brought water for you. Water, and a magic pill," she said, tears running down her bare unmasked cheeks.

"Will I be a skeleton when I die?" Max asked, and she pressed him harder, and wished he would talk and talk because healthy people talked and the deathly ill fell silent. Bill stood by her side holding a glass of water.

"Did you give him Tamiflu?"

"A dose three hours ago. He threw up soon after. I don't think it got absorbed."

"Give me the rest."

Max's Tamiflu was different from the adult dosage. It was a week's worth of pink powder to be diluted in water provided with the package in little foil-sealed plastic cups. Eva accepted the drink from Bill and, before giving it to Max, tasted it first with the tip of her tongue. It had a bitter, cherry-like taste.

"The pill's in the drink, Max," she said clearly and slowly. "You have to drink it and not throw up no matter how sick you feel. Do you understand me?"

Max did not respond but took the drink. Eva held his head and slowly poured the suspension into his mouth, encouraging him to swallow. When the glass was empty, she held him upright, praying that he would hold down the medication.

"Mommy," he said in a stifled, queasy voice. She bent closer to his face, which gleamed in the dark like a pale spot.

"It'll be fine, my dear, dear boy, just don't throw it up, just breathe quietly, like this," she whispered, showing him. "Do you want me to sing you a song?"

He didn't answer and she sang, *Hush little baby, don't say a word, mama's gonna buy you a mocking bird. And if that mocking bird won't sing, mama's gonna buy you a diamond ring. And that diamond ring turns brass, mama's gonna buy you a looking glass. And if that looking glass is broke, mama's gonna buy you a baby goat ...*

She sang and stroked his face, and when she forgot the words, she started over again.

"Mommy ..." he said and then sent a fountain of warm fluid into her neck and shoulder, vomit and cherry odors mixing in one.

"It's okay, pumpkin, it's okay," she muttered and rocked him back and forth until he fell asleep, hot, limp and untreated.

Eva had imagined it before, in graphic and alarming detail. She had brought home butterfly needles and IV catheters designed for kids. There was still a bag on her belly. She would hydrate him while he slept. She would wake him up and give him Tamiflu again. Without a word spoken, Bill handed her the First Aid bag, and the IV catheter, stepping softly so as not to disturb her grief. He kneeled next to her, helping to bare Max's tiny arm. Eva let him tie the sling over his elbow. With dismay she noticed how the needle jumped back and forth in her hand, and stabilized her hand with another.

"It's okay, I'll do it," Bill offered quietly. She nodded, handing him the butterfly. It was unbearable to observe. He got the vein on the first try and carefully pushed in the catheter.

It was quiet, very quiet. Together they bound the fluids to the roof of Max's car-bed and sat silently side by side, watching the drip flowing down, drop by drop, in the dim light. Although their silence felt oppressive after a while, Eva could not speak. If she kept watching Max, never wavering and never closing her eyes, he would get well.

As time passed, measured by the trickling drops, Eva wandered between the states of denial and tearing pain. Both were liquid and unreal. She craved certainty, but it kept eluding her, condemning her to wait. Occasionally she grabbed her stethoscope and listened to Max's lungs, as if waiting for an answer. His lungs were filling and ripening, the inflammation claiming them.

Eva reminded herself that bulimic patients usually absorb at least half their food despite vomiting, but, slippery and elusive, hope quickly turned into despair. She rocked, swallowed tears, and pressed Max's hot fingers. Her attempts at rational thinking spindled out fantasies, and, through a watery film, all the while watching Max's round tender face, she imagined how she would sit and look at him when he was not breathing any more, and how she would disappear into nothingness next to him and stop breathing herself. Later, spurred by hope, Eva imagined them running away and living in a warm, lush forest in a hut built of dry branches and big fragrant leaves – where deer would visit them in the mornings, timidly stepping forward on long graceful legs, and where water was abundant in a stony brook nearby. She rocked and waited, trying to hypnotize Max into life with her imploring gaze. After a while she heard Bill's long-winded snores, with high-pitched spikes at their ends. Eva sat visualizing them for a long time, her eyes on Max watering from effort and love. The fluid bag was half-empty when Eva heard the screech of tearing tape. The sound startled Bill awake.

"What's that?" he asked.

"I don't know."

"It's her. She has to go before something really bad happens."

"What could be worse than this?"

Bill stepped out of the room without answering. Eva felt lonely after he left, and cold. She extended her hand to touch Max's forehead. He turned and coughed, weakly at first, then doubling over. Eva held him tight, convulsing with him, as if togetherness could ease his illness. There were screams and banging in the next room. Max's cough subsided at last, and, drenched in sweat, he lay back. His lips moved, but she couldn't hear what he was saying. *I can't hear my son's last words!* she thought, and, furiously, got up and bellowed into the darkness, "*Quiet!*" The banging stopped for a second and then resumed.

"Open up, you crazy bitch!" Bill was shouting.

"You wait here, Max, I'll be right back," Eva whispered, quickly touching his forehead with hers. She didn't wear a mask. He was her boy, herself. Max didn't react, and Eva repeated it again and waited a couple of seconds before leaving. *And then she just left him*, the narrative in the mind condemned her.

"She's in the bedroom," Bill said when Eva entered the hallway. "Talk to her."

Eva tried the doorknob. Galina recited something ominous behind the locked door.

"Max is sick! Open the door!"

"Go away!"

"Is the rest of Max's Tamiflu still in there?" she whispered. Bill nodded in affirmation.

"I have a master key somewhere," she said. "Wait."

Eva ran to the living room and pulled out a drawer, fumbling in desperate haste. Here it was, strangely shaped, long and square, lent to her by a neighbor once after Max had accidentally locked himself in the bathroom. How could Galina have become so crazy again?

"Here," Eva said, handing the key to Bill.

Galina kept talking to herself in agitated bursts. Bill unlocked the door. Tape rustled. The door was not budging.

"A knife," he said, leaning on the door with his shoulder. Eva brought a box cutter. Bill made an incision along the frame. Galina fell quiet.

"Step back," Bill said and pushed the door open.

Galina sat on the bed with a hand on her mouth, her red nail polish shining. All of the chest drawers had been pulled out, Eva's socks and underwear spread on the floor. With gleeful greed, Galina was eating Eva's Tamiflu capsules out of her own palm.

"You lie to me!" she mumbled, her eyes fixed in the mirror opposite her. "I feel Flu in my body. Why you lie to me?"

A hysterical hiccupping reflex attacked Eva, tickling her throat. She tried to force it down, but reasoning made it worse. Continuing to shake, she watched Bill throw himself on Galina and snatch the Tamiflu away. When he throttled Galina by the throat and her eyes went big and glassy, Eva's fit ceased. Galina gagged.

"Bring me a pot!" Bill commanded. Eva obeyed, and Bill took Galina by the hair, threw her head back, and stuck three fingers into her mouth. "Vomit! Puke!" he yelled. His face was terrible.

Galina bit him, hard.

"Fucking bitch!" he cried, withdrawing his bleeding hand. He punched her, continuing to hold her by the hair. Her head rolled back like a doll's. She screamed and kicked. Bill snatched a pen from the table and stuck it into her mouth. She bit it, too, sending a stream of black ink down her lips and chin. Wincing, Eva stepped around Galina's thrashing legs and fetched a shoe spoon from the closet. Then she sat down on Galina's arm in an attempt to restrain her. Galina bellowed and thrashed.

"Tape!" Bill barked. Eva fetched tape and together they bound Galina's legs. When Galina bit Bill's shoulder, he punched her again. She squealed.

Bound like a mummy, Galina became mute and refused to open her mouth.

"I'll punch all your teeth out, you hear me?" Bill whispered menacingly, leaning close to Galina's ear. "*Open your mouth!*"

Eva shone the light into her face. Helpless, crazy, and pitiful, Galina looked at her. Her face was a grotesque smudge of rouge, mascara, and ink. Her lower lip hung down, baring a row of yellow teeth. It was the face of a mental patient. Eva couldn't recall what she looked like before.

"Open your mouth!" Bill yelled again.

Galina opened her mouth.

Eva could watch no more. Swaying as she walked, she returned to Max. The last drops of fluid were tinkling into his vein. It was dark and quiet again. Eva was tired, a terrible emptiness nagging at her insides. She touched his hand. He moved his fingers and squeezed her thumb.

"Mommy," he said. She put her head next to his on the pillow, their hair touching.

"I love you," she whispered, drifting into his hot feverish world.

When Eva woke up it was noticeably colder. She propped herself up and glanced around. The candle was still high, dripping wax icicles. Eva's leg was numb. Max was asleep. She felt his heat. She freed herself and got up to stretch and massage her leg. It tingled, filling her with an unbearable sweetness that made her want to scream. The wind started again. She could see the pale moon through the window. The fluids were disconnected from Max's arm, the catheter taped over. Yawning, she grabbed the flashlight from the top of the bookshelf and went out into the hallway. Bill sat at the empty table. Hearing Eva's footsteps, he turned.

"Hi! How's Max?"

"Sleeping. Where is Galina?"

"She left."

"She left?"

He nodded. Eva paused, relieved and uneasy.

"I gave Max some Tamiflu while you slept. I think he tolerates it better in smaller doses."

"He didn't throw up?"

Bill shook his head. "No. He's fine. He'll be fine."

Eva looked at him in silence.

"Drink urine and be happy!" he chuckled wryly. "I kept her vomit too. In case we need it."

Eva nodded, nauseated.

"You need to wear a mask. Here," he reached into a drawer. She accepted it silently.

Time moved through the night and into the morning with its moist grey winds, tiredness, and Max's wheezes. Eva felt them physically as if it were her own body struggling for breath. She breathed with him and helped him cough when he had to, and gave him the remaining Tamiflu suspension, and changed him when he peed on himself, and sang to him when he opened his eyes. She waited, measuring out her patience. Her thoughts were caught in a web of guilt. *If only she had not left him ... If only she had not brought home the virus ...*

"You didn't infect him," Bill insisted. "Galina did."

Eva didn't ask for an explanation, and Bill did not offer one.

The candle burned down and was replaced by another. Around midday Eva drank half a glass of water, refusing food. Max was better in that he was not worse. Emotion left her little by little. She felt formless, like the sea. She was just there, holding Max in the lap of her incidental presence. She was quiet. As long as she was there he would be there too.

"Eva, Eva, you must sleep. Do you hear me?"

She heard his voice through the mist of what was left of herself. *This is what a catatonic state must be like*, she thought. Very slowly, she forced her eyes to roll upward. They felt unbearably heavy. Her head pulsated with bursts of pain. Her body ached as if all her bones had been broken.

"Here, drink this," Bill said, lifting her up. Glucose solution. Eva obeyed.

The morning was sunny. She squinted. "Blinds," she whispered. The blinds were drawn. She drifted off again, swimming into a bright circle of fire. *No, no!* she wanted to scream, but the sound was blocked, and she realized she was isolated by soundproof glass. She floated in some wet prickly substance. Fire was all around her. She glanced down and saw the earth. *I am in space,* she thought. Her thoughts were slow and awkward, too big for her head. Acute loneliness was consuming her. *Why can't anyone hear me?*

"Eva, can you hear me? Eva?"

She opened her eyes again. Bill could hear her. She smiled but was not sure he could see her smiling. Something was blocking her mouth.

"I can't hear you," she heard. She nodded. He put a hand on her forehead, and she remembered. Max was sick.

"Max?" she asked. The effort finally, truly, woke her. She was sweating. The heavy pounding in her head was unbearable. Bill's face appeared painfully close to her. She tried to avoid it but her head was leaden. In a strange voice Bill said,

"He's better."

His voice trailed off. She was relieved, but couldn't be sure it wasn't all a dream. She looked for Bill through the pain and difficulty to focus. Something was wrong.

"Am I sick?" she mouthed. The face approached her again. Bill was saying something slowly. The sound of his voice hurt her but she knew he spoke like that to be understood by her. She thought he said "water." Water, she thought, and saw a river. She was entering a river, slowly, like in the movies: she could only see herself submerging, without feeling the sensations of cold or wetness on her body. When she put her head under the stream she understood why she couldn't understand Bill. He was speaking to her underwater. It was strange. Her pain was almost gone. She had trouble breathing. *If the end is like this,* she thought, *it's okay.*

39

ill stood over her for a while. Eva breathed in sudden sharp heaves. Morning light hushed by the blinds fell on her face in thick grey stripes. She looked haggard, her orbs large and dark, her cheeks hollow. That's how the dead looked. A strange blue woman lay in front of him, and he was responsible for her. Bill felt like he had never laid eyes on her before in his life.

Bill swallowed. His saliva was thick and viscous. His mouth was parched. He wished he could talk to someone, about death, or water, or anything at all. His loneliness was almost as bad as his thirst. Rainwater vessels had stood outside on the air-conditioners for the past thirty-six hours, empty and dry. Bill waited desperately for rain, or at least for some morning dew. Wasn't there supposed to be dew in the mornings, sometime around daybreak? There was none. And there was only one bag of water left, one bag for the three of them. How could there be no rain when they needed it so badly? He switched on the radio. Reporters talked of the new vaccine, still inaccessible in most areas but "on its way," to be brought in by military convoys. Martial law had been initiated a week earlier but no one had seen any soldiers, and no one had brought any supplies to the VA hospital – which, Bill reasoned, would have been their first priority. A confused kind of hope filled him with rage. The President was still well and about to address the shattered nation from one of his hidden locations. Bill sneezed into his mask, blessed himself, and scratched his beard. When he returned to the bedroom, it was full of shadows and close, sick air that made him claustrophobic. Eva wheezed under the blankets, showing just her fingertips and the side of her grey hollowed cheek.

He bent closer to her, looking for signs of awakening or guidance, something that would make them partners again. "Don't die!" he said into the void. She did not hear him. It didn't make sense talking to her any longer. He pulled her sleeve back and lightly pinched the skin on her forearm, then watched the fold slowly disappear. She was dehydrated. It wasn't too bad yet, not for another couple of hours. He carefully bent over the bowl containing Galina's vomit and covered it, wincing. Without water, all of the Tamiflu in the world would be useless. He didn't dare touch what water had come with Max's supply. There was just one bag of fluid left, and no one else to get water but him.

Bill was weak and light-headed. "Am I a hero?" he asked aloud. No one answered. He was standing in Max's room, the bag of fluid in his hand. Automatically, he glanced at the wall where a yellow, wooden clock shaped like a chicken nonchalantly moved its battery-operated red legs: *tick-tock, tick-tock.* "Seven a.m.," Bill said and then repeated himself, "Seven a.m." Max turned to his side, his breathing inaudible.

"Max?"

Max slept, his cheeks slightly flushed, his eyelids trembling. He must have been dreaming.

"Buddy! Talk to me!" Bill whispered, putting his hand on Max's hip. "Wake up!"

Max opened his eyes.

"Your eyes are clear. You're breathing well," Bill said.

"Sleep, daddy, sleep," Max murmured indistinctly.

Tiredness hit Bill suddenly. *How come I didn't think of that?* he pondered gratefully, leaning on Max's car-bed and shutting his eyes. I just have to sleep, first drink a little, then sleep, take counsel from my pillow. Through the mist of fatigue he forced himself to get up, took the bag, hung it on the bed, and connected the last of the fluid to Max's catheter.

"Some water," he mumbled. "You don't mind sharing, do

you?"

Max opened his eyes for a second, registering that something had been done to his arm, but he didn't protest. Bill had been wearing his latest mask for four days now; it was fetid and oily, probably useless. Still – because it was the only one he had left – he kept it on. He washed and disinfected his hands and carried on as a survivor. He'd eaten a spoonful of Galina's vomit the previous night, and took another one now. For some time he sat on the floor among the plastic dinosaurs, trains, and Legos, watching the play of light and shadow on the blinds, created by the poplar branches moving in the wind outside. When his eyes became so heavy that he couldn't keep them open, he disconnected the bag with the fluid, weighing it in his palms like a woman's breast, and took off his mask, squeezing the bag to allow a spurt of water into his mouth. It had a delicious sweet and salty taste. Bill stopped, took another spoonful of vomit into his mouth, his taste buds screaming with disgust, and swallowed, placing his lips around the hole in the bag again, drinking until it was almost empty. "Okay!" he said then, with fake calm. "Save one sip for the road."

He slept in Max's room. His mask lay on the floor, covering the paw of a bear whose fluffy paws were touching a yarn of dust. Wrapping himself in his sable he lay down on the couch, the taste of her vomit still in his mouth, and stretched his limbs. His body ached, especially his legs. When he was a boy he had it often. The family doctor said it was because he was growing. Other memories came and went. *I'm just tired*, he thought. *Water.*

He woke up shivering. "Daddy," Max was saying. "I'm thirsty."

Bill propped himself up on an elbow. Max was sitting in his bed clutching a plush T-Rex.

"What time is it?" Bill asked.

"I'm thirsty," Max repeated.

Bill hung his legs down, rubbed his eyes and glanced at the chicken clock. Three p.m.

"I gave you water earlier."

"No you didn't!"

"I gave you a drip. Well, never mind. There's no water. I'll get some."

"Where's mommy?"

The question surprised and frightened him, and he scratched his beard, as had become his habit over the past weeks, concurrent with not shaving. He got up and dragged himself out the door, heavy like a knight in iron armor. In the hallway he stopped, panting. For several seconds, he listened wondrously to his own breathing, as if it were something occurring apart from him. Holding on to the wall, he entered the bedroom.

"Bill!" Eva cried weakly.

Bill stopped, happy and confused. He had been sure he would find her dead, blue and cold on the striped pillows.

"How's Max?"

"He's better. He's thirsty."

"Water," she whispered dreamily and smiled, closing her eyes. She looked pale and vulnerable, but she was alive. Bill took her pulse and counted for thirty seconds, then multiplied it by two. Ninety-eight. He glanced at her with a puzzled expression.

"I'll be well. We'll survive," she whispered, stroking his hand with her fingers. Her tone was full of hope. He felt how his own face became distorted, his mouth forming an eight, cheeks folding around his eyes. He cried, unashamed of the tears dropping into the thick of his beard.

"Sh-sh," she said continuing to stroke him. "Sh-sh..."

"Eva!" he said painfully. "I'm sick, Eva. I'm sick. I'm sick. *I'm sick...*"

He wept, their eyes interlocking even though he could not read her expression through the tears.

"Water?" she asked.

"There's none!"

Eva nodded and closed her eyes again.

Tears refreshed him as if he'd just washed his face. Squeezing her hand, he said,

"I'll go get water."

"Thank you," she answered.

Bill felt stronger now, his wheezing letting go. *Maybe it's nothing*, he thought with a glimmer of hope. Maybe he wasn't sick after all. He wandered into the kitchen and put Motrin on his tongue. Back in Max's room he washed it down with the last swallow of fluid while Max watched him squeezing the bag.

"I want to drink!" Max demanded loudly. Bill savored the robust sound of the boy's voice.

"I'm going out. I'll bring you water," Bill nodded, forcing a smile. "You'll be fine."

As he packed empty plastic bottles into the backpack and zipped up his black quilted jacket, a desperate plan formed in his head. With a last little bit of hope, he peered out the window into the cloudless, bleached sky and shook his head. No rain. Then he threw his backpack on his shoulder and re-entered the wild.

Measuring his steps down the black staircase, Bill saw himself crossing Stuyvesant Town and coming out to the East River where, along the boardwalk, he would find a promontory of stones he should be able to navigate without too many acrobatics. He would squat on the rocks and submerge the bottles in the river, watching bubbles escape their necks and gurgle on the surface. Maybe there would be corpses, floating facedown like rotting logs, but the river was vast, and if a body came too close, he'd push it away with a stick. He'd fill the bottles and wash his face and maybe even take a sip or two before coming home. The water was bad, surely not for drinking and maybe a little salty too, but they had to survive until the next rainfall. After fulfilling his task, he would take his camera and snap a shot of the water rippled by November wind, of the hard, rainless sky, and of the high buildings in Brooklyn – or was it Queens? – on the opposite shore. The light would be brilliant, and yet the sun hung low enough that there would also be sufficient shade to accommodate his loneliness.

Bill continued down the stairs, holding carefully onto the railing. His breathing echoed in the darkness. Something rustled on the lower stairs, and he stopped to listen in and rest. A rat, he decided. Or maybe Ska? He wouldn't be surprised to see Ska, happy and fat on rodent meat. He passed by the forgotten mailboxes, pushed open the main door, and came out into the sun. The swaying poplars dropped dry brown leaves that whirled as they fell to the ground with a slight rustle. As Bill breathed in the fresh air, his chest wouldn't expand, and he tried harder, finally collapsing in a cough. Sweating, he walked on and turned the corner, stepping slowly to conserve his energy. He hadn't eaten anything in twenty-four hours but did not feel any hunger. Thirsty people don't feel hungry, he told himself. The Con Edison power station revealed itself, its four ominous towers rising into the sky like those of a crematorium. Where was his camera? He wanted to capture this: the lonely expanse, the empty statue of an urban empire. He opened his bag. There were his flashlight, four empty bottles, a box of matches, the keys from his own apartment, old scraps of papers, but no camera. "Of course, of course!" he mumbled, reaching into the inner pocket of his jacket. Here it was. As he opened the lens, another thought occurred to him. Where were the keys to Eva's apartment? He pushed the thought away, took the shot and then another, holding the camera out at arm's length to shoot himself with the power station in the background. "C'mon!" he muttered then, going through the backpack and searching his pockets again. With a sense of growing panic he emptied his backpack, letting its contents fall on the grass. He took off his jacket and patted the pockets in his jeans, until, shivering with cold and anguish, he accepted that the keys were gone. He rushed to retrace his steps, in the mad hope that he had dropped them on the way. He squealed, clutching his head. Galina's insane, defiant face stood in front of his eyes. She was leaving like a winner. "She took my keys!" he cried into nowhere. "The bitch took my keys!"

He tried the entrance door. It was locked, locked like it always was. The windows of Eva's apartment did not even face this way. She wouldn't hear him. And she was still too weak to walk. In his mind's eye he saw Max's and Eva's blue and stiff corpses decomposing in the apartment upstairs. Little Max would be crying for daddy, for water, until his life ceased to be.

Suffocating in angry tears, Bill yelled, "Eva! Eva!" His voice was weak and squeaky, and weakened further with each subsequent call. He crossed the road and picked up a stone. The door had a glass window interlaced with wire. He swung his arm and hit the glass, again and again. He wept and coughed and called Eva until he had no strength left, then just stared at the entrance, hoping someone would arrive to go in or come out. He sat on the steps for a long time, crying and calling out into nothingness. The windows around him were dark and empty – as if he, Eva, and Max were Stuyvesant Town's sole survivors. Several times, seized by a hope that he had overseen the keys, he searched his backpack again. At dusk, exhausted and cold, he went through it one last time. His glance fell upon the only keys that offered themselves to him time and again: the keys to his own home.

"Home sweet home," he muttered and called again, with tired desperation, *"Eva!* Please! Anyone!"

There was no response, and after a long minute of waiting he left, shuffling through the dry fragrant leaves with his heavy feet.

As soon as Bill had left and she could not see him any longer, Galina started her ascent. She unlocked the door quietly so no one would know that she was there. The White Angel talked in her head, and she hushed him down. The little boy needed her. She would bury him. He wasn't heavy, and the grave was close by. Or she could take him down to where she had found the apples.

Galina entered the apartment and tiptoed to Max's room. Max lay in bed like an angel. She would wrap him in his sheet with little giraffes printed on it, and take him with her. The White Angel said the boy was gone, but the hope to find him alive tightened her throat. Stepping soundlessly on the carpet, she came closer and peered into his face. Max opened his eyes.

"Daddy said he'd bring me water and ice cream."

Galina didn't touch him, keeping her distance from the virus. "I miss you. Look what I bring!" she said. She reached into her pocket and gave him an apple. Max ate the apple. The White Angel was quiet. Galina tiptoed to the bedroom. Eva moved and moaned in her sleep.

"Why did you do it?" Galina asked, standing away, hands on her hips. "Did you know?"

Eva slept, a pile of blankets around her.

"Max was next," Galina whispered, shuddering. "You knew that?"

She hesitated, wondering whether she should leave an apple for Eva as well, and finally placed one next to her pillow.

Lock the door, the White Angel said. She found the master key and locked the door, hiding the key in her pocket. *You're dirty!* the White Angel said. *She infected you!* In the bathroom Galina took off her clothes and rubbed herself all over with disinfectant. For the next hour she paced through the apartment incessantly, talking to the Angel. When her thirst became unbearable, she ate another apple. It was dark outside. She lit a candle and went back into Max's room.

"Where's mommy?" Max asked, and Galina whispered sternly, furrowing her forehead,

"Mommy sleeping. Don't disturb her."

Max fell quiet, too weak to argue. Then he spoke again. "I'm thirsty. Where's daddy?"

"He is not daddy. I tell you secret," she lay down on the floor, resting her neck on the plastic frame of his bed. "You see angel?"

"No," Max said sheepishly.

"I see angel. Angel give me apple and bring me back to you."

"Can I have another apple?"

"One apple today, one apple tomorrow."

"That's too long. Can you ask the angel to bring the apple now?"

"I'll ask."

"I want my mommy."

"Mommy is sleeping."

"I want daddy."

"Hush! He is no daddy! He is bad man! He want to eat you!"

"He said he'd bring me water!" Max said with an astonished look.

"He go to get a big knife, like this, and come and eat you. Then I come and save you!"

Big-eyed she spoke to him in a rapid staccato of horror, and Max gazed at her, frightened and lonely, and cried.

"You cry, cry is good," she said. "I close the door so you are safe."

"Don't close the door!" he cried. "Galina! I'm afraid! Don't close the door!"

She closed the door and locked it. Now he was safe.

You're dirty! the White Angel told Galina again, and she ran to the bathroom to disinfect, wondering why the Angel was speaking so cruelly to her.

Eva called from behind her own locked door. She called for Max and Bill.

Galina kept quiet. When she was tired of Eva's cries, she turned up the radio.

The Flu was ending. The vaccine had arrived in New York. Power stations were ready to resume operating in California. The President was hopeful.

Max cried again, in a tiny voice. Galina gave him another apple and locked the door again. "Sleep baby, sleep."

Eva dragged herself to the door of her room. Galina heard her clearly, seeing her movements with her mind's eye: how she got out of bed and fell, and then crawled on all fours, reaching the door to scratch on it like an animal, trying to turn the knob while still on her knees. She tried again, three times in all. Then Eva's clothes made a swishing sound as they rubbed up along the doorframe; Eva had managed to pull herself up and was now standing. Galina sat like a watchdog, chewing on her apple, the key secure in her pocket.

When the door opened Galina was surprised. She hadn't known the room could be unlocked from within. Eva emerged like a ghost.

"Max!" she called hoarsely. "Max!"

She looked awful, too weak for a battle. Galina remained seated. "Go back to bed," she said briskly.

"Galina," Eva pleaded, sliding on the floor, her eyes huge and wet on her mortally thin face. "Please. I want Max."

"Why did you do it then?" Galina shrieked, rising from her chair and towering over Eva, intense and wild.

Eva crawled toward her. "Please," she said.

"You wanted to get rid of him. Tell me, how can mother want to eat child?" Galina cried in a shrill spiral of righteousness.

"You're sick," Eva said, trying to suppress a new cough.

Galina thought Eva looked guilty. *Let her die,* the White Angel said.

"You're crazy!" Eva whispered, struggling to rise again to her feet.

"Don't come closer!" Galina yelled.

Eva stepped forward and leaned on Max's doorknob, turning the handle back and forth. It was locked.

"Max!" she cried. It wasn't much of a sound. She coughed, pressing her lips to the door. "It's mommy! Max, Max?"

Galina continued flatly to watch Eva's pitiable, wheezing being.

"Mommy," Max cried, and Galina jumped up, furious and erect.

"You infect him! I give you apple! I here for Max!" she yelled, stomping her foot indignantly.

Eva crouched on the floor, mumbling, coughing, and crying. "Max, my dear, Max, can you hear me, my boy?"

When she passed out Galina carried her back to bed.

Eva woke up in complete darkness. It was cool and still. The pounding in her head had abated, only thirst remained: severe thirst, which exacerbated her despair. She cried tears of rage and hopelessness, coughed, and passed out again.

There was nothing left, just waiting for the death that would claim her and her little boy. She was to blame. If she had listened to Bill and hadn't given her the Tamiflu, Galina would be dead, and the rest of them safe and healthy.

Bill, where are you Bill? Max, my boy, I want to hold you again, one last time. Why can't we at least die together?

40

nna was glad to be awake, back to lifeless reality. Permeet sat up in bed, stretching his body, yawning loud like an animal, his teeth big and strong.

"Back to the death ward?" he asked.

"I'll come."

It was dark outside. Lightning illuminated their faces, seeming to photograph Anna's mournful expression and Permeet's body as he carried the bedpan to the window. Thunder roared a second later and a heavy rain poured from the skies, drumming against the pane.

"Good," Permeet said, shutting the window. "This will wash away the stench."

They had some cookies, multivitamins, and water. Permeet glanced at his watch.

"He should be here by now."

They played Scrabble to kill time while waiting for the ambulance to come. DEATH, Anna wrote, carefully, letter by letter fitting in the tiles. WARD, Permeet countered vertically with quick precision. He burst out laughing, and she followed him, holding her belly and tapping her feet on the floor. Two hours passed.

"I guess, that's it. Something must have happened," Permeet said. "What now? Death ward? Or a day off?"

"I'll come with you," she repeated.

"Let's go then."

Under a big yellow umbrella, arm in arm, they strolled down the street.

"My wife and I moved here just three months ago," Permeet said. "We were expecting a furniture delivery the day the pandemic broke. Hard to believe."

"It was a different world," Anna agreed.

He shook his head, muttering something, remembering.

"Yes, you can say that. A different world," he said. "Can you heal me?"

"Time will heal."

"Aren't you a healer?"

Anna took her time to respond. The rain was all around her. *I'm drained,* she thought. Shock passed quickly, and even fear and compassion seemed to have waned. Now everything felt merely drained. Nothing left to cling to. No purpose, no hope, no life. No Ben. No miracle. No home.

"I used to be," she said. "It feels, though, as if I never was, that it was all a mirage: my whole life. It hurts to look back. I never even had a child. And yet, I live, while little kids die..."

A man appeared around the corner in front of them, water dripping down from his dark receding hair, his hands clutching his shoulders. He coughed when they approached, a deep, hacking cough convulsing his body.

"Do you need help?" Permeet said. "I'm a doctor."

"Yeah, so am I," the man said.

"You need to go to the hospital."

"No, thanks, colleague. I'd rather die at home. I could use your help getting there, though. 207 Second Avenue. Over Momofuku. Apartment 4 …"

The man was heavy, leaning on Permeet and Anna's arms. Several times they had to stop to give him water and let him cough.

"What's your name?" Permeet asked.

"Bill Jacobs."

"I'm Permeet Khanna. This is Anna."

"Hah. You rhyme. Khanna and Anna."

Bill became nervous and impatient when they reached his building. Fumbling with his keys, he said, "Thanks again. I'll manage from here." As he unlocked the door they all smelled death inside. Bill looked at them impatiently, his cheeks tense, his eyes bloodshot from strain.

"It's okay," Permeet said. "Go on, we'll wait just in case."

They heard him gasp as he opened the door, and Anna hurried up, seized by horror and pity. The memory of her own horrifying homecoming sprang before her eyes in all its graphic revulsion, and for a split second Ben's smell returned to her.

"You need water!" she heard herself shouting. "You need care!"

She reached the door. The pungent smell of decomposing flesh made her eyes water. She wanted to run away, but she searched for Bill. He had staggered to the window and was leaning out, retching. In the cold grey daylight, on the bed, lay a cadaver barely resembling a woman, her short, checkered skirt still intact, her face gone.

"Who is she?" Anna asked.

Bill's face distorted into a miserable silent howl. He looked like an English bulldog, the skin around his mouth and chin gathering into many folds, his eyes red and woeful. "Get me out of here," he cried like a baby. "Please. I want to get out …"

He made a step toward Anna and Permeet, who had followed her up, and they took him by the arms, leading him, slack and sobbing, out and down like a drunk.

"You haven't been here in a while," Permeet said outside.

Bill stopped. "You'll get sick now, too. That air was bad. I told you not to come in."

"Nonsense! The virus needs a nice warm temperature to survive. It's long been dead."

Anna shivered. Bill spoke the truth. It was the Avian Flu itself that they met in his apartment. The smell of death was the face of the virus. Bill sat down on the pavement.

"Bring me to VA," he said.

"Is that where you worked?"

Bill stared at Permeet as though he hadn't heard him. He breathed audibly, unevenly.

Anna and Permeet urged Bill to walk on. They stepped over puddles in silence, looking at the wet empty street and listening to Bill's wheezes. The rain stopped and the clouds hung like amorphous beasts in the brightened sky. Bill shivered again. A car approached. Permeet jumped into the street to wave his arm with the youthful vigor that didn't cease to surprise Anna, whose every movement had been humbled and slowed by the Flu. The car passed. Dejectedly, they rested for a moment and then continued, retracing their steps eastward.

Bill's condition worsened, and although he continued to move his legs automatically, he was losing his grip on reality, delirium infecting his reason. On 23rd Street they passed a row of corpses lying facedown in a puddle and entered the hospital ramp, pushing Bill along. On a bench in front of the entrance they sat down to rest, Bill's head hanging loosely against Anna's shoulder.

"He's a goner," Khanna said evenly.

"I can help him. I nursed my friend. She was worse than him. And didn't they say more people are getting well now?"

Bill opened his eyes. "I lost the keys," he blurted. "There's a little boy. Max. And Eva. They're sick and thirsty. 10 Stuyvesant Oval, 10C. Ten, ten. Easy to remember. No, no, write it down! The babysitter stole my keys; you have to break down the door... Eva Leigh."

"Eva Leigh?" Anna cried. "I know Eva Leigh!" Energized, Anna urged Bill to drink more water, holding his head pressed to her breast, smoothing his wet oily curls. "I know Max. I know Eva," she whispered urgently. "I can help. I can help ..." Gently, she rocked Bill back and forth, embracing his bony shoulders as though he were a baby.

Permeet was already on his way into the ER, a mask fastened tight on his face. The hospital had the look of an

355

abandoned warehouse. Patients lay in their beds under the dim blue lights, soundless except for their labored breathing and occasional coughs and moans. He spotted a nurse who sat at the bedside of a pregnant woman, attempting to find her vein, but it was too supple from dehydration. Permeet quickly pulled a glove onto his hand and took over, in one push inserting the catheter and untying the sling on the woman's arm.

"I'm Dr. Khanna," he said to the nurse. "Who is in charge here?"

"The Flu's in charge, I guess. There're only four doctors left in the whole hospital."

"I'll help. There's a new Flu victim, also a physician, in the hallway. Do we have any supplies left? I.V. fluids, Corticosteroids, NSAIDS?"

"People steal, you know. Here's Dr. Lessing, ask him!"

Dr. Lessing came out to have a look at Bill.

"Hopeless," he said while Bill looked at him miserably. "Take him home."

"I'll stay with him," Anna said, continuing to stroke Bill's forehead with her free hand.

She stayed in the ER throughout the night. Dimly, while attending to Bill, she remembered the deck of cards, with its Joker popping up, and the King that was supposed to protect Eva; Anna couldn't remember which suit. Where was the King now? Eva was sick. Anna expected to find her dead in her bed, her little boy beside her. Anna couldn't bear to see any more death, not in the intimacy of a home. Wearily she changed Bill's wet clothes and tucked him in under several blankets. She forced the remainder of her drinking water into his mouth and gave him Motrin, at least to alleviate his suffering somewhat. She held his hand and wiped the sweat from his forehead. Then, called upon by Permeet, she helped the rest of the staff carry corpses outside in order to free beds for new patients. It was a small blessing that there had been only three new admissions during Anna's seven hours of duty. She planned to stay till the morning. She was drained and afraid, and the Joker laughed in her face. In the dark she wouldn't find Eva's house, anyway. She didn't even have a key.

Bill emerged from a bout of delirium. She held his hand. *"Eva,"* he said urgently. "10 Stuyvesant Oval. Apartment 10C. Give her the camera in my bag," he wheezed. Anna obediently found the camera and put it in her pocket.

The staff disinfected the water brought down from the roof and, after drinking some themselves, the caretakers hydrated the patients. The night was humid and dark. A truck with food arrived in the early morning hours, causing a joyous commotion. Everyone got a can of Ensure, Anna accepting hers gratefully. When she returned to Bill's bedside with a pitcher of water in her hands, he was dead. Anna closed his eyes. Five-twenty a.m., her watch said. The pregnant woman had died thirty minutes earlier. Anna felt the camera in her pocket. The sun would rise soon. "He's dead," she told Permeet, when she had found him. He squeezed her fingers with absentminded compassion.

"It's the worst place. When I'm here, I think we are all going to die," she said impassively, only her body shaking.

When the sky had brightened she crossed 23rd Street and entered Peter Cooper Village. The alleys looked cleaner here; the shit bags and abundant garbage lay scattered only on the lawns, leaving the inner alleys clear. It was quiet and fragrantly wet. Anna slipped on the moist leaves twice but did not fall. The sky overhead was spotted pink. Another day was starting, the sun oblivious to their miseries. Squirrels were scurrying around. They were hungry, coming close to Anna and pleadingly standing up on their hind legs, expecting a treat. Far away someone screamed and Anna quickened her pace. Would she even recognize Max? Vaguely, she recollected a round face and a happy smile on the picture at

Olga's and Vladimir's, of Max on a swing.

The sun was rising, it discus full and perfect over the river. Anna raised her arms, inhaling deeply and standing on her toes. It was pleasant. Exhaling, she slowly bent to her ankles in a bow to the rising sun. She was silent. The step from hope to despair was short. She kept her hope hidden.

Slower now, she walked on, lost in the maze of identical brown brick houses with green window frames. The house numbers were confusing. With the help of a map on the alley, she finally found the right building. The air was chilly and full of purple morning tenderness. Approaching the entrance, she heard a voice. Its cadence was Russian. She stopped, suppressing her breath and looking around. *No more apples,* the voice mumbled woefully. Goosebumps ran through Anna's skin. She must have been hallucinating; but it wasn't Ben's voice, she was sure of that. *I told him not to go to her,* the voice continued. Anna took a fearful step forward. *No, no!* the voice said. *I'm good!* A figure moved frantically back and forth in front of the basketball court.

"Who's there?" Anna called out in Russian.

The figure froze.

"Who's there?" Anna repeated, coming closer. A woman in a dirty tattered coat crouched behind the wooden back of the bench.

"Don't be afraid, I'm Russian too," Anna said, moving slowly. Suddenly she became aware of the situation's almost cinematic irony: two Russian women lost in a dead American city, talking to themselves, hearing voices. The woman stared at her from above a huge green mask of the kind used by construction workers. Her hair stuck out in tangles. Threateningly, with her hands, she ordered Anna to halt.

"Are you sick?!" she shrieked.

"No, no …" Anna replied.

"Who are you?"

There was an unmistakable provincial tinge to this voice, to its soft guttural consonants and hushed *A*s. Anna felt a kinship to the woman – though not quite enough to let down her guard. She answered clearly and kindly. "I'm Anna. I heard that Dr. Eva Leigh and her little son who live in this building need help. But I don't have the keys."

"I have the keys," the woman said triumphantly.

Aha, Anna thought. *The babysitter.* The woman looked at her closely, her gaze changing, "Anna Borisovna? You treated me, remember? I'm Galina."

They locked into a quick tearful embrace.

"A lot has happened. The Angel sent you to me. You have water?"

Anna opened her bag. As Galina drank, choking on large greedy gulps, water trickling down her chin, Anna watched her with unease. There was something broken in her face. Or was it just thirst and hunger and the burden of loneliness? Of one thing Anna felt certain: providence had intervened. Its hand was unmistakable. If she could just ingratiate Galina, win her trust with her kindness and the commonality of their heritage …

"Shouldn't we go up?" Anna suggested, using a careful, kindly voice. Galina had not yet handed over the keys.

"Where is the man? Bill? Is he coming too?"

"He died this morning," Anna said. "About two hours ago."

"Good, you see, the Angel was right. Sometimes he gets things wrong. He told me to bury the little boy, but he was alive. And then he gave me apples after the old lady died. Eva should know he's dead, we must tell her …"

"He left something for her," Anna said, understanding scarcely a word Galina was saying.

"Don't give it to her!" Galina shrieked, moving closer. "She'll be free. He planned to kill the little boy. She knew it, but I don't blame her, she was in love."

The sun rose higher, painting the rooftops yellow.

"He ate people. I know," Galina whispered, her eyes big.

"It'll be fine," Anna said, patting Galina on the arm. "Look at the sky, it's beautiful, isn't it? The end of the Flu is coming."

Galina jerked, calling Anna to silence. "Listen!"

Anna listened. The birds chirped their morning songs. The trees creaked in the light breeze. Two squirrels ran by, chasing each other through the damp leaves.

"It's beautiful," Anna smiled.

"Did you hear him?"

"Galina," Anna said, rising to her feet. "I told you. He died. Now hurry, let's go up?"

Together they crossed the street and Galina unlocked the door. "No light!" Galina hissed, and Anna obeyed, putting away the candle. The door to the staircase closed behind them, sealing them into the fetid air, with its dark, fecal stench that penetrated their masks. Holding on to the wall, Anna went first, prompted by Galina's quick whispers. When they had climbed three flights, however, Galina's footsteps ceased behind her.

"Galina!"

"Why does he talk to me like this?" Galina whispered frantically. "Did I deserve it?"

"Just keep coming, one step at a time. We'll manage," Anna backed down a few steps and tried to take Galina's hand.

"It's not clean there!"

Galina released the keys into Anna's outstretched palm and fled down the stairs, whispering insanely. Anna continued her climb alone. Somewhere on the pitch-black staircase she tripped over something, and, hearing a faint groan, realized it was alive. "I'm sorry!" she yelled, terrified, her voice echoing in the staircase. "Do you need help?" There was no answer, only the sound of a body recoiling along the floor. Anna looked for matches but she had lost them in the haste and panic. She gave up and hurried away, up and up the steps. Out of breath, she reached the tenth floor, its hallway numbers just recognizable in a thread of thin daylight from a window at the end of the corridor. Here was 10C. She knocked hard, calling out Eva's name, praying for an answer. It was quiet. She inserted the key with anxious hands, the door gave in, and she stepped inside, continuing to call out in a trembling voice,

"Hello! Eva, Max! It's Anna! Bill sent me!"

Anna found her matches and struck one twice, the sudden flame of her candle flickering to form giant shadows on the walls. Anna walked into the empty living room and blew out her match. A red blanket lay on the floor next to the brown rests of several apples. Anna proceeded to the end of the hallway, turned the handle, and entered a dimly lit bedroom.

"Hello?" she whispered in the direction of the bed, as cautiously as if a voice any louder would magically summon death.

"Bill?" Eva whispered back, and Anna ran in and saw her face – bluish and starved but alive – and took it into her hands.

"*Anna,*" Eva whispered, confused, attempting to sit up. "How ...?"

"Bill," Anna said and stopped herself.

Eva gave her a long look.

"Max?" she mouthed.

"I'll go and look, don't worry dear. Here, here's some water," Anna said.

Max lay in his little yellow car-bed listlessly, smacking his lips, a plush tyrannosaurus by his side. He didn't react to Anna's entrance, just tracked her movements with big, expressionless eyes. At the sight of water he let himself be propped up and drank avidly. Anna gathered him up then. His cheek touched hers. He had no fever.

"Mommy," he said quietly.

Anna carried Max into his mother's bedroom, his little

hands locked around her neck.

"Max?"

"Mommy!"

Like a little fish, Max squirmed out and leaped into his mother's bed. Eva wrapped her arms around him, kissing his head, and tucked him in beside her, under the blanket, his cheek on her breast. For a while no one spoke, the women weeping and Max quiet and at peace.

"Bill asked me to give you this," Anna said softly, placing the camera on the night table.

Eva nodded and pressed Max closer to her. She did not ask questions, and by her silence Anna assumed that she understood.

"Where's Galina?" Eva asked hoarsely.

"Outside."

"Don't let her in. No matter what happens, don't let her in!"

Max tucked himself in closer to his mother. Eva's eyes were moist.

"I'll run out and bring you more water and food and medicine."

"Don't let her in!" Eva whispered again.

"Providence," Anna muttered, running down the staircase, and smiled, full of bliss. For the first time in so long she was overcome with a desire to sing. Ripping her mask off, in a clean and trembling voice she sang *The Blue Scarf*, a Russian love song from wartime, and its melody echoed back to her – stronger, purer, and sadder, bringing tears to her eyes.

Galina was gone.

All the way back to the hospital Anna continued singing, words and melodies flooding from her – from depths of memory she didn't even know she possessed.

"Isn't it amazing?" she said to Permeet when she arrived. "I can sing again!"

41

Greg recognized salvation as soon as he saw the impeccably white house sitting atop a volcanic cliff. There was the blue sky, and the sparkling alien ocean, and the severe gray of the stone. In the house, as soon as dust covers had been removed from the colonial-style furniture, there was fizzy wine, opened with a pop. And there was Tony: considerate, gentle, powerful Tony.

The ice with Brian and his wife was broken with the first bottle of Champagne – when they sat down, showered and squeaky clean in fresh bathrobes, at the heavy wooden table set with china. Their encounter on the yacht sparked a chain of good-humored jokes they would make over the next weeks. Greg played the piano with his healthy right hand and sang clearly and grandly. The melody galloped forth chordlessly, naked and vivacious in a refreshing way. Applauded, Greg bowed like a concert pianist would, all flair and smiles, pressing his good hand to his chest.

Their early conversations, when they gathered around the fireplace after a good meal – listening to the wind and the rumbling ocean – concerned their respective Flu-time adventures. The Flu was not yet over, of course, but here, in Tony's idyllic oceanfront retreat, it seemed a plague from the past. Greg mentioned Lora's death but didn't dwell on it, instinctively choosing a less morbid mood. His descriptions of Randy and Booger and Rudolph-the-Rhinoceros were met with much laughter. Tony slapped his knees and cried, wiping his eyes with the back of his hand.

Greg talked about his Russian family, growing up in Coney Island, and singing. The tales he shared came out like chapters in a book, sweet and remote, and separate from him. They were ballads of Greg-the-Troubadour, displayed on the table like presents in festive paper. Only his memories of Eva and Max were palpably alive – if also scant and incoherent, scarred by worry and fear he didn't want to feel. There was no working cell phone or landline on the island and Greg was guiltily grateful for this.

"Bird Flu attacks the satellites, rendering them nonfunctional," Tony explained, his voice dry and scientific. "Just before they croak the sick birds shoot up in a final burst of manic energy and puncture the satellites with their beaks..."

Tony's daughter-in-law looked up from an old magazine, puzzled. Brian slapped her on the head, "He's *joking* you fool!"

Tony treated all three of his houseguests kindly and teasingly, as though they were little children. He insisted on cooking and taking care of the household. He also changed Greg's bandages. Although he never touched Greg beyond the mechanical necessity of a nurse, those moments were charged and intimate. There was a hungry insistency in Tony's gaze. Greg pretended not to notice.

The house was built out of wood and had a nice old smell, airy and cozy, with large panoramic windows and simple wooden furniture. It had four bedrooms and a fireplace with a ceiling-high brick chimney in the living room. There was a pool and a deck overseeing a small green garden grown on soil Tony had had shipped from LA. A windmill right behind the garden supplied electricity. The wings of the mill perpetually turned and the ocean waves rolled over the lava stone. This was the rhythm of their hours at the house: tedious and identical, repeating itself through a spiral of days. All was swaddled in a benevolent, healing repetition. The water came from the well, clean and fragrant, and different in its chemistry from all water Greg had known previously. There was no past and no future, just the blissful rest of the spared. There was enough food to last them a couple of months; Tony had seen to this well in advance. As days passed by, the worries about getting sick left Greg little by little, too.

United by danger and solitude like shipwrecked survivors, the four co-habitants became very close, in a way similar to the forgotten, innocent collusions of childhood. Despite his worries, Greg was happy. In fact he couldn't remember a time in his life when he'd been happier. This too he kept to himself.

They devoted themselves to comfortable sustenance and diversion, staying up late and getting up at noon. They swam in the pool, sunbathed, read old magazines and spy novels, played table tennis and tended to the garden. In the evenings, old and expensive wine bottles were uncorked in symbolic appreciation of survival, as though in an offering to the gods of life. Scrabble and cards were played until late at night, and sometimes, after Brian and Gloria had retreated to bed, Greg and Tony would play chess by the warm light of an antique crystal chandelier. They did this listening to the moans of pleasure from upstairs with the tacit self-indulgence of older men.

"You're a good player," Tony remarked after losing his first game.

"I'm Russian, remember?" Greg said with a cackle.

Greg wasn't particularly attracted to Tony, but when Tony's interest seemed to drift away from him, Greg flirted to retrieve it. It wasn't love or desire, but rather more like winning a cool's guy's attention in high school.

Greg's birthday was celebrated with cake, candles, and cheer. On the radio there was music and good news. Everyone got drunk and swam in the pool, later watching the stars from the garden. Brian and Gloria left, giggling and rubbing their hips against each other as they went.

"Aren't you afraid I could infect you?" Greg abruptly asked

Tony later, over tea.

The wood in the fireplace crackled, sending sparks around. Brian and Gloria made love noisily upstairs. Gloria especially was loud – as though she were proud of the pleasure being given and received. She had reason to be proud, Greg mused, listening intently.

"Does it turn you on?" Tony asked quietly.

Greg shrugged his shoulders. The question made him realize he had a hard on. Or maybe it was the question that had aroused him.

"Yes," he said finally.

Tony gazed at him with intense sadness.

"I'm dying to kiss you."

Greg leaned back, suddenly tense, and Tony laughed and looked away.

"That's the damage of words. They ruin the moment. They betray weakness even if they're true. *Especially* if they're true," he muttered a moment later.

Then: "Let me just touch you then, massage your shoulders."

He got up and walked behind Greg's back, putting his hands on Greg's shoulders and pressing his thumbs deep into Greg's flesh. As Tony worked his hands deeper and lower into his back, Greg's erection returned. Within minutes he grew malleable and as soft as honey. Obediently, he turned over and let his pants be unzipped. Then he wailed and groaned, losing himself in the tender yet violent sex, the rough fabric of the sofa grazing his face. He came into one of its cushions, taking pleasure at smearing its pattern, rocking violently back and forth. He and Tony collapsed on top of each other, breathing loudly. Exhaling pleasure and relief, Tony sat up. His face looked noble and old, not at all like the face of a man who'd just banged another man. Brian and Gloria were quiet, sleeping or perhaps listening to the echo of activity downstairs.

Greg lay on his back, his slim body beautified by Tony's gaze. He stretched, his penis still erect, and laughed.

"Why are you laughing?"

"I don't know. I'm happy," Greg said.

"You are? You liked it?"

Greg raised his eyebrows like Eva used to do in his previous life, and Tony switched gears. "Well, happy birthday, darling! Let's open some more Champagne!"

Being with Tony was easy, their love enclosed by the island and possible only due to its isolation. Like a kid on summer vacation, Greg laughed and played, while waiting for a wake-up call to reality, which encroached with every eaten can and emptied bottle, with every word of good news on the radio.

42

Anna rose refreshed. Although the sun hadn't yet risen, she did her sun salute in the living room by the light of a candle. Eva and Max were sleeping in the bedroom holding hands, beautiful and young in their convalescence.

Life was waking up all around her, and Anna was merry. Even the arthritis that used to bother her around this time, during the weeks leading up to winter, let her be. Trucks carrying food had been arriving regularly, so it was just a question of when basic services such as heat, water, and electricity would be working again. For now, Anna was serving the two: the woman and the boy – and praying for the others. She brought mother and son bottled water, juice, dried fruit and cans of tuna fresh off the truck that pulled right into Stuyvesant Town.

Eva still coughed a lot, was weak and sweaty, and complained of continuing muscle aches in her chest. Her heart skipped beats. She spent most of her time in bed with Max, softly reading to him when it was light and sleeping long hours, from dusk to dawn. She did not talk much with Anna, just said *thank you* and *please* and gave occasional absent smiles. Max was quiet too. Anna hadn't known the little boy well before he was sick, but the smile she remembered from the picture in Olga and Vladimir's apartment was gone from his face. She prayed to see that smile again sometime. On a couple of occasions Max asked Anna questions about the bad daddy and whether he would be coming back with a big sharp knife, and Anna would lovingly tell him a story of Bill-the-hero – the story Max wanted to hear. More difficult was answering his questions about Galina, and in hushed tones Anna would just say, "She was sick," and Max would nod and fall silent.

Anna did not think much about her widowhood, her apartment, or the time when she would leave Eva's house and be on her own again. Ben's voice had vanished – forever, she hoped. And in front of them lay a big wonderful life to be lived by her and Max and Eva.

Anna stretched, bowing to the sun, and thanked providence for delivering her here. After she was finished she had crackers and water. On the kitchen counter she had scrubbed clean of dust she lay out a white napkin and arranged vitamins for Max and Eva, humming as she worked. A fire-truck siren howled on the street, and hearing it Anna clapped her hands like a child. She had missed the city's sounds: its screeching and honking, its sirens and children's laughter. She had loved these sounds like people she knew – as we love what we own without realizing it. So much had to be recovered, so many wounds had to heal.

While Anna stood by the window, the houses all around began lighting up one by one in a silent, single firework of illumination.

"The widows are yellow!" Max yelled. "Wake up, mommy!" Eva rose tousled, thin and excited, and ran to look. They turned on their own lights and then held one another and shouted, together with all their neighbors and the whole world, "Light! Light! *Light!*"

Water spurted out of the taps brown and angry, smelling of feces and rust. They let it run until it was good first for cleaning the bathtub, then for bathing, with bleach added, and soap. "Bubbles!" Max cried. "Bubbles!" and for the first time Anna saw that old smile on his face. She laughed, and Eva laughed with her. They kneeled together, dipping their red, hardened hands into the water.

Tossing off their filthy clothes, Eva and Max got into the tub together, shivering and happy. They bathed and rubbed their skinny bodies with fragrant soap, Max splashing, Eva growing tired and tearful from joy and exhaustion.

"Let's watch TV?" Eva asked after the bath.

"TV, TV!" Max cried.

In the living room, they looked at the colorfully lit screen in wonder.

"When I was your age," Anna told Max, "television had just been invented. We used to run to our neighbors' house and marvel at the moving pictures. There were only black-and-white then."

"Why?"

"I don't know. It started out black-and-white."

Anderson Cooper, his silver hair twisted in a smart forelock, cried onscreen, showing empty streets, mass graves, and photographs of former colleagues, now dead.

"I can't watch this," Eva said and walked out, muffling herself into a thick mohair robe. "I'll charge Bill's camera." Anna switched the channel to cartoons.

Back in the living room, Eva looked at the phone with dread and hope. "Let's call," she said in a barely audible voice, and Anna dialed Olga and Vladimir's number for her.

"Hi," Eva said. "It's me. Max is watching TV."

Exhausted, Eva and Max were napping in the freshly made bed. Only then did Anna take a bath herself. Dipping her head under the fine white foam, pinching her nose, she exhaled bubbles. "Ah!" she cried, surfacing. Fragrant water dripped down her hair, overwhelming her with delight. "*Ahhh ...!*" After her bath she changed her bed sheets and rested on the sofa in the living room, drowsy with comfort. Then she set out to clean the house. Dipping the parched mop into a bucket of sudsy hot water she washed the floor. She dusted, scrubbed, polished, and tossed all the dirty clothes into the tub to soak. From time to time she sat down in front of the TV to rest, weeping along with the unknown mourners onscreen. Olga called twice in three hours and they wept together. Olga and Vladimir were both well, but still there was no news from Greg. "It's three hours earlier in California," Olga said hopefully. "Maybe they don't have power yet?" Anna agreed even though this rationale did not make sense to her.

Late that evening Eva woke up and sat with the telephone on her lap, summoning courage to dial Paris. There was no international connection, and she put the phone down with uneasy relief.

"I would give anything for a glass of wine," she laughed nervously.

"I'll make tea," Anna offered, and made sweet tea with milk powder, served in fine white cups with silver rims. "I found them in the closet while I was cleaning today," she said. "Do you mind?"

"Mind? On the contrary: I haven't used these in years! They're Lalique, my mother's wedding present. It's a perfect occasion to drag them out."

They drank in the descending dusk, every light in the apartment burning brightly. Eva lay on the sofa, her legs tucked under the robe. Max huddled next to her.

"I can't wait," she said softly. "To know. It makes me nervous."

"The waiting can be wonderful if you expect good news," Anna said.

"That's what's so awful about matters of life and death, isn't it? I pick up the phone to ask a question today, and each question has the power to kill. These are simple but magic acts. I wield the power of sentencing. It seems to me better if I *don't* call. It seems I can save a life. And I wait, in hope and dread. I just want to be happy."

"You will be," Anna said kindly. "No matter what happens now. More tea?"

Eva drank her sweet, hot tea trying to remember the name of Robin's mother. She could picture her clearly: a kindly, overweight woman with closely cropped hair. She used to feed Eva and Robin apple strudel and ask them anxious questions about their plans for the evening. She always wanted to sit with them when Eva came over, and once she had even wept loudly behind the wall after Robin had closed the door in her mother's face. Robin had giggled, but Eva had felt badly for her mom. "Oh don't pity her," Robin had said. "If not for her, I'd have a life." "*Don't* you have a life?" Eva had asked. "Please," Robin had rolled her eyes. "I'm still a *virgin.*"

Like other friends' parents, Robin's mother had always been just a guarding and guiding presence. She needed a name now. Her child was dead. Eva leafed through her old phone book until she found it: Debra Steinberg. The name didn't want to attach itself to the face she remembered, and she repeated it several times, trying to glue the two together.

What would a mother want to know about her dead child? Everything, Eva thought, her eyes resting on Max. Everything, to extend her child's life through new memories. Debra would want to know everything. But did one say everything? Would Debra Steinberg want to know that her daughter had had sex while patients died around her? That she took an overdose after her lover had died and she had fallen sick herself?

"I don't know what to tell her," Eva said, pages of the phone book rustling under her fingers.

"Don't worry. She'll ask. If not today, then later, when she's ready."

The idea that it needed not be a final account of Robin's end calmed Eva, as if their friendship still had a chance of resolution. Still, Eva dialed the number twice in a row, having gotten it wrong on the first try. Debra answered right away.

"Debra? This is Eva Leigh. I don't know if you know... that Robin died of the Flu while working at the hospital."

That's how it was. Debra didn't ask questions. Eva said what people always said. That Robin was a wonderful person. That she had loved her mother. That she had saved people.

"The guilt!" she exclaimed after hanging up a second later. "I almost forgot the guilt I'd felt. Today has been such a good day."

Anna glanced at her expectantly.

"I wasn't a good friend to Robin," Eva explained. "I wasn't a good mother, either. I infected Max. It makes me sick to talk about it." Eva pressed her forehead to her knees, her weakness weighing on her.

"Time will heal," Anna whispered.

In a little while the phone rang, startling them. Eva's hand trembled when she picked it up.

"Greg! You're alive! ... Yes, yes, we're both alive. Max, it's daddy's calling! You take the phone, Max, take it!" Tears streamed down Eva's face.

"Daddy! Look, I have a plane!" Max cried, tossing the phone away and picking the plastic toy up from the carpet.

Eva wept, holding Max's hand. "Daddy's OK, honey," she said as much into the phone. "He's coming home on the first flight he can find. He loves you."

"He's coming now?"

"No, not now. Later, when the big planes start flying again."

Giving scarce details, Greg told Eva about how he had survived: about the miraculous coincidence of choosing Tony's boat to hide in and about the hospitality he'd been granted during the weeks in the remote ocean house. It had been "an easy and innocent time," Greg said, a phrase that confused Eva, though no emotion was greater than her relief, and her happiness, at hearing his voice. "I'm happy for you," she said instinctively. *I can't wait to see you again,* she wanted to add, but remained silent, leaking fresh tears.

"More tea?" Anna offered, smiling.

That night, when the sun had set, Eva was quiet, and Anna waited for her to speak.

"It's funny how quickly shades of life come back into play,"

Eva said. "When the call comes, you think there's only black and white, life and death. And then you know it's white, and after the first relief, still crying, you form sentences that fit the narrative started much earlier. You don't say, 'I love you,' even if you do, or 'I miss you,' because there're all the *what*s and *if*s, and it gets too complicated."

"It's good," Anna said soothingly. "It means there's a future."

Putting Max to bed, Eva sang a lullaby in a low, husky voice. Listening, Anna took a napkin from the table and wiped away tears.

Eva returned and sat back on the sofa in the same position, her naked ankles sticking out from her bathrobe. "Max used to be different before," she said. "He'd have never allowed me to have a conversation or talk on the phone. He was very possessive. I'm worried about him."

"Everything needs time. It's early for all of us."

"You're right. You're always right, I noticed that. In a good way."

Anna smiled, "And yet I have no one to call."

They sat in silence. Eva didn't ask questions and Anna didn't want them.

"Tell me about Bill," Eva asked finally.

Anna spoke with her eyes closed, recounting the events of that day. As she talked, Bill's reference to Galina ("the babysitter stole my keys!") came to her mind, and she mentioned that too, retaining nothing for herself. Weeping for him, Eva turned on Bill's camera and looked at his documentary of the Flu. Bill in front of Con Edison by the river. Galina's rouged face. Eva holding Max on her knees. A dead man on the street. Looted stores on First Avenue. A pack of hungry dogs. An excavator by a mass grave. She flipped through the pictures quickly. Then she froze.

"Oh my God."

A young woman in a checkered skirt lay on a bed, eyes open, hands folded on her chest. There was a shot of her full body, then one of her face, then one of her eyes, dark and blank under the thin lines of high eyebrows; then one of her pale lips and, finally, one of her graceful hands with unpainted bluish fingernails. All of them were dated the second of November.

"She was dead," Eva said in a constrained voice. "Grace died weeks ago; she was dead all this time, and he knew it. He'd been exposed. He took pictures of her. He never told me."

"He did," Anna whispered, putting her arm around Eva. "He asked me to give you the camera."

The city glared with lights. They could hear music playing. A few fireworks brightened the sky far away. Eva cried for Bill and Robin and all those who were not coming back.

"We would have died without you," she said, squeezing Anna's hand. "I don't know if I have even thanked you."

Anna hugged her. The Flu was over, the Joker gone.

"Shall I brew another pot of tea and read your cards?" Anna asked Eva with a sly smile.

"Yes, yes!" Eva laughed eagerly.

Anna closed her eyes. The future lay before them, vast and long. They'll live; that was all that mattered. Max will forget the time of the Flu. His smile will return to him forever. Eva will remember until time will heal her too. Anna knew she would not see them often. The Flu had brought them together and its memory would keep them apart.

"I thought you didn't believe in cards," Anna smiled, opening her eyes.

"I don't," Eva laughed. "But I'd do anything for another cup of tea."

The End

About the Author

Elena Bruck was born in Moscow, Russia, studied Medicine in Vienna, Austria, and is currently an assistant professor of psychiatry at one of New York's hospitals. She lives in the East Village together with her husband and two children.